ADVANCE PRAISE F(

This book came to the attention of the publisher at PREP Publishing through an independent Reader's Report prepared for the author through PREP. Here is some of the advance praise given the book prior to its publication:

"You share a remote part of the world and a remote history with readers."

"The trial is well written and holds the reader's interest."

"The manuscript is unique and offers a 'new twist on a popular theme' by sharing a remote part of the world and a remote history with readers."

"The love letters written throughout the manuscript are well done."

"The journal gives a very real sense of what life was like in colonial Africa in the early twentieth century, and I greatly enjoyed the descriptions."

To Kulwinder and Kamal, with best wishes

A Novel by Pally Dhillon

KIJABE
An African Historical Saga

PREP Publishing
Fayetteville, North Carolina

PREP Publishing
1110 1/2 Hay Street
Fayetteville, NC 28305
(910) 483-6611

Cover design by Chris Pearl

Library of Congress Cataloging-in-Publication Data
Dhillon, Pally, 1944-
    Kijabe : an African historical saga / Pally Dhillon.
    p. cm.
    ISBN 1-885288-21-2
        1. East Indians--Africa--Fiction. 2. Africa--Fiction. 3. Sikhs--Fiction. I. Title.

PS3554.H55 K55 2000
813'.54--dc21   00-028574
                                                     CIP
Printed in the United States of America
First Edition

This book is a work of fiction. The events, characters, and plot are products of the author's imagination or are used fictitiously.

WITH GRATITUDE

My sincere thanks to family members for their support and help in providing historical data from memory and to some special friends for their encouragement over the past two years when I struggled and needed inspiration to continue with the book.

Special thanks to Chris Guin and Anne McKinney of PREP for editing the manuscript and for giving me their professional guidance in making my dream of publishing Kijabe become a reality, and to Chris Pearl for his creativity and professionalism in designing the cover.

The publication of Kijabe spans four generations. It started with journals written by my grandfather which were picked up by my father, who formatted the writings into notes in English, followed by my compiling them into a manuscript. Finally, my son-in-law, Dr. Daniel Zanotti, completed the process when he took some of the photographs for the cover.

Kijabe turned out to be an accurate account of my grandfather's pioneering days in Africa and an imaginative reflection of what could have been, should have been, but for the most part, wasn't.

Pally Dhillon

EDITOR'S FOREWORD

Books are often the story of a writer's persistence, and this one is no different. Pally Dhillon, a successful corporate computer executive, became intrigued by the story of his family's history in Kenya, East Africa, and wanted to find out more about his grandfather's mysterious murder. His curiosity led him to archives of old newspaper clippings, and he journeyed back into the thick of Africa to discover answers to the mysteries surrounding the life of the Asian transplant who became a great African leader in the early part of the twentieth century. What began as a mission, and a labor of love, became a story that had to be told to the world, and thus was born the African historical saga which you will read. Be prepared to see Africa at its most menacing. You will be awed by the wonder and terror of colonial Africa untamed. Be prepared to smell the fragrant odors of the manicured gardens in African plantations. You will be introduced to Africa at its core, tribal level, and you will experience the primitive customs of tribal Africa through the eyes of the Asian transplant who fathered a dynasty.

The Sikh religion is a part of the background of this book about Africa, as Sikhism was the religion practiced by the 6' 4" Indian who came to Africa to help build a railroad and ended up helping to shape a country's politics. When the Asian Mehar Singh came to Africa, he brought his religion with him, and it shaped the way he lived, loved, pursued politics, and died. Mehar Singh was a member of a group of enterprising pioneers who, fortified by their fierce determination, survived unbearable African environmental conditions, dangerous animals, and hostile tribes in order to plant roots and lay the foundation of modern Kenya. The author encourages you to consult the Glossary at the back of this book as well as the Appendix of Characters.

For anyone who wants to believe in a rags-to-riches story, Kijabe will entertain. For those who enjoy a love story, Kijabe will charm. For anyone who yearns to taste and smell the culture of Africa at its wildest, Kijabe will enthrall. And for those who enjoy a historical family saga rich in anecdote and detail, Kijabe will thrill. This book is a fictional account of a true story. The characters are fictional, and any resemblance to real people is purely coincidental. PREP is pleased to publish this astonishing historical tale that brings Africa to life. And if you haven't had enough of *Kijabe* when you finish this book, visit the author at his website http://www.kijabe.com.

Anne McKinney

CONTENTS

DEDICATION

Kijabe is dedicated to my father, Sardar Gurbux Singh Dhillon, who began the research that led to this book thirty years ago but passed away before he could see the book which honors his curiosity, intellect, and persistence. Thanks to him, I was able to pick up his notes and research and compile the data which led eventually to this book. I hope he is happy with the final product.

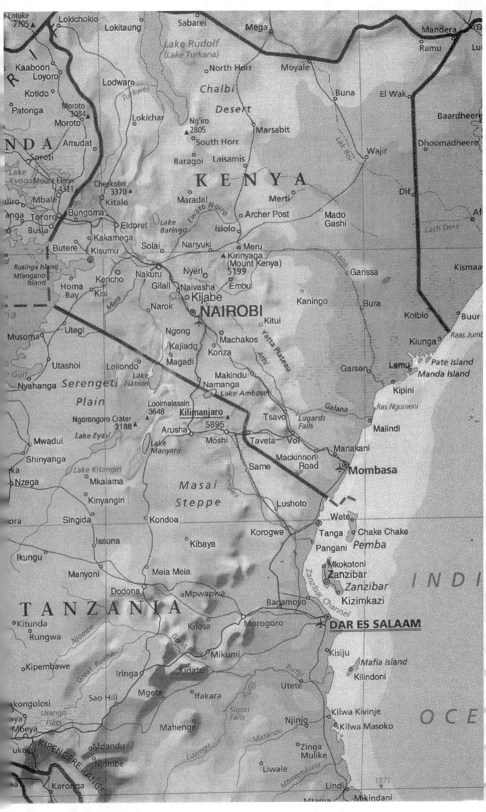

KIJABE

An African Historical Saga

Chapter I

"There is one God.

He is the Supreme Truth.

He, the Creator, is without Fear or Enmity.

He, the Omnipresent, pervades the Universe.

He, being unborn, cannot die to be born again.

Through His Grace, All may worship Him."

The Mool Mantra

Guru Nanak Dev Jee

"Daughter-in-law Charged in Murder of Slain Political Leader"
began the newspaper article.

SharanJeet Kaur Dhillon, daughter-in-law of slain political leader Mehar Singh Dhillon, was arraigned today in the lower court, and charged with murder in the death of her father-in-law.

In an emotionally charged courtroom, filled to capacity with Mehar Singh's political supporters and mourning family, testimony from distraught relatives and police officials, as well as physical evidence incriminating Mrs. Dhillon, was presented before the court.

One legal expert called the arraignment "a mere formality," stating that the physical evidence was so overwhelming that the case was predestined to move quickly to trial in the higher court.

Although the murdered Sikh leader's family refused to comment, SharanJeet Dhillon loudly proclaimed her innocence, stating that she was pleased that the case was moving to the higher court. She contended that once all the evidence was seen, she was certain justice would be done and her innocence and good name cleared.

The high-profile case will be tried at the High Court in Nairobi, as soon as the selection of a Judge and Assessors is complete.

1

Akash sat on the edge of the bed in his grandfather's room, helping Satbir Kaur go through Mehar Singh's effects. In accordance with Sikh tradition, his grandmother was preparing to give away her dead husband's clothes and other belongings, and she had asked Akash to help with the ordeal of sorting through the drawers and closets.

"Here, Akash beta why don't you go through this and see what's in it?" she said, placing a large box on the bed beside him.

Akash reluctantly turned to the work at hand. He had to return to Britain shortly after the trial, and he was still having a hard time getting used to the fact that his grandfather was gone.

He pulled off the yellowed tape that sealed an old box shut and began examining the contents. In the top of the box were several old turbans, still tinted faintly red from dust ground in over the years. Beneath them, he found a number of thin books with worn covers.

He picked one up from the top of the box. There was no title on the cover, so he opened it, and he immediately recognized his grandfather's tight, neatly formed handwriting.

"Manjee ! What is this? I never knew Bapu Jee kept a journal!"

Satbir turned to see what he had discovered. "Oh, those," she said. "I wondered where they'd gotten to. He started those journals on the dhow coming into Mombasa and kept writing in them all during those early years. I often wondered why he bothered—he never let anyone read what he'd written."

She turned away suddenly, her eyes filling with tears.

"I guess this is why he bothered," she said, her voice thick with sorrow. "So there would be something left when he was gone. It's hard to believe he survived all that, just to be gunned down in the courtyard of his own home."

Akash set the journal down, and hugged his grandmother to his chest. He held her as she sobbed quietly, letting go of the tight control she'd held over her grief since the funeral.

She said, "You two are so much alike, so tall and handsome. You look much like he did that first time I saw him, when I was fresh off the boat from India."

"I wish I had known him better," Akash said. "It always seemed as though there would be more time."

"Your grandfather always told me, 'Time is the one thing there's never more of. Use what time you have in the best way possible, for none of us can go to the local duka and buy a few extra hours,'" she replied somberly. "Why don't you keep the journals, at least for now?"

Akash hesitated before asking the question on his mind.

"Manjee," he began, "Anar has been asked to write a series on Bapu Jee's life for the paper. Do you think he would have minded my sharing the stories in the journals with her, for the articles?"

"No, I think he would be pleased," she said. "Everyone says 'Mehar Singh was a great man, a true leader, but your grandfather was more than just a great man. Some of what he was is in those volumes, and I think he would be glad to see someone introduce the people he so loved to the man behind the political figure."

"Thank you, Manjee. You don't know how much this means to me."

Akash had a hard time containing his excitement at finding Mehar Singh's journals. He knew he'd made an important discovery and he felt more alive than he had at any time since he'd learned of his grandfather's murder.

"Go," Satbir told him. "Go off in a corner somewhere, and spend some time with the journals. I'm almost done here, anyway, and it's obvious you'll be of no more use today."

Akash needed no further encouragement. He gathered the journals into his arms and retreated to a quiet room in the guest wing of the Kijabe mansion, where he was unlikely to be disturbed. He opened the first volume with eager anticipation and suddenly he was transported to an older, wilder, and more fascinating Kenya than the one he'd known. The journal was written in Urdu, an Indian language that Akash and Anar had learned in school, and the language in which his grandfather was most proficient.

3

The long sea journey is finally over. I can barely contain my excitement, as the little dhow in which we crossed the Indian Ocean is coming into port at Mombasa!

The trip was difficult. At times it seemed as though the monsoon winds that drove us across the ocean would snap the mast or suck the little ship beneath the waves. When the storm changed directions, we had to bail water from the ship while the sailors tacked against the raging winds, struggling to keep us on course. For a while, I thought it would be the waters of the Indian Ocean, and not the infamous lions of Tsavo, that would take me from this earth.

At least I have not been ill. Kala and many of the others have been seasick for most of the trip. Of course, I had to make fun of him—my tall friend, so proud of his physical strength, laid low by the rocking of a boat. But he knows it was only in jest, and now his misery is over anyway. They are turning the dhow to pass between two taller ships, and we're going into the docks. The perilous sea voyage is over!

The white sandy beaches look like paradise and glisten beneath the burning sun, and the rich green of the landscape is broken here and there by the red tile roof of a European-style house or the glint from a tin-roofed shed.

Down on the wharf, chaos reigns. There are sailors and traders and businessmen from all over the world. I can hear them shouting back and forth in every language. It seems that everyone here has something to sell, and the language barrier is bridged mainly by money and the sound of bartering goods for goods.

Ships from Britain, Europe, and even America are unloading cargoes of ironwork, cloth, olive oil, and a thousand other things the Africans want. In exchange, they are loading ivory, rhinoceros horn, cinnamon, and even forced labor, some of whom are children who appear to be orphans, bound for the colonies. I can see that this unsettled land offers vast opportunity. It is said that men with small fortunes are turning them into large ones without ever leaving the port.

I'll have to work to build my future, but I know this country will be the making of me. I have dreamed of this from the moment I first heard that the British were recruiting Indian nationals to work on the railway project to link Nairobi with the coast. I am strong and I am ambitious, and I have not come here only to work on the railway. I have come here to make my fortune.

Life in India was good, but I want something more—not the sedate life my father and my father's father led, but a life that makes the blood sing in my veins. Hunting lions, taming a continent, forging a living out of the steel of my will and the bounty of nature—that's why I've come to Africa. Adventure and opportunity, a new life in a new land; what more could I ask for?

LATER ON MARCH 24:

We unloaded our things from the dhow and went to find a place to stay for the night before we explored the port of Mombasa. As we walked into the city, I heard the constant roar of the Indian Ocean, as it broke over the coral reef that rings this side of the island. We walked beneath the coconut palms, and the fresh sea air was tinted with the faint scent of the brilliant purple bougainvillea that grows in proliferation in the rich African soil.

Dozens of the Arab dhows sat rocking with the current, anchored in Mombasa's harbor. Tall men in long white gowns like nightshirts were screaming admonishments at the nearly naked African boys who scampered about, shouting insults in return.

The Arab women, veiled in black and swathed head to toe in the black Buibuis, appear mysterious and exotic as they lounge beneath the mango trees listening to the eerie melody of a nearby musician playing the Arab flute. Although their features are veiled, I can feel their sensuousness, and they fascinate me. All this clashes with the raucous noise from the wharves, just as the stench of rotting fish vies against the smell of coffee drying in the sun and the cloying sweetness of jasmine.

The air is hot and thick with humidity, clinging to us like a warm, damp cloth and as we get deeper into the city it seems tinged with a faintly foul odor.

Although I have been accustomed to cramped spaces in India,

*narrow alleys and overhanging balconies seem to push in on us
from all sides. The towers and minarets of the temples and mosques
rise above the lower buildings, proclaiming the heavy Arabic influence on the island, but there are traces from the Portuguese
occupation, as well.*

*Through these confined passageways, scores of Arab traders
move slowly, jamming the alleys with hand-pulled carts, caravans
of camels moving no more than two abreast, and donkey trains.
In the close quarters, the smells of the animals mix with those of
dried fish, curry, cinnamon, and unleavened bread baking in nearby
houses and shops. The unfortunate combination of scents threat-
ens to turn the stomach. At least they turn mine.*

*We decided to get off the streets for a bit and found a tavern
to wash the taste of the thick air from our throats. After a few
drinks, Kala jokingly suggested that we challenge the natives at
kabbadi, the sport we played the most in Punjab. This sounded
like a good idea to me, so I found a couple of Africans who could
communicate with us, and before long we were gathered in a field
at the edge of town.*

*I drew the circle in the center of the field and carefully ex-
plained the game to one of the natives, who translated for the
others. Kabbadi is a good game in this respect; its rules are few
and simple, so the Africans were able to catch on quickly. I explained that the sport is played with five men on each team, and a
circle is drawn and then divided by a line in the middle about 12
feet in length. Then two spots are marked at a distance of 25 feet
on each side of the dividing line. Every team member on the two
opposing sides takes turns going into the other half and, without
taking a breath, has to reach the marked spot and return to the
center line. A member of the defending team has to try to tackle
and hold the opponent until he takes another breath. The defense
scores a point if it is able to hold the person down, and the offense scores a point if the intruder can make it all the way back to
the dividing line without taking a breath. Kabbadi is designed to
test one's stamina and strength as well as speed.*

I watched as the first three rounds passed, leaving the game tied at one point each. Then it was my turn. I took a great breath, filled my lungs, then darted past my defender. Touching the opposite side of the circle, I raced back, trying to avoid my opponent. As I ran for the center, he lunged at me, grabbing me around the waist, but I slipped away from him and made it back to the center to score.

Then I was defending against an opponent both quick and strong. As he tried to sprint past me, I caught hold of his arm, but the young African twisted in my grasp and evaded me, sprinting for the edge line. He touched the line and came rushing straight for me, as though to run me down.

With his head and shoulders, he feinted to the left, but then he shifted his body, turning suddenly to the right and putting on a burst of speed. I dove for him, circling him with my arms. He strained and struggled against me, trying to reach the center of the circle before he was forced to take a breath. We were almost evenly matched; I could not pull him towards the edge, but he could gain no forward momentum, either.

Then suddenly he went slack against my straining, throwing me off balance. Both of us tumbled to the ground, and he rolled off of my chest and across the center line. Once he scored, my opponent let out the breath he'd been holding explosively. Once again, the score was tied, this time at two points apiece.

Only one player remained for each team—a huge but slow-looking African for them, and Kala for us. I wished my big strong friend luck—not that he needed it. I knew there was no way that his opponent would defeat Kala, since Kala is about my height at 6' 5" but bigger and stronger. With his huge frame and hairy body, he reminds me of gentle giant—gentle since I know his kind disposition. Of course I was right.

The African went first on the offense, trying to run Kala down and use his raw strength to score. Even though Kala is big, my friend was not as bulky as his opponent but every ounce of Kala is pure steel; he locked his arms around his opponent and lifted the big African completely off the ground, carrying him to the edge of the line, and held him there until *the African was forced to take a breath.*

Then it was Kala's turn on offense, and he so quickly eluded his lumbering defender as to make the game's earlier drama seem farcical by comparison. We won the kabbadi match, by a score of four to two, but I am impressed with the strength and resourcefulness of these Africans! You can learn a lot about a man when you play a game with him.

And at least the Africans were good sports about their loss. They took us back to the tavern and bought the first round of drinks in honor of our victory. Tired from the game and the excitement of our arrival in Africa, we made our way back to our lodgings. This first day in my new country has nearly overwhelmed me, and I have tried to put it all down as closely as I can remember, for it is a day I hope never to forget.

JOURNAL OF MEHAR SINGH, YEAR ONE, VOLUME I - MARCH 29, 1916

Only four days out from Mombasa, and already the scant moisture and occasional coolness the ocean had lent to the air is only a memory. The lush vegetation of the coastal zone, populated with exotic birds and butterflies in vivid colors, is behind us now. We are passing from a land of near desert into an area studded with anthills and scraggly green thorn bushes.

The ox cart continuously creaks and sways beneath me as we travel, and my arms and hands are so tired by the end of the day that I fear I am writing poorly and am not sure my handwriting will be legible later. But my writing is an escape from the primitive conditions I now find myself in.

This is a miserable way to travel. It seems that walking would be as fast, though little more pleasant. The hot African sun beats down on us, baking the dust from the red earth that sticks to the sweat of my skin and coats my body. The air is so hot and flat that it is hard to breathe. Every breath is flavored with the faintly metallic taste of the iron oxide that lends its color to the scorched red earth which rises with the passing of the carts to coat the nose, the throat, the lungs.

In the distance, wild animals roam the plains seeking the scant shelter of the low bushes or grazing in the tall grass around them. I see giraffes, impala, Thomson's gazelle, zebras, and wildebeest, as well as lesser-known creatures like the kudu, a grayish-brown antelope with white markings and the eland, a larger antelope with spiral twisted horns.

The animals stay well clear of us but they do not seem intimidated, seeming to regard the passage of the ox carts as no more than a minor distraction. They might stop to stare, or make a noise to object to our intrusion, but soon they snort as though in contempt, then return to their grazing. The herd animals swish their tails to rid themselves of the flies and tick birds riding their backs, though the birds are impervious to these attacks, and the flies quickly return.

The bee-like sting of the tse-tse flies bothers us, but for some humans and animals, the sting is more than a bother as the sting carries the sleeping sickness. Already some of the animals are infected but, fortunately, none of us seem to have contracted the disease. Even going to bed at night is an adventure in this country because when we try to rest, mosquitoes descend upon us like a living blanket, the air thick with their incessant buzzing.

This afternoon I saw my first lion. We had heard their roars in the distance, but we were never close enough to see them. Today, as we passed through a bend in the road, we spotted a herd of zebras grazing alongside wildebeests and Thomson gazelles. I was admiring the doe-eyed, deer-like gazelle and the wildebeest, which some call the gnu, and marveling at the way the wildebeest looks like hybrid of a horse and an ox with its oxlike head and horns and its horselike mane and tail. I was so absorbed that, at first, I didn't see the solitary lioness stalking silently through the tall grass. When I finally spotted her, she was watching the zebras, which were grazing close to the stand of grass where she was concealed. Her entire body was as tense as a bow string, and the tip of her tail twitched as she silently advanced toward the zebras, one step at a time, stealthily, with infinite patience.

Several of the zebras raised their heads, as if sensing movement nearby, and the lioness froze in place until they returned to grazing.

Then only the quivering of her flanks revealed her tension as she waited for her unsuspecting victim to drift within range; she had picked her target.

When the zebra was close enough, the lioness rose, almost as if taking flight, and began her charge in one smooth, fluid motion. The herd of zebras scattered and ran from the lioness, but with an explosion of power from her muscular flanks, she quickly overtook her intended prey. In a distance run, the zebra would have outpaced her, but lions seem built for raw speed and striking power. Her hooked claws tore into the frightened animal's rump, and she pulled the zebra to the ground in a stunning display of her awesome strength.

In the same motion, she lunged for the zebra's neck and strangled her prey, clamping steel-spring jaws shut over its throat to suffocate the animal. She stayed in that position for several minutes, until the zebra's struggling and trembling was over, and her victim was still, unconscious or dead.

Now that the zebra was motionless, the lioness was joined by her mate, a magnificent male lion with a full, dark mane. She was in heat, and the mating pair had drifted away from the pride. The two lions tore into the zebra, and I could hear the sound of bones being crushed in their powerful jaws. The lioness ripped open the zebra's chest, and stuck her whole head inside its body, going after the liver and heart.

We were resting so we watched from afar as they fed for most of an hour, then headed for the shade of some nearby bushes, their bellies visibly sagging as they walked away from the zebra carcass. As soon as the lions were a safe distance away, the jackals, hyenas, and vultures swarmed in to finish off the remains of the victim.

From a distance, it was a magnificent spectacle of nature's glory. But I cannot help but think that from the zebra's perspective, this would not be the case. It also reveals the treachery of this new land in which I find myself. This has been a sobering reminder of our need to be vigilant in life, and we are all aware, as we travel to Tsavo that, by all accounts, lions prefer the taste of man to zebra.

Akash closed the journal, reluctantly returning to the present. He was supposed to meet Anar for dinner, and he couldn't wait to share this discovery with her. He knew that she would be as excited about the journals as he was. As he prepared to see his beloved, his thoughts wandered back to earlier days, when as a youth he had helped in his grandfather's successful election campaign that had made the Asian transplant one of Africa's most respected leaders.

Chapter II

"I have fought against White domination and I have fought against Black domination. I have cherished the ideal of a democratic and free society in which all persons will live together in harmony and with equal opportunities. It is an ideal which I hope to live for and achieve. But, if need be, it is an ideal for which I am prepared to die."

Nelson Mandela, 1964

"Mehar Singh Wins Landslide Victory" "Kenyans Vote No to KANU Corruption!"

It was 1966, and newspaper headlines proclaimed his grandfather's victory. The winner's ruggedly handsome grandson, Akash, beamed as he listened with the rest of the family gathered around the radio in the campaign headquarters at the family's mansion in Muthaiga to hear outgoing Kenyan African National Union Secretary Michael Kariuki's concession speech. At 150 pounds and 6 ft. 1 in. tall, the broad-shouldered young Akash was shorter than his 6 ft. 4 in., 240-pound grandfather and didn't wear the neatly tied turban always worn by the patriarch of the family to signify his membership in the Sikh religion.

However, like his grandfather, Akash seemed to have the naturally captivating mannerisms and handsome smile of a born politician, and his charm was noticeable as he quickly strode towards the entourage of cars ready to leave

12

for the campaign headquarters in Ngara.

According to newspaper articles Kariuki had already called the president, who was also the head of the Kenyan African National Union or the KANU, as most people referred to the political party, to inform him of his concession to Mehar Singh. He'd called a press conference outside the Law Courts in Nairobi and his speech was being broadcast live.

Dressed in his customary starched khaki pants and shirt, the defeated KANU leader Kariuki was as gracious in defeat as he had been vicious during the campaign. In a conciliatory tone, he said, "My heartfelt congratulations go out to Asian leader Mehar Singh Dhillon. He is a worthy and deserving winner of this contest. He knows Kenya, and he is a true Kenyan. He knows its people and its problems. I promise to cooperate with Mehar Singh in shaping the future of Kenya. I am available to work in any post within KANU that I am offered."

The multiracial crowd at the campaign headquarters burst into shouts and applause as the speech was heard. Then cheers turned into a roar of triumph as they saw the turbaned, imposing Mehar Singh uncoil his tall body and step triumphantly out of the black Mercedes. Walking protectively in front of the popular new leader, Akash and his father forced a path through the crowd so that Mehar Singh could take the podium.

"Friends," was the first word uttered by the new leader in the strong, deep voice with an Indian dialect that had become familiar to Kenyans. At the sound of his voice, the crowd grew respectfully silent.

"It's been a long and difficult fight. Kariuki played every card he had, and he made it difficult. At first he tried to make you believe that I would represent only Maasai interests. When that didn't work, he campaigned on the fact that I was a 'foreigner,' an Indian immigrant and not a true Kenyan. But now you've all heard him publicly refute that statement in his concession speech.

"The first leg of this race has been won. But it's not I who have won—it is you. All of you. Without your support, I could not have achieved this feat. You all know that no Asian—or European—has ever been elected secretary of KANU. You all know that when we announced my candidacy for this post, we were laughed at, considered a joke.

"Now *they* have heard the punchline of that joke—but it's us, not them, who are laughing. Now, finally, we'll have the opportunity to see real change in Kenya. The change that you, my supporters, want. The change this country needs can come to pass. And it is all thanks to you. My friends."

Pushing his way through the crowd, Akash's father struggled to make his way to the podium, carrying a telephone with a long cord. "Bapu Jee," he said. "I'm sorry to interrupt this moment. But I think you'll want to take this call—it is Mzee."

To his countrymen, President Kenyatta was simply "Mzee" (Muh-zay), a Swahili word meaning the "old man," a title of the greatest respect and affection in East Africa. Revered as a godfather and regarded as a hero to the average Kenyan, Jomo Kenyatta had become the first president of their independent country when it broke free of colonial British rule. The newly elected Asian secretary of KANU would be reporting to President Kenyatta.

Murmurs ran through the crowd, then quickly cascaded into silence as everyone listened intently to hear what the country's leader had to say.

"Yes, Mr. President," Mehar said in a booming voice which resonated throughout the room, smiling as he spoke and nodding to his roomful of admirers as though to make them a part of his conversation with the beloved country leader. "Thank you, sir. I am proud and honored that the people of Kenya have entrusted me with this position. Yes, sir. I look forward to working with you, as well. Yes . . . I'll be there tonight. Kwaheri, Mzee."

He hung up the phone, and the crowd grew restless in the silence.

"The president called to congratulate us on our victory," the tall, turbaned Asian informed his supporters. "He told me he's looking forward to working with me and wants me to report this evening for a planning session. Now it's official. We've won the election, friends."

The crowd exploded into pandemonium. Corks flew from champagne bottles and kegs of strong beer were tapped as the celebration began in earnest. Jubilant Sikhs started the traditional Bhangra dancing. All around Akash, his grandfather's ecstatic supporters clapped one another on the back, and a group of enthusiastic Maasai began to chant, "Kala Singha! Kala Singha! Kala Singha!"

Akash and his father, Santokh Singh, helped Mehar climb down from the podium. As his father and grandfather walked side by side in front of him, Akash was struck in a fresh way by their physical dissimilarities. The old man towered above his 5 ft. 9 in. son, and the patriarch's imposing presence seemed to diminish his firstborn in every respect. But Akash knew that his soft-spoken, tenderhearted father was devoted to his strong, overpowering grandfather. Led by Mehar and his eldest, the family retreated to the sanctuary of a tented pavilion near the back of the building to give the newly elected leader a chance to gather his thoughts and reflect on all that had happened.

Akash could barely contain his joy. He'd worked in his grandfather's campaign headquarters since the early days, when Mehar Singh had been elected Member of Parliament for the Maasai district. Because Akash wanted to study law and go into politics like his grandfather, he'd followed Mehar Singh's political career closely, and he'd worked with his grandfather and Joseph Ole Likimani on the campaign for the KANU secretary's post. A Maasai politician, Likimani had been instrumental in his grandfather's political success. A big man at 250 lbs. who stretched to 6 ft. 2 in. tall, Likimani was a jolly fellow whose perpetual smile revealed a missing front tooth, which was customary for Maasai men.

Although they had opposed each other in Mehar Singh's successful bid for the Member of Parliament position representing the Maasai district, like strange bedfellows Joseph Likimani and Mehar Singh had formed an alliance. Over time, friendship and respect had grown into a strong political and personal bond and, now as a team, they were a significant force to be reckoned with. With Mehar Singh's recent defeat of the Kikuyu Michael Kariuki for KANU party secretary, Likimani had pulled off a major coup and a historical first in African politics. An Asian outsider would now occupy one of Kenya's most important political posts. Important positions within KANU and KADU, the Kenyan African Democratic Union, had always been reserved for natives, but Likimani had felt strongly that Mehar Singh, even though not a black African, could beat Kariuki for the position if he had the right help.

Mehar Singh himself had been confident that, if he could sway the will of the people, President Jomo Kenyatta would support him. Mzee had always held Mehar Singh in high regard and he'd expressed his appreciation on many occasions for Mehar's deft handling of thorny political situations.

On the other hand, they'd been aware that Charles Lare, the vice president of KANU, would be a venomous obstacle to Mehar's candidacy. At 5 ft. 11 in. with piercing black eyes and short, curly hair, Lare stood taller than the average Kikuyu and had an ability to intimidate even veteran politicians. Unlike the fair-minded Kenyatta, Lare was a jingoist who strongly opposed the intrusion of immigrants into African politics. Likimani and Mehar Singh had spent eighteen months planning Mehar's campaign for KANU secretary before declaring Mehar's intention to run.

Akash had been allowed to sit in on those planning sessions and he'd even contributed a few ideas which the veteran politicians had embraced. Over many weeks of late suppers and drinks, they had developed their strategy while simultaneously confiding in some Members of Parliament and seeking their advice. The first step in their strategy had been to forge an alliance with the Jaluos from Kisumu and the Makambas from Machakos. Africa was a nation of tribes to a large degree, and the support of the tribes had to be cultivated.

With many of his front teeth pulled as was characteristic of his Jaluo tribe, the powerful Jaluo leader Oginga Odinga had ambitions to be the next vice president of Kenya and replace Mzee when Kenyatta retired. There was no love lost between the 5 ft. 8 in., potbellied Odinga and the tall, intense Charles Lare, two Africans of enormous ambition, but their mutual hatred had less to do with tribal differences than their conflicting personalities. Odinga was simple, outspoken, and loved the people. Lare was a clever and manipulative man who kept his true motives hidden.

Likimani and Mehar Singh had traveled to Kisumu to spend a week with Odinga at his cattle ranch in the Nandi Hills, about thirty miles outside of Kisumu. They took with them several cases of Captain Morgan's black rum, which they knew was a favorite of Odinga's. On the second day of their stay in Nandi, Likimani broached the subject of the alliance as they sat around the fire over drinks and a dinner of roast dik-dik, a delicious small antelope cooked on the large charcoal fire pit.

Likimani started off by attacking the Kikuyus; he knew that would generate empathy in the Jaluo leader. The arrogance of the Kikuyus made them a common enemy for Odinga's people as well as the Maasai. He reminded Odinga of incidents where the Kikuyus had voted against the Maasais and the Jaluos, and he spoke of how they considered themselves to be the superior Kenyan tribe. It wasn't difficult to inflame the Jaluo leader's resentment against the cocky Kikuyus who would use every opportunity in their power to gain advantage.

Likimani then proposed the idea of Mehar Singh's running for the KANU secretary's post and simultaneously supporting Odinga in his bid for the vice presidency and the number two man in the country. The Jaluos had been expecting some sort of proposal for an alliance, so they were not totally surprised. The plan pleased Odinga, so they shook hands to seal the deal and then refreshed their drinks.

Mehar's campaign to win the post of KANU secretary had thus begun. Odinga was receptive to their running side by side for the KANU secretary's post and the Vice Presidency, but he wanted to learn more about the opposing Kikuyus. They agreed to meet in another month at Mehar Singh's Kijabe residence to finalize details.

Before the meeting, the master politician and campaign strategist Likimani discovered through political contacts that Michael Kariuki had been involved in questionable dealings with some large Asian building contractors and had used his influence to sway certain officials in the awarding of lucrative Kenyan government contracts. Asian businessmen had rewarded him with large lump sums of cash deposited in foreign banks, Mercedes Benz automobiles, beach resort vacations, and airline tickets. Underground sources in Nairobi had obtained this information and furnished it to Likimani, who had paid dearly to acquire documents proving Kariuki's involvement in the corruption. Despite the high price, Likimani considered the information worth its weight in gold, because he knew he could use it to discredit Kariuki and erode his support within the KANU. Tom Kaplanget, chief editor at the *Daily Nation*, one of Kenya's two English-language speaking newspapers, was a friend of Likimani's. So Likimani turned over the information to Kaplanget, who agreed to release the news in accordance with Likimani's timetable. Likimani and his assistants spent the next six months collecting corroborative evidence, preparing to break the scandal at the worst possible time for the African insider.

The following summer, Odinga brought his party to meet with Mehar and his supporters at Kijabe. Mehar Singh's wife, Satbir Kaur, had been busy organizing the cooking and accommodations for the guests. The 5 ft. 5 in., slightly plump lady of the house was an industrious woman who had been an important helpmate to the husband who was nearly a foot taller than she. With dark, deep set eyes and a pleasant gentle air, she competently managed their mansion at Kijabe, built on five acres with thirty bedrooms which frequently provided a safe and luxurious night's respite for many Asian traders on their way in and out of Maasai territories. A large warehouse on the Kijabe estate had been converted into a meeting room, with accommodations set up so that food and drinks could be served continuously. Waiters were dressed in white kanzu and red fez caps as they served under bright floodlights.

Mehar Singh felt this was a critical meeting and would establish him as a serious candidate for the KANU party position. It was agreed that the *Daily Nation* news story would break the morning after the president announced the election dates. Investigations and follow-ups to the scandal were sure to follow. Mehar Singh would announce his candidacy a month after the story broke, and a week after that Odinga would follow suit.

Their strategy was well planned by Likimani, a master at detail who was known for his thorough follow-up on every aspect of a plan.

The news broke as planned on a Friday morning. This was to give the general public something to discuss over the weekend at bars, sports clubs, churches, mosques, temples, and other meeting places.

The whole country was shocked that the popular Michael Kariuki, a leading public figure in Kenyan politics and the secretary of KANU, would be involved in such corruption. Kariuki quickly issued a radio announcement and newspaper interview denying the allegations. In his statement, he alleged that his political enemies, the Jaluos, were behind the false allegations, which he insisted were fabricated in an attempt to discredit him before the election.

The damage to Kariuki's image was done. President Kenyatta immediately ordered an investigation to be conducted by Chief Justice Harris. The Kikuyus were in disarray.

When Mehar Singh announced his intention to run against Kariuki a month later, the repercussions were felt throughout Kenya's entire political structure. For an Asian to run for the KANU secretary's position was unthinkable, impossible, just not done. For Mehar, it was a tremendous risk politically, but if he succeeded, it would be an equally great victory.

Mehar's candidacy rekindled excitement among members

of the Asian and European community. They began holding political gatherings all over Nairobi and in the smaller towns and cities. The Europeans already had three Members of Parliament, but for an Asian to run for secretary of KANU was unheard of.

Mehar Singh now had to campaign not only in Maasailand but also throughout Kenya. If his candidacy was to have any chance of success, he had to take his message to the people. Likimani organized the entire operation and he intricately planned everything in advance: their transportation was arranged; speeches and press releases were written; press conferences and parties were scheduled. The good-humored Likimani was an exceptional campaign manager, and he loved being at the center of this controversial candidacy.

When Oginga Odinga announced that he was running for vice president of KANU, there was no mention of the alliance. The decision had been made in a back room to delay revealing the coalition between the Maasai and the Jaluo rather than alienating the Kikuyus and giving them the opportunity to present a united front.

The highly confident Charles Lare almost nonchalantly ignored his opponent's candidacy for the vice presidency.

Mehar Singh required funding for his election campaign, so he and Likimani soon were visiting prominent Asian, African, and European figures in Nairobi, Mombasa, Nyeri, Nanyuki and Kisumu. Likimani organized group parties with cocktails at which the host would give a speech and then introduce Mehar Singh. The formula for those meetings was successful, and in a short time they had raised the capital needed to keep the campaign moving.

Joseph Likimani relentlessly organized travel throughout Kenya so that the Asian could come face to face with his potential supporters. They traveled to Western Kenya and visited Machakos and the Makambas as well as Kisumu and the Jaluos. They traveled to Eastern Kenya to pay their respects to Nyeri and the Kikuyus, then to the coast to visit Mombasa and the Arabs, and then on to Southern Kenya to pay homage to

Narok and the Maasais. Mehar Singh also made a trip to the Northern Frontier District in the far northern part of Kenya that borders Somalia.

At every stop on the campaign trail, Mehar Singh was warmly received. The tall, imposing Asian with the booming voice was asked many questions about his plans for KANU and Kenya as well as his views on Kenya's multiracial society, education, and jobs. His responses were articulate, and he answered fluently in English, Swahili, Hindi, Punjabi, and Maasai.

Meanwhile, the incumbent Kariuki had pulled his political campaign team together. Well established in political circles, he felt confident enough to run for reelection despite the scandal, and he expected the full support of the Kikuyus. President Kenyatta kept a low profile, distancing himself from the rumors, the candidates, and the election itself.

Kariuki's campaign emphasized that Mehar Singh was a regional representative for the Maasai tribe and did not have the national exposure which Kariuki had as the secretary of KANU. Kariuki also aggressively stressed that his opponent was not a black African, a fact largely ignored by local media and most voters.

Mehar Singh played the corruption card to the hilt in his campaign as he highlighted his achievements as a Member of Parliament and his success in representing the remote Maasais. He claimed that he had brought the tribal, almost primitive, Maasais into the political structure of Kenya as he campaigned on the "Multiracial Kenya for Everyone" slogan. On many of his campaign stops, he took some Laibonis with him, and they were effective as they stood up, spoke in Swahili and provided testimonials for their Sikh Member of Parliament.

The *Daily Nation* and the *East African Standard* ran front page headlines every day as they followed the two candidates. The papers played on the Asian vs. African angle and printed interviews with other Members of Parliament, local leaders, and people on the street commenting on the candidates and their stands on the issues.

The election date was set for a Thursday. Throughout the nation polls opened early on a blustery, rainy day. Some Kikuyus started disturbances in Nanyuki and Nyeri, but overall voters behaved well as they were transported from the villages to the polling booths on government, KANU, and candidate-sponsored trucks and buses. Candidates attempted to maintain contact with voters through announcers who drove around the countryside in open Jeeps using megaphones to encourage people to vote for their man and make the difference.

After polling booths closed down, votes were counted over the next two days.

Oginga Odinga had campaigned vigorously for the vice presidential position but his efforts had been overshadowed by Charles Lare's well-organized campaign. Odinga had encountered serious problems raising funds for the campaign and his popularity had been mainly amongst the Jaluos and Luos. While Odinga suffered from lack of national visibility and insufficient financial support, Charles Lare, on the other hand, not only had campaign experience but also enjoyed the financial resources of the affluent Kikuyus as well as personal wealth. Despite the late announcement of Mehar Singh's affiliation with Odinga's campaign, Lare soundly defeated Odinga in the race for the Vice Presidency.

In the race for the KANU secretary's position, early returns showed a close race. Mehar Singh had gathered his family, friends, and campaign team at his mansion in Muthaiga while the incumbent Kariuki awaited the results from his house at Limuru, on the outskirts of Nairobi.

As the evening approached, it gradually became clear that Kariuki was going to lose. Final results were announced the next morning, and it had been a landslide victory for Mehar Singh!

After the results were made public, the last of Michael Kariuki's supporters filed out of the meeting room where the losing candidate had thanked his supporters, and then he followed Charles Lare into a side room where they could speak in private.

"That was certainly a fiasco," Lare said sharply. "I would have thought a three-legged mule could have taken the race from that old man. I didn't realize I'd backed a two-legged mule."

"I didn't know they'd gotten the details of the bribery scandal until it was too late to stop the story," Michael Kariuki whined.

"And why didn't you tell me about your bribery scheme?"

"By the time the story broke, I thought . . ."

"No, you *didn't* think," Lare snapped. "If you *had* thought, you wouldn't have accepted bribes from those crafty and manipulative Asian contractors until after the election. If you *had* thought, you wouldn't have been foolish enough to claim that your Asian opponent wasn't fit for the secretary's position because of his foreign connections."

Kariuki protested, "We were trying to control the damage from the story. It seemed best to continue the campaign as originally planned and hope the scandal would blow over. . ."

"The only thing that's over is your political career, and you're the one that blew it."

"It's not that bad," Kariuki countered, "I can still. . ."

"What you can still do is listen to me and do exactly what I tell you," Lare said, then added menacingly, "if you ever want to hold political office in Kenya again, that is."

"What do you need me to do?" Michael asked.

"That Asian Mehar Singh bears watching. Kenyatta favors him greatly, and people are flocking to him in droves. We want you to give him any help he needs as he assumes the KANU secretary's post. Gain his confidence and get as close to him as you can, so we will know his plans and be prepared the next time."

"After the smear campaign I ran against him, he will probably think I'm offering assistance to sabotage his efforts in some way," Michael said. "How can I convince him to take me into his confidence?"

"That's your problem," Lare replied impatiently. "A politician of your experience should be able to come up with a solution.

If necessary, try pretending that your career is in shambles, and you've realized that forging an alliance with him is your only chance at a political future. That should make it easier—you won't even have to lie."

Chapter III

"Let me tell you that Jomo Kenyatta has no intention of retaliating or looking backwards. We are going to forget the past and look forward to the future. I have suffered imprisonment and detention, but that is gone and I am not going to remember it. Many of you are as Kenyan as myself...let us join hands and work for the benefit of Kenya, not for the benefit of one community."

Jomo Kenyatta, 1963

As the first Asian ever elected to a high post in Kenya, Mehar Singh knew he was part of history, and his feeling of triumph made him recall vividly the greatest day in the history of Kenya—August 12, 1963—when the African country had achieved independence and Jomo Kenyatta, the great leader, had been named the first Prime Minister. Celebrations had been held throughout the country, and Africans, Asians and Europeans had rejoiced during the "Uhuru," or Freedom Festival.

That had been only three years earlier, and now Mehar would be working closely with the great "Mzee," whom he had come to revere. Mehar Singh found himself transported back mentally to that Independence Day when the Mzee had stood before the crowd so that all could look upon him. The prime minister had turned from side to side so that everyone could see his gray-bearded face. In his mind's eye, Mehar could picture Kenyatta clearly; the great leader's eyes were shining as he held back tears of joy. From his wrist dangled a silver-handled horsehair flywhisk, or "Mgwisho," one of his trademarks, and he swept it forward in a theatrical gesture.

In a clear commanding voice Kenyatta had called out, "Harambee!" (Hah-rahm-bay!).

Mehar had joined with thousands of others and, like a single thunderous echo, the words returned,"Haaa-raaam-bayyy!" It was a Swahili word meaning, "Let us pull together," and it had been selected by President Kenyatta as the national motto.

A devoted nationalist, the new prime minister became a staunch protector of Western political and economic interests in Kenya, and he came to be widely regarded as a stabilizing force in black Africa. Like most Kenyans, whether of African, Asian, or European descent, Mehar had proudly watched the leader's rise to glory. In the aftermath of his own election, Mehar found himself reflecting on the background of the political giant with whom he would now be working.

Kenyatta had been born on October 20, 1891, at Ichaweri in British East Africa, which later became known as Kenya. A member of the Kikuyu tribe, he was named Kamau wa Ngengi. Educated at the Church of Scotland Mission at Kikuyu and baptized a Christian, he worked as a government clerk in Nairobi, where in 1922 he joined a political protest movement. By 1928, as secretary of the Kikuyu Central Association, he was the chief advocate for Kikuyu land rights. From 1931 to 1946 he worked and studied in Western Europe and Moscow. His influential book *Facing Mount Kenya,* which he wrote in 1938, had begun as his thesis for the London School of Economics.

On returning to Africa, Burning Spear Beaded Belt, as Jomo Kenyatta was then known, was elected president of the new Kenya African Union, which later became the Kenya African National Union, or KANU. In 1952 he was charged with leading the Mau Mau rebellion against the British and, despite his denials, he was sentenced to seven years in prison. Released in 1961, he assumed the presidency of KANU. In 1963, when Kenya gained independence, Kenyatta became prime minister.

In 1964 he was elected president of the new Republic of Kenya. Elected for a five-year term, Kenyatta had to preside over a tribal land.

Although no Asian had ever attained such a high post as Mehar Singh, Asians had run for office at the city council level and several Asian lawyers and business figures represented constituencies throughout Kenya.

In his earliest political attempt, Mehar Singh had been encouraged by his friend Harry Fosbrooke and his closest African and Asian friends to run for the parliament seat representing the Narok area in Maasailand. A highly regarded Englishman who had lived in Kenya for many years, Fosbrooke had become District Commissioner for Narok, and he believed in Mehar. A big man at 220 lbs. with blond hair and gray eyes, Fosbrooke was seldom seen without a cigar in his mouth, and the good-natured, soft-spoken Brit was a definite asset to Mehar Singh's political career. With the support of Fosbrooke and others, Mehar was hopeful that nearly all of the Asians and many of the Maasais would accept him as their representative.

Mehar had joined the Kenya African National Union, KANU, rather than the Kenya African Democratic Union, KADU. The KANU was a party dominated by the Kikuyus with some Luo, Jaluos, and Makambas.

In his first run for political office, his primary opponent had been an independent candidate named Joseph Ole Likimani, a Maasai educated in Narok, Nakuru, and Nairobi who taught school in Narok. Mehar Singh's campaign had been centered on the issue of setting up a moratorium in the Maasai territories. He wanted to leave the land as it was and stop all new development of farms and tourist lodges. The nomadic Maasai favored his plan, as it would allow them to maintain their cattle herds and have ample grazing land, which they would share only with the wild animals.

In contrast, Likimani's campaign had emphasized the fact that he was a native of Narok and knew what was right for his fellow countrymen.

27

Mehar Singh had traveled extensively throughout the territory with his wife and sons. They camped in remote areas and spoke to the Maasais in their native tongue. He was fluent in the local language, Swahili, and would argue for hours with the "Laibonis," the Maasai headmen. After fierce debates, they would chat amiably over a feast of goat meat and the local alcoholic drink "Chaanga" which was brewed in the manyattas, or Maasai villages.

One of the biggest challenges for the Kenyan Government was to find a way to get the Maasai registered to vote. This was difficult, as they lived in remote areas of the country with no means of transportation except cattle and donkeys. And since they had never voted before, this was a new concept for them. Getting the Maasai registered to vote had been a critical factor for Mehar, as they represented a large portion of his district.

The Maasais would walk and run for miles to travel from one village to the other, to go to school, and to shop at the Asian dukas. Their young men, Moraans, were famous for their magnificent physiques and incredible stamina.

Because they had come to know and trust Mehar Singh as a successful Asian businessman, Mehar was treated by the Maasais as one of their own and held in high esteem. On one occasion during his campaign for office against Likimani, the local Laiboni had invited him to one of the special Maasai ceremonies which are restricted to Maasais and special invitees. To the Asian transplant, the Maasai customs seemed strange and their ritual ceremonies were quite different from those of the Sikh religion which Mehar Singh and his family practiced. Mehar gained a special appreciation of the cultural differences between him and the Maasai when he accepted that particular invitation.

Mehar had been invited to the ritual circumcision of girls who were about to be married in a ceremony held at the big manyatta in Moricho, just south of Narok. Mehar had learned that Maasai girls are treated and behave in much the same way as boys until they are old enough to carry out small chores. A

Maasai girl then becomes an assistant to her mother, while boys of that age go out herding cattle. A young girl would gather fresh cow dung to repair the huts and split strips of olive wood for cleaning out "kibuis," and she would help her mother milk the cows and be taught to construct mud huts.

As soon as the girl started showing an interest in boys, usually at about eight or nine years of age, she was permitted to go off with the layonis, young boys who had not been circumcised, so that they could explore each other's bodies. When she reached the age of eleven to thirteen and was ready to make love with the Moraans, she was no longer a virgin.

If a girl liked a particular Moraan, or Maasai warrior, he was invited to drink milk with her on a fixed day in a ceremony called Ngibot. The girl would inform her mother that she wanted to have the Ngibot, and the milk would be set aside for them for two or three days beforehand. All the Moraans and the young girls, Nditos, would dress up in beads and smear themselves with red ochre before entering the manyatta.

As a guest at the ceremony, Mehar Singh also was dressed and decorated for the Ngibot. They took his shirt off and painted his face and chest with red ochre, and then, with great care and respect, they removed the turban which they knew distinguished him as a member of the Sikh religion and tied his long hair in a ponytail. They then applied red soil to his entire head, just as they had done to themselves. They also handed him a long spear known as "Makuki," a symbol of manhood and bravery. He was also given a "Rungu," a short wooden club rounded at the end like a tennis ball.

Once they were all prepared, everyone ate the curdled milk and the dancing began. An older Ndito, who had already proven her "worth" to the Moraans, was then chosen to perform the Milk Ceremony.

A kibui of milk, previously treated with olive ash that makes it stay fresh for days, was presented by the older Ndito to the chosen Moraan and placed at his feet. When he had drunk all he could, the Moraan led his new sweetheart to a hut, followed by the other young men and girls. The couple spent the night making love, and subsequently both were known as "asanja," the Maasai word for lovers.

A Moraan could have as many as fifty asanja or lovers at any one time, and unmarried Maasai girls could take just as many. An asanja always had priority over other lovers and a girl would retain her status as the asanja of a given Moraan until she got married.

Mehar Singh sat alongside the Laiboni, or the Maasai witch doctor, during the whole ceremony, drinking the locally brewed Chaanga and eating the roasted meats. No foreigner had ever before been invited to this Maasai ceremony as they were private and the tribe likes secrecy. The witch doctor told Mehar Singh that an uncircumcised girl could not become pregnant, so unmarried Maasai practiced coitus interruptus. In the event of accidents, abortions were performed. If an abortion could not be performed, the girl was given a clitoridectomy and a marriage took place immediately.

Mehar Singh had also participated in the ceremonial killing of the ox the day before the girl's circumcision ceremony. The day before the circumcision, the witch doctor planted an olive sapling just outside the manyatta, or group of Maasai huts. Then, with Mehar's help, an ox was killed and split down the center, and the right side of the carcass was kept for the women. Any woman within sight of the slaughter was given a piece of the meat for good luck. The left side of the ox was for the men, and from it certain portions were removed and cooked separately for use in the re-naming ceremony, for it was customary that the girl would lose her name and be given a new one.

Neither Mehar nor any other man was permitted to watch the actual circumcision. Early on the morning of the circumcision the girl went between her mother's hut and the fence enclosing the manyatta. She bathed with water specially prepared for the ceremony and, while she was bathing, a hole was made in the roof to let in light for performing the operation, which would be carried out by one of the older women.

During the circumcision, the girl was held down by several women, and she could scream and fight as much as she wished for there was no disgrace associated with this.

The circumcision consisted of removing half an inch of skin around the clitoris, which was cut out to a depth of a quarter of an inch and a slash made below it towards the vagina. The reason given for this crude and cruel surgery was that it enlarged the vagina, making childbirth easier. It was believed that removal of the clitoris would prevent sexual arousal and prevent promiscuity.

Mehar was told that, for the next four months after the ceremony, the girl was to remain in her mother's hut, during which time she was fed only on meat and fat. On the day she was to leave the hut, her betrothed would be present. She would be shaved and every particle of body hair removed so that she was made to look as beautiful as a bride and was then presented to her husband.

After the circumcision ceremony, Mehar Singh spent the night at the manyatta and was offered, as a token of Maasai respect, any woman he wanted for the night. Mehar had always found attractive the tall Maasai women with their attractive sculptured facial features highlighting their cheekbones.

On his subsequent travels through Maasai land, Mehar Singh had worked hard to get voters registered. He coordinated with local government officials and arranged for taxis and buses to transport Maasais to the election booths. Temporary voting booths were set up in some remote areas in the manyattas where the Laibonis lived. This election was predicted to be a historic one; everyone expected the highest voter turnout in the history of the region.

The central election headquarters was set up at the District Commissioner's office in Narok. Days before polling day, Asian traders were camped on the shores of the Narok River and the celebrations began. Cases of Scotch whiskey, barrels of beer, and hundreds of chickens and goats were prepared to be barbecued. Mehar Singh's family was in the midst of this celebration, as this was the first time an Asian had run for a major political office outside of Nairobi.

Election booths closed at six in the evening, and the counting was to be completed by four the next afternoon. Voters had been coming in at a regular pace to place their ballots. The Maasais had to be instructed very carefully on the process as this was the first time most tribesmen had voted. The Maasai had been a nomadic tribe with little interaction with the outside world, so they were apprehensive and had to be coaxed into the process. The reasons why they should vote and what the candidates might do for them had to be explained in detail to the tribesmen. The Maasai who had dealt with Mehar Singh trusted him and his judgment completely.

Throughout Kenya, there was tremendous anticipation after the polls closed. Everyone was anxious to learn the outcome of the election—whether Mehar had been beaten by his African opponent or had broken new ground, as one of the first Asian candidates to win a major election outside of Nairobi.

A huge crowd had gathered outside the District Commissioner's office to hear the election results. Fosbrooke was outside the office promptly at ten o'clock in the morning, and he had his assistants lined up with the ballot boxes. As he rose to announce the result, the Maasais began their ritual dance in which they jumped as high as possible in the air and threw spears. Fosbrooke had to wait while the assistant district officer calmed the excited Moraans.

The announcement was heard in silence. First, Fosbrooke announced the count for Likimani. He had received 23,019 votes. The crowd wasn't sure what this meant, as there was no indication of the percentage of the electorate eligible to vote or of the actual turnout on polling day.

Fosbrooke continued, "Mehar Singh has 25,905 votes— and the winner is...Mehar Singh."

The margin was closer than anyone could have predicted.

It was 1964. The crucial first step in his political ambitions had been taken and now he could start planning his future. Mehar Singh was on his way to starting a new career and making contributions to the country and the people he so dearly loved.

The Dhillon campaign headquarters had been set up in a huge tent beside the Red River at Narok. His friends came by that whole day to congratulate him and chat. Maasai well-wishers crowded the area, singing and drinking.

At sunset the Moraans continued their traditional dancing in which they challenged each other and jumped as high as possible with their spears while dancing around in circles and singing.

Some Maasai women, or siangikis as they were called in the Maasai language, joined their men in the ritual. Mehar had learned that the Maasai culture was quite primitive in the way they treated sexual relationships. Sex was allowed between any consenting individuals, and the Moraans or siangikis could choose a different partner any time they wished. As a ritual of courtship, a Moraan would walk outside a hut in the manyatta and plant his spear in the ground to signal that he was spending the night with the woman there. It was customary for a Maasai Moraan or Maasai elder to offer his wife to his guest. This was a tradition that the Maasais believed was the ultimate in hospitality and if the guest refused, it was considered an insult. The women had no control over these decisions.

As the traditional dancing progressed into the night, it became more erotic and more alcohol was consumed. Gradually, Maasai couples drifted off into the bushes in the dark African night. Some of the couples couldn't wait and did not even move away from the gathering.

The party was over about four in the morning. It had been a grand affair with the Maasai voters and the candidate feeling quite pleased with the outcome of the election.

After the election, Mehar Singh, his wife Satbir Kaur, and their sons, daughters-in-law, and grandsons packed up and made the forty-mile journey back to the residence at Kijabe. A vacation was in order, they decided, after the long, grueling campaign, and they traveled by train to the coastal town of Mombasa to spend some time at the beach.

Mehar Singh was now a political figure, and he was approached frequently by strangers who would offer advice, tell him what they thought was wrong with the country, and offer their help.

Chapter IV

"The survival of our wildlife is a matter of grave concern to all of us. These wild creatures amid the wild places they inhabit are not only important as a source of wonder and inspiration but are an integral part of our national resources and of our future livelihood and well-being."

Julius Nyerere (1961)

When he was a young man Mehar Singh had left India for Africa to help build the railroads, and he had adopted Africa as his homeland. Akash, on the other hand, had been born in Africa and grew up amidst the family businesses his industrious grandfather had built, many of which centered on Kenya's growing tourist trade. The family owned several hunting lodges, which made for an adventurous and exciting lifestyle. During school breaks, Akash went on hunting safaris with his father and uncles and they let him hold the seven millimeter rifles and the big elephant guns, the .420 and .450 millimeter rifles.

Safaris varied depending on the tourist's tastes; some desired to hunt the "big five"—elephant, rhino, lion, leopard, and buffalo—while others just wanted to photograph the majestic animals in their natural habitats. In difficulty, hunters ranked the leopard first, followed by lion, buffalo, elephant, and rhino. A preference for hunting the carnivores was shared by most big game hunters who had to finish off the wounded animals.

Akash spent his school vacations with his uncles at the various

Dhillon businesses. He visited the sawmills at Mau Narok, the stores at Loliondo and Narok, and the game lodges.

Educated at private schools in Nairobi, Akash was, like most students of Indian or European descent, actively involved in hockey, cricket, soccer, badminton, volleyball, and rugby. He had a knack for sports and excelled at a young age. At fifteen, he was chosen to play cricket for the Combined Asians against the Combined Europeans.

His debut was memorable as he scored eighty-nine runs and contributed to his team's winning. He played hockey for the elite Sikh Union Club and was a prolific scorer. His selection to the Kenyan national hockey squad was a record as he was the youngest player ever to be named at that level in East Africa.

As he turned eighteen, Akash completed his "A" levels which in Kenya, modeled after the British educational system, followed high school graduation. Active in debates, he excelled at oratory and was the school debating captain. He was itching to travel and go overseas, and since his ambition was to get into politics, he was leaning towards law school.

After applying to colleges and universities in Britain, Akash received favorable responses from Cambridge, Oxford, Cardiff, and Edinburgh based on his impressive academic credentials. He decided to visit some of the campuses before making a decision.

His friend Khurshid was also planning on studying in England. They'd been childhood friends and constant companions. To Akash, it was exciting to envisage the two of them going to a new country together, and having a lifelong friend nearby would facilitate the transition of living in another country. Perhaps surprisingly, Akash's father did not support his son's decision to leave home. In Santokh Singh's view, his oldest son Akash needed to take over the family businesses, and he didn't need to get his head filled with theories from law school or leave home for England and perhaps get sidetracked into staying abroad for social or professional reasons.

After his grandfather won the KANU secretary's post, Akash

used the patriarch's latest success to advance his argument. In what almost seemed like a well-prepared legal defense, Akash argued with his father that with men like Mehar Singh making inroads into Kenyan politics, the country already had great leaders. Moving into its first century of independence, however, Akash warned, Kenya would need great legislators—and the best law schools were in England.

After many verbal wrestling matches, Akash's father agreed to take counsel with Mehar Singh, and he told Akash that together they would come to a decision. Mehar told his soft-spoken, pot-bellied eldest son that, while he agreed with his desire to have Akash take over the family businesses, Mehar felt that studying abroad, especially in England and at one of the top universities in the world, was a valuable opportunity. Mehar admitted that Kenya—indeed, all of Africa—offered no schools that could match the education Akash could receive abroad. The young man was bright and the best universities in the country were ready to accept him and credential him. The family had the financial resources to support his studies in Britain, and the opportunity was too valuable to let it slip away.

Once Mehar Singh blessed the decision, there was no holding back the excited young man.

Akash and Khurshid flew on Lufthansa to Frankfurt where they stayed for two nights. They took the short flight to Munich to visit the old Bavarian city and they were in awe, as they wandered through the narrow streets, admiring centuries-old architecture. In Munich, they discovered the Hofbrauhaus beer halls, and after a long drinking session, Akash and his friend visited some of the local nightclubs.

The young men found a busy club, and it wasn't long before they were surrounded by beautiful blonde German girls. Language was a problem as only a few of the girls spoke any English, but they managed well enough, using gestures and body language. They danced nearly all night, enjoying the company of the friendly German girls.

After two days in Munich, it was time to continue on to England. They made the connection to Heathrow from Frankfurt on a British European Airways jet. In London, a family friend, Hardev, who lived in Mill Hill, North London, met them at the airport. A resident of England for ten years, Hardev owned a chain of supermarkets. Originally from Eldoret in Kenya, he'd been a friend of the Dhillon family for as long as Akash could remember.

It was convenient staying near the Mill Hill Underground Train Station, and Akash and Khurshid traveled all over England using the best designed and most efficient subway system in the world. Mindful of the main reason he was there, Akash called to schedule appointments to visit the universities, and the young men visited Oxford, Cambridge and Cardiff. Akash decided against the Scottish University, as it was too far from London, and the winters were extreme and would restrict his sports activities. In a rented Ford Cortina, Akash enjoyed driving on the fast motorways, admiring the carefully landscaped campuses of these historic universities and the quaint, Gothic atmosphere of the towns in Oxford and Cambridge.

Akash chose Oxford, and Khurshid decided to study Engineering at Cambridge. The two friends would be on opposite sides of the ancient rivalry.

Akash was elated at the prospect of spending the next few years at a historical institution which had an excellent sporting curriculum. He called his parents and informed them of his decision, but he was careful not to sound too excited as he didn't want his father tortured by the thought that he might be leaving Kenya for good.

College terms didn't start for another four weeks, so the two young Kenyans decided to spend the time touring Britain in a rented Volkswagen Kombi van. Starting in Wales, they visited Harlech Castle and then they were off to the Midlands and Manchester, followed by Glasgow and Edinburgh, returning through Newcastle, Sheffield, and finally back to Hardev's home in Mill Hill.

Play and freedom soon gave way to work and a scheduled lifestyle, and once Akash started his law education at Oxford, he was engrossed in his studies. Although the academics were grueling, he discovered that he could manage his time so he could participate in extracurricular activities including debate as well as hockey and cricket.

Historically one of the leading universities for sports, Oxford played in the premier London Hockey League, the most competitive in England. Oxford's perennial rivalry against Cambridge was a major event on the sporting calendar. Aside from the long tradition of the rivalry, by playing against Cambridge Akash got to face his friend Khurshid, who received his varsity colors at hockey.

Akash especially excelled at cricket and at Oxford he was thrilled at the opportunity to play against the Indians, New Zealand, Australia and the West Indians. In the most exciting match of his life, he scored "124 runs not out" against the West Indians, his best performance ever and the highlight of his cricket career. The West Indians had Garfield Sobers, Rohan Kanhai, Lance Gibbs, Conrad Hunte, and Wes Hall playing that day, all giants who became legends in the cricketing hall of fame. Oxford had drawn the match against the touring Caribbean superstars.

Akash would never forget that day. He had come in to bat at number three in the order and had held the innings together throughout the day. Then he faced the devastating speed of Wes Hall and the guile and spin of Lance Gibbs. At the end Oxford was 389 with nine wickets down. Akash and Mike Twilliger had held out the last five overs with the menacing West Indians crowding the batsmen to get the last wicket in before the fading evening light and threatening rain clouds.

Most of the games played by the West Indian touring side were televised, and there was considerable interest among East Africans living in Britain, who enjoyed watching one of their countrymen playing at that level. There were headlines in all the Sunday national newspapers in England and in East Africa.

Akash had distinguished himself, and he was offered the opportunity to play for a full season with Warwickshire in the English County Championships. He was tempted, but playing professional cricket was something he hadn't considered. He thought about his conversations with his grandfather and father and realized that he couldn't allow anything to derail his goal of eventually returning to Africa. He declined their offer.

The British universities played each other at cricket, and the hockey league played matches all over England, so Akash visited all the major cities. A socially gregarious person, Akash made friends easily all over England. At most of the games he would run into Kenyans and East Africans, and as they conversed in Swahili they were grateful for the opportunity to speak with others in the language of their homeland.

Although he had promised his father and grandfather he would return to Africa, Akash began to feel very comfortable in England. He began to understand how his grandfather and people like his grandfather could expatriate and choose another country as their homeland. Akash knew he had to be careful never to communicate this to his father. How different this civilized, literate country was from the untamed jungles of Africa, his homeland.

Chapter V

"God Himself shapes men as vessels, and brings
them to perfection. In some is put the milk of loving
and kindness, others ever are set on the fire of passion.
Some lie down to sleep on cushions, others stand to
watch over them. God regenerates those on whom He
looks with grace."

Guru Nanak Dev Jee

From a distance in England, Akash continued to follow Mehar Singh's political career closely. He spoke to his father and uncles frequently and pored over the stories in the political sections of the Kenyan newspapers. By all accounts, Mehar Singh's political star was rising, not only within Kenya but also throughout the African countries.

His grandfather's popularity as KANU secretary grew by the day. Mehar's pleasant mannerisms and firmness in making decisions became a frequent subject of conversation, and his neutrality in dealing with tribal matters surprised even the Kikuyus.

President Kenyatta liked the tall, turbaned Asian, and he invited Mehar Singh to accompany him on several state visits to the African countries. Kenyatta was a consummate politician, and taking Mehar on state trips was an excellent strategy as it presented an African and an Asian representing Kenya and enhanced the country's multiracial image. Kenyatta knew that this public relations event was extremely important for the tourist industry, a mainstay of the Kenyan economy, which was extremely sensitive to any rumblings of internal or ethnic turmoil. Kenyatta seemed to seize every photo opportunity to project a unified, tranquil nation as the 6' 4" turbaned Asian stood smiling next to the black African who was six inches shorter.

In an effort to strengthen the East African Community of Kenya, Tanzania and Uganda, Mehar was busy developing trade agreements, common railways and airlines, and tourism packages. He traveled to Dar-es-salaam and Kampala to meet with the heads of state of Tanzania and Uganda to get an historic economic agreement approved, and he was establishing a reputation as a brilliant negotiator and strategist who could establish consensus among unlikely parties. Mehar seemed to have a knack for persuading people to analyze one another's viewpoints, and this enabled him to get tough negotiators from different countries to work together with a common goal in mind.

It was agreed that the three heads of state would meet in Dar-es-Salaam and sign the pact. Mehar and the entire cabinet accompanied Kenyatta on the trip to Tanzania for the meetings and celebrations.

Mehar had developed an excellent rapport with the Tanzanian leader, Julius Nyerere, affectionately known as "Mwalimu" or "the teacher" by his followers. The Ugandan leader, Milton Obote, initially had reservations about dealing with an Asian mediator, but he was soon at ease with Mehar Singh's easygoing and humorous yet insightful style. The political friendships Mehar had forged helped tremendously in securing the agreement.

Mehar Singh's stature as a politician and negotiator became known throughout the East African countries. He was now established as one of the leading politicians in Kenya, whose authority and power were sanctioned by the president.

Indeed, because of Mehar's political successes, Kenyatta assigned increasing political responsibilities to Mehar Singh, and the Asian was placed in charge of many critical domestic and international issues.

On one occasion, Mehar was sent to the Kenyan/Somali border in Northern Kenya to settle the feud between the Somali

"Shifta" terrorists and Kenyan tribesmen. The struggle had been going on for years over water rights in the desert region. Raiding Shifta parties had attacked Kenyan villages in the middle of the night and taken their women, goats, cattle, and food. Whenever both the Shiftas and the Kenyans met at a watering hole there were fights. Both groups traveled in Jeeps and Land Rovers armed with powerful rifles, and casualties were rising every year.

Apparently fearless about traveling to the front line to mediate in the dispute, the rugged Mehar drove to Wajir in northeastern Kenya and then deep into the Shifta camps, where he tracked down and developed a relationship with their leader Waria Mohammed. He and the Somali leader hit it off instantly. They had a similar sense of humor and shared many political views. Waria invited the Sikh to come to sit with him at the campfire, drinking home-brewed liquor and sharing "Marungi," a green leaf that prevents sleepiness and has mildly intoxicating effects. Mehar Singh discussed the issues and tried to understand the Somalis' point of view.

By establishing trust, Mehar was able to set up a series of meetings between the Shiftas and Kenyan villagers. After much negotiation, it was agreed that the two parties would take turns in drawing water from the wells, and each group was assigned certain days of the week. If the agreement was violated, the party that broke the pact would lose its rights for the next month.

The agreement was brilliant in its simplicity, and it was so simple that everyone easily accepted it. The historic agreement was completely credited to Mehar Singh, and the settlement was widely reported and publicized by KANU and the government, which further strengthened Mehar Singh's public image.

The Sikh leader continued touring the land, speaking eloquently and bluntly, and calling for peace and harmony. His recurring themes were for Kenyans to reject tribalism, to be one people and one nation, to work hard, seek education, practice tolerance, and support the rule of law, the government, and the president. A commanding orator, Mehar was able to articulately and fluently express his views in Swahili, and the country came to be full of converts to his way of thinking.

Although Mehar came to be accepted as an "African at heart," his beliefs about Africa and politics were formed mostly from his religious views, although he rarely discussed his Sikh religion with non-Sikhs. About five hundred years old, the Sikh religion had evolved from a need to defend oppressed Hindus from their oppressors, the Mughal Islamic invaders in India. To Mehar Singh's knowledge, Sikhism was the only religion in the world that fought for human rights of another religion. Mehar's values had been formed by The Holy Sikh Book, The Guru Granth Sahib, which had been compiled by a number of the Sikh Gurus and contained a selection of teachings from other religions.

As a Sikh, Mehar recognized God as the Creator and Sustainer of the universe, and Sikhism emphasized the need for each person to live a life of physical, moral, and spiritual self-discipline. Devotion, discipline, and humility were the cornerstones of the Sikh faith, and Sikhism taught that the true believer was a man of action with an overwhelming sense of self-reliance. Sikhism especially rejected distinctions of caste and creed, and from its inception the Sikh Gurus or founders gave women equal status with men. Ethics and morality were the basis of Sikhism, and Mehar had always liked the point made by Guru Nanak: "Greater than Truth is truthful living." Sikhism enjoined its members to cultivate essential virtues including a love of truth, contentment with one's lot, patience, perfect faith, compassion, and the practice of virtue. Sikhs were encouraged to avoid vices including lust, anger, greed, worldly attachment, and pride, which Sikhism considered the main enemies of man.

One Sikh tradition which Mehar enjoyed centered on the serving of food, "langars," at all times of the day to anyone who visits the Gurudwara, Guru's Place, or Sikh temple. Everyone would sit together as one, to break the caste and the rich/poor separation. In the Sikh Religion there were ten Gurus, and the second Guru, Angad, had started this tradition. This religion which taught tenderness toward others was probably what had produced the tender-hearted Mehar.

Perhaps because of his religion, Mehar Singh was sensitive to the plight of the less fortunate, and the poverty of the average Kenyan touched him. With the political clout he now had, Mehar Singh wanted to help the poor. In a widely publicized act, he organized all the Sikh Gurudwaras, or temples, throughout Kenya to set up Sunday as the day when they would pool their resources and drive though the cities and villages and set up camps where they served langars, or the temple of bread, to everyone.

This gesture made Mehar even more popular with all races throughout Kenya. The Africans became more aware of the Sikh religion and its traditions, and they gained a new respect for the Sikhs. Although the Sikhs were not active in converting others to their religion, some Africans liked what they saw and the image of the strong, fearless Sikhs made them want to convert. Suddenly some Africans started wearing turbans and maintaining beards, and some participated in the temples where they cooked and served food to the congregations.

The Sikh Temple at Makindo, on the trunk road from Nairobi to Mombasa, was a popular stop for travelers. The Sewadars at this Temple were mainly the newly converted African Sikhs, with their dark skin in sharp contrast to their white turbans.

As Mehar's popularity grew, there were rumors about Mehar Singh's being a serious contender for the vice presidency of Kenya in the next election. The possibility that he was being groomed to be Kenyatta's successor was openly discussed in the press and by his constituents.

In the background, however, the ambitious Kikuyu Charles Lare desperately wanted to succeed Kenyatta as the next Kenyan leader. Lare's camp grew increasingly concerned as Mehar Singh's popularity increased daily among Kenyans of all races, and they grew alarmed watching the photographs and news articles which appeared about Mehar Singh almost daily in the national newspapers. The popular Asian was shown meeting with Africans in the remote villages as well as with

Europeans and Asians at sports and social events throughout Kenya.

Charles Lare and his advisors held secret strategy sessions, trying to develop a plan to overcome the Sikh leader's growing popularity. It was becoming obvious that the Asian Sikh would be a major hurdle and could block the politically ambitious Kikuyu.

Chapter VI

"If you desire to play the game of love with me,
Come into my lane, placing your head on your palm,
If you want to tread on this road,
Lay down your head, without any reservation."
Guru Nanak Dev Jee

Anar was the granddaughter of Shahbaz Khan, an orthodox
Moslem from the same village in the Punjab as Mehar Singh.
Shahbaz Khan had migrated to Africa in the same dhow—a
small ship with lateen sails used mainly along the coasts of
Arabia, East Africa, and India—with Akash's grandfather. Religion
was the top priority for Khan, and it was imperative that his
granddaughter eventually marry a man of the Moslem faith.
Born in Arusha, a beautiful town on the base of majestic Mt.
Meru in Northern Tanzania, Anar was a beautiful girl with
hazel eyes, a button nose, and a radiant smile. Everyone who
saw her knew she was destined to break a few hearts when she
grew older.

Her name was taken from the Indian word for pomegranate,
a sweet fruit with a multitude of red seeds full of sweet nectar.
Her parents were wealthy in a town dominated by the
Sherwanis, the elite of the richest Asians in East Africa, owners
of sugar mills and coffee plantations. Her family owned businesses
ranging from sawmills and supermarkets to wheat farms and a
host of other corporations. With two brothers and three sisters,
Anar was the youngest in the family and she had the sweet

47

disposition often associated with the youngest in the birth order.

Shahbaz Khan had established a mosque in Arusha on the shores of picturesque Lake Duluti. That magnificent setting on the outskirts of Arusha possessed the ideal climate, with tall acacia trees, a magnificent view of the majestic Mt. Meru, and a unique combination of plant life that made the site of the mosque a calm green all year round. The mosque was private yet accessible to residents from Arusha as well as to travelers passing along the main road from Arusha to Moshi.

As the other major city in Northern Tanzania, Moshi was located fifty miles from Arusha at the base of snow-capped Mount Kilimanjaro, the highest mountain in Africa. Moshi was dominated by the business-smart "Chagga" tribe, which resided at the foothills of Mt. Kilimanjaro. The Chaggas were an intelligent, ambitious tribe of Bantu-speaking cultivators who practiced irrigation in the rich highlands. Like the Kikuyus, they were driven inland from the coast by northern invaders, and they were supposed to have displaced a small race of men carrying big bows and communicating in unintelligible speech who had been driven higher and higher up Mt. Kilimanjaro until they eventually vanished.

Shahbaz Khan had come to be established as the Moslem leader in the northern part of Tanzania. Educated at the College for Islamic Studies in Lahore and fluent in the Urdu poetry and dialect, Shahbaz had studied other religions in great depth, especially the Sikh religion and literature. It was unusual for a Moslem to study those subjects because of the historical conflicts between Moslems and Hindus and the fact that Islam was the reason for inception of the Sikh religion.

One unique quality about Shahbaz was his progressive thinking with regard to equality for the sexes, although his views on this subject weren't shared by his peers in the clergy. His Sunday congregation was growing weekly, and his fame was spreading throughout Tanzania and Kenya. Shahbaz Khan had a knack for preaching religion at a level that was down to earth so that everyone could relate the concepts he preached to their daily lives.

Shahbaz came to be regarded as a controversial figure as he sometimes sang hymns from the religious Sikh holy book, the "Granth Sahib," in a tune that was folksy and in sync with the day's fashionable pop music. Besides, a Moslem singing Sikh hymns was unheard of and almost sinful for someone from the Islamic faith.

Anar was almost five years old when she started singing with her grandfather. She also sang with her Sikh friends in the local Gurudwara in Arusha. From the first moment that this young bird opened her mouth, it was obvious that her sweet voice was special and destined to be famous. However, she was introduced to controversy at a young age, for Orthodox Moslems frowned upon a young Moslem girl singing in the Sikh Temple. They would regularly complain to her father, Manzur Khan, a 5' 10" bald man in his fifties, but his response was always the same: "Her grandfather taught her the truth about God. If it is Allah's wish that she preaches in Sikhism, then let it be. The almighty will take care of her."

The Sikh religion fascinated Anar and she began reading books about the "Sikh Gurus" and about Indian history. She even began singing the Shabads, songs containing the Guru's message with music added, so she was actually singing the most sacred of Sikh sermons. When Mehar Singh learned of his friend Shahbaz Khan's granddaughter's being a religious singer, he contacted her father and requested that the sixteen-year-old Anar preach the Shabads at the Singh Sabha Gurudwara in Nairobi. The recital was to be on Baisakhi, the holiest of the Sikh religious days commemorating the formal crowning of the Sikhs by the tenth Guru, Gobind Singh.

The Sikhs were no more happy about the young bird's singing their religious sermons than the Orthodox Moslems had been. The announcement that Anar would appear on Baisakhi caused uproar among the Sikhs in Nairobi. Many were offended at the idea of a Moslem reciting the Sikh holy scripts, and protest marches were organized as local businessmen sponsored broadcasts on the Asian Voice of Kenya denouncing the decision to have Anar sing at the Sikh temple on Baisakhi.

Amolak Singh, the Gyani or head Sikh Priest in Nairobi, was adamant that the young girl would sing. Amolak Singh was an impressive figure and even more so when he was adamant about something. He dressed in the religious long white kurta, or gown, which was nearly four inches below his knee with tight-hugging pajamas underneath. On his head he wore the traditional white turban, like Mehar, but around his waist he sported the kirpan, or sword, along with four other symbols of the Sikh religion. His beard was white and neatly combed with touches of black sprinkled throughout as it flowed freely and hung down his chest. He and the tall, turbaned Mehar made an impressive duo and they were hard to resist as they visited many of the angry Sikhs at their homes until they were able to defuse the protest. They persuaded the Sikh leadership that this was an honor that someone from another religion had shown a desire to learn the Sikh religion and now excelled at preaching. It was probably a gift from God, they argued, so it must be accepted, they insisted.

Anar was nervous as it was going to be a tremendous test of her singing, character, and composure to face one of the largest Sikh crowds in Nairobi on this holiest of Sikh holy days. The crowd was expected to be even bigger because of the controversy surrounding her appearance. Anar prepared for almost two months, carefully selecting her favorite Shabads and practicing them daily.

Anar's father, Manzur, grandfather Shahbaz Khan, and her three best friends, Pammi, Shahnaz, and Jagi, accompanied her on the drive to Nairobi. They made the trip on Saturday, the day before Baisakhi. By arriving early and staying overnight, Anar would be able to get plenty of rest before the service, as she was scheduled to begin reciting at ten in the morning.

The drive was uneventful; the girls joked and sang among themselves. The trip from Arusha to Nairobi took almost six hours over dirt and tarmac roads. The drive took them around the base of Mt. Meru, over Ol-Donyio-Sambu, and crossed the border between Kenya and Tanzania at Longido, a small outpost where they checked their documents and tried to formalize the customs process. Then they passed through Namanga, the entry to the famous Amboseli Game Reserve. They saw the usual animals en route to Nairobi—the zebras, wildebeests, impalas, Thomson gazelles, and a herd of elephants accompanied by newborn calves stumbling on the road past Namanga.

When they reached Nairobi, they stayed with the Querishy family in Westlands, on the outskirts of the capital. Abdul Querishy and Anar's father had been school friends and had played hockey and cricket together for the Sir Ali Moslem Club in Nairobi. Abdul had prepared a feast for their arrival, with Biriyani and Beef "Ghosht," Manzur's favorite. After dinner, the host served hot spiced tea, sweet Julebis, and Ghulab Jamans, the traditional Indian sweets. They sat around the table and played a game of gin rummy. Everyone went to bed early as the big day was almost here.

The party arrived at the Gurudwara, or temple, at nine thirty on Sunday. The Sikhs in the car park and in the grounds of the temple whispered to each other and kept staring at the beautiful young girl. Mehar Singh greeted them and embraced his friend Shahbaz and blessed young Anar by placing his hand on the top of her head as she reached toward him. Anar entered the huge temple accompanied by the proud and smiling Shahbaz and Mehar Singh. According to Sikh Custom, she bent down on her knees and bowed to the holy "Granth Sahib." There was a strange silence as everyone fixed their eyes on the gorgeous Moslem girl.

The spectators admired her natural good looks and her wholesome, traditional style. She wore the colorful baggy trousers with a long tunic known as the salwar kameez which was the traditional garb worn by Sikh women, and her pretty face was set off by small walians, or earrings, which her grandmother had given her on her sixteenth birthday.

Anar sat on the "ladies' side" of the temple, the right side facing the holy Granth Sahib, in accordance with Sikh custom.

Her father sat on the left-hand side.

A local Gyani from Nairobi, Dharam Singh, initiated the ceremony by singing the Shabads and doing the Kirtan, the Guru's message in a collection of musical hymns regarded as the means by which the soul could be reached. He had started at six in the morning with Asa-Ji-Di-War, prayers performed early in the morning which lasted for three hours.

Dharam Singh rose after finishing his allotted time, and the head Gyani announced to the congregation that Anar would now recite a few Shabads. There was excitement as everyone shuffled to get a better view. A local musician from Nairobi accompanied her on the tabla and she played the harmonium.

Anar began with her favorite Shabad, "Jo Mange Thakar" (Whatever you may ask from God). As soon as she began to sing, the congregation was spellbound. They sat in silence and listened to the magnificent voice and the holy words. It was evident that this voice was going to grow into an extraordinary religious medium. She sang two more Shabads, "Mitr Pyare Nu" (Please tell my plight to my most respected friend) and "Sache Sahiba Kiya Nahin Ghar Tere" (Oh, true lord, in thy house is every treasure).

Anar started to rise after finishing her recital, when an elderly Sikh gentleman who had been enjoying the performance said, "Wait. . ." Everyone was taken by surprise, apparently thinking the Moslem girl singing Shabads might have offended the older gentleman.

The old man tried to get up, stumbled, and was helped to his feet by his young grandson. He was one of the Sikh pioneers in Kenya, Khushal Singh, who owned a flourishing laundry business. He cleared his voice and requested that Anar sing one of his favorite Shabads.

Anar began singing the Shabad requested by the old man, "Mohe Lagtee Tala Beli" (My restlessness yearns for you, my lord), and by the time she had finished her recital, there were mounds of East African coins and paper currency in her lap and all around her. According to Sikh custom, they had showered her with money as it was customary to do with preachers singing holy Shabads.

Devout followers from the congregation, old and young alike, approached Anar and made their donations. They patted her on the back, wished her well, and thanked her for performing. The young woman was moved to tears of joy, which flowed down her fair pink cheeks.

As she left the Singh Sabha Gurudwara, there were hugs and words of congratulations. Her trip to Nairobi and the recital had been a huge success. The drive back home was a happy one with the girls giggling and joking. They discussed the atmosphere in the Gurudwara and the reaction of the congregation. The happy travelers crossed the Longido border outpost late at night where the African Immigration Customs officer waved them by. Everyone except for the driver was asleep by the time they pulled in front of the house in Arusha.

The next day, there were photographs in the *East African Standard* and the *Daily Nation*. The headline in the *Nation* was **"Moslem Girl Spellbinds Religious Sikhs,"** and the front page on the *Standard* had Anar's picture with the caption **"Sikh Religion Preached The Moslem way!"**

In addition to her musical talent, Anar was a top academic student in her class. She was skilled in hockey and tennis and played the tabla, piano, and guitar. Back home after her riveting performance, Anar continued to grow in beauty and grace.

By the time she was eighteen, Anar had become a well-known personality in Tanzania and Kenya. She continued to perform in the temples reciting religious songs, and she sang famous Indian and English "pop" songs in her home.

After completing her General Certificate of Education "O" levels, the equivalent of high school graduation in East Africa, she began her undergraduate studies at the Royal Technical College in Nairobi, one of the two universities in East Africa. This meant moving away from home in Arusha and living in the dorms in Nairobi. Her ambition was to be a journalist for an international newspaper. She was constantly picking up newspapers and publications from all over the world and spent her free time reading articles and analyzing writing styles of journalists from different nationalities.

The years in Nairobi attending the Royal Technical gave Anar the chance to excel in the musical field as there were plenty of opportunities to practice and try playing different instruments. As she grew into a young woman, Anar's self-confidence and outspoken qualities became apparent. She had been influenced by her grandfather, Shahbaz Khan, a great champion of women's equality, and she was quite independent and accustomed to getting her way.

Nairobi was the most cosmopolitan city in Africa with an abundance of sports clubs, and Anar joined the Nairobi Sports Club where she played hockey and tennis. The club had one of the few heated swimming pools in Nairobi at that time, and Anar began taking swimming lessons. As with everything else she had begun in her life, she became an expert swimmer in a few weeks.

After completing her undergraduate degree at the age of twenty-one, she started thinking of completing her journalism education in London. When Anar mentioned this to her parents, it caused an uproar as she would be the first person and the first girl from the family to leave Africa and go overseas. There was an uncomfortable silence in the Khan household for days.

But Anar was determined, even stubborn, about going to England to study, even though her father was totally opposed to sending her. This youngest daughter, however, knew how to get to him. Her sweet smile and pleading eyes were convincing after a time, and in the background her logical and practical mother envisioned a future where her daughter would be professionally qualified and have a career.

Nevertheless, it was socially unacceptable in the community to send a young girl overseas, and even when Anar's parents were ready to let their bird fly free, they weren't ready to face their community and friends. They spent days brooding about the social pressure they would face and finally decided that her aunt who lived in Willesden in North London would be a suitable guardian for the young girl. Anar could stay with Aunt Jamila and pursue her studies from there.

Not soon enough for her tastes, Anar found herself on an East African Airways jet bound for Heathrow, and she landed in England on a cold February morning. The early fog and rain fascinated her as this was in total contrast to the tropical East African climate and warm mornings. As she came out of Customs and Immigration, her aunt Jamila and pen pal, Dee, were waiting for her.

Friends for almost ten years, Dee and Anar had met a couple of years back when Dee visited Anar in Tanzania. They had visited the Ngorongoro Crater as well as the Serengeti and the Maasai Mara game reserves, and they'd spent time on the beaches in Malindi near Mombasa.

Half Danish, Dee now lived on her own in a two-bedroom flat in Wraysbury, a suburb on the outskirts of London near Heathrow airport. Both girls were about the same age and had common interests including sports, politics, music, and theater.

Anar settled in quickly and adapted to the English lifestyle as her friend sought to help in any way she could. Anar had to wait until September to start her journalism courses, so she decided to travel around Britain and see the country. The eight-week experience was what she needed to attune her ears to the different British accents ranging from London to Manchester, Leeds to Scotland, and Liverpool to Wales. In her travels through Britain, Anar made it a point to visit some East African Asians who had settled in English cities and who were family friends from Tanzania. Sensitive to the situation her family was in, Anar wrote home weekly describing her experiences and telling them how she missed everyone and the African climate.

Dee had her summer vacation in July, so the two of them decided to spend two weeks on the continent in France, Belgium, Switzerland, and Germany. Anar had never been to Europe and traveling with Dee was always fun. They drove off in Dee's Ford Cortina and crossed the channel using the ferry at Dover. The first stop was Paris and all of its magnificent sights, the

Eiffel Tower, Notre Dame, the Louvre, and Versailles. Walks along the Champs-Elysees found the girls being admired, followed, and teased by the young French men, who tried to win the attentions of the attractive ladies. Dee and Anar left France for Brussels, visited Waterloo, and then moved on to Switzerland. They spent a few days in Zurich and Geneva and then traveled to the beautiful Bavarian cities in Germany.

Two weeks went by quickly, and it was time to head back to Dover and home. The trip had been a wonderful experience, and it allowed Anar to see the historic legendary sights of Europe and compare them to the African jungle which had been her home.

By the time September arrived, Anar settled into her own flat in Hampton Hill on the River Thames. She had a few English friends whom she had met through Dee, and Anar made friendships with Kenyans in Britain, some new friends and some old acquaintances. Her usual pattern was to meet Dee on Friday evenings at some of the popular English pubs and then go dancing at a party with Australians, English, European, and Kenyan students.

Anar also found herself introduced to a new cultural experience called dating. Dating was never the "in" thing in Kenya and Tanzania, but she discovered that she quite enjoyed it. She met Jeff, an Australian law student with a great sense of humor, and Dave, short for Davinder, a Sikh from Kenya, who was studying Aeronautical Engineering at the Imperial College in Kensington. She decided that she quite liked this international custom of dating!

Chapter VII

*"Africa is a paradox which illustrates and high-
lights neo-colonialism. Her earth is rich, yet the products that come from above and below the soil continue
to enrich, not Africans predominantly, but groups and
individuals who operate to Africa's impoverishment."*
Kwame Nkrumah, 1965

After a year away from home, Akash was homesick and yearned
to visit his family in Kenya. He decided to fly via Rome over the
Easter weekend and enjoy the sights in Italy before breathing
the African air.

Akash was met inside the Embakasi airport in Nairobi by a
number of armed security guards and was quickly ushered
through the airport into a chauffeur-driven, black Mercedes
limousine with Kenyan Government registration plates. Being
Mehar Singh's grandson was going to reduce his anonymity.
As he was escorted to his destination by the security vehicle
and during the next few days, Akash realized the power his
grandfather had come to wield and the influence he commanded.
Government ministers visited the house on a daily basis. Security
guards, Kenyan police, KANU, and other government cars
were continuously parked outside the house. From the time he
had landed at Embakasi airport in Nairobi to the day he left,
he was followed by plainclothes government officials.

Akash spent most of his time at the family beach house in
Malindi on the Indian Ocean. He'd flown there with his parents

and amused himself fishing, snorkeling, swimming and relaxing in the thatched grass huts. He relished the opportunity to drink again from the coconuts, the African favorites called "Mandafus." His favorite libation was to pour rum or vodka into the coconut shells so that the alcohol mixed with the coconut milk to make a refreshing concoction. It was nice to be home, and he began thinking about the day when he would be back for good and living in his Kenya, his country.

The moment he stepped off the plane, he realized how good it felt to breathe the tropical African air again, and he realized anew that Africa was, indeed, home. The concrete jungles, rich in their history and architecture, were no match for the real jungles of Africa with its flat, yellow prairie lands surrounded by mountains. He'd missed the sight of a lion and lioness playing together, he'd missed motoring by the long stretches of scrubby grassy brush which nature had provided so that the smaller creatures could hide from their larger predators. He'd missed catching an occasional glimpse of two lions sharing the carcass of a zebra while the hyenas circled, waiting for their turn after the bigger animals satiated themselves. He'd missed the sight of white birds landing on the backs of gentle elephants, and he'd missed the sight of a hippopotamus immersed in a nearby swamp with his long crocodile-like face protruding thoughtfully from the dank water. He'd missed the spectacle of the tall mountains always rising in the background so that the skyline was etched with the undulating curves of a majestic tree-studded mountain range. He'd missed the sight of country scenes when he traveled the country roads past the mudhuts, the gates made out of sticks, and the natives dressed up in their plumage. He'd missed the genteel, manicured plantations with their fertile gardens tilled by servants which his family owned, and he missed the status of being a Dhillon in a country where that name was synonymous with respect and privilege.

Mehar Singh met Akash on the first night of his arrival and wanted to spend a day with him. The KANU secretary's political schedule was extremely hectic, but they settled on a day which was going to be a flight to Marsabit in the North of Kenya so that Mehar could give a speech at a political rally. Akash was excited at the prospect of accompanying his famous grandfather on an official function as he always enjoyed watching the master politician and orator in action.

Before they embarked on the flight from Ngong Airport, they stopped to watch the start of the East African Safari, the world-renowned automobile rally held each year over the long Easter weekend. The contest took drivers throughout Kenya over extremely rough dirt roads. It was a rugged test of stamina, skill, endurance, and driving skills. Some cars were sponsored by the manufacturers, but there were also many private entrants. Local favorite Joginder Singh, a past winner, was known as the "Flying Sikh." Mehar Singh waited till Joginder's Mercedes was up on the ramp and then stepped up to shake Joginder's hand and wave him on.

On the flight to Northern Kenya from Wilson Airport on the west side in Ngong Hills, Akash and his grandfather admired the beauty of the countryside below. It was a brilliantly clear day, and they were awed by the herds of elephants moving below them. Each sensed in the other a love for the sensual beauty of Africa. This was a heady experience for young Akash, sitting next to one of Africa's power centers, and he became aware that the man sitting beside him was not the man he had known as grandfather growing up.

Mehar Singh loved his grandson deeply and he spoke to the young man about the politics in East and Central Africa and the rivalries between different factions as he confided his ambitions to be the next president of Kenya. He reminisced about his past and told Akash stories of how he had sailed to Africa, worked on the railways, moved to Nairobi, and entered politics. His grandfather had told some of the stories before, but each time he added other details and Akash was fascinated at the new insights.

Mehar Singh was in a philosophical mood as he advised Akash, "Without love, we are nothing."

"God created human beings in the form of flesh and implanted a spirit within them that is free, loving, and lovable. There aren't enough prayers to replace a loving being on earth. God entrusts us to be kind and loving to our fellow beings.

"We are here to help each other, to care for one another, to understand, to forgive, and to serve one another. We are here to have love for every person born on earth. Their earthly form might be black, brown, or yellow, handsome, ugly, thin, fat, wealthy, poor, intelligent, ignorant, male or female. Each spirit has the capacity to be filled with love and eternal energy.

"At the beginning of life, each of us possesses some degree of light and truth that can be more fully developed. As to how it develops during one's life span, it is up to the individual being. We cannot measure these things. Anything we can do to show love is worth it. It may be a smile, a word of encouragement, or a small act of sacrifice. We grow by these actions.

"Not all people are lovable, but when we find someone difficult for us to love, it is often because they remind us of something within ourselves that we don't like. We must love our enemies, let go of anger, hate, envy and bitterness.

"I believe God would be extremely pleased with the spirit when a person dies and the spirit moves on, if that person had loved all and refrained from hating any of the people encountered during that person's life on earth."

Akash had never heard his grandfather talk in this manner.

"I want you to grow to be a person who loves his fellow human beings, who hurts no one deliberately, and listens to everyone. Be a Kenyan; we belong here. This is our country now. Come back and make a contribution and help the Africans in any way that you can."

Akash felt honored that he was being exhorted by his grandfather to come back and follow in his footsteps. But Akash had already felt the spirit inside him stirring to do just that. As he looked down from their small plane at the rich and primitive landscape which was Africa, he realized his sense of belonging on African soil.

As his grandfather continued to talk about Africans and

their customs, Akash was fascinated by his grandfather's vast knowledge of the country and its people. What impressed him the most was how this simple man cared so much for the average African and how he totally understood their thinking and needs.

Before he returned to college, Akash spent another day listening to his grandfather reminisce about his humble beginnings at the old family mansion in Kijabe. Then Akash returned to Oxford after three relaxing and educational weeks that would influence his political life forever.

Chapter VIII

"Avval aalah nur upaya kudrat ke sabh bande,
Ak nur te sab jag upjia kaun bhale ko mande."

The first, Allah (god) created the light,
All creatures belong to his divinity nature
All nature was created from his light,
How can some be good or some bad.

Bhagat Kabir

Anar and Akash were introduced at the Lord's Cricket Ground in Marylebone in North London where she had gone with her Australian friend Kay and her boyfriend Jeff to watch the cricket test match. Jeff had known Akash for a year as they had belonged to the same cricket club in Ealing and played on the same team.

The "ashes" were at stake with England playing Australia. England and Australia were playing each other in a series of matches based on a tradition which had started years back when Australia did the unthinkable and beat England for the first time, and a devout follower subsequently burnt the cricket "stumps." Since then the ashes were rumored to be kept in an urn containing the remains of bails used in the test match of 1882-1883.

As Akash was introduced to Anar, he shook her hand and, looking into her hazel eyes, he felt an unusually powerful attraction. His eyes lingered on hers and he held onto her hand longer than he probably should have. Anar liked what she saw, too, and she smiled the slow and sensuous smile which always made her look ravishing. As she smiled, beautiful dimples in her cheeks emerged that enhanced her sculptured cheekbones and pretty face.

Akash was his usual charming self that day, and his easy manner and calm voice made Anar feel at ease. They quickly discovered that they shared the same East African ancestry, so conversation was easy. To Akash's delight, Anar understood the game of cricket and they even agreed on their favorite players. She was able to converse with him about the technical details of the game as everyone watched the test.

After the match was over, they all went to the local pub, The Cricketeer, in St. John's Wood. Akash and Anar found themselves reminiscing about the African lifestyle and how they missed it. To even the most casual observer, the attraction between these two was obvious. As the night wore on and it became clear to the two of them that a powerful connection was being made, they began to feel slightly embarrassed and had difficulty keeping their eyes off each other.

As they left the pub at closing time, 11 p.m, Akash offered to drive Anar back to her flat in Hampton Court. She readily agreed, and the drive was quiet and relaxing. Akash had turned on a Billie Holliday cassette, and Anar reclined the luxurious passenger seat and lay there with her eyes closed, listening to the soothing voice of the legendary American blues singer.

Dropping her off outside the flat, he brushed his lips lightly against her fingers, squeezed her hand, and promised to call her the next day.

Inside her flat, Anar couldn't get him out of her mind. She liked being near him and had felt at ease talking to him. It was going to be a long night and an even longer wait till the morning when he would call her. She had never felt such a strong physical attraction to anyone before.

In his own digs, Akash found himself lying in bed thinking of her, her gray eyes with the sparkling green tint, and that toothy, spirited smile. He wanted to call her right then but didn't want to seem anxious. He drifted off to sleep thinking of her dazzling smile and the way it lit her whole face and exposed her feelings. He felt a strange warmth all over his body.

Promptly at ten in the morning he called. She answered on the first ring and had to restrain herself from nearly screaming his name. After chatting for almost an hour, they arranged to have dinner in Windsor.

After he picked her up at seven, they stopped for a beer at The Hampton, a pub around the corner from her flat, and sat on the patio overlooking the Thames. In a bold gesture, he took her hand and looked deeply into her eyes, and she returned his gaze and drew closer to him. The chemistry was there and the physical attraction was strong, so he reached toward her, held her face in his hands, and kissed her softly on the lips. Like a magnet, her mouth found his, and she kissed him back as they held each other for a few minutes.

Anar finally turned away from him and asked him, "What about dinner?"

Feeling bold but brave, he replied, "I'm really hungry but I want you in my arms. Let's go. We'll continue later."

After enjoying a great meal at The Steak House in Windsor, where they held hands for much of the evening, they headed back to her flat and finished a couple of bottles of red wine. As they sat on the couch, Anar offered to make coffee, but Akash asked, "How about some Grand Marnier instead?"

"Sure, there's a bottle in the cabinet behind the television," she replied.

As they lay on the couch and caressed, Akash delighted her with stories about his grandfather and his exciting adventures when he came from India and settled in Kenya. Anar was fascinated and wanted to hear more. She knew the Dhillon family was a wealthy and prosperous one, and the journalist in her wanted to find out more out the patriarch who had built the family fortune and established its good name.

At about three in the morning, they decided to turn in for

the night. Akash was in no shape or mood to drive back, so Anar fixed up the couch for him with the extra sheets and pillows. A social and gregarious person who frequently had friends sleeping over, she was prepared for house guests at all times.

Akash held her close as he got ready for bed and whispered, "Anar, I am really fond of you and want to see more of you and be near you. You are special to me."

He kissed her softly for a long time with their lips and tongues doing most of the communication, and then he stretched out on the couch and dozed off. Anar smiled as she stood looking at the man she had met so recently. She knew she had met a soul mate, a kindred spirit, and it wasn't just their East African backgrounds. It had been a nearly instantaneous recognition on both their parts that they were on the same wavelength. As she gazed at the stranger in her house, she felt that it was unimaginable that she would ever be without him in her life. For the first time in her life, she was in love with a man, and she knew it.

He was up early in the morning and left before she awoke, leaving a note that he would call her later in the day.

During the next month, they saw each other regularly, and they found they had similar tastes in movies, theater, museums, libraries, and even the temples in Southall and Shepherd's Bush. At the temple, Anar wanted to do Kirtan, and she made a request of the holy man, or the Gyani, that she would like to sing. He had no idea she was a Moslem, as the name Anar could have been a Sikh name, so he put her name down in the day's scheduled preachers.

As usual when she sang, the "sangat," or Sikh congregation, was spellbound and they swayed from side to side enjoying the Guru's teachings. This was the first time Akash had heard her sing in a temple. Like her other listeners, he was awed by her talent and powerful voice. The Gyani was so impressed that he invited her to come and sing whenever she wanted to.

The young lovers were inseparable, and they encouraged

each other with their college work. At the London School of Economics, Anar was on her way to becoming an international journalist and Akash was distinguishing himself at Oxford University studying law.

Akash and Anar had a holiday coming up and, since they had never been to the United States, they decided to plan an excursion to America. This trip was a chance for them to get away from London and be on their own with each other. It was planned on the spur of a moment, as they debated between a trip back home to Africa or America.

The Trans World Airlines plane landed in Los Angeles on a typical smoggy afternoon. They had made reservations at the Beverly Hilton. The cab ride to Beverly Hills took longer because of the continuous traffic jam on the Interstate 405. They checked into the hotel with their eyes searching for any show business personalities. They thought they saw Tom Selleck but he was too far away to be sure.

Akash made reservations at Spago's, as they wanted to see where the rich and famous spent their time. They were alone, the food was superb, and the California wines were perfect.

The next day was spent shopping at Rodeo Drive, driving around Beverly Hills, and they took a tour of the stars' homes. In the evening they had reservations to see Ray Charles at the Universal Amphitheater. Before the concert, they dined at Benihana's as Anar had taken quite a liking to the Japanese cuisines and especially sushi.

The concert was better than Akash had expected. He had been a fan of Ray Charles for years, and he was in awe of the musical genius who had been blind since the age of seven. The musical giant stumbled slightly as he came onto the stage, even though he was guided by a young man. He tried to find his way around and listened to the thunderous applause all around him, but he couldn't see where those people were. Then he sat at the piano and alternated between piano and an organ before he got up clumsily to play the saxophone. As he sat on the piano stool, he constantly stomped his feet and rotated his legs and waist as if to get up and touch the fans that he knew were somewhere out there. As he sang, he looked towards the audience. It was a riveting performance. This man who could not see his admirers could nevertheless see into their souls, and his music and lyrics touched them deeply.

After the concert, Akash turned to Anar, "It's funny . . . he's blind, and yet he doesn't let it hold him back. But there are so many people with no physical limitations who are afraid to strive for their dreams.

"These 'normal' people have all their senses but some of them don't have any use for them. They take it all for granted and spend time fussing over useless material things, competing with others, and arguing over nothing."

After doing the tourist rounds to Disneyland and Universal Studios, they drove north in their rented car along the Pacific Coast Highway, stopping at Santa Monica and Malibu before traveling on to Santa Barbara. There they decided to stay for a week, not sightseeing, but just spending time with each other and enjoying being on their own.

The young lovers paid no attention to anything or anyone around them; they were engrossed in each other as they windowshopped on State Street and walked along the beach. This was a rare time for them to really get to know each other, and they could feel their relationship blossoming.

One day at lunch time, as Akash and Anar strolled along the beach and past the palm trees, surfers, sunbathers, and swimmers, a pleasant warm feeling encompassed both of them. The lovers walked with arms around each other's waists, and Anar had her head tilted on one side as she always did. Every now and then Anar would rest her head on Akash's shoulder and they would stop and kiss gently as the warm sea breeze touched their happy, smiling faces. They were so much in love that they had no worries in the world. After they walked past the pier and the beach resorts and hotels, they reached the park where the beach curved and extended into the ocean. Akash found a clean, green spot with no one in sight. They lay next to each other on the grass and touched each other all over while whispering loving words. Chatting as usual, and losing track of time, before they knew it the gorgeous California sunset was visible with all its picturesque glory and beauty. As he looked into the depth of her inviting hazel eyes, all Akash could see were reflections of love that he had grown accustomed to over the past few months. They smiled at each other, held each other, and hugged without a thought of time.

He whispered to Anar, "When we are together, I forget completely who we are. The happiness I feel transports me to another world.

"When I'm with you, it's as though I were an eagle soaring freely in the clear blue sky without a care in the world. You are so special to me, Anar, and you make me feel so wonderful that nothing else and no one else matters when we are together. It seems that we are surrounded by everything that is beautiful and serene in this world.

"As we travel through life, we see thousands and thousands of people. We get to meet hundreds and we get to really know a few. Out of these few, there are some special relationships or bonds. I feel that we have that special friendship. There is a magic about what we have. Almost by instinct, as though we were destined to know each other, you seem to know me and I you.

"This is the nicest feeling I've ever had. When we're apart, I miss hearing your voice. I yearn for your touch. I long for your scent. And when I am with you, looking at your face, I know that I love you. I never thought I could miss anyone as I miss you. I've always thought of myself as totally independent and self-reliance, and I was brought up in the Sikh religion to aim for that. Now, here I am, looking into the eyes of a beautiful Moslem girl who sings the Kirtan better than any other Gyani I've ever heard, and I feel I have discovered a part of myself that I didn't know had been missing. I am a different person now than I was before I met you. I feel completed. I feel satisfied in a new way. I am most alive when I am with you.

"When we're apart, I miss your sensuous lips, your warm

comforting hug, your voice on the phone, your giggles, and your laughter."

Anar giggled the giggle he loved, and then she kissed him. She didn't mean to kiss him as passionately as she did, but her emotion overpowered her. Here was a man who gave expression to her most private thoughts, and here was a man who described the essence of what she'd been feeling.

She'd never fallen in love until she met Akash. He made her feel special, as though she was the only person in existence on this planet. He spoiled her in every way possible, fussed over her, cared for her, and made her laugh with his unique and often strange sense of humor. They'd known each other for only four months, but their friendship seemed to go back in space and time. They knew that what they felt, the greatest lovers in history had experienced throughout the centuries.

Their stay in California was unforgettable for both of them. They had left England as friends, and they would be returning as a couple, with their relationship cemented in every way—physically, mentally, intellectually, and spiritually. The memories they would take with them would forever give them an unforgettable bond.

Without warning, a jangling telephone shattered their time of peace and joy. It was three o'clock in the morning when it rang.

With pain in her voice, Anar's mother reported that Anar's father, Manzur Khan, had sustained serious injuries in an automobile accident on the notoriously dangerous stretch of road between Nairobi and Mombasa. Nearly in shock after hearing the news, Anar dropped the phone and left it hanging by the cord as she wailed and collapsed on the couch. Then she stared off into open space, as though in a catatonic state. All she could do was look at Akash and shake her head.

Akash quickly picked the phone and continued the conversation with Anar's mother after explaining that her daughter was too distraught to talk. Anar's mother revealed that her husband was conscious but in a critical state. His lungs had been punctured and there had been extensive chest injuries as he was thrown out of the car. She said she was grateful that it hadn't been worse, but she didn't sound grateful.

Akash and Anar were up all night as Akash made arrangements to fly with her from LAX to Heathrow, where she would make the connection to Nairobi.

Chapter IX

"Once again the creed of the Individual Creator
was proclaimed from the soil of the Punjab.
A real perfect man appeared who woke up and
shook India from her slumber of dream."

Sir Mohammed Iqbal,
On Guru Nanak DevJee

The flight from Heathrow to Nairobi was lonely and depressing. The youngest child and probably her father's favorite, Anar had been close to her father and the prospect of seeing him hurt was traumatic.

Upon arriving at the Aga Khan Hospital in Parklands, she found her father asleep and bandaged from head to toe. Anar sat at his bedside throughout the evening and when he finally awoke, she whispered, "Aba Jaan? It's me, Anar. I'm here."

At the sound of her voice, her father dissolved into uncontrollable tears. She held his hand and they began to talk.

Anar learned that the accident had been a head-on collision and her father was lucky to be alive. Two local pickup trucks had been racing, and as they went around a bend, they hit her father's Peugeot 504. The accident had happened near the Sikh Temple in Makindo and then it had been hours before Manzur was admitted to the Aga Khan Hospital in Nairobi.

As Anar spent most of the next week in the hospital, a change began to occur in her personality. She wanted to be alone, and she hardly ate or spoke to anyone. She refused to see her friends. She would lie on the couch and, after four weeks, she was still

71

in Kenya with no plans to return to London in order to resume her studies.

When friends visited, she would retreat into another room and gaze out into the garden. In what seemed clearly to be a clinical depression, Anar was despondent and unable to be freed from her state of mind by anyone or anything. Although her mother desperately tried to convince her to go back to London and continue with her life, she got no response from her daughter.

Akash had never been away from Anar for this length of time since they had met. He longed to be near her and speak to her. When he telephoned, Anar was quiet and would merely listen to Akash talk. These weeks of separation were driving him crazy. He decided to write and express his feelings. He felt that putting his feelings in a letter might allow her to see what she couldn't seem to hear. A letter might somehow show her how much he cared for her and missed her. He didn't know if it would work, but he had to try.

Anar, my soul,

I miss you so much and I feel for you under these conditions. If we were together, I would hold you close to my heart, let our heartbeats talk to each other, hug you forever, and never let you go.

I'm going to write to you and try to put into words these feelings I have for you. Please forgive me, my darling, for my amateurish writing and clumsy thoughts. You know that you are the writer in this couple; I am only the legal mind, and I regret that I cannot produce the elegant and eloquent phrases which would do justice to my feelings for you.

How can I capture what I feel on this page? These are such strong emotions that words can't even begin to touch the depth of what I feel. This phenomenon may be expressed simply by the word "love," or at least it may be the closest word in the English language. So let me say that "I love you" from dawn to sunset, from moment to moment, in between the breaths I take, and any time that is left over.

The dream goes on and my wish is for this joyful, serene, blissful and happy "sleep" to go on infinitely. My love for you strengthens and deepens by the day, and now that I know you so well, I feel you to be an extension of myself. When you hurt, I hurt. When you cry, I cry. When you feel joy, your joy thrills me. When I do not see the beauty of your face or hear your magical voice, I feel that I am only half alive. Without you, I am only half of what I could be.

You bring out the best in me. You make me feel as I have never felt before. You listen to me and often anticipate my next thought or sentence, and I do the same for you. Our interests are so alike that is scary at times even though our personalities are different. I agree with you so frequently that it could be perceived that I was doing it deliberately but the crazy part is that I'm not; we simply agree on many things.

The heartaches, the skipping of heartbeats, the everlasting desire to be with you all the time, are feelings that young teenagers are supposed to experience. I would never have dreamed that I could go through this.

We long to touch and caress each other and our lips have to be forced apart. I can't explain this and I wish I could. When I am with you, there seems to be no track of time and it passes so quickly that it is not fair as our time together is limited.

I love the way you hold and hug me. Could there be a better fit? I love the way you close your eyes when I hold you and how you keep your eyes closed when I kiss you or when you rest on my shoulder. I love the way you touch me when we walk or sit or chat. I love the way you hold my arm when we walk. I love the way you sneak up on me and hug me from the back.

At times I think of pinching myself to find out if this is a dream or reality that I am experiencing. I could go on and on, I do love you and will forever.

I find it amazing how this trickle of emotions has blossomed into an ocean of everlasting love that is so strong yet is unconditional with no demands. I long to be near you, yet even when I am far away and I can hear your voice it seems that you are within me and beside me.

I can look into your beautiful eyes that intrigue me to such an extent that I can gaze at them forever. I wish that everyone could experience the happiness that I do when we are together or when I think of the times we have spent with each other.

True love is rare to find, and I am so lucky to have found one. So now, you know how treasured you are to me. I do hope that you feel the same. It is exceptional to come across someone so special whom you can love and trust and feel completely at ease with as though they were part of your own essence, body, and mind. I have that with you.

When I lie down or when I am sitting, I close my eyes and think of your caressing fingers running over my arms and body, and your soft, tender, moist, inviting lips touching mine in the distinctive way that only you can kiss. As we kiss longer, our lips become more passionate, and they move sensuously with our tongues becoming inflamed. As our hips move closer and closer with our chests close, our heartbeats seem to synchronize so that it could be one heart beating. As our fingers and hands take over, our body temperatures soar.

When the concept emerges that I will not be able to see you, I feel very sad. I do know that whatever is meant to be, will be, and I believe I now know what a writer meant when he wrote, "Absence makes the heart grow fonder."

My love, I can't live without you, and I can't exist without you. You truly must come back here as soon as you can. Every fraction of a second I am away from you, it seems like being in a vacuum. I feel as though I am adrift on a sea without my life vest, and my mind is always with you *rather than being centered on the work I need to be doing. Please also know that when you ache, I ache. When you are in pain, I feel the pain. When you mourn, I mourn. I am your alter ego, and I am experiencing everything you are going through. But the pain you are in must end, and we must return to our normal, happy selves. As long as you are in agony and feeling depressed, you imprison me there as well. I beseech you to set me free as you free yourself from this tortured state.*

I love you so much and will never stop as long as there is air I breathe.

I love you and wish you were here right now. You must come back soon, my love.

Yours,
Akash

Anar had been reading the letter at her father's bedside. She began sobbing as she read the last lines. Her father asked what was wrong, but she was embarrassed and explained that it was a note from a dear friend who missed her and was trying to encourage her. Manzur insisted that he was going to be fine and said she make plans immediately to return to London and continue her career. Anar made no protest. If her misery created misery for Akash, then she had to do everything in her power to end it. Her father was right.

Anar returned to London after almost six weeks in Africa, but she was a new woman when she returned. As daddy's little girl, she had come to realize that her father was never going to regain his former state of health. He was mentally alert but would be bedridden for the rest of his life. He was wealthy and would be well cared for, but her staying in Kenya would not change things for him. And her sadness and depression would not change the situation. She realized she had to choose happiness, and she had to choose it for Akash as well as for herself.

After she returned, Akash took some time off and made sure she settled back in her routine. After staying with him for the first two weeks and feeling the comfort of his companionship, she moved back into her flat. He went out of his way to pamper her and did whatever was necessary to make sure that she was comfortable and her mind was directed towards something other than Kenya and her father.

The two young lovers were back together now, and stronger than before.

Chapter X

*"Guru Granth Ji manio pargat Guran ki deh, ja
ka hirda sudh hai khoj sabad mein le."*
Consider Guru Granth as the living body of Guru,
With a pure heart, one can realize him in the
Shabad.

Sikh Ardaas (prayer)

Akash was an avid soccer fan and his support of the Manchester
United Football Club bordered on fanaticism. Dee was visiting
with Anar, and he was at his flat watching a live BBC transmission
of the sold-out fixture against Liverpool FC being played at
Anfield, the home ground of Liverpool.

These two titans of English soccer played in the First
Division, and their old rivalry had added tension since the
winner would top the league. Their managers, Bill Shankly for
Liverpool and Matt Busby from Manchester, were revered as
gods in their respective cities.

The famous Liverpool fans, known as the "Kop," were in
peak form, singing and shouting slogans. The United fans were
also out in force and trying to outdo the home crowd.

The match featured some of the best players in the land
with Bobby Charlton, Dennis Law, George Best, and Alex
Stepney on the Manchester side and Tommy Smith, Emlyn
Hughes, Ray Clemence, and Ian St. John starring for the
Merseyside team.

The game finally got under way, with Charlton unleashing

one of his famed long-range thunderbolts at the Liverpool goal only to be matched by a spectacular full-length save by Clemence. On the other end, Stepney had to match his counterpart with an equally fine stop of a hard shot from Ian St. John, who sprinted through the United defense. The two premier teams were displaying power and finesse, and their skills were at a high level.

Halfway through the first half, the mercurial Irishman George Best picked the ball in his own half. After a quick interchange with Dennis Law, he took off on a run that evaded three Liverpool defenders before he finally went around Clemence to slide home a spectacular goal for the visitors. The United fans screamed their support at the top of their lungs as Akash watched the replay.

The phone rang, and Akash reached absently for the receiver, his thoughts focused on the match.

"Akash? It's Khurshid." His friend's bleak tone and hesitant voice caused Akash to snap out of his reverie.

"What's the matter, Khurshid?" he asked.

"I—you'd better turn to the News Flash on the ITN Network . . . it's about your grandfather."

Akash switched the station and listened in growing shock.

". . . at home in his Kijabe mansion. At this time, police are still investigating the slaying of the KANU secretary . . ."

The rest of the newscast was just noise in Akash's mind as he sat there in shock, taking in what he'd heard.

"Akash? Akash . . . are you still there?"

"Khurshid? I think I . . . let me call you back later, okay?"

His friend replied, "All right. Let me know if there's anything I can do."

As soon as he cradled the receiver, it rang again. He hesitated, too numb to answer. After the fourth ring, he picked it up. It was Anar.

"Akash? Oh, thank God you're there. I've been trying to call and I couldn't get through."

In a quiet, stunned voice, he said, "Is it . . . true? Bapu Jee? Killed?"

Anar said, "I'm afraid so—it's on all the news channels. Have you heard anything from your family?"

"No," he answered. "I suppose I should call dad and find out what happened."

"Go ahead and call, then, but stay at the flat 'til I get there, meri jaan. I'm on my way over there now. Oh, Akash, I'm so sorry."

Chapter XI

As Thy light is in life, so life is in Thy light.
Thy Incalculable Power permeates this Universe.
Thou art the true Lord. Whoever Truly Adores
thee, may cross the Sea of Life.
For in Thy Adoration lies our Salvation.
Says Nanak: "Let us Glorify that Creator who does
as He feels best."

—Rahras Sahib (Evening Prayer)

Mehar Singh's youngest daughter, Kulwant, was in the Sikh Temple next to the mansion in Kijabe, where she conducted religious teachings for the local Asian children. She heard a sound which was repeated several times and assumed it was one of the African pickup trucks backfiring.

She was interrupted by Mwangara, the senior house servant, who was out of breath as he stumbled into the temple.

"Kuli. . .there has been an accident. . .your father is hurt. . . come quickly."

Kulwant's initial reaction was confusion. She was right in the middle of her lessons and had difficulty comprehending what the African was saying.

"What are you saying? Hurt? Where? Take me there."

Kulwant panicked, running as fast as she could with the African servant. As she entered the yard, Mehar's daughter-in-law, SharanJeet, met them. SharanJeet was an impressive figure,

80

about 5' 9" and 140 lbs. She wore clothes tailored to highlight her slim figure which left nothing to the imagination. She was a strikingly beautiful woman with beautiful black hair that hung down to her waist which she usually tied in pigtails. With an erect bearing, she was a tantalizing-looking woman and there was an arrogant air about her that was intriguing.

"Help ... get help...Bapu Jee is hurt. Go call the postmaster."

Kulwant was in shock and didn't know what to do, so she followed SharanJeet's directions and ran to the village post office, about half a mile down the hill in the township. She could hardly stand as she screamed to the postmaster, "Uncle, please come to the house. Quickly—Bapu Jee has been hurt."

They both got in Anand's Austin Prefect and drove as fast as they could back to the house.

The Dhillon mansion was spread out over several acres, with numerous buildings and outhouses. The large fenced yard had a gated main entrance, and steps led up from the yard into the central building. Mehar Singh was lying near the steps next to the tall water tank.

The 5' 5" impish Kulwant ran to her father's side. Her normally mischievous brown eyes were somber now, and she stooped over him, her long black oiled hair hanging down her back and tied in a single pigtail. Mehar's tall body made him look like a fallen giant as he lay there on the ground bleeding, barely conscious, and trying to speak. She sat down on her knees, cradled his head, and held to his lips some water in a glass Mwangara had brought from the house. She put an ear next to his face and tried to make out the words he was whispering, but they were impossible to comprehend.

Postmaster Anand sat next to Kulwant and noticed that Mehar Singh was struggling with his breathing. As soon as he saw the blood from bullet wounds, he asked the servant Mwangara to call for an ambulance and summon the police. The nearest hospital was on the escarpment, about a 30-minute drive away. The police station was a 20-minute drive.

It took Mwangara, Anand, and Kulwant to slowly lift the

6' 4" political leader and carry him inside the house, and they laid him on the floor in the living room. Kulwant was holding his head in her arms when he looked into her face, moved his lips slightly to utter something she couldn't understand, and passed away. Kulwant screamed, "Bapu Jee.....Bapu Jee..no ..."

Everyone in the yard heard her cry and knew it meant the death of the family patriarch.

Chapter XII

"There is no society of angels, whether it is White, Brown, or Black. We are all human beings, and as such we are bound to have done wrong to you. It is for you to forgive me, and if you have done some thing wrong to me, it is for me to forgive you. . . You have something to forget, just as I have."

Jomo Kenyatta, August 12, 1963

Within twenty minutes, an ambulance and a fleet of police cars accompanied by reporters and the Criminal Investigation Department officials were on the scene. The estate was cordoned off, the servants were gathered, and Inspector Bhardwaj, in charge of the CID team, set up his control center in one of the outbuildings at the Kijabe mansion.

Bhardwaj instructed photographers to take pictures of the whole area, and he interviewed the African servants, Karanja, the gardener, and Mwangara, who worked inside the house.

The Africans repeatedly stated that they were nowhere near the house at the time of the incident. They had been working at the outlying buildings, taking care of the small maize plantation.

In the meantime, Mehar Singh's wife, Satbir Kaur, had arrived from Nairobi accompanied by her son-in-law, Bawa Singh. The 5' 9" slim young man was an arresting figure, as he walked with a slight hunchback and had a face full of pockmarks left by the smallpox which had ravaged him as a child. The local police in Nairobi had informed Mehar's wife and son-in-law of the tragedy.

Mehar Singh's body was still in the house but had been covered. When Satbir Kaur stepped out of the automobile in front of the mansion, she was overcome with emotion. Bawa had to support her weight, to keep her from collapsing.

Satbir Kaur struggled as she climbed the stairs and into the house. As she saw the white sheet covering the body of her husband, she burst into tears and began to wail in a high-pitched voice. She lifted the sheet covering the body and touched Mehar Singh's face. Her hands became bloody from the wounds on his temple, and she kept screaming hysterically as she looked at her hands and recognized the blood of her beloved husband.

SharanJeet was in the bedroom and came out when she heard the screams. She ran towards Satbir Kaur and embraced her with tears running down her face.

She told her mother-in-law, "Manjee, the Africans killed Bapu Jee, the Africans did it... I saw them running away."

SharanJeet joined Satbir Kaur and her daughter Kulwant as they sat next to the body. Kulwant appeared to be in shock and was silent as she gazed into space.

Thirty minutes later, Inspector Bhardwaj sent a messenger to tell SharanJeet that he wanted her to come to see him.

He asked her, "Please sit down as I am going to ask you questions about what happened . Where were you when the shooting took place?"

"I was inside the house when I heard the shots. . .I saw the Africans running away after the shots were fired."

"How many Africans were there?" asked Bhardwaj.

"Two or three I think," replied SharanJeet.

She kept looking away, biting her nails and moving her body nervously. SharanJeet described to the inspector how she had asked Kulwant to call the postmaster after discovering her father-in-law's body. Bhardwaj continued the questioning for almost forty-five minutes.

It seemed obvious that SharanJeet's story had inconsistencies, and each time she repeated her statements she changed some of the facts.

News of Mehar Singh's murder sent shock waves throughout the continent. Reporters found the nearest phone to broadcast the details as soon as they became available.

The initial news flash on the Voice of Kenya Radio broadcasts was of a robbery attempt at the Dhillon residence by a band of local Kikuyus.

". . .it is believed that the popular Kenyan political figure was killed by Kikuyu bandits while attempting to foil the robbery attempt. Mehar Singh's body was discovered by his daughter-in-law, SharanJeet, who apparently discovered him lying on the steps of his Kijabe home. He had been shot several times, and there was blood on his forehead and chest."

This was a major incident in Kenya as a leading political figure had been murdered. The initial rumor was that black Africans had committed a political assassination.

In the morning Satbir Kaur, accompanied by SharanJeet, Kulwant, Inspector Bhardwaj, and the rest of the family traveled back to Nairobi. They had been asked to spend the previous night outside the family home so as not to contaminate precious evidence.

The journey was quiet. Family members were sobbing quietly or just staring out of the moving Land Rover. Someone asked if they could stop at the Sikh Temple in Pangani to offer prayers, and as they sat down to pray, each member of the party kneeled in front of the Holy Book and recited a different prayer. Satbir Kaur knelt down and prayed for her husband's "atma," or soul.

When Satbir had finished her prayer, SharanJeet sat down on her knees, put her hands together to pray and quietly whispered, "Oh God, please forgive me, I didn't mean...didn't mean to do anything... to Bapu Jee."

Seated next to SharanJeet, Satbir Kaur was shocked to hear this statement, which she interpreted as practically a confession of guilt, although she could scarcely believe her ears. As SharanJeet got off her knees the two women exchanged looks, and Satbir was overcome with anger. She wanted to strike out at this woman who had practically admitted to killing her father-in-law and Satbir's husband. Her son, Hardial, was by her side now and wanted to know what had transpired. At 5' 11" and 220 lbs., Hardial was a ruggedly handsome man with a tanned brown complexion. He wore the white turban signifying that he was a Sikh. Those who knew Hardial knew that he was a proficient hunter, and he had a long scar on one of his thighs to prove he'd been the victor in a fierce battle once with a leopard. After Satbir told her muscular son with the piercing eyes what she'd heard, he had difficulty controlling his emotions, but logic prevailed and he walked over to Inspector Bhardwaj and shared the information his mother had told him.

The Inspector's suspicions after the previous day's interrogations in Kijabe were confirmed. SharanJeet was handcuffed by Bhardwaj and the Askaris, or Kenyan police, and she began to scream and protest that it was the Africans who killed Mehar Singh.

Satbir was furious as she ordered Inspector Bhardwaj, "Take her away…take the bitch away, I don't want to see her face again."

SharanJeet was taken to the Parklands Police Station and she was charged on suspicion of the murder of Mehar Singh Dhillon. After her booking, she was taken to the Nairobi Prison pending bail.

In the meantime, Mohinder Singh, SharanJeet's husband, had flown back to Nairobi from Dar-es-Salaam in Tanganyika. Mehar Singh's second son, Mohinder Singh looked the most like his tall father of all the sons. At 6' 3", he was nearly as tall as his father, a muscular fellow who sported a white turban and carried himself erectly and proudly. He had heard the tragic news on the radio and went straight to the prison in Nairobi to visit his wife.

SharanJeet sobbed as she repeated to her husband the same version of her story that she had told Inspector Bhardwaj.

"Don't worry," Mohinder assured her. "As long as I'm here, I'll make sure you're freed. You're going to be fine. I'll go and arrange for bail."

Mohinder, SharanJeet's parents, and some friends managed to raise the bail money, and SharanJeet was home with her family within hours.

The Dhillon family gathered at the home of son-in-law Bawa Singh in suburban Eastleigh. When they learned of the bail arrangement, the other brothers, Rajinder and Hardial, had to be restrained. They wanted to go to SharanJeet's parents' home and avenge their father's death.

Mohinder visited Bawa Singh's house to see his mother and join the grieving family. As the discussion turned to SharanJeet, Mohinder was very defensive and insisted that she was innocent and that he would stand by her. As the discussions grew more heated, he walked out and went to his in-laws' house to be near his wife.

Mehar Singh's body was brought to the mortuary in Nairobi and an autopsy arranged. Because of Mehar Singh's popularity throughout Kenya and neighboring countries, friends and political allies from all over Kenya would be coming to visit the family at Bawa Singh's house in Eastleigh.

No one could believe that the popular political leader had been killed, and they were shocked that a family member could have committed the murder. Rumors of all kinds began to circulate as everyone searched for an explanation for this family tragedy and speculated as to motive. In Africa, as elsewhere, things were often not as they seemed, and for some reason, the way things seemed did not make sense to anyone.

Chapter XIII

"Friends and Comrades, the light has gone out of
our lives and there is darkness everywhere. I do
not know what to tell you and how to say it. Our
beloved leader, Bapu, as we called him, the father
of the nation, is no more."

Jawaharlal Nehru (1948),
on Mahatma Gandhi's assassination

Akash and Anar flew back from Heathrow to attend Mehar Singh's funeral. Anar would be staying in Kenya for a while. She'd been writing freelance for the *Sunday Times*, and they had asked her to create a series of feature stories on Mehar Singh because of her connections with the slain leader's family.

Funeral arrangements were set for Sunday morning to allow time for people to travel from all over East Africa to Nairobi.

Announcements for the funeral ceremony had been made on Voice of Kenya Asian broadcasts as well as in the national newspapers, *The Nation* and *The East African Standard*.

According to Sikh customs, Mehar Singh's body, at the city mortuary, was washed with yogurt and oil. A new turban was tied and he was dressed in new white clothes. His body was placed on a wooden platform and covered with a red sheet which was then covered with flowers. Holy water, amrit, was sprinkled on the body as the Gyanis recited prayers.

The cremation ceremony was preceded by prayers at home. Then the wooden platform was lifted and placed on an open truck. Women cried and wailed as the funeral procession started on its way to the crematorium with smartly dressed Kenyan policemen on motorcycles leading the truck followed by a long entourage of cars, pickup trucks, and lorries. The next stop was the Sri Guru Singh Sabha Temple in Nairobi where the body was laid before the Holy Granth Sahib and more prayers were offered by the Sikh priests, the Gyanis.

After the prayers, the procession of more than two hundred cars traveled to the crematorium in Karioker, on the outskirts of the capital. The body was carried from the truck to the pyre by the slain leader's sons Hardial, Rajinder , and Mohinder as well as Mehar Singh's brother Harbans, Joseph Likimani and Oginga Odinga. Shorter than his brother at 5' 11", Harbans nevertheless bore a striking resemblance to the deceased, as he was lanky, dark, and gangly with a strong and intimidating presence. Mehar's eldest son, Santokh, was in Loliondo at the time and too ill to travel. The body was laid to rest on a recently constructed high platform of wood. Then more prayers were offered by the Sikh priests as the sons poured ghee onto the wooden platform and the body.

Mohinder picked up a torch to light the platform, but the other brothers Rajinder and Hardial quickly intervened and reached to grab the torch. Mohinder had alienated his family with the stand he'd made to protect his wife so he had aligned him against the family, in their opinion. There was pushing and shoving among the grown boys until Mohinder backed off, and then the platform was lit jointly by the other two brothers. As soon as the flame reached the ghee, the pyre burst into flames.

Onlookers watched for half an hour as the pyre burned. Eventually they began to leave in small groups but the Gyanis kept praying as long as the fire burned.

The funeral procession returned to the Sikh temple and, as is Sikh custom, more prayers were said, and prominent members of the Sikh community made speeches, praising Mehar Singh's achievements in life and politics. Strangely, there was no mention of the murder and no word of the circumstances of his death.

His first political opponent and steadfast friend and supporter Joseph Ole Likimani gave an emotional speech in which he spoke of his first meeting with Mehar Singh and how they ran against each other in the election. He sobbed intermittently throughout his speech as he praised the Sikh leader and bemoaned the irreplaceable loss this was going to be for all Kenyans and East Africans. He emphasized Mehar Singh's honesty, integrity, and leadership as well as his genuine love for his fellow human beings and Kenya, the adopted country he so dearly loved.

Likimani broke down and had to be helped from the stage as tears streamed down his face.

Oginga Odinga, the tribal leader who had supported the Asian Sikh, was among the mourners and praised his friend in a brief eulogy.

Kenyatta had sent his aide, Makora Masharia, to extend his condolences and speak at the temple. Mzee had telephoned Satbir Kaur at the Muthaiga home and expressed his shock and sorrow at the loss of a personal friend, and at Kenya's loss of a political giant. He promised to do everything possible to bring justice to the murderers.

The sadness felt by the Asians was deeply echoed by the Africans, who were sure they had lost a leader, a close friend, and one of the few politicians who understood their problems.

The brothers Hardial and Rajinder, along with Mehar Singh's brother, journeyed to the crematorium the next day to pick up the ashes. The last remains were then taken and scattered in the Tana River according to Sikh customs and in accordance with his wishes.

Chapter XIV

"In this dish are placed three things: Truth,
Harmony, and Wisdom. These are seasoned with
the Name of God which is the basis for all;
whoever eats it and relishes it, shall be saved."

Guru Arjan Dev Jee,
commenting on the nature of the Granth Sahib

SharanJeet would be tried within the Kenyan judicial system, which consisted of two major courts and several lesser tribunals. The major courts were the Kenyan court of appeal, with a chief justice and five associate judges, and the high court of Kenya, with seven junior associate judges.

Mohinder Singh began the preparations for his wife SharanJeet's trial by hiring a top-notch defense attorney. A handsome, flamboyant lawyer from Scotland who wore a kilt, Michael Anderson had an impressive record in criminal cases, but he knew her defense was going to be a challenge. His efforts to prove his client's innocence would be hampered by Mehar Singh's stature in the Asian, African, and European communities. Michael knew there would be strong opposition from the slain leader's political allies, and he would face all the resistance which the financial resources of the family could bring to bear. Most importantly, he had to contend with the unrelenting commitment of Mehar's sons to be revenged for the unexpected loss of their father.

The prosecution was well prepared; they wanted this case to set an example for the rest of the country. They were under intense pressure from the government and even from President Kenyatta himself to make sure that justice prevailed. The case had received an incredible amount of publicity, not only because it involved the murder of one of Kenya's most popular and unique leaders but also because he was murdered in his own home and under such unusual circumstances.

Chief Justice Peter Njonjo, the first black African judge in Kenya, was appointed to try the case. Kenyatta had personally called and instructed him to make sure that nothing went wrong in this important political trial and to see that justice prevailed.

The defense objected to having the trial in Nairobi. They felt their client could not get a fair trial in the capital and wanted to move the trial to Mombasa.

Chief Justice Njonjo denied the defense's motion, ruling instead that the case would be heard in Nairobi.

The trial was the talk of the land, and it was reported extensively in all the East African English and Swahili newspapers as well as in the press internationally.

The Trial: Day One

"I heard a gun go off, and Mehar Singh told me to go to the kitchen."

SharanJeet Kaur

Akash drove his father to the courthouse for the first day of the trial. His father was silent during the trip and seemed visibly upset. The main courthouse was located in the center of Nairobi, near the Parliament buildings. He turned into the parking lot and pulled the Mercedes into an open slot. It was a good thing they'd come early; the parking lot was almost full, and it was clear that the courtroom was going to be packed.

They walked towards the main entrance, shaded by trees planted in landscaped beds with fragrant flowers and shrubs around the perimeter of the parking lot and along the side of the building. The courthouse was one of the old Empire structures, built by the British during the height of the colonial expansion period. The huge columns and the long flight of steps that ran around three sides of the building made the courthouse look quite imposing, an effect which was softened by the pale peach color.

As soon as they started up the steps, a mass of television and newspaper reporters swarmed towards Akash and his father. In a circus-like atmosphere, they were shouting questions, each one trying to be heard over the din. Akash pushed ahead of his father and shouldered a passage through the crowd. They made their way into the courtroom and found a seat at the end of the row where most of the family was sitting.

There was no mistaking the sons of Mehar Singh; they were

all dressed similarly, in khaki pants, white shirts, and with the distinctive white turbans which were a sign of mourning. Tall and broad-shouldered with neatly trimmed black beards, their facial resemblance to their father was sobering although none was quite as tall as Mehar had been. The women were dressed in the traditional outfit known as salwar kameez, all in somber, muted colors, save Akash's grandmother, Satbir Kaur, who wore the white that signified widowhood.

A portrait of the president dominated the back wall of the room. It was as though Jomo Kenyatta was staring down at them, keeping a watchful eye on the proceedings. The high ceilings and ceiling fans stirred the air but did little to mitigate the heat created by so many people crowded into the building. At least a dozen of the Kenyan policemen, the Askaris, stood against the walls around the room, appearing tense and looking ready to deal with any trouble that might arise.

Akash sat next to his father in awkward silence as two police officers brought his aunt into the courtroom. The crowd that thronged the proceedings fell silent for a moment when SharanJeet first appeared, then the buzz of their conversation increased. Photographers from the African and international press snapped pictures of the distraught woman.

SharanJeet's long black hair was, as usual, gathered in pigtails, which made her look younger than she really was. A strikingly attractive woman, her light blue salwar kameez was set off by the blue-black darkness of her hair and by the midnight blue chunni scarf wrapped loosely around her neck and trailing over her shoulders and down her back. SharanJeet walked with a self-confident, almost arrogant air, her head held high as she glanced around the courtroom. Her uncomonly beautiful features caused an appreciative murmur amongst the packed courthouse gallery.

The booming voice of a court officer stilled the crowd as he ordered the onlookers to rise. He announced the assessors as they entered, then called out, "Chief Justice Peter Njonjo, presiding." The swish of the judge's robes rubbing against his legs seemed loud in the utter silence of the courtroom, as the man who would decide SharanJeet's guilt or innocence took his place before the crowd.

SharanJeet appeared before Chief Justice Njonjo and three assessors, who spoke both Punjabi and English. The charges against her were read before the court.

"That the accused, SharanJeet Kaur Dhillon, did commit murder on the person of her father-in-law, Mehar Singh Dhillon, and that she shot him with a .32 caliber automatic pistol and killed him in cold blood."

Once the charges were read, Justice Njonjo said, "How does the accused plead?"

SharanJeet's attorney, Michael Anderson, answered for her.

"Your honor, my client pleads not guilty."

There were murmurs from the crowd at this statement and Akash could understand why. The physical evidence implicating SharanJeet was almost overwhelming. How could she possibly hope to prove her innocence?

Assistant Superintendent T.S. Sheridan conducted the prosecution's case. He rose and stood before the court, to make his opening statement.

"This is a simple case," he began. "The state will prove that the accused, SharanJeet Kaur Dhillon, for reasons as yet unknown, did plan and execute the heinous murder of her father-in-law, the noted political figure Mehar Singh Dhillon.

"The facts speak for themselves. The accused planned for the murder to take place at a time when most of the family would be away from the mansion at Kijabe. She arranged the absence of her sister-in-law, Kulwant, and once Kulwant was at the temple, she lured Mehar Singh back to the house under false pretenses. When he returned to the house, she drew a gun, which she had already loaded and kept near for this very purpose, and she shot and killed him.

"All the physical evidence which will be presented before this court will support these facts. Please note that I said *all* the physical evidence. No one else could have committed this heinous crime. Every shred of physical evidence collected at the crime scene incriminates the accused. SharanJeet Kaur Dhillon was the only person who had both the means and the opportunity to kill Mehar Singh. The state will prove, beyond the shadow of a doubt, that SharanJeet Kaur Dhillon is guilty of murder."

When Sheridan was finished with his opening statement, SharanJeet's lawyer, the energetic Michael Anderson, rose from his seat at the defendant's table. The crowd again grew silent as they listened to the kilted Scottish lawyer who seemed strangely out of place in this African courtroom.

He began, "Mr. Sheridan would have the court believe that this is a simple case. The state will present piece after piece of physical evidence, nearly all of which is circumstantial. They will attempt to use the deceased's notoriety and the country's shock at his death in an effort to influence this court to make a hasty decision regarding my client's guilt.

"What the state will not do—indeed, what Mr. Sheridan will avoid at all costs, as he in fact has done in his opening statements—is discuss motive. They will not discuss my client's motive for murdering her father-in-law because there is no motive. Not for murder.

"I will not stand before this court and attempt to deny that the weapon that took Mehar Singh's life was wielded by my client. What I will do is prove, before this court, and before the people of Kenya, that my client's actions were not premeditated as the state claims, and that her intention was never to murder Mehar Singh. I will prove that the gun went off in the middle of a struggle between SharanJeet and the deceased, and I will prove that my client's possession of the gun was provoked when the deceased intentionally demeaned and insulted her.

"I will also prove that Mehar Singh initiated the struggle that ended so tragically, when he tried to take the gun away from my client. Whether Mehar Singh's death resulted from self-defense or from involuntary manslaughter is a matter for the court to decide. But I will prove that in no way is my client guilty of murder."

After opening statements were given, Sheridan rose from

his seat to begin presenting the prosecution's case. Justice Njonjo ordered him to call his first witness.

"Your honor, the prosecution calls Assistant Police Inspector Koch Keino."

The tall athletic-looking Inspector Keino came forward, was sworn in, and sat on the witness stand.

"Inspector Keino, can you please tell the court, in your own words, the events that transpired after you arrived at the Dhillon family residence in Kijabe on the evening of February 20th?"

After clearing his throat, the inspector replied, "I arrived at the Dhillon home around 8:30 p.m. The victim's body was lying on the floor inside the house. A sheet was covering his body and bloodstains were clearly visible on the white cloth."

"Where was SharanJeet Dhillon when you arrived?" Sheridan asked.

"The accused was sitting in a chair approximately four feet away from the body."

"What, in your opinion, was her emotional state?"

Michael Anderson objected that the inspector was not a psychologist and was, therefore, not qualified to testify as to SharanJeet's mental or emotional condition. Sheridan countered with the statement that Keino had seen the families of murder victims before in his capacity as a police officer, and thus was at least qualified to compare SharanJeet's reactions to those of others he had observed. Judge Njonjo allowed the question.

Keino answered, "She seemed remarkably poised considering she was sitting so close to the body of her father-in-law." He paused and then he volunteered, "Also, there was no sign that she had been crying."

On further questioning, Inspector Keino revealed that one bullet was found in the front door of the house, a second under a meat safe in a connecting passage between the sitting room and kitchen, and a third bullet was taken from the body of Mehar Singh Dhillon.

Sheridan said, "The prosecution has no further questions for this witness, your honor."

Anderson cross-examined Assistant Inspector Keino.

"Inspector Keino, you stated that you have experience in dealing with the reactions of victims and the families of victims of violent crime, is that correct?"

"Yes."

"And wouldn't you say that shock, and even denial, are frequent and natural reactions to such events?"

"Well, yes. . .I suppose so."

"Then Mrs. Dhillon's lack of visible response to her father-in-law's violent death could actually be a natural response to the events that she witnessed, is that not also true?"

Sheridan objected that Michael was leading the witness. Michael stated that he was only asking Assistant Inspector Keino to answer a straightforward, yes-or-no question. The judge ruled in Anderson's favor.

"I suppose that you *could* say her response was a natural one," Keino began.

"Yes or no, Inspector Keino. Could SharanJeet's apparent lack of response to Mehar Singh's death indicate that she was in shock and denial, after witnessing such a violent event?"

"Yes, it could," he answered grudgingly, with an annoyed sound in his voice.

"Thank you. No further questions, your honor."

Anderson returned to the table, and whispered something to SharanJeet. Akash couldn't hear what he said to her, but he had to admit that the lawyer was doing his best to defend SharanJeet. With the exception of the physical evidence presented, it appeared that he had nullified most of Keino's damaging testimony.

The prosecution called a second police officer, Assistant Inspector Tom Price.

T.S. Sheridan said, "Assistant Inspector Price, can you please describe the wounds you observed on the victim's body?"

"There was an entry wound on the left temple, the victim's right wrist was shattered by a bullet wound, and there was a third wound in the left shoulder which also appeared to have been made by a bullet," he said. "There were exit wounds in the victim's back and shattered wrist, and ballistics reports indicate that the bullets found in the door and under the meat safe are consistent with the exit wounds on the victim's body."

"Was any evidence found at the crime scene that would indicate the type of weapon, Inspector?" the prosecutor asked.

Price responded, "We found three shell casings, which appeared to have been fired from a .32 caliber pistol."

"And was such a weapon found at the crime scene?"

"Yes, sir. A .32 caliber automatic pistol was found in a partially opened drawer in the living room of the Dhillon residence."

"Was this weapon dusted for fingerprints?"

"Yes, of course - it's standard procedure."

"Will you please tell the court, Inspector," the prosecutor persisted, "whose fingerprints were found on that weapon?"

"There were a number of older partial prints on the pistol grip, but the only clear set of latent fingerprints were those of SharanJeet Kaur Dhillon."

"Thank you, Inspector Price. No further questions."

Michael Anderson stood up from the table to cross-examine the witness.

"Inspector Price, you say that a .32 caliber automatic was at the scene of the crime?"

"Yes, that's correct."

"And can you please repeat to the court exactly where that weapon was found?"

"It was in a partially opened drawer in the living room," he answered.

"So we are to believe that this cold, calculating killer, who allegedly planned every detail of this murder so carefully, not only tossed the murder weapon into a convenient drawer after the crime was committed, but also left the drawer open, so that the police would have an easier time finding the murder weapon?" He paused. "Isn't it more likely that the gun was placed there by someone else, to cast suspicion on my client?"

"I can't speculate as to why the gun was placed there. I can only say that the pistol was found in that drawer."

"Thank you, Inspector. No further questions, your honor."

Aside from that question, SharanJeet's lawyer didn't cross-examine Price. Akash guessed that this was probably because the officer's testimony was almost entirely confined to statements backed up by physical evidence, and thus would be all but impossible to refute.

The prosecution called its final witness of the day, an African Police Constable named Mustafa Mohammed.

"Can you please tell us what happened after you arrived at the scene of the crime on the night of February 20th, as best as you can recall?"

"Certainly," Mohammed said. "I interviewed the accused, SharanJeet Kaur Dhillon. She told me that she was present when her father-in-law died. When I asked her who killed him, she said 'I heard a gun go off, and Mehar Singh told me to go to the kitchen. Then he shut the door, and as I was walking towards the kitchen, I looked back and saw him falling down.' She also told me that she had not seen anyone outside the house," he added. "She said she didn't know who had fired the shots, and that the African servants had not been present."

There were no further questions for the constable, and again Michael Anderson did not cross-examine the witness. At a gesture from Justice Njonjo, the court officer rose, and said, "This session is adjourned. Court will reconvene at 9 A.M. tomorrow."

Santokh Singh rose from his seat, and Akash followed his father out of the courtroom.

Chapter XV

"True Lord, in thy house is every treasure.
He on whom thou bestoweth thy grace may
attain to it, for that we acknowledge thy glory.
May thy name remain forever in our hearts for
then our minds will remain filled with thy
heavenly music. Says Nanak: "Since thy name
is my only sustenance, is there anything that is
not in thy house?"

Anand Sahib Guru Amar Das Jee

That night the family conversation was about the trial. Akash understood their obsession with the day's events but he did not share it. He wanted to see his grandfather's killer brought to justice, but in the end, nothing would bring him back or fill the void that losing Bapu Jee had left in their lives.

Akash was eagerly anticipating a brief distraction from the pervasive gloom that seemed to hang over the family—he was meeting Anar for dinner. He hadn't told her about finding his grandfather's journals yet, and he looked forward to having the rare opportunity to surprise her. He carefully packed the books in a canvas tote bag in the boot of his Mercedes.

After arriving at the restaurant a little early to position the surprise in an appropriate place, he checked on his prior arrangements. He'd ordered a dozen white roses delivered to the restaurant, and they were at the table, just as he had specified. He thought of how best to present the evening's big surprise, and he took the mâitre d' aside and explained what he wanted to do. Then he sat down at the table, concealed the rest of the journals behind him, and waited for Anar to arrive.

She stepped into the room and murmurs of appreciation could be heard through the room. Akash understood why. At the worst of times, Anar was beautiful, but tonight, she seemed more radiant than usual. She spotted him and smiled, which magnified her radiance.

It hardly seemed that anything could make her more gorgeous. But Akash was willing to bet that his surprise would bring out another smile. He knew the journalist in her would be delighted at this discovery of a famous man's memoirs.

He rose from the table and met her halfway across the room, taking her hand gently in his own as he pulled her into a quick embrace. His arm found its way comfortably around her waist, as he walked her to the table.

Her eyes widened when she saw the roses, flawlessly arranged in a Waterford crystal vase.

"Oh, Akash," she said. "They're beautiful!"

"Pale and ugly," he said, "next to you." He cupped her face gently with his hand. "Why do they say, 'Her skin was as soft as a rose petal,' anyway? They should say, 'The rose petal was as soft as Anar's skin.'"

She blushed and he saw the shy smile that had endeared her to him the first time they met.

"Hush, you," she begged. "You're embarrassing me."

He pulled her chair out from the table, then went around to the other side and sat across from her.

"I hope you're ready for this," he said. "I hear they have a very special menu here."

As if on cue, their waiter appeared at his side.

"Would you like to see a wine list, sir?" he asked.

"Oh, no. Let's let the lady decide," he answered, gesturing towards Anar.

The waiter shifted quickly to the other side of the table and said, "As you can see, we have a most rare and unusual selection tonight," as he handed the first volume of Mehar Singh's journals to Anar. It looked like a wine list—sort of. A brief look of confusion passed over her face as she realized she had not been given the wine list, and then on her puzzled countenance appeared a look of sheer amazement as she studied the "wine list" and realized what she was holding.

"Where on earth did you find this?" she exclaimed. "I had no idea your grandfather kept a journal."

"I don't think anyone knew, except for Manjee," he answered, referring to his grandmother. "And there are more than a dozen volumes all together. We found them boxed up with some old clothes in one of Bapu Jee's closets. Manjee said she thought it would be all right if you used them as background for your articles."

"You're as sneaky as you are wonderful, meri jaan." Her eyes glinted mischievously as she added teasingly, "I will have to find some way to pay you back for all these wonderful surprises."

They had a wonderful dinner and then retired to Anar's for a nightcap. He'd told her most of what was in the first journal during dinner and the drive home, and she was anxious to explore the other volumes. There was an English league soccer match on TV, so Akash watched while she read from the second volume, nestled against him on the couch.

JOURNAL OF MEHAR SINGH DHILLON, YEAR ONE, VOLUME I - APRIL 6, 1916

We've finally arrived at the base camp, which it took us for-ever to reach as it followed the line of iron tracks snaking their way inland to Nairobi. This country is rugged and tough, and that's why they need us here: to tame the wilderness and build a railway that will permit humans to travel through it. The work camps are set up outdoors, in makeshift tents on the African veldt.

The cooks work in shifts, preparing communal meals for the workers. Various ones specialize in cooking meals that conform to the dietary restrictions of the Sikh, Hindu, or Moslem cultures. I hear them squabbling, arguing over cooking facilities, uten-sils, anything they can think of to take offense at. Their petty arguments echo the tensions that have long existed between these opposing religions. (I wonder if God isn't somewhere laughing at their silly quarrels, as God is probably essentially the same God in all religions.)

And yet, it is not so quarrelsome among the rail workers. There is some conflict, to be sure, but it seems as though we all feel a common bond. As we lay down the rail lines, we are building the framework for this new, modern Kenya. Though the African workers were born here, and the rest of us chose to come to this land, already it feels like home. We are all Kenyans, and this beautiful country will be the only home we have for years to come.

As we settle in for the night and I try to sleep, I hear the roaring of lions combined with the laughter and howling of the hyenas, the snorting sounds of zebras and wildebeeste, and the trumpeting of elephants nearby. I have been told that the animals were near, but seldom came close enough to see. As I drift off to sleep, the sense of danger and the thought that I have come all this way only to feed some large animal, as the zebra fed the lions, plagues me. Will these sounds ever lull me to sleep in this strange, new land, or will anxiety always be my bedtime companion?

JOURNAL OF MEHAR SINGH DHILLON, YEAR ONE, VOLUME I - APRIL 7, 1916

Today was the first day of work for us. There are fifty men in each work party, and each of us is assigned to different tasks. Because Kala and I are both very strong, we are assigned to place the "sleepers," the wooden logs that rest between the rail tracks. The work is hard and the day long. I can barely keep my head up and my eyes open long enough to write this, but in many ways it seems that the body's exhaustion frees the mind to roam. I know that in years to come, I will want to remember these first months in my new home.

Anar kept reading for what seemed like hours. She'd never read anything like it. She, like Akash, had grown up in Africa, so she was enthralled at seeing a much-more-primitive Africa through the eyes of an Asian transplant who became a legend and whose career in Africa obviously started with hard physical toil. She was surprised at the elegance of some of his writing.

JOURNAL OF MEHAR SINGH, YEAR TWO, VOLUME III - JULY 12, 1917

It's been a long, hard journey thus far. The railway snakes its way slowly towards Nairobi, but many of those who came with me to Africa are with us no more; some have returned to India, and others have died. Living conditions are harsh, and many are struck down by malaria, yellow fever, typhoid, cholera, and other tropical illnesses. The work goes on, but the work crews grow steadily smaller, leaving more work for those who remain.

More than the hard work and illnesses, it is the fierce man-eating lions of Tsavo that cause our numbers to dwindle. These rogue lions prey on the rail workers, mostly attacking at night, but sometimes they take their victims even in daylight, boldly attacking as we work on the tracks or travel between the tents. It is their land, they seem to be telling us, and they do not want it tamed. Will Africa ever be tamed? I have my doubts.

Several of the foremen, armed with hunting rifles, keep watch over us as we work. But somehow these lions always manage to elude them. Even the bravest among us have an almost superstitious fear of these beasts, who seem able to come and go as they please. They appear as if from nowhere, take down one of the workers, and drag their prey into the tall grass before the armed men can get a decent shot.

Though dozens of these man-eaters have been killed, more always come to take their place, and nothing seems to deter them from hunting the men who work on the railroad. All too often the roars of these fierce predators and the screams of their dying prey pierce the still African night, waking us all and filling the camp with terror.

To fill our scant free time and take our minds off the lions, we engage in familiar activities such as kabbadi, wrestling, and card games. Wrestling is especially popular among the Indian workers. Back home, every village had its own wrestling champions, and they would challenge the best wrestlers from another village. Wrestling allows us to use the wiry strength we develop in the hard labor of rail work. It reminds us of home and gives us something to occupy our minds besides the predators outside and our friends inside being preyed upon by disease.

It is night, and the sound of the lions hunting has dwindled. Tomorrow will be here soon, and with it, a full day's work. Each morning I wonder if this might be the day the lions come for me— if this day might be my last. Part of what I sought by coming to Africa was adventure, but this is more adventure than I wanted. Still, the work goes on, the railroad moves inexorably towards Nairobi, and in time, Tsavo and its man-eaters will be behind us— soon I pray.

JOURNAL OF MEHAR SINGH, YEAR TWO, VOLUME IV - AUGUST 17, 1917

My dear friend Kala and I have left the rail camp winding its way so slowly towards Nairobi. We're going ahead to the capital to seek better opportunities there. I've heard there are better jobs with higher pay and greater opportunity for advancement.

Several Indian companies are contracting to supply the labor and materials for laying down the sleepers for the rail line. I've discussed it all with Kala, and we agreed that if there are better opportunities in Nairobi, we want to be among the first to get the best jobs that can be had. We've worked so much, and have had so little time to reflect, that I seem to have missed the wonders of nature that surround me.

Now, as we travel towards Nairobi, at first the beauty of the landscape is nearly overwhelming. The sky seems farther away here, the clouds higher. Distances are deceiving in this still, clear air, especially after the rains have fallen. It seems as though I could reach out and touch the distant hills and mountains that define the horizon. Africa is a tantalizing place, and so sensuous. I am coming to love the sight of the scraggly open plains with their backdrop of mountains majestically rising and undulating in the background. The woods are filled with storks and nightingales, and wildflowers carpet the ground after the rains.

Once again, I am spending some of my time aboard a cart pulled by six oxen. On our journey, we stop frequently to rest the bulls and give them water and time to cool down. Each night we make camp near a hillside, using the terrain to provide some minimal protection against the predators that stalk the night.

The driver backs the cart onto a slope, and we light huge fires at each corner of the camp, hoping that the flames will frighten off some of the beasts. The route from Tsavo to Nairobi has one of the densest populations of wild animals in Kenya. Herds of elephants and buffalo pass right through camp, and the roars of lions surrounds us.

The open savanna is truly beautiful. Grassy plains are dotted here and there with the delicate, lacy, olive-green branches of the acacia trees, which lean against the horizon like giant bonsai. The stately baobab trees, which we use to make rope, look as though they've been ripped up and replanted upside-down, their branches reaching upwards like arms to pull nourishment from the sky.

Herds of zebras and gazelles thunder across the plains, sometimes fleeing predators and sometimes seeming to run just for the sake of running, raising clouds of dust in the stagnant air. Large herds of wildebeests and zebras move slowly across the plains in the oppressive heat, like dark lava flowing inexorably towards new pastures.

The dust raised by the ox cart coats my throat and makes my eyes burn. The cart shudders and jostles, and the back of my neck stings as my own salty sweat irritates the dust ground into my skin. Three hundred miles from Tsavo to Nairobi, but it seems like three thousand, and the trip from Mombasa seems a distant, pleasant memory by comparison.

JOURNAL OF MEHAR SINGH, YEAR TWO, VOLUME IV - SEPTEMBER 3, 1917

This morning we arrived in Nairobi. Kala and I went to the office of Prem Singh, whose company has contracted with the British government to supply cut logs to be used as sleepers for the railway project.

As we talked of home, we discovered that Prem Singh was actually related to Kala by marriage. He and Kala spoke of family back in India, and after that we agreed to join his company.

We'll stay here in Nairobi for a couple of days, and then we'll go to work at a small railway outpost in Kijabe, on the Rift Valley Escarpment.

JOURNAL OF MEHAR SINGH, YEAR TWO, VOLUME IV - OCTOBER 30, 1917

We've been at Kijabe for a couple of weeks now. Kijabe is located on the escarpment about sixty miles from Narok in the Maasai district and on the route between Nairobi and Kisumu. At the base of the Escarpment, there are sulphurous hot springs, and people come from all over Kenya to partake of the medicinal waters at the spa here. The land here is beautiful, and our working conditions are safer and less arduous than at the site in Tsavo.

This morning, Joseph, the big Kikuyu who leads the work crew, came and fetched me from where I was working. He took me to the other end of the job site and showed me a huge boulder that had fallen in the path of the rail line. He challenged me to try and move the stone. As the African workers had already tried to no avail, he felt certain that I would be unable to do it.

"Come on, Kala Singha," he said, "let's see you move the rock."

We Sikhs, with our turbans and beards, all look alike to the Africans. Because Kala Singh is the tallest and strongest of the Indians in the work crew, the Africans have taken to calling all of us Kala Singha. It's become our ethnic nickname, but we don't mind it!

I looked at the boulder, examining the ground around it, and saw that I could probably move it with a lever. I told them I would wager a month's salary that I could move the rock by myself. Joseph and several of the other Kikuyu workers eagerly took the bet.

I found an iron rod and hooked it under the stone, wedging it in the ground. Then I shouted a Sikh prayer, "Jo bole so nihal!" and heaved against the boulder with all my strength. The rod slipped in the ground; I had picked the wrong spot and couldn't get enough leverage to move the rock. The Kikuyu workers began to shout and laugh among themselves as the prospect of winning excited them.

When I removed the iron bar, they started clapping each other on the shoulder, thinking they had won. But they grew quiet again, as I bent down and felt the ground around the edges of the stone. When I found a spot where the earth was not as loose, I stood again and positioned the iron rod beneath the stone in this new location.

I yelled another holy cry, "Sat sri akaal!" and threw my entire body against the bar. Straining with every muscle, my feet scrabbling for leverage, I felt the stone begin to move. With a sudden burst of strength, I levered it over, and then it quickly picked up speed and rolled down the hillside.

The Africans were amazed, and they gave me the name "Mwanake," which in their language signifies a man of great strength. This was a sign of enormous respect, and I didn't know what to say. Tribal names have great significance to the Kikuyu and are rarely given to foreigners. I thanked them for honoring me so, and I smiled and bowed to show my pleasure.

JOURNAL OF MEHAR SINGH, YEAR THREE, VOLUME II - JULY 20, 1918

I went back to the shop today. I hated to see it with the doors and the windows boarded over. It has been months since I wrote in this journal; long, painful months as I sought to regain my strength and recover from my injury.

After several years of hard labor, I had grown tired of the railroad business. I decided to open a small general store, a duka, as it is called in the local language. The location I chose was Ruaraka, about twenty miles from Nairobi. Kala had left several months earlier to join the Kenyan police force. I asked him if he wanted to join me in this new venture, but he was content with his new life, so I started the shop on my own.

I dealt mainly in staples such as groceries, fruits, vegetables, blankets, sugar, and flour. Nearly anything that was a necessity could be found in my shop. Though the business started doing well, I had trouble learning the local language, Swahili, a fairly new dialect that originated on the coast which is made up of elements combined from Hindi, Arabic, and English as well as several

African languages. I hired a tutor to come in twice a week to teach me Swahili as well as English, which I also needed to master, since most correspondence with my suppliers is in English.

The shop did well from the very start. Local Africans seemed to love being around us, and they came to the shop not only to buy maize-meal, sugar, and tea, but also to visit. They would sit around the shop, laughing, joking with us and drinking Indian tea which we brew all day.

Since I needed help around the shop, I hired Nika Singh, a young Sikh who comes into the shop often. We became friends and his help was valuable, although at times he could be a bit impetuous. Though the majority of my customers are friendly, this part of Africa is still quite wild and mostly unsettled, so I kept a gun in the shop, loaded and ready in case it should be needed in self-defense.

I still remember that morning as though it was yesterday. I was attending to some customers who were provisioning for a trip into the Serengeti when curiosity got the better of young Nika. He picked up the gun and was pointing and aiming it, as though he were practicing shooting. If I had noticed him doing that, I would have stopped him, but I was busy with my customers until it was too late.

The gun went off in Nika's hand, and the bullet went through my leg. I suppose I am lucky. Someone could have been killed. But the ordeal I went through in the following weeks did not seem like any kind of luck.

Nika and my shocked and terrified customers helped me to a chair. There was no doctor in the village, and nothing in the shop to treat the wound properly, so Nika arranged for an ox cart to take me to the doctor in Nairobi. The 20-mile journey was long and painful. With every bump in the road, the pain stabbed through my leg. As I drank shot after shot of whiskey to relieve the pain, I grew delirious. When bumps in the road caused the wound to open and start bleeding again, they would clean and bandage my leg again before we continued on our way.

When I finally arrived in Nairobi, I was taken to see my old friend Krishan Lal, a doctor who lives and works in the capital. Though he expertly treated my wound, it never healed properly. There are still fragments of the bullet in the leg, and he's told me that I will probably always walk with a noticeable limp.

My convalescence took six months. Without me here to manage the store, the business had to be closed. The ordeal of being shot, my slow recovery, and having to close my business left me weak and disheartened.

I tried everything to return to health. I turned to the age-old Indian village remedies to regain my strength. Twice each day, I would drink a spoonful of buttered ghee in a glass of hot milk with almonds. I taught the African servants to massage my injured leg, and I would lie on a bed on the patio, while one of them poured hot mustard oil on the leg and vigorously massaged all the way from my toes to my upper thigh.

Now that I have regained my strength—and my normally positive attitude—I am once again looking at possible business ventures. I found a buyer for the store. There is nothing for me there now but memories of pain and loss. The British government has just announced the decision to allow Indian traders to start doing business in the Maasai district. This part of Kenya is unsettled, and the British are hoping that the Asian and European traders will develop it for them.

I am determined to explore this untapped market. I have convinced some of my European friends to back me in this venture, though others think I am crazy. The Kikuyu and Maasai people are considered dangerous and unfriendly, and there are even rumors that they are cannibals, but I don't believe it.

I met a man named Shamboo Dutt who is interested in trading in the Maasai district. Now that I've sold the shop in Ruaraka, we have formed a business known as "Mehar Singh, Shamboo Dutt, and Company." We came up with the idea of a traveling duka. Rather than having a fixed location where the natives must come to buy their supplies, we will have a shop on wheels. As we travel through the Maasai district, we will make stops at designated towns and villages.

Since the Maasai are largely a nomadic people, this seems the ideal solution. We'll carry the shop to the customers, rather than rely on customers coming to the shop. We've purchased a large four-wheel cart and twenty oxen. The cart can carry two tons of merchandise, and I'll be the wagon master. As soon as the last of the stock arrives, we'll begin our first trip into Maasai lands.

I am excited about this new venture, although it is an irony that after worrying so much about being murdered by a wild animal, I found myself wounded and maimed by an accidental gunshot by a boy. It has changed my life, but as things often change for the better and our misfortunes frequently pave the way for new successes, I anticipate my new path in life with eagerness. I will practice the dedicated self-reliance which the Sikh religion has taught me to do. If it is God's will that I prosper, then I shall.

JOURNAL OF MEHAR SINGH, YEAR THREE, VOLUME II - AUGUST 9, 1918

We have left Kijabe, traveling towards Narok and the remote tribal areas of the Maasai district. I led the wagon carefully down the escarpment in Kijabe and over the Siabei escarpment, through a landscape of small, open plains dotted with silvery-white leleshwa bushes. During the evenings, as the sky grows dark and we make camp for the night, I use some of the drier bushes for firewood. The leleshwa gives off a pleasant odor as it burns, and it is plentiful.

The first night out was unusually still and quiet, and the stars seemed as close as the end of my arm. Though my leg still pains me from time to time, I am largely at peace with myself. Despite the excitement of starting this new venture, there is something about the beauty of the night, clear and cold, which calms and relaxes me as I prepare myself for the journey ahead.

JOURNAL OF MEHAR SINGH, YEAR THREE, VOLUME II - AUGUST 18, 1918

As we neared the Siabei River today, I was exhilarated at the sight of abnormally tall acacia trees as well as wild fig, olive, and cedar. Each morning, I rise with the sun and the party travels until late afternoon. Even so, we are only covering about ten miles each day. The land around us is breathtaking in its beauty, especially when the steep walls of the Rift Valley are visible. There are wild animals in abundance; wildebeest, zebra, impala, and gazelle, giraffe, ostrich, dik-dik, jackal, and warthog. Most of the animals keep their distance, frightened by the noise of the cart and the smell of humans.

Though all the country we are traveling through is Maasai land, I have as yet seen few of the Maasai people. Near the middle of the day, we spotted several of the "Moraan" (young single men of the warrior class of the Maasai tribe) herding cattle. Nearby, women and children were working and playing in a small manyatta, or mud hut village. But that manyatta was neither populous enough nor prosperous enough to warrant stopping to trade—even the cattle were thin and sickly-looking.

By late afternoon each day, all the workers are tired and the oxen will go no further. I order them to stop and make camp for the night. Oxen are untied and let loose to graze, and I assign a few men from the party to watch over the animals in case there are lions or Maasai poachers in the area. Another man is sent in search of firewood. I have the workers build huge fires out of the biggest logs they can find, in hopes that this will keep night predators, both human and animal, at bay.

Later in the evening, just before it gets dark, I order the oxen brought in closer to camp. Valuable animals are kept in the middle of the enclosure, with bonfires lit at all corners. We ring the camp with thorny acacia bushes as an added deterrent, and once the camp is as secure as we can make it, we bed down for the night. I am not totally accustomed to sleeping with the treacherous night sounds all about me, but my early days building the railway acclimated me to this type of night.

JOURNAL OF MEHAR SINGH, YEAR THREE, VOLUME II - AUGUST 20, 1918

This morning, the wagon train made its first stop at a manyatta not far from where we had made camp the night before. The huts in the village were made of fine twigs, leleshwa or sage, which were shaped into a dome-like structure, covered with a layer of grass and leaves, and then plastered with fresh cow dung. There were three entrances to the manyatta, and these "gates" were opened at dawn and closed again at dusk.

The Maasai were excited and intrigued when they saw our traveling duka arrive in their village. As I spoke a little of the Maasai dialect, I was able to conduct the trades. The villagers purchased blankets, sugar, matches, wire of copper and steel, red ochre, beads, flour, and pieces of tire to make sandals. They had no concept of money, and instead bartered with me for whatever they needed. They exchanged live goats and sheep as well as skins and hides for the items they wished to purchase.

When the trading party left the village, we tied the animals taken in trade to the back of the wagon. I made arrangements to pick up the skins and animal hides when we come through the village on our way back to Nairobi. We are establishing relationships of trust and friendship with many people whom I feel might be loyal trading partners for years.

JOURNAL OF MEHAR SINGH, YEAR THREE, VOLUME III - SEPTEMBER 12, 1918

Though it only lasted for several weeks, our first trip into the Maasai lands was a great success. Shamboo and I were encouraged by the results, and we now have many offers from people who want to join the new venture. Already we are talking of purchasing a second cart and planning "trade routes" through the Maasai country in order to provide our goods to as many customers as possible. I think I may finally have found a way to make the fortune I sought when I first came to Africa. Perhaps there was a silver lining in that gunshot which ripped me from my first occupation as a shopkeeper.

JOURNAL OF MEHAR SINGH, YEAR FOUR, VOLUME I - JANUARY 27, 1919

As our trade journeys into Maasai country continue, Shamboo and I have come to be friends with many of the Maasai. They have the reputation of being fierce warriors. Our customers no longer wait until the traveling dukas stop in the villages; they come right up to the wagons, stopping us on the open savanna as we travel across the Maasai lands.

Lately it has gotten to the point where we often run out of goods to sell and trade long before we have visited all our intended destinations. The Maasai have started to request specific items that we don't have in the wagons. The business has become a greater success than I could have imagined, and other traders are rushing to copy our methods.

To stay ahead of our competition, we have begun carrying more stock, adding additional items which the Maasai tell us they would like to buy. I am naming the sites where our wagon trains most frequently camp at night, and I have chosen names such as Sukhi Nadee, which is Indian for "a dry river;" Khambee Simba, Swahili for "a lion camp;" Khambee Chai, Swahili for "tea-making station;" and Majee Choombie, which in Swahili means "salt-water camp." I have decided to use timber or aluminum sheets to construct permanent shops at those locations. As the number of fixed-location stores increases, I will invite friends and relatives to come over from India to help me run this growing business. India is full of ambitious and strong young males who will come to Kenya and get involved in the backbreaking work of developing this new land, and I know I can recruit them as the need arises.

Not only do the permanent sites generate additional business, but they serve as fixed "warehouses," where the traveling dukas can replenish their stock when the Maasai have traded for everything that can be carried in a single cart. In this way, we are developing a series of outposts which are stepping stones on our trade routes through Maasai country that make our operation more profitable and less cumbersome.

The traveling duka expeditions carry their own cooking supplies and condiments, such as onions, ghee, Indian spices, and flour for the Indian bread called "chapatees." These items are all for the trader's own use. In one corner of the wagon, under a small roof constructed to protect valuable items from the rain and the scorching African sun, we also carry large barrels of Scotch whiskey.

On one trip, three of our company's wagons left Kijabe together on a trading journey to Maasai country. When I called a stop for the night, the workers all started drinking whiskey after the hard day's journey. After quite a few drinks, the crews started arguing over who was going to cook the evening meal.

One group volunteered to cook, and the others went back to drinking. While a cook kneaded the dough for the chapatees, others prepared spicy curried goat meat. Everyone enjoyed the evening, as we sat around the fire drinking and eating delicious food.

The next morning, as preparations were being made to depart, several workers were trying to find drinking water to boil for tea. They found an empty kerosene can lying near the water cans. It was discovered that the cook had kneaded the chapatees with kerosene oil, but everyone had been drinking so much that they hadn't noticed! It was a miracle no one was sick the morning after.

Akash reached over and pulled the journal gently from between Anar's sleeping hands. He laid it on the coffee table and, after gently easing himself away from her, found a quilted down comforter and covered her with it. He stood for a moment, enjoying the angelic innocence that stole over her face when she was asleep. Then he found a pad and pen, and left her a note for when she awoke.

"My dearest heart,

I'm sorry I could not be here when you awake. The sun will rise dimmer for lack of the added radiance of your beauty. I have to be ready to go with the family to court first thing in the morning, and so I leave. I will see you soon, my love, though never soon enough.

Your soul,

Akash

The Trial: Day Two

*"So you are testifying that you heard
her say that he was killed with a panga,
which we know to be a long Swahili knife,
even though it was obvious that he was
not."*

Prosecutor Sheridan

On the second day of the trial, the prosecution began by calling two African police constables to testify.

Sheridan, the prosecutor, began. "Please state your name, for the record."

"I am Constable Lotobonye Sangura."

"How did you come to be at the scene of the crime?"

"Mwangara, an African servant who works in the Dhillon household, came running in and reported the shooting. We armed ourselves and went immediately to the Dhillon's compound." The witness was referring to the senior house servant at Kijabe, a 60-year-old Kikuyu whose gray hair signaled his age. Mwangara was known for his infectious giggly laugh and amiable disposition, and he had worked at the Kijabe residence of the Dhillons for many years.

"What was your impression of the defendant?" the prosecutor asked.

Sangura replied, "It seemed as though she was in shock. She was outwardly calm and it didn't appear that she had been crying, but she was clearly irrational."

Sheridan pursued this angle. "What do you mean?"

The constable replied slowly, "At one point, she went over to her father-in-law's body. She took his head in her hands and turned it to the side so that it was facing towards us, and in Swahili, she said, 'Can't you see? This is not an injury caused by a bullet. He has been cut by a panga.' Mrs. Dhillon could obviously tell as easily as you or I that Mehar Singh's injuries were not caused by a panga. She was either hallucinating, or she was hysterical."

"So you are testifying that you heard her say that he was killed with a panga, which we know to be a long Swahili knife, even though it was obvious that he was not," stated the prosecutor. Then he continued. "Then did you question the defendant as to how the victim was killed?"

"Not at that time," Lotobonye said, "I was taking a statement from Mwangara. Inspector Potter took SharanJeet's statement."

"What happened after you took the servant's statement?"

"When I came back I noticed the accused lean back as if she was going to fall. Kulwant, the victim's youngest daughter, said she was going to make some tea for SharanJeet. I told Kulwant she didn't have permission to go into the kitchen, and as I was going after her, I noticed a cartridge case lying on the kitchen floor."

Sheridan took a sealed evidence bag from a table in the front of the courtroom. "Is this the shell casing that you found in the kitchen of the Dhillon home?" he asked.

"It appears to be the same one, or it's one just like it," Lotobonye replied.

"Can you tell the court what kind of bullet this type of casing would be used for?"

"This cartridge case is for a .32 caliber bullet," he answered. "The same type of bullet as that which killed Mehar Singh."

The policeman then gave testimony pertaining to the arrest of five African employees whom he saw outside the house. After extensive questioning all had been released the following morning.

SharanJeet's attorney, Michael Anderson, had lodged a complaint that one of the Dhillon women had slapped his client, pushed her around, and poured water over her.

On cross-examination by Anderson, Constable Lotobonye stated that he had seen Kulwant slap SharanJeet, and pour water on her head.

Anderson said, "In response to the prosecutor's questioning, you stated that you didn't ask SharanJeet at that time about how Mehar Singh was killed. This implies that you spoke with Mrs. Dhillon on this matter at some later time. Is that correct?"

Lotobonye hesitated before answering, then replied, "Yes, I did."

"When did that conversation take place?" Anderson asked.

Lotobonye replied, "Later that night, shortly before we left for the evening. Mrs. Dhillon seemed to be in distress, and I went over to ask if there was anything I could do for her."

"And what did Mrs. Dhillon say to you at that time?"

"She said, 'I didn't mean to do it. He tried to take the gun away, and it went off. I never meant to kill him.'"

At this statement, a cacophony arose from the gallery. Mehar Singh's son Rajinder Singh leapt to his feet and shouted, "Liar! Who paid you off? Was it Mohinder? He won't save his viper of a wife that easily!"

Justice Njonjo banged his gavel, calling the court to order. Facing Rajinder, in a commanding voice he said, "Mr. Dhillon, if you cannot restrain yourself, you will be removed from this courtroom."

After a few moments, the courtroom again grew calm, and the judge ordered Michael Anderson to continue his cross-examination.

"Inspector Lotobonye, this statement from the defendant completely contradicts the story she gave to the other police officer that night. Why haven't you presented this evidence before now?"

Lotobonye paused, looking embarrassed. "No one ever asked me," he said. "No one asked what SharanJeet Dhillon said to me that night, and I didn't realize that the story she gave me was different from the one she gave Potter."

"Yet this evidence is not present in your statement before

the magistrate, either."

"No one ever asked me if I had a conversation with Mrs. Dhillon," he said. "It never came up."

"It never came up?" Anderson raised his voice in anger. "It never came up, so you decided to keep vital evidence, evidence that might have saved my client from the anguish of imprisonment and trial, to yourself?"

"I. . .I'm sorry. I didn't know. . .I wasn't sure whether to believe her. . ."

Anderson looked angry enough to throttle the inspector. With an obvious physical effort, he reined in his anger and turned away from the witness, returning to his seat.

"No further questions," he spat over his shoulder.

But Chief Justice Njonjo did not relieve the witness. Instead, he turned to Inspector Lotonboye and said in an angry voice, "This is ludicrous. I find it difficult—no, impossible—to believe that an officer of the law could be stupid enough to suppress evidence in this manner, especially when doing so is in direct contradiction with your own statement before the magistrate."

"I assume that you are familiar with the penalties for perjury," he said disgustedly. "Be aware that I can impose additional jail time for contempt of court, and if I discover that you have provided this court with false testimony, I will not hesitate to do so. You are an embarrassment to that uniform, an embarrassment to the law, and an embarrassment to all of Kenya."

"One man has already been killed," he said. "If anyone involved in this case gives incomplete, inaccurate, or intentionally false testimony which results in an innocent person being sentenced to death, then they are as guilty of murder as the person who took Mehar Singh's life. The witness is dismissed. For now."

The prosecutor called Assistant Inspector H.G. Potter to the stand.

As Sheridan handed the constable a piece of paper, he asked, "Do you recognize this statement?"

"I do."

"Can you please tell the court what this is?"

"It is my report, specifically the sections of that report which refer to the actions of SharanJeet Kaur Dhillon on the day of the murder."

"Would you tell us how the statement was taken?"

"She was asked if she understood English. She stated that her English was not good, so she was questioned in Punjabi. Ranjit Singh, who was present as interpreter, translated our questions for Mrs. Dhillon's benefit. Her answers were translated back to us and recorded in English. After we finished recording her statement, it was read to the defendant, and she placed her signature on the document to verify that it was accurate."

Describing SharanJeet's physical condition at the time she gave her statement, Assistant Inspector Potter noted, "She was calm, and did not appear to have been crying." He added that when she was asked to give a statement, she did so in "a clear, calm voice."

"Thank you. Can you read the statement aloud, please?"

In his strong, deep voice, the constable read, "I asked the victim's daughter-in-law her identity, and she stated for the record, 'My name is SharanJeet Kaur Dhillon, wife of Mohinder Singh. We have no children. My husband is in Tanganyika on business.'"

"Then I asked if she knew of any reason why someone would want to kill her father-in-law. She said, 'No. There has been no trouble in the household at all.' I asked her to relate the events that she witnessed that night. 'Around six o'clock this evening,' she said, 'I was in the kitchen preparing food. My father-in-law, Mehar Singh, came into the kitchen and asked me why I was not at the temple. I answered that I would come as soon as the food was ready.'"

"'Then,' she continued, 'I went out the kitchen door to the lavatory, which is about 25 yards away. I heard a sharp noise, like a shot, and when I came rushing out, I saw Mehar standing in the doorway—the same door I had come out of. His hands were empty. He told me to go and call Kulwant, and he said he was going to shut the front door. I went around the house, and as I approached the gate of the compound I saw four Africans near the steps.'"

"I asked her if she recognized them, and she replied that she did not. She then stated that she felt giddy, and that she heard another shot. Mehar's youngest daughter, Kulwant, called out to SharanJeet, and the two met across from the entrance to the Dhillon compound."

Potter pointed to SharanJeet. "She said that she sent Kulwant to call the postmaster, and once the other woman left, she entered the compound. Then she said, 'I saw Mehar Singh lying on the ground close to the front steps. I saw blood running from his body, into a depression in the ground.'"

"SharanJeet stated that she poured water over the victim's lips, and because she felt dizzy she put her own head under the water tap. She said she then went indoors and got a gun, which her husband kept in a sideboard drawer. She said she went to the kitchen door and fired two bullets into the air, and then she said went to the front door, past the body, and around the corner of the house, and fired two more bullets into the air. She said she fired the shots hoping to scare off any robbers still near the house."

"SharanJeet stated she had been taught to use the pistol by Sunder Lall, a brother-in-law. When I asked her about the bloodstains on her dress, she said they resulted from helping to carry Mehar Singh's body into the house. She concluded her statement by saying that she was walking back around the house when she saw the postmaster and Kulwant running towards her."

"Was anything else of note found at the crime scene?"

He responded, "Yes. A holster containing an automatic pistol was found in one of the bedrooms. At the time, I was unable to tell whether it had been fired recently."

"Thank you, Inspector," Sheridan said. "I tender the witness, your honor."

Michael Anderson cross-examined the witness, asking, "Inspector

Potter, you have told the court that SharanJeet's statement was rendered in English, and that she signed it to verify that it was accurate. Is that correct?"

"Yes, it is," he replied.

"And yet, you've just told the court that Mrs. Dhillon explained to the officers present that her English was not good. In fact, the assessors in this case were specifically chosen because they were bilingual in English and Punjabi, and this was necessary because the defendant cannot speak English well. Was the written statement which the defendant was asked to sign in Punjabi, or in English?"

"I just said it was in English!" Potter answered.

"Then you admit that SharanJeet Kaur Dhillon had virtually no idea what she was signing when she placed her signature on this document, this piece of evidence that is one of the lynch pins of the prosecution's case?"

"No, that's not what I meant," he said. "Ranjit Singh read it to her, translating it into Punjabi."

"Nevertheless, Mrs. Dhillon was unable to comprehend the written statement which you had her sign. She had no way of knowing, and this court has no way of knowing, whether the document she signed represents her true testimony on the events that transpired that night, is that not correct?"

"I . . . suppose so, when you put it that way," Potter said. "I never thought. . ."

"Exactly. You never thought. No further questions." Anderson turned and stalked across the room, to fling himself into his chair.

This concluded the second day of testimony. Akash and his father rose and filed out of the courtroom. The sequence of events that led up to his grandfather's death was both more and less clear. The prosecution's physical evidence against his aunt was strong. But the conflicting testimony of the police officer confused the matter. As a future attorney, Akash realized he should be enjoying the courtroom spectacle and all the legal posturing. But he would be glad when all this was over, so he and his family could put the horrible incident behind them. It was hard to enjoy a trial intellectually or legally when it was a source of agony and causing such a schism in the family.

Chapter XVI

*"Does not the history of the world show that there
would have been no romance in life if there had
been no risks?"*

Mohandass K. Gandhi

Anar sat on the couch, with the pile of journals around her,
reading while she waited for Akash to arrive. She had reached
one of the parts she'd wanted most to read about -Mehar Singh's
first meeting with his future bride.

JOURNAL OF MEHAR SINGH, YEAR FOUR, VOLUME II - JUNE 26, 1919

*Now that my business has become successful, I decided that I
am financially stable enough to have my wife, Satbir Kaur, join
me in Africa. Our marriage was arranged according to the village
traditions when I was only ten years old. The two families agreed
that we would live together after she turned sixteen. I never saw
her when I was still in India, so this was the first time I would ever
lay eyes on the woman who will be my wife.*

*Satbir is only 16 years old. She came over from India with my
brother, Harbans Singh, and his friend Teluram. My dear Kala
went with me when I traveled to greet them when they arrived in
Nairobi.*

*In traditional Indian fashion, Satbir has her head and face com-
pletely covered with a cloth made of malmal, called a "chunni."
She is very shy and will not look up to see me; though we are to be
married, we are still total strangers. She keeps trying to peek
through the chunni without being noticed, so she can catch a glimpse*

of me. I caught her doing that quite a few times.

I arranged for us to stay for a time at the quarters of Munshi Ram and Company, until we are ready to go to our home in Kijabe. After we ate, we spent some time socializing and finally, everyone left us alone for our first night together. It was awkward at first, introducing myself to my new bride. To ease the tension between us, I began by telling her stories about my life here in Africa, and the things I have seen and done.

Satbir listened intently to my voice, and hardly spoke at all. She kept looking at her hands and wouldn't lift her eyes to look at me. I talked late into the night, as it is important to me that she know everything about our new life. Finally, I got close to her, held her face in my hands and lifted the chunni off her. Her shyness prompted her to look away from me. I missed a couple of heart-beats as her facial beauty stunned me and my lips were eager to touch hers. I hugged and held her and she surprised me by hugging back quite affectionately. We stayed in that position for at least twenty minutes. At last, just a few hours before dawn, we drifted off to sleep.

We spent a week together in Nairobi before I took Satbir to the house in Kijabe. The wilds of Africa are not so wild as they once were. I have a manicured plantation with servants to offer my new bride. A number of retail stores have opened in small townships throughout the Maasai lands. The government now has a district office and a police post has opened in Narok. So the land where I am taking Satbir to start our family is part of the new Africa I have been helping to build. It is still wild in places but becoming more and more civilized.

JOURNAL OF MEHAR SINGH, YEAR FOUR, VOLUME III - AUGUST 19, 1919

Satbir has been here for only a little more than a month, but already she has made the house in Kijabe into a home. Her won-derful cooking is already near-legendary, and traders throughout Maasai land plan stopovers at Mehar's house, ostensibly to visit and discuss business with me, but it is plain that my wife's culinary talents have as much to do with these visits as anything.

Truly I am blessed, to have such a woman at my side. Not only is she beautiful and caring, but she is an excellent hostess. Her gracious manner is often enough to soothe the tempers of men who are bitter rivals in business, but who behave as though they are close friends whenever Satbir is around. She is much more than I could have hoped for, and soon we will start our family together. I can hardly wait for the day when this house will be filled with strong sons and beautiful daughters, with their mother's sharp wit, flashing eyes, and inquisitive mind.

JOURNAL OF MEHAR SINGH, YEAR SIX, VOLUME II - MAY 12, 1921

The Dhillon house in Kijabe has come to resemble a small railway station, with traders stopping in as they passed on their way to Nairobi or Narok. The warm hospitality and exquisite food that Satbir offers my colleagues has also increased my business.

But the guests we normally entertain will seem as nothing to the crowd that will be here this week. Four days ago, Satbir gave birth to twins. Only one of the children survived: my first born son, whom we named Santokh Singh. We are about to hold a huge celebration for this blessed event, and even more traders are expected to stop in to congratulate us on our good fortune. Many barrels of whiskey, as well as goats and chickens, have been set aside for the festivities. I have also engaged the services of an excellent chef.

Some of my guests will be disappointed, for I know the chef will be no match for my dear Satbir, but she is too weak to labor in the kitchens over so large a feast. Still, no one will leave the table hungry, and if the meal is not up to my wife's usual standards, it will still be a memorable occasion.

JOURNAL OF MEHAR SINGH, YEAR EIGHT, VOLUME I - FEBRUARY 12, 1923

Satbir has birthed a second set of twins. Again only one of the children survived— another boy. This second son we have named Mohinder Singh.

I continue to conduct business throughout Maasailand, and trade with these nomadic tribesmen is more prosperous than ever. I have also persisted with the sometimes outrageous incidents that have made me even better known throughout the Maasai country.

Last month, an Indian trader bet me a barrel of good Scotch whiskey that I could not kill more than a single lion at one time. Though it could have been a dangerous bet, I was never one to back down. Besides, in some ways it is my reputation for being fearless in the face of danger that has made my reputation with the Maasai people, and that reputation is part of what makes my business successful.

After agreeing on the parameters of the bet, I went into the wilderness and shot two zebras to use as bait to lure the pride of lions which was in the area. I surrounded myself with rocks and hid behind the cover of some bushes, with the dead zebras directly in front of me.

Night fell, and in the fading light the lions approached the fresh meat. As they neared the waiting feast, I noticed there was an unusually high number of males among them. They circled the bait cautiously, then pounced on the corpses, rending the flesh from the zebras' carcasses.

I had two loaded rifles with me. Once the dangerous predators were busy tearing the zebras apart, I quietly came out into the open and started firing. I have always been a good shot, and before I was done, I had killed seven of the lions. When I returned to camp, we all sat around the fire and shared the whiskey. The other traders congratulated me on my courage and achievement.

JOURNAL OF MEHAR SINGH, YEAR EIGHT, VOLUME II - OCTOBER 14, 1923

This is the first time I had taken the entire family on a trading expedition. We traveled in a wagon and set up camp at Khambee Simba, which means "Camp of the Lions." Satbir was a little nervous, but she was excited to be making this trip with me.

After tea on the first day I told Sabir I was going to check on the cattle. She wanted me to take my gun but I told her I didn't need it. I left the campsite and started towards an open area half a mile from the wagons. As I strolled through the low grass, I felt the cool night breeze of the African savanna on my face. In the

distance, I heard birds chirping and the Thompson's gazelle, zebras, and wildebeests were all grazing near our cattle.

I was deep in thought and enjoying the calm beauty of the
evening when I looked up and saw a lioness racing towards me,
roaring angrily. Now I regretted not bringing my rifle. I looked
from side to side, trying to find some place where I could take
cover. There was nothing; no trees or bushes, not rocks, nothing
but the tall grass.

The lioness was speeding towards me, and it seemed there
was nothing I could do. As she came nearer and nearer, I untied
my turban and waved it from side to side, swinging it around my
head as I retreated towards the wagons, hoping to confuse the
raging beast. I ran as I had never run in my life, before or since. My
legs flew beneath me, barely touching the ground, and I ignored
my limp and the pain from the leg, which had never healed properly
after I was shot. I raced towards the camp, my lungs afire, not
looking back, never looking back, certain with every step that I
was about to feel the lioness's claws as she brought me down
from behind.

As I neared the camp, some workers with the caravan saw me
racing away from the lioness, waving my turban like a madman.
Several people ran into the tents and got their guns. They fired a
few shots in the air to scare the lioness away. The Africans started
making loud noises with the kitchen utensils, trying to scare off
the enraged beast with the noise.

Satbir came out of our tent and when she saw my predicament she
did not hesitate; she snatched several burning brands from the
bonfire in the center of the camp, and charged towards the lioness
and me, waving the flaming torches to frighten the lioness. She
threw the burning sticks at the charging animal, but the lioness
ignored the fire and commotion and continued to chase me.

By now, I had retreated back to the camp; the shots and noise
had distracted the lioness just enough that I was able to barely
stay ahead of her. As we ran into the camp, one of the traders,
Pyara Singh, aimed his shotgun at the lioness and fired both barrels. His shot stopped her in mid-air. She fell only a few feet from

the wagons. I collapsed in relief and exhaustion. In all my time in Africa, I have never come so close to death.

Later we discovered that the lioness had several cubs in the bushes with her. When I approached, she thought her children were in danger, and that was why she attacked with such ferocity.

Everyone was full of praise for Satbir and myself, lauding my resourcefulness in using the turban to distract the lioness and her bravery in charging towards the fierce lioness and trying to ward her off with the flaming brands. But when we were alone, Satbir had more words for my foolhardiness in going so far from camp without my rifle than for my "resourcefulness."

I took some of the Africans back to the area where the lion cubs were. The young lions were lost without their mother, and it was a simple matter to capture them and bring them back to the camp. We are keeping them in one of the wagons. Satbir arranged for the lions to be fed, filling large bottles with goat's milk, and bottle-feeding them.

Some of the traders were apprehensive about having the wild lion cubs around, but there are more than enough interested hands to feed and care for the animals. I had some of the workers build a barbed wire cage on one of the wagons, so the lion cubs were free to move around on the wagon as we traveled.

We continued onto Wasonyeiro, about thirty miles from Narok. I have built a small store there, with a number of rooms for travelers to rest, providing a stopover through Maasai country. The Maasai bring skins from their cattle to the store to exchange for goods, and I ship them to Nairobi, where they are sold to Old East African Trading Company, a wholesaler who specializes in animal skins. There they are cleaned and treated for export to Europe and Asia. Already this newest venture has begun to prosper.

JOURNAL OF MEHAR SINGH, YEAR 10, VOLUME II, AUGUST 19, 1925

We were finally packed, and everyone, even the youngest of my four sons, was excited about the trip. It had been some time since I had visited India, and my father has written constantly, *asking us to come for a visit so that he could meet his new grandsons.*

I booked our passage to India on the S.S. Khandalla, one of the largest and most comfortable ships on the sea. We carried our bedclothes and food, prepared our own meals, and slept on the floor. We also carried three lion cubs with us. The other passengers were terrified of the wild cubs and complained constantly to the ship's captain, but they were safely caged and posed no real threat to anyone's safety.

JOURNAL OF MEHAR SINGH, YEAR 10, VOLUME II, AUGUST 30, 1925

After we arrived in India, I took my family to Punjab, where I presented the lion cubs as a gift to the Maharajah of Patiala. He was so pleased that he offered me a position in his ruling cabinet, along with a large parcel of land for my family and me. Though I was flattered, and I thanked him for his generous offer, I had to decline. I have made a home for myself and my growing family in Kenya, and I have no desire to leave Africa.

After our audience with the Maharajah, we went on to my father's home. It was wonderful to see my parents again after so long, though it was a difficult adjustment for the children, especially the youngest. In Punjab, the days were extremely hot and humid and the children found it unbearable. They all slept on the roof at night to take advantage of the cool, pleasant breeze. During the day they had to lie down on a wet "sand bed." This was their daily routine until it was time to leave India.

Unfortunately, I had to cut our visit short and return to Africa earlier than we had planned. All of the children became sick because of the hot weather.

When they were healthy, the boys enjoyed watching kabbadi games between the villages and accompanied me on trips through the wheat fields. But the constant heat and humidity proved to be too much for them, especially the babies, so I ended my visit and we returned home, to Kenya.

JOURNAL OF MEHAR SINGH, YEAR 25, VOLUME I, MID-MAY, 1940

In order to see that my children were properly educated, I had enrolled my sons in the Khalsa School in Nairobi. For the last several years, I continued to run the chain of shops in the Maasai lands as I expanded and diversified my business interests.

I decided to go into the timber business and start a sawmill, so I discussed this venture with my friend, Udham Singh, who was working for Ralston and Kaplan, solicitors in Nairobi. Udham advised me to approach a European named Newton, who was in the lumber business, about a possible partnership.

I was introduced to Mr. Newton, whose wife had a forest concession in the Maasai District. After negotiating with Mrs. Newton, I bought a share of the concession and we became partners. A new company was formed named Newton Timber Company Limited, with offices and a timber yard in Nairobi.

Together we opened a sawmill at a remote jungle outpost in Maasai land called Endulele. The mill was operated by steam engines, the cheapest form of energy for this type of work. Since there was no natural spring or river around, water had to be brought from Kijabe, thirty-five miles away.

I drafted a contract with Messi's Express Transport in Nairobi to supply the operation with 5,000 gallons of water a month. Next I purchased huge water tanks from Hartz and Bell in Nairobi and had them transported by Express Transport.

My company was given an exclusive contract to transport all the timber from the sawmill to Kijabe and carry water for the steam engines on the return trip. After one year, a "posho" mill was installed to grind the local maize and supply flour to the local Maasai in the district.

Nika Singh wanted to do a special favor for me, to make up for the shooting incident, so he arranged the engagement of my eldest son, Santokh Singh. He introduced the families and arranged the marriage to Dr. Pawitar Singh's daughter, Jasbir Kaur.

The young couple had never met and would see each other for the first time on their wedding night. Everyone accepted these traditionally arranged marriages, as they strengthened ethnic and family ties amongst the Indians and solved the problems that resulted from the lack of opportunity for Indian youngsters to meet each *other alone.*

Dr. Pawitar Singh was working for the British government and was posted at Nyeri in the Kikuyu District. Santokh and Jasbir were married in Nyeri, during the Easter holidays. The bridegroom traveled one hundred miles from Nairobi with a huge marriage party. The ceremony was very elaborate with many separate celebrations leading up to the main festivities. The guests were extremely pleased and congratulated me on a marriage that brought two Kenyan Sikh families together.

JOURNAL OF MEHAR SINGH, YEAR 25, VOLUME III, OCTOBER 27, 1940

The Second World War has come to Africa, and the Maasai warriors have been looting and burning the Indian traders' stores in an effort to get rid of the foreigners. I have sent word to all my trading stores requesting that everyone temporarily move to our main location in Wasonyeiro, for safety's sake. All the Sikh traders agreed to come and stay there. Each night, two or three men stand guard. The Maasai frequently attack the store but we have driven them off every time.

There is a tall acacia tree in front of the building, and I constructed a long ladder to climb up the tree. Then I built a small platform on the tree and covered it with a tarpaulin. During the hostilities, Satbir and the children go up into the acacia tree house to sleep after dinner. I would fire blank shots into the air each night to try and scare off attackers. After a time, things died down, and there was peace, of a sort.

Eventually, the District Commissioner came from Narok and spoke to all the traders. He warned us that it was getting more dangerous for us to stay in the store and said everyone should come to his guarded camp. I thanked him but refused his offer. Everything we have built is here, and it is our home. I feel strongly that I and my family should stay at the store as long as we can, guarding ourselves and all we have built together.

Anar looked up from the journal volume she was reading as Akash came into the room.

"Did you read this morning's article?" she asked.

"Yes, I did. It was some of your best writing," he said, "and I don't just say that because of my fondness for your subject matter."

She closed the volume she was reading and laid it on the table in front of her.

"In some ways, the journals are terribly frustrating," she said. "They record the things your grandfather thought were important at the time, and, like life, they refuse to stick to the subject at hand." She smiled. "I keep wishing I could just ask him about things happening just outside the events in the journal. I guess I'm just being unreasonable."

"No, you're not," Akash said, with a contemplative look. "Believe me, I find myself wishing the same thing, every single day. It's still hard to believe he's gone."

The Trial: Day Three

"The three of us, the postmaster, the African
servant Mwangara, and I carried Bapu Jee
into the house, but he was gone, in my arms,
when we lowered him to the floor."

Kulwant

The prosecution opened the third day of the trial with testimony from Dr. H.M. Arnell, the government medical officer from Nakuru who had performed the autopsy on Mehar Singh. The doctor stated that the cause of death was shock due to a penetrating bullet wound, and she testified that the bullet had been extracted from his body.

Sheridan moved quickly to a new allegation against SharanJeet. Mehar's 18-year-old daughter, Kulwant, was called to the stand. She claimed that SharanJeet was visited by an unknown Sikh on February 20th, the day on which she was alleged to have killed her father-in-law, Mehar Singh.

"Please describe the events you observed that morning," Sheridan said.

Kulwant obliged. "Mohinder Singh, SharanJeet's husband, had been away on safari for several days at the time of the murder. His business frequently took him away from home. On the morning of February 20, there was only Bapu Jee, myself, SharanJeet, and one small child in the house. Bapu Jee and I went to the Sikh Temple about ten o'clock in the morning, leaving SharanJeet behind to get on with her work in the house.

"About an hour later, I came out of the temple and noticed there was a car outside the gates and a turbaned Sikh was standing close to SharanJeet. When the man saw me, he immediately got into the car and drove away, while SharanJeet ran back to the house.

"When father returned from the temple, I told him of the incident. He was angry and refused to eat lunch. He asked SharanJeet who the man was and she replied that it was her brother, Harbhajan Singh. When my father asked why the man had driven away when he saw me, my sister-in-law gave no answer.

"Father told her it was not good for her to be seen alone with strange men, and that he had forgiven her on previous occasions when there had been incidents similar to this one.

Kulwant added, "My father reprimanded SharanJeet, saying, 'Let my son return home and I shall settle the matter with him. You will be sent back to your parents because such things cause damage to our reputation.' He was very angry.

"Later," she continued, "My father had a small snack at afternoon tea time and left to visit his friend Anand, the postmaster. I asked SharanJeet to go to the temple with me in the evening, as we usually did, but she declined, saying that she needed to stay and prepare dinner. I left for the temple at about 5 p.m. SharanJeet was alone save for the African servants when my father returned from his visit.

"After I had been reading our Holy Book for about half an hour, I heard a noise like a gunshot, closely followed by two similar sounds. On coming out of the temple, I saw SharanJeet standing inside the front doorway of the mansion. As I was closing the door of the temple, I heard another shot. I rushed towards the mansion and met SharanJeet along the way.

"When I asked her what was wrong, she replied, 'Nothing. Don't go to the house, go to the post office and call Bapu Jee.' I did as she said, and ran to fetch the postmaster."

"Did you notice anything unusual about your sister-in-law's

behavior at the time?" asked Sheridan.

"Yes," replied Kulwant, "though I didn't think anything of it at the time. She had one of her hands wrapped inside her head veil, which she was holding tucked under her other arm."

"When I got to the post office, Bapu Jee was not there. The postmaster returned to the house with me, and as we entered the gate of the compound I saw my father lying on the ground in front of the steps. He was very nearly dead and could not speak."

I asked him, "'Who shot you?' but his whisper of an answer was too faint to hear. I knew he was desperately trying to tell me something. His lips moved, but no sound came out. I ran and fetched some water and poured drops into his mouth."

"The three of us, the postmaster, the African servant Mwangara, and I, carried Bapu Jee into the house, but he was gone, in my arms, when we lowered him to the floor."

Kulwant was visibly upset at having to relive the death of her father.

"I know this is difficult for you, Miss Dhillon," the prosecutor said. "Can you please tell us, what was SharanJeet doing during this time?"

The young woman cleared her throat, and said, "SharanJeet was in the courtyard, but she made no effort to help us carry my father into the house. When I asked her, 'Where were you when Bapu Jee was shot?' she offered me no reply."

"Will you please describe what you saw after you carried your father into the house?" Sheridan asked.

"My father's walking stick was lying near the kitchen door," Kulwant replied, "and there were blood stains on the floor. He had a wound on his right hand and another on the left side of his head, which was bleeding profusely. I did not see SharanJeet go near Bapu Jee at any time."

Mr. Anderson cross-examined Kulwant. "Miss Dhillon," he said, "I want to go back to the car that you claim you saw outside the gates on that morning. I have noticed that your testimony about it is a little vague. Could you please tell the court what kind of car it was?"

"I. . . I'm not really sure," she said. "I think it was some type of four-wheel drive vehicle."

"You aren't sure? You think? Miss Dhillon, do you understand the importance of this proceeding? Your testimony could send your sister-in-law to her death. Can you at least tell us what color the car was?"

Kulwant hesitated for a long moment, then said in a wavering voice, "Blue. The car was blue."

Anderson said, "And you are certain that this mysterious car, about which you can tell us so little, was blue? It couldn't have been white, or black, or even silver?"

"No. Well, maybe," Kulwant answered. "The sunlight was beating down on the car. I think it was blue, but it's hard to say for sure."

"So you have no idea what kind of car it was, and you can't even say for sure what color it was, and yet you expect us to believe that such a vehicle exists, and that whoever drove it had a meeting with the defendant?"

"Yes, it's true," Kulwant said. "You have to believe it, because it's the truth."

"Since you are having such trouble with the car," the defense attorney said, "perhaps you will have better luck with the man. Can you please describe him to the court?"

"I don't — it was too far to see clearly," she said. "They were all the way at the house, and I was at the temple. He was clearly a Sikh, though. Tall, wearing a turban, with a neatly trimmed beard."

"He was so far away that you can't describe his features, yet you noticed that his beard was trimmed neatly?" Anderson asked.

"I think it was trimmed. It seemed so, at the time."

"You have stated before the court that this mystery man visited your sister-in-law while you and Mehar Singh were in temple, and yet you offer no useful description of the man or the vehicle he was allegedly driving. How are we to believe that this man ever existed?"

"Because I saw him," Kulwant said, her voice rising. "I saw him that morning, talking to SharanJeet."

"And yet you have conveniently forgotten what he looks like - it seems odd that your memory is clear on every matter which is damaging to the defendant, yet so vague about anything that might be used to help her."

Justice Njonjo announced that court was adjourned until 10 a.m. the next day. Akash got up and followed his father across the courtroom; the family was gathered around Kulwant, offering her comfort after the ordeal of having to relive that horrible day. She and Akash's grandmother held each other and cried. He wished there was something he could do to console the women.

Kenya had lost a great leader, but for Akash's family, the loss was more personal. They had lost their patriarch; the man who had brought the Dhillons to Africa and given the family a sense of direction had been snatched away from them. Until the trial was over and his murderer punished, there would be no closure. Akash's family would hang in limbo, moving neither forward or back, until the case was resolved.

Chapter XVII

"For lovers priceless is the moment of togetherness,
Enjoy it as the inevitable separation hangs over
you."

A Sikh Village saying

Anar sat at the typewriter, with the journal entries she had photocopied for her story next to her on the desk. This would be the last article in her series on Mehar Singh's early life, and she wanted it to be the most powerful. She decided to read this last set of entries one last time before writing the story.

JOURNAL OF MEHAR SINGH, YEAR 30, VOLUME I, MID-FEBRUARY, 1945

As tensions between the Sikh traders and the Maasai gradually eased, I decided it would be a good time to expand the business. I sought a new concession in Nyeri, at the foot of Mount Kenya. This majestic mountain crowns the land that bears its name, tall and glorious. In all of Africa, only Mt. Kilimanjaro stands higher.

Newton Timber Company Ltd. had been quite successful. But after two years Mr. Newton had to retire from the business for health reasons. He had a weak heart and wanted to settle down in Ngong on the outskirts of Nairobi.

I am not an educated man. I still struggle with reading and writing the English language and also have difficulty in speaking it clearly, but I can write quite well in my native tongue. After considering the matter, I decided that I needed to try and find another partner whose language skills were stronger.

An Asian entrepreneur named Chunilal Aggarwal was interested in joining the firm. We negotiated a deal, and soon I had a new partner. Like the first, this partnership lasted two years, but this time it was I who decided to move on. Withdrawing my interest in the company, I purchased a plot of land in Nairobi and built a bungalow there.

After the Second World War ended, there was a severe shortage of food in Kenya. The government asked the public to try and grow enough food to support themselves. I was allocated 250 acres of land on a three-year lease to start a farm and grow maize, a type of corn which is a staple of the African diet. My land was at a place called Loliondo, about twenty miles from the border between Kenya and Tanganyika, four thousand feet above sea level. The surrounding valley is covered with dense, high-altitude forest; there are cedar and wild olive trees in proliferation, as well as the loliondo from which this place takes its name and a variety of other trees.

My sons, Santokh and Mohinder Singh, started a retail store in Loliondo. The main inhabitants of the region were the three Maasai clans: Loita, Purko and Leitayo. The Dhillon family still had our home base in Kijabe.

I began by purchasing twenty oxen, six cows, and farm implements. Then I started training the oxen to work in harness and plow a straight line. It took me about a month to get the animals working as a team, but once I had accomplished this, the rest came easier. That first year, the farm produced three hundred bags of maize. I also built a posho mill to grind corn grown by the local Africans into flour, and the mill also provided an additional source of income.

To improve the mill's efficiency, I repaired an old Dodge car engine, attached a pulley to it, and coupled it to the grinding mill. When I started the engine and fed maize into the grinder, it worked perfectly. The engine ran on "voco," a mixture of diesel and kerosene, and the maize was turned into flour and sold to local Africans around Loliondo.

After a time, I put my son Rajinder in charge of the farm. The

141

*other brothers worked at the shop and drove trucks as well as the
passenger buses which delivered mail twice a week between Narok
and Loliondo. Before the bus route was started, runners handled
the deliveries, and the mail only came once a week. More than
500 East Indians lived in the Maasai area.*

*One of the most frequent visitors at the shop in Loliondo was
a Sikh who migrated to Kenya from the same village in India as
me. Affectionately nicknamed "Lambardar," which means "the Chief,"
he had worked on the railway construction project and had always
seemed a loner. When traders moved into Maasailand, Lambardar
came with them. He wasn't interested in setting up a shop but
would travel alone on foot, camping in the wild and hunting for
food. Every few months, he would visit the Dhillons to buy bullets
and other supplies.*

*The Maasai knew and recognized him. Lambardar would spend
many nights at their manyattas visiting their wives and the young
siangikis. Once he disappeared for a long time and eventually the
Maasais reported that they had found his turban next to his remains. It was suspected that he fell prey to a lion or a leopard. I was
saddened by the loss of a friend who had traveled with us from
India, but I wasn't surprised. The African life was filled with dangers, and those who lived mainly in the wild were exposed to
constant peril.*

JOURNAL OF MEHAR SINGH, YEAR 31, VOLUME II, JUNE 16, 1946

*The oxen on the farm were well trained by now, and they were
fed on cottonseeds. After a few months, my cattle started looking healthier and in better shape than the Maasai herds.*

*The Maasai pride themselves on the quantity and quality of
their cattle. They believe that all the cattle on this earth belong to
them and they have a right to rustle and keep these. They constantly bargain, sell, and buy to replenish their stock. Most trades
take place at cattle auctions, or "mwanandas," which are held at
different places within the district and are festive occasions.*

*All us Indian traders camp our dukas in large tents organized
in a semicircle, fenced by thorn bushes. On display are beads,*

spears, simis, and almost everything normally sold at a store. This is a major social event with the Maasai reuniting with their friends and relatives as well as meeting traders.

Auctions take place in a specially constructed compound. A high platform is built for the auctioneer, the district officer, the Maasai laibonis, or witch doctors, and other officials. Cattle are channeled through a narrow alley into a circle enclosed by concrete blocks. The Maasai constantly chew tobacco and spit and there is a prominent smell of cow dung. Buyers and sellers point at cattle with their long sticks and the auctioneer sanctions the trades. Once the trade is complete, cattle are channeled through the alley on the opposite side of the entrance.

The Maasai have become envious of Dhillon cattle and they have tried to plan their cattle-rustling raids. Once we learned of their intentions, Rajinder was instructed to carry a gun whenever cattle were out grazing with the herdsmen. We would normally graze the cattle about three miles from the shopping complex, over hills covered with rich green grass from the short rains. The Maasai had noted this pattern and had planned their rustling strategy accordingly.

Cattle worked on the farm in the morning and in the afternoon were taken to the watering hole. As they had planned, one late afternoon, the Maasai Moraans waited in ambush and attacked Rajinder and the African herdsman Kipragut. Kipragut ran away as soon as he saw the Moraans coming. My son, Rajinder, was not so lucky, and he was captured and held by three of the Moraans as the leader struck him on the head with a round wooden club known by the Maasai as a "rungu."

He was lucky to survive the experience; he recounted the tale to me after making his way back to the camp at Loliondo. When the leader struck him, Rajinder fell down and lay still on the ground. He was still conscious as he lay on the ground and he could understand the Maasai talking in their native language as he was fluent in the local dialect. One of the Moraans told the others that the Sikh was not dead and suggested that they cut his head off with the "simmi," a sharp knife.

The leader said, "Let me hit him on the head with my rungu and if he moves then we will chop his head off, otherwise, we will leave him."

They all agreed to this plan. Rajinder braced himself for the blow and prayed that he could be motionless when he was struck. The Maasai warrior hit him hard on the back of the head. He was hurt and his head throbbed but he did not move.

The leader of the raiding party said to the others, "He's dead, let's go before they come looking for him."

The Maasai left him for dead and took off with the cattle. Bleeding profusely and close to losing consciousness, Rajinder realized then that if he stayed until nightfall, the hyenas or other night predators would finish him off.

My son has always been strong, and he tried to make it back to the shop in Loliondo. The complex was at the opposite end of the hill and, although it was not a long journey, in Rajinder's injured state it must have seemed a thousand miles.

Everyone at the shop was worried. The herdsmen should have been back with the cattle by now; they were long overdue. We kept watch on the trail they would use when they returned, and I organized a search party to go after them if they were not back by dark.

About 6:30 p.m. in the evening, Jasbir Kaur, Santokh's wife, saw someone stumbling, getting up, waving his hands, and whistling as he came down the trail. Rajinder was a master at whistling and he could play different tunes. He also could make a piercing, high-pitched single note that carried well across the plains.

Jasbir cried out to us, and we ran to help Rajinder, who was bleeding profusely. We brought him inside the house and prepared him to be transported to the hospital a hundred miles away in Narok. Rajinder was drugged for the journey as traveling over rough terrain would be extremely painful. He bled steadily for most of the four-hour trip from Loliondo. I thought he was going to die.

It took my son two months to recover from his injuries. The Maasai had stolen all the cattle and, without them, the family could not continue to work the farm. I had no other choice: we gave up the farm while Rajinder was in the hospital.

In Loliondo at the time of the rustling incident, there were few police constables called "Askaris." The European district officer was away on safari, so no police action was taken for days. When the district officer returned, he took statements from me and the herdsman, Kipragut, and then they traveled to the hospital to take Rajinder 's statement. Though a police report was filed, no cattle were recovered and we received no compensation for the loss of our property.

Even after they stole the cattle, the Maasai would come to my shop to gather information and check on what was happening. Early one morning, at about 7:30, three Moraans came into the store as we were having breakfast. They talked loudly among themselves, using abusive language toward the Sikhs in the Maasai dialect which the Dhillons understand.

After finishing breakfast, I went to the sales counter and asked the Maasai what they wanted to buy. The Moraans persisted in using abusive language. Finally, I had had enough. I stepped out of the shop into the verandah and got hold of one of the Maasai. The other two started attacking me. When the rest of the family saw what was happening, they came out to help. After a struggle, we tied the Maasai up and handed them over to the police.

When the district officer came back, the Maasais complained that the Dhillons had beaten them and refused them service at the store. The district officer issued warrants for the arrest of all the family. He did not bother to take statements from us or check into the allegations.

I requested that this district officer not be allowed to sit in judgment at our trial, as I felt it was obvious that he was biased, but my request was refused. I then sent a telegram to the Chief Justice in Arusha, the nearest judiciary authority, explaining the details. To my relief, the case was transferred to Arusha, where I engaged a solicitor to defend my family in court.

At the trial, the Maasai claimed I had used a piece of wood ten feet long and six inches wide to beat them up. The solicitor *defending the Dhillons asked for a recess and went to the nearest lumberyard to get a wooden specimen that matched those dimensions.*

When he returned, he presented his argument that he would challenge anyone present to lift that wooden piece by themselves and swing it and do harm to another person. The family was acquitted, and the court ruled that the Maasai had no case.

JOURNAL OF MEHAR SINGH, YEAR 32, VOLUME III, NOVEMBER 11, 1947

At the store in Loliondo, our main trade was in cattle skins or hides and sheep. I started buying sheep and when the stock reached two or three hundred, I would take them into the Kikuyu lands to be sold. One night a leopard got into the yard and slaughtered about 30 or 40 sheep.

The following morning, I reported the incident to the district officer and got his permission to kill the leopard if he returned. This turned out to be a cunning animal; though we searched the forests and plains surrounding the complex for two weeks, the leopard could not be found.

Around the same time, one of the family's dogs delivered a litter of puppies. A small box was made for the puppies where the mother could come and feed them. The night after the puppies were born, the leopard came back. It leapt over the fence and got inside the compound. As the bitch slept, the leopard grabbed her by the neck, nearly killing her.

It was about 11:30 at night when we heard the dog screaming. First on the scene were Hardial and Rajinder, who ran into the yard to check on the commotion. They found the bitch badly mauled, hardly breathing, moaning, nearly dead. The Sikhs were furious and were more determined to kill the leopard. A trap was set inside the courtyard; the trap was baited with fresh goat meat tied to a wooden pole and small bells were tied on strings wrapped around the meat.

The third night, the leopard came back and grabbed the bait. Hardial was on watch; he heard the bells ring when the leopard grabbed the goat meat. He moved quietly as he carefully aimed at the leopard and fired. The animal was wounded slightly and managed to jump over the fence and out of the courtyard. Hardial couldn't track the animal in the dark. He cursed the leopard, but there was nothing he could do until morning, so he went back to bed.

The next morning, the herdsman, Juma, came to take the cattle out. As he approached the fenced "boma" where the animals were corralled, he saw the leopard hiding behind some gasoline drums. Juma ran into the courtyard and shouted for Rajinder to wake up and come outside. He told Rajinder that the leopard was about one hundred yards from the building.

Rajinder was unaware that his brother had wounded the leopard the night before. He loaded his gun and approached the boma. As soon as he was within range, Rajinder aimed at the leopard and fired.

There was no charge from the gun and no shot rang out. He reloaded the gun and fired again, but the same thing happened. By this time the leopard came out charging at the Sikh. Rajinder reloaded his gun with the final bullet. As the leopard pounced on him, Rajinder thrust the gun barrel into the animal's mouth and fired. Nothing happened. The bullets he was using were old British army stock and had proved defective. He cursed the British, the makers of the bullets, the makers of the rifle, and anyone else he could think of.

While the struggle between the tall, strong Sikh and the vicious leopard was going on, Juma caught hold of the leopard's tail and chopped it half off with his "simmi" knife. Enraged, the leopard turned from Rajinder and started towards the young African. The herdsman ran as fast as he could with the animal in pursuit.

Abruptly, the leopard turned back and attacked Rajinder again. The young Sikh pitted his strength against that of the vicious animal. They wrestled in the dust, Rajinder trying to avoid the slashing claws and razor-like teeth of the leopard.

Hardial heard the growling beast and the cries of his brother and noticed the open door. He let out a cry of alarm to alert the rest of the household, and he ran with his gun into the yard, *where he saw Rajinder struggling with the leopard. Hardial aimed his rifle carefully, looking for an opening where he could aim and shoot at the animal without hitting his brother.*

Rajinder seemed to get a better grip on the leopard's coat and lifted the beast off his chest by brute strength. Hardial had only a moment, but it was all the time he needed. He slowly let out the breath he'd been holding and gently squeezed the trigger. There was a sharp noise, and the force of the bullet knocked the leopard out of Rajinder's grasp and into the dust beside him. The beast was dead before it hit the ground. It was quite a sight to see the beautiful spotted leopard lying next to the brave and fallen Sikh.

The big cat had badly mauled Rajinder. In addition to the two-inch laceration on his arm, his wrists looked nearly severed from his arms. We rushed him to the same hospital in Narok that had treated his injuries after the assault by the Maasai rustlers. The difficult four-hour journey and loss of blood took its toll on the young Sikh. This time, it was five months before he recovered.

When he returned from the hospital, Rajinder's body was marked with grim reminders of his struggle with the leopard. He had a permanent imprint on his thigh, shaped with the exact dimensions of the leopard's claw. This turned out to be quite an attraction for the tourists; in the evenings they would sit near the outdoor fire pits and my son would proudly display the claw mark on his thigh and tell the story of his battle with the leopard.

Visitors took pictures to take back to their own countries, so they could tell stories of how they met a "real big game hunter" who had wrestled a leopard with his bare hands. Rajinder's wrists were badly damaged and it was months before he fully regained his strength. We skinned the leopard and had the head mounted by the Zimmermans in Nairobi. It will remind later generations of the family of our tough pioneering times during those early years in Africa.

JOURNAL OF MEHAR SINGH, YEAR 39, VOLUME I, MARCH 2, 1954

All of the business ventures I started have flourished. My knowledge of Swahili and English has become proficient, and people seem naturally drawn to follow me. I have come to be recognized as a leader of the Asians in the Maasai reserve. I have even somewhat grudgingly earned the respect and admiration of the local Kikuyus and Maasai.

For the last couple of years, I have formed a strong friendship with the British District Commissioner for Narok, Harry Fosbrooke. The Englishman has been in Kenya for almost twenty-five years and he loves our country and its people. We greatly enjoy each other's company, and we go on big game safaris for weeks at a time, hunting and exploring remote areas of Kenya.

It was my friendship with the District Commissioner that sparked my interest in politics. Fosbrooke came from a political background, and gradually, exposure to his views and ideas began to have some influence over me.

Kenya used to be under British rule, but the Africans started to organize politically, rallying behind the popular leader Jomo Kenyatta. Kikuyu legend claims that at the dawn of time, the divider of the universe created Mt. Kenya as his dwelling place and bestowed the adjacent lands on the Kikuyu people.

These lands, known as the White Highlands, were a great source of bitterness to the Kikuyu tribesmen. They believed they had been tricked out of land given to them by "Ghai," their name for God. This land had been owned by individual tribesmen and paid for by the Kikuyus. But the British government appropriated the land and dispensed it to the colonials on the grounds that, without modern farming methods, the Africans would ruin this rich and fertile land.

Lord Delamere rushed through legislation written solely for the benefit of the whites. His mandate was that no African or Asian was permitted to own any of the land known as the White Highlands. Four-fifths of the best land in Kenya was owned by less than five thousand whites, and a million Kikuyu were expected to use the other one fifth set aside for them.

Many of the Kikuyus hurt by this injustice joined the Land Freedom Army movement and engaged in a rebellion which was the forerunner of the Mau Mau movement. The Kikuyus were denied any major additions to their reserve, and they were never reconciled to the loss of their original lands. Resentment grew, and the militant faction started gathering strength under Dedan Kimathi, who had given himself the title Field Marshal Sir Dedan Kimathi.

Tired of having its grievances ignored, the African community, and especially the Kikuyu, moved toward more radical means. Outbreaks of violence occurred in 1951, and the following year the secret Kikuyu society known as the Mau Mau began a campaign of violence against Europeans and disloyal Africans.

In October 1952, the British declared a state of emergency and deployed troops to stamp out the rebellion. Jomo Kenyatta, leader of the Kenya African Union, a predominantly Kikuyu political party, was arrested and charged with organizing the Mau Mau. In 1953 he was sentenced to seven years in prison in Kipunguria. Before the rebellion was quashed three years later, 11,000 rebels had been killed, and a total of 80,000 Kikuyu—men, women, and children—were confined in detention camps; on the other side, some 100 Europeans and 2000 pro-British Africans lost their lives. Although it was a military failure, the Mau Mau rebellion brought recognition of African grievances and efforts at correction.

The Mau Mau movement continued to be active throughout Maasai Land. The Kikuyus lived in huts deep in the forests. They had gruesome initiation ceremonies for new members conducted by their witch doctors, and some Mau Mau rituals were very cruel. They would chop some, but not all, the legs off cows and sheep belonging to the Europeans, and animals would be left to crawl helplessly on the ground. Occasionally English farm women were raped, grossly mutilated, and tortured before they were killed. Initiation ceremonies included drinking of blood mixed with urine, animal brains, and other revolting things.

Upon their initiation, the Mau Mau had to swear an oath, stating, "I swear I will fight for the African soil that the white man has stolen from us. I swear I will always try to trick a white man and any imperialist into accompanying me, strangle him, take his gun and any valuables he may be carrying. I swear I will offer all available help and further the cause of Mau Mau. I swear that I will kill, if necessary, anybody opposed to this organization."

The founders of the Mau Mau movement were Bildad Kaggia, Fred Kubai, James Beauttah, and Makhan Singh, an Indian Communist party organizer who was inexplicably allowed by the British government of Kenya to return to that nation after several years of exile from Kenya. Makhan Singh spent 11½ years in detention for his part in the Mau Mau rebellion, longer than any African Nationalist.

I had started a new sawmill at Mau Narok, a small town about 170 miles from Nairobi, right in the middle of the White Highlands. I was able to acquire this contract through the influence of Harry Fosbrooke. The terms of the contract granted me right to all the trees for 100 yards on either side of the road through Mau Narok, which was on the Narok-to-Nakuru route. This timber was then transported by truck to Elmenteita, the nearest railway station. From there, it was sent to the Timsales Corporation in Nairobi, the main buyers for timber in Kenya.

The sawmill had state of the art equipment. I had purchased Allis Chalmers and Caterpillar tractors, Mercedes Unimog four wheel drive trucks for moving logs from the forest to the sawmill, and seven-ton Mercedes and Thames Trader trucks for transporting timber to the rail tracks at the Moolraj and Sons storage depot in Elmenteita.

Mau Mau rebels frequently visited the sawmill and were given food by the workers. I arranged to have extra food and groceries stored for the terrorists and instructed local workers to give the Mau Mau whatever they asked for and not to resist. I did this to ensure that they left my workers and the mill alone. Though I do not support their violent means of bringing about change, occasionally providing food for the rebels has been a small price to pay for the safety of my employees.

JOURNAL OF MEHAR SINGH, YEAR 40, VOLUME II, JULY 14, 1955

My dear friend Chand Singh, another tall Sikh from my native village in India, is dead. He was slightly over 7' in height and towered over everyone. On my suggestion, he had opened his duka at Ndasegera, right in the heart of Maasailand, about fifty *miles from Narok. He grew to be one of the finest traders I knew, and I'm sure being bigger in stature than his customers didn't hurt his ability to make deals and get respect! He was a strikingly handsome man, too, and always wore stylish, bright-colored turbans and kept his beard impeccably neat. If you ever met Chand Singh, you never forgot him. I will miss that strong old bull.*

Chand had his regular customers from the surrounding Maasai manyattas, and he was a designated stop for our bus service from Nairobi, Kijabe and Narok through the Maasai lands and on to the Tanzanian border town of Loliondo.

The Mau Mau primarily located their camps mainly in the Aberdare Mountains, but they had gradually begun to infiltrate the Maasai District. The rebels were able to acquire firearms there from a sleazy, alcoholic Sikh named Ujaggar Singh.

Every community, town, or group has someone that everyone would like to forget and, for the Sikhs in the Maasai District, it was Ujaggar Singh. That bloody Sikh made his living by supplying anything and everything that was underhanded, crooked, immoral, or illegal. The Kikuyus and especially the Mau Mau loved him as he satisfied their need for those items that could only be procured outside the law. He was a lowlife who attracted similar vermin.

The Mau Mau rebels decided to pay Chand Singh a visit one cool summer evening. As usual, my friend had already finished his usual three drinks of Johnny Walker whiskey and he was settling down for a fine dinner of curried impala, an antelope he had shot that evening. Every night, Chand would go walking through the land around his shop, where an abundance of antelopes and zebras roamed the plains. He would shoot one of the animals and then get the Maasai to help him carry it back to his store.

His Maasai wife Ondiki had learned to prepare the Indian dishes from Chand Singh. Her cooking was spicy, with a lot of garlic, ginger, Indian Masala spices, and red chilies grown in her garden, just the way he liked it.

On the night of his death, Mau Mau rebels sneaked out of the thick African vegetation and circled Chand's duka a few times to make sure he had no visitors. Once they were certain that he and his wife were alone, they slammed the side door down and rushed into the kitchen, where they circled the couple. Chand Singh started to run for his rifle but realized he would never make it.

They grabbed him and held him down while the leader demanded food, money, bullets and guns.

"Kala Singha, lete paisa na chukula pamoja na bunduki na rasasi," the leader shouted.

Physically strong with an aggressive nature, Chand Singh was well known for his temper. He managed to free himself and ran for the bedroom where he kept his .303 rifle and a revolver.

One of the Kikuyu intruders, who had a scar across his whole face, swung at Chand with his simmi knife. He caught the Sikh merchant on the arm and forced a deep cut. As Chand stumbled, the other three jumped on him and started hitting him with wooden rungus. He was repeatedly hit on the head even after he lay motionless. After a while, the leader, who answered to the name Kamau, decided they had hit him enough.

They tied Ondiki to the chair and started looting the shop, stealing everything they could carry. They drank all the whiskey in the shop and then finished off the beer. It was nearly dawn when they finally left the duka, drunk and well fed. The raiding party stumbled into the bushes on their way back to the camp, carrying some loot and dragging the rest in bags. They took Chand's rifle and revolver with them.

Ondiki managed to get free from her bonds and ran to her husband's side. Chand Singh was unconscious and hardly breathing. She tried to talk to him, but he was bleeding profusely and incoherent. He kept mumbling something to her, but she couldn't understand what he was saying. They had no neighbors; in fact, no one lived within miles of the shop. The nearest Maasai manyatta was at least a five- mile walk.

She thought of going there, but decided to stay, get some water, wash his wounds, and give her husband another drink. She lay with him on the floor and tried to keep him warm by cuddling *next to him. Chand had loved her from the first day she had come into his shop. He had always thought Maasai male and female facial features were very clearly defined and attractively sculptured, and she was a special beauty. Only eighteen years old with an almost-perfect figure, Ondiki was mischievous and had teased him in the shop.*

Chand told me that he had approached her father the next day and offered a dozen cows and 25 goats as well as a lump sum of money to marry her. The father negotiated a little, as is customary, but he was thrilled with the match and the bargain he had made for his daughter. Ondiki loved Chand Singh, cared for him, looked after him, and made him happy in every way. They had been married for almost three years.

She hoped to stay with him until the morning and get some help when the Maasai customers came or the Dhillon bus stopped on the way to Loliondo. This was a scheduled day for the bus to deliver mail by mid-morning.

But Chand was having difficulty breathing and was in a lot of pain. From his labored breathing, Ondiki was afraid that his ribs were broken and his lungs damaged. He was struggling to stay alive and had been bleeding throughout the night. She gave him a few more drinks of Scotch to help ease the pain, but by 5 a.m. he was nearing death.

He leaned towards Ondiki and tried to say something, but the words would not come out. His eyes were half closed. He looked at her and his love for his beautiful Maasai wife was clear in his eyes as he painfully bid his farewell.

She was sitting on the floor with his head in her lap. He forced a smile through his smashed face and reached up to hold her face in his hands, but he didn't have the strength to reach her. He kept looking at her and finally stopped breathing in her arms.

Ondiki wasn't speaking but tears ran down her delicate and sharply etched cheeks. She sat there until the first Maasai customer walked in and saw her.

All of this I learned from Ondiki, after the funeral. However, I first heard of my friend's death from a runner who was sent after our bus made its scheduled stop. Soon the tragic news was relayed throughout Maasai land and across the country.

Chand's murder caused a panic to spread through the ranks of the Asian traders. Some of the Gujaratis decided to pack up and move to Nairobi, where they would be safe in the midst of a larger community. All the Sikhs decided to stay despite the potential danger.

Chand Singh's body was transported to Nairobi in an open British Thames Trader truck. His body was placed in a bed on the truck and covered by a white sheet, but as the bumpy journey progressed, the sheet had turned red in a number of places with blood from his many wounds. The sheet covered his whole body including his face. As flies landed on the sheet, near the blood, the nearest person would wave them away.

Nearly all the Sikh traders in Maasailand accompanied the procession from Ndasegera though Wasonyeiro, Moricho, Narok, Kijabe, Limuru, and on into Nairobi. Some of the traders sat on the lorry with the body, praying and reciting from the Sikh holy books. The others followed in their Jeeps. The procession stopped at every small town and village. As oncoming vehicles approached, the procession would stop, and people going in the opposite direction would climb up onto the lorry, lift the sheet from his face, and pay their respects to the tall and popular Sikh.

My sons rode in the truck with Chand's body. I was already waiting for them in Nairobi, when the funeral procession arrived. According to the Sikh religion, Chand Singh was cremated in Karioker, on the outskirts of Nairobi, with almost all the Sikhs in the capital showing their presence and solidarity.

Sikhs throughout Kenya were furious and wanted revenge. They had lost one of their own and wanted to fight back. There was even talk of taking up arms and going into the Aberdares after the rebels.

I gave a long emotional speech describing how it was I who had originally written to Chand Singh and convinced him to come over to this country. I spoke in detail of how I had set my friend up in the duka in Ndasegera and helped him learn the business. Then I closed my speech with a forceful statement, as I addressed my friends and fellow Sikhs, "Kenya is our country now. We chose this land for us and for our generations to come. We have worked hard to make a life for ourselves. Let's make sure that our hard work and that of our forefathers is not wasted. This is an isolated but tragic incident and the murderers will pay. We must work within the system and not take law into our hands. Let the authorities take care of the guilty ones. I want everyone to be calm and go home. Try to be cautious as you go back to your homes in the city or in the remote areas. Try not to be alone wherever you are."

I repeatedly beseeched the angry Sikhs to be calm and allow the authorities to handle the situation. In the end, common sense prevailed, but the tense atmosphere in Kenya continued throughout the existence of the Mau Mau movement.

Anar turned back to the keyboard and collected her thoughts. She held the shape of the whole series of articles in her head as she wrote the final piece from Mehar Singh's early life, the story that would sum up the story of those years that led him inexorably into the political arena.

The Jungles of Civilization
by Anar Khan
Special Correspondent to *The Sunday Times*

If these early days in Mehar Singh's life have a message for modern times, it is surely this: then as now, man is the greatest predator there is.

Much has been made of romanticizing the adventurous spirit of Africa's past; of Kenya's past. The man-eating lions of Tsavo stalk through the annals of our literature, assuring us that there was a time when life in Africa was wilder, freer, more dangerous.

Yet even then, even for Asians like Mehar Singh who settled in what was then British East Africa, the greatest danger was never hiding in the tall grass of the savannah.

During those pioneering years, Mehar Singh faced down nearly all of Africa's greatest "killers." He was chased by a lioness, his son was mauled by a leopard, and the whole family was involved in the dangerous sport of hunting elephants and rhinoceroses. Yet the friends and family of Mehar Singh who were attacked by wild animals mostly survived. Nearly all whom he lost in those early years died at the hands of their fellow Kenyans.

Our country has not lost its danger as it has embraced western culture and civilization. Rather, we have internalized the savagery, the old hatreds and tribal resentments dressed up in three-pieced suits, and sent them off to the office. Beneath the thin, cracking veneer of civilization, Kenya and the Africa of today has no less death to offer the unwary explorer. It is only a more civilized death.

So don't look for irony in the fact that Mehar Singh survived the dangers of wildest Africa, only to be killed in the supposed safety of his own compound. Now, as then, the greatest predator that man needs fear is man.

The Trial: Day Four

*"If you really want a child, come and sleep
with me."*

Mehar Singh

SharanJeet was allowed to remain seated in the dock when her
trial reconvened in the Supreme Court in Nairobi. She was
dressed in a light pink salwar kameez dress with a dark em-
broidered chunni with white daisies partially covering her head
as she entered the courtroom escorted by a European policewoman.

She was escorted to the witness box to be questioned by the
Crown Counsel, Mr. A.G. Howard. As before, since SharanJeet
had limited knowledge of English and spoke only Punjabi fluently,
the prosecutor's questions and SharanJeet's responses were relayed to the court through a translator.

Mr. Howard said, "Please describe to the court the events
that took place on the morning of February 20th."

SharanJeet said, "That morning, I got up later than usual,
because I was feeling sick. When I went into the kitchen, I saw
my father-in-law, Mehar Singh. When I came in, he said to me,
'What is this about your being sick? If you really want a child,
come and sleep with me.'"

Murmurs spread through the courtroom and then silence
resumed.

"Who else was in the house when this alleged incident took
place?" Howard asked.

"There was only myself, Mehar Singh and his daughter Kulwant."

"Did anyone hear this statement which you claim Mehar Singh made to you."

"No. When he said that, we were alone in the kitchen."

"Did you discuss the alleged incident with anyone?" he asked.

"No," she replied. "I wasn't sure what to do. Mehar Singh had never before made such a remark to me, and I was never aware that he was interested in me in this way. The whole situation made me very uncomfortable. I did not mention it to Kulwant."

Howard said, "After your sister-in-law went to temple and Mehar Singh went to visit his friend, did a car come to the house?"

She answered, "No. No one came to the house when I was there alone."

"Mrs. Dhillon, your sister-in-law, Kulwant, has stated under oath that she saw you speaking to a Sikh in front of your Kijabe residence, and that when this man spotted her, he got into his car and drove away. Are you stating, under oath and with full awareness of the penalties for perjury, that Kulwant's statement is untrue?"

"Yes," SharanJeet said. "I don't know why she said that, but it was untrue. She never told Mehar Singh about this incident that was supposed to have taken place, and so, of course, he did not threaten to tell my husband about it."

"Did you or did you *not* lure your father-in-law back to the house under false pretenses?"

SharanJeet shifted in her seat, then answered, "Well, yes. I called him back from the post office with a false message about guests arriving."

"So," Mr. Howard said. "You laid your plans, you made sure the house would be empty, and then you arranged for the victim to return from the village?"

"Yes, but it's not like you are trying to make it sound," SharanJeet said. "I just wanted to talk to him alone - to discuss the incident that had taken place that morning."

"What was the point in bringing up this incident again? What did you think it would accomplish?"

"I don't know," SharanJeet said. "I was upset by the things he said, and my feelings were hurt. I wanted to confront him. I wanted to talk this matter over with him and make him apologize to me."

"What happened after Mehar Singh returned to the house that day?"

"He came into the sitting room, and I told him that he should not jeer at me for not being able to have any children. I told him not to say that he would sleep with me and to treat me like a daughter."

"What was his reaction to this confrontation?"

"He shrugged his shoulders," she said, "and told me, 'I will go on saying what I want to you, and if I want to, I will sleep with you. I can force you, if I want, because you have no children.'"

Rajinder jumped out of his chair and shouted, "Why are you lying, you *kutee*. . .Bapu Jee would never do that, how could you make up this story. . ."

Justice Njonjo quickly interrupted Rajinder and ordered him to restrain himself or leave the courthouse.

"Did you fear that he was going to force you to sleep with him?"

"I don't know. . .I can't say. I was upset."

"Were you afraid?"

"It wasn't a question of fear. My feelings were hurt. I was upset, and I didn't understand why he was talking to me in this way."

"Mrs. Dhillon," he asked, "how did you react to your father-in-law's statements?"

"I was angry and distraught," she said. "I went into the bedroom to get away from him, and I remembered the pistol that my husband keeps under the pillow. I thought I would force him to listen to me. I threatened to commit suicide if he would not stop saying those things and treating me the way he was treating me."

"When you took the pistol into the kitchen, allegedly to threaten to kill yourself, did you bother to check and see if the weapon was loaded or cocked?"

"No," SharanJeet said. "I was too upset. I never even stopped to check if the safety was on."

"Then you had no intention of committing suicide?"

"Yes, that's right. I didn't really intend to kill myself at that time. I just wanted Mehar Singh to listen to me. I thought if I did this, he would take me seriously. I came into the kitchen with the handgun, and I said, 'Bapu Jee, stop saying such things. If you don't stop, then I'm going to shoot myself.'"

The Crown Counsel then asked, "And how did your father-in-law react to your threats?"

"He came after me," she said. "He got hold of my wrist, dragged me towards him, and I fell on him. The pistol went off."

"When did the first shot go off?"

"At the same time the he pulled me towards him."

"Who pulled the trigger?"

"I don't know. I wrested my hand loose and ran. As I reached the doorway, he embraced me with both arms. In the struggle the gun went off again. . .I don't know how many times."

"Your finger was on the trigger. The gun was in your hand. You must have pulled it, didn't you?"

"I have no idea - he was struggling with me. It all happened so fast . . . I just don't remember."

Akash thought that his aunt was close to the breaking point. But before the Crown Counsel could finish his line of questioning, Chief Justice Njonjo called a recess for lunch. Before the adjournment the judge gave a stern warning to the assessors.

"From information I have received, there is reason to believe that someone will seek to discuss this case with you. Although you are merely assessors, it is important that you do not discuss this case with anyone at all. This matter is of utmost importance to the integrity of these proceedings. I tell you now, and heed what I say—if anyone approaches you before the trial is concluded, it is your duty to tell me immediately and I will have that person, whoever it is, jailed for contempt of court."

After the lunch break, Mr. Howard continued his line of questioning.

"Before the recess, you stated that you had no recollection

of pulling the trigger. After the first shot, what happened?"

SharanJeet said, "Mehar Singh was still holding me, and I was struggling to get free, moving back towards the kitchen."

"When were the other gunshot wounds inflicted on your father-in-law?"

"I don't know," SharanJeet answered. "I never heard him cry out, and I didn't see any blood."

"How did you get away from him?"

"When we got back into the kitchen, he let me go," she said.

"Are you saying that you didn't pull the trigger in the kitchen?"

"No, I did not shoot the gun in the kitchen."

"Then who did?"

"I don't know."

"Mrs. Dhillon, you have already stated that there was no one present but yourself and the victim. You stated that you went and got the gun in order to confront your father-in-law. You said you didn't remember who shot the gun. Yet now you claim that you did not shoot him. By your own admission, there was no one else present, so who else could have shot him?"

"I tell you, I don't know," she said. "I was running from him. I ran out into the compound and through the gate. When I turned and looked back through the fence, I saw him lying at the foot of the steps. I still didn't think he was hurt, but I wondered if he had tripped and fallen down."

"Did you turn and peep through the fence because you were afraid something had happened to your father-in-law?"

"I don't know," SharanJeet said. "I think . . . I believe I was trying to see how close behind me he was."

The Crown Counsel had no further questions for SharanJeet. Now it was time for her lawyer, Michael Anderson, to try to undo some of the damage done.

"SharanJeet," he said, "I know this is very upsetting for you, but try to think back. Do you think that first shot, when Mehar Singh came at you and grabbed the gun in your hand, could have caused the wound to his head that eventually killed him?"

"I . . .yes, I suppose so. He lunged at me, and grabbed my

hand, pulling me towards him. That was when the gun went off in my hand, and the way he was pulling me towards him, the shot could very well have struck him in the head."

"Now, SharanJeet, I want you to try and tell me what you told the African constables when they took your statement on the night of the murder. Can you repeat to me what you told them that night?"

"I'm sorry, but no, I can't. I was still in shock. I don't even remember talking with the African constables."

"Then you don't recall telling them that Mehar's head wound was caused by a panga knife?"

"I told you, I don't remember talking to them at all," she said. "But I don't think that I would have told them that. A bullet wound and a panga wound do not look anything alike."

"Thank you, SharanJeet. I have no further questions, your honor."

The trial was adjourned until ten o'clock Monday morning.

Chapter XVIII

"On every pointer spear, the head of Sikh was hanging
Streams of blood dripping, the sight will give panging
Sikh prisoners shackled in chains, shouted this voice of cry
O! our true saviour preserve thy honor, don't let panth shy.
Rabindranath Tagore
In praise of Banda Singh Bahadur

"So why haven't you told me any of your African adventures, Akash jaan?"

They were sitting on the couch at Anar's, sipping Chardonnay and relaxing, as Akash tried to wind down from the difficult day in court.

"What do you mean? Are you teasing me?"

"A little, maybe. But with your family running the game lodges and safari trips, surely you must have had some interesting times growing up."

"You do know about the Chinese curse, 'May you live in interesting times,' don't you?" he asked, teasing back.

"There were some adventures, I must admit," he continued. "Since you insist on teasing me, I should horrify you and tell you about my baptism."

"Your baptism?" Anar asked, intrigued in spite of herself.

Akash didn't need any further encouragement.

"Just remember, you asked for this story," he warned.

"I was only five years old, and it was the first time I ever went to Ngorongoro. I accompanied my father and one of the tourist safari groups down into the crater."

"Laiboni Dangoiya felt that it was his duty as a special friend of the Dhillon family to pay his respect and baptize me according to Maasai tradition. He sat me down on a small stool while he sat on a higher one. I could see his enormous pot belly which was only partially covered by his red blanket. His two front teeth were missing like most Maasais. The tribe suffers a lot from tetanus which could result in lock jaw. They pull two of their front teeth when they're young so that, in case of lock jaw, they can still feed medicine made from tree roots and branches through the gap. When the Laiboni spoke, spit would fly freely in all directions from the gap.

"Dangoiya blew his nose by blocking one nostril with his thumb and from the other shooting a shaft of silver mucus onto the grass. He wiped the residue from his upper lip with the palm of his hand. Then he rubbed my face with his bare hands and started spitting in my face, rubbing the spit all over my face while he recited the words of the ritual in the Maasai language.

"Now, I hadn't been sure what to expect of the Maasai baptism, but after a few minutes, I was quite certain I was baptized enough. I kept looking over at Papa, to see if I could get up and leave yet, but he just nodded at me and indicated that I should try to be calm and stay still.

"Laiboni Dangoiya prayed for my good health, my sexual prowess, and my feelings towards other human beings and family members. He followed this by picking up a handful of red soil in his hand. He rubbed the dirt in my face and spit several more times into his face, as well. Then he rubbed the spit and the dirt all over my cheeks, lips, forehead, and mouth.

"The ritual continued for about ten minutes. I was really getting fed up and thought I was going to throw up, but Papa asked me to sit there for a few more minutes as Dangoiya would feel insulted if the ceremony was stopped before it was complete. I could barely wait for the moment when I could get up and run away. As soon as the Maasai chief said his final prayer, I leapt to my feet, ran from the gathering, and jumped in the back seat of the Land Rover. I think I did throw up.

"Papa later told me that Dangoiya also wanted to circumcise me, but he had explained to the Chief that it was not permitted by the Sikh religion.

"To further honor our family, Dangoiya asked Papa to promise that I would marry one of his daughters. I would be allowed to choose whichever one I found most pleasing. And me only five years old!

"This last gesture was considered to be the ultimate in respect coming from a Maasai elder. Fortunately, Papa was able to persuade the Maasai elder that we could put off that particular decision until a later date."

He looked into Anar's eyes, and gave her a sly grin. "I'm not supposed to go back and choose until sometime next year," he said.

She grabbed a pillow from the couch and swung it at his head.

"You're impossible!" she said.

"No, only highly improbable," he retorted. "I have to tell you, I was glad to get out of there that day - I don't think I could have survived being 'honored' any more."

"Come here, you." She pulled him close, and leaned over to kiss him. At the last minute, she dodged his mouth and licked him on the side of the face. "Now, don't you feel honored?" she asked.

Akash groaned. "You're never going to let me live this one down, are you?"

"Well, I thought you were going to tell me something nice and respectable - about your first safari, or something normal," she said. "After sharing that story, you deserve whatever teasing I give you - and believe me, I'm going to give you a lot."

"I can't even remember my first safari," Akash said. "After a while they all just sort of blended together. By that time, the family businesses had expanded to include grocery stores and sawmills, as well as tourist lodges in the game reserves and safari adventures for hunters and photographers alike.

"I guess the safari part of the family business really started taking off in the 1960s, mainly within Kenya and Tanzania.

"We ran hunting trips all over Africa, but the safaris into the Serengeti Plains and the world-famous Ngorongoro Crater were by far the most popular and were always full of excitement. We ran two basic routes; one tour would start in Nairobi and travel through Narok, passing Loliondo in Tanzania, and then finally through the Serengeti to Ngorongoro. The other was Nairobi to Namanga, with a stop at Longido on the Tanzania border, through Arusha, to Lake Manyara, and on to Ngorongoro.

"The Lake at Manyara is famous for the prides of lions that climb the tall baobab trees and rest there. This is one of the few places where one can see lions resting in trees. The lake is a soda lake or Magadi lying along the base of the Great Rift Valley Escarpment.

"The Crater at Ngorongoro is truly a natural wonder. The crater walls are 2,000 feet deep. The circumference of the crater is about a hundred miles. There is a steep and rough trek that curves down the slopes onto the floor of the crater. The only vehicles permitted are the four-wheel drive Willys Jeeps, Land Rovers, and Toyota land cruisers, and even they don't have an easy time of it.

"Tourists would normally stay overnight at one of the lodges and then take a day trip into the crater with packed lunches supplied by the lodge kitchens.

"Inside the crater, there's a lake and the Larai Forest with tall acacia trees scattered amongst the dense bushes. The lake has a large number of hippos and is surrounded by beautiful African flamingo birds. They add color to the scenic environment with their bright pink feathers.

"The Larai Forest is the favorite stopping ground for herds of elephants that come down on a regular basis from the rim of the crater and then go back up on the other side. It's a joy to see these huge animals come down the steep slopes where they almost tumble over and then watch the epic struggle against gravity as they go up the other side. The picnic area at Larai is the perfect spot; it is on the edge of the return trip back to the lodges on the rim.

"The crater at Ngorongoro had four lodges on the rim. The Ngorongoro Crater Lodge was the oldest and had the best view from the rim. The Dhillon's Forest Resort Lodge was built in the forest about four miles away from the rim. It had the reputation of having the best chef in Ngorongoro.

"Suleiman was an Arab who had worked for German, French, and English families in Africa. He was also an expert at making curries. Frequently guests from other lodges would come and dine at the Forest Resort, which was the highest compliment for the local chef.

"Cradled in the dense forest, the lodge had an unusual look and atmosphere while offering the advantage of being in the midst of the animal habitat. There was a salt lick in front of the main balcony, which elephants and buffalos came to at dusk every night and crowded around. Tourists would sit in the balcony, gathered around the log fireplaces, sipping Kenyan Tusker and Allsop beers or other cocktails and photographing the unique African scenic drama.

"The lodge had one hundred beds in rooms which were built in an L-shaped formation with fireplaces and private bathrooms. It was fairly common late at night for the tourists to see or hear elephants and buffaloes almost on top of them in the compound as they retired from the lounge area to their cabins.

"The north side of the crater had the flat savanna type of African grass, and that's where all the lions, cheetahs, and leopards were found. They stayed in this part of the crater along with zebras, impalas, Thomson gazelles, wildebeests, jackals, wild dogs, and hyenas.

"There were about ten black rhinos in the crater and the guides who drove Land Rovers for the safaris had given them nicknames. George was one of the more popular ones. The tour guides would drive towards these large animals and then speed away, and the rhinos would sense the moving vehicles and start chasing after them.

"As the animals came close, tourists would get amazing photographs of these beasts in full charge. Drivers waited until the last minute, then sped in a different direction, and the rhinos would go racing by, as they were unable to turn around in a short area.

"The famous Olduvai Gorge is on the slopes from Ngorongoro to the Serengeti plains. It is renowned because of Dr. Leakey's archaeological research, which uncovered fossils millions of years old. The earliest hominid found at Olduvai is the man-ape, Australopithecus, with his heavy brow and small brain. He was thought to have been slight and swift with an arm fit for slinging rocks and sticks.

"Olduvai is a Maasai word for a small cactus-like bush. The Maasai use the leaves of this plant to make ropes and tie their cattle, and it's also used to make frames for the mud huts and tie belongings on donkeys used to transport goods from one manyatta to another. The Maasai affectionately refer to the donkeys as their four-wheel drive Land Rovers.

"The road from Arusha to Ngorongoro was steep once it passed Lake Manyara, past Mto Wa Mbu, 'The Mosquito River' and Kampi Ya Nyoka, 'Camp of the Snakes.' As it neared the crater rim, past the little store kept by the Indian Pika Patel, the road became narrow and it was difficult for two trucks to pass each other.

"Elephants crossed these roads regularly and would sometimes lie down or sit in the middle of the road. It would be hours before they moved on their own or were distracted enough to move without danger of charging the trucks."

He looked down at Anar, who had shifted to rest her head in his lap. He brushed a strand of hair away from her face and kissed her gently on the lips.

"Go on," she said. She saw that talking about the past was easing some of the day's tension from Akash. "I love listening to the sound of your voice."

Akash continued.

"Tourists would come from all over the world; our clients

at that time included a lot of high-level dignitaries. Prime ministers and presidents from many countries came to visit Africa and go on safari with my father and uncles, who at that time were well known as famous hunters.

"Even the Indian Prime Minister, Indira Gandhi, and the German Chancellor Adenauer stayed at our lodge in Ngorongoro and went on safari with Papa when they came to Africa. In the guest book at the lodge, Indira Gandhi wrote, 'If there is a heaven on earth, and if it is not this spot in Ngorongoro, then it must be somewhere near here.'

"The Dhillon safaris had a reputation for being elaborately planned. No expense was spared, and each trip was supplied with the amenities possible in the African bush. We carried generators for power, air- conditioned tents, portable flush toilets, bars with an assortment of wines and liquor, and food that compared favorably to the top restaurants in Nairobi. There was always a chef on hand who was a master in European, Indian, and Oriental cuisines.

"Safaris were planned so that a set-up party always preceded the tourists or VIPs to predetermined locations along the route. Roads were mainly dirt tracks running through the game reserves. Most traveling was done on four-wheel drive vehicles, but even these would sometimes get stuck in the mud. Riverbeds were always deceptive and the black cotton soil was treacherous. As a crossing was attempted, often the vehicle would sink until the mud was halfway up the hubcaps.

"To free trapped vehicles, the Africans would try to push the jeeps, chains would be put on the wheels for added traction, or another truck would try to pull out the stuck vehicle using steel chains. When none of this worked, a steel winch was used and the winch would be tied around a strong tree. The hook would be connected to the Jeep and then, using a rotating pulley and handle, the chain moved, gradually pulling the trapped vehicle free.

"Once advance crews arrived at the predetermined spots, they set up tents, lit campfires, and began preparing the evening meals. When exhausted tourists arrived in the late afternoon or early evening, trailing plumes of golden dust behind their land rovers and land cruisers, they had all the amenities waiting for them.

"Dinner was served by candlelight under the clear starlit African skies by waiters dressed immaculately in white. The dining area was brightly lit with gas fired lamps and lanterns."

Anar laughed as she pictured this unusual image.

"Your guests weren't exactly 'roughing it,' were they?"

"No, but that's what set our safaris apart from the rest. Most people who think they want 'adventure' wouldn't be interested in the adventure of sitting around a smoking campfire eating thin stew from a common pot." Akash grinned. "Nobody packaged adventure quite as comfortably as we did.

"In the morning, after the tourist parties departed from the campsite for hunting or photographic expeditions, the set-up crews dismantled everything and moved on to the next site."

"It does sound like great fun, when you take the comforts of home along with you," Anar admitted. "Assuming that your home is an expensive hotel with a four-star restaurant, of course."

"It was an unusual way for someone my age to spend his summers," Akash admitted. "I was more reluctant to return to school than most boys."

He looked thoughtful for a moment and then said, "Now that I've started to talk about it, there is one safari trip that stands out. I was eight or nine years old, and the Maharaja of Ranipur had come to Africa on a hunting expedition, accompanied by Apa Pant, the Indian High Commissioner to Kenya.

"The family had planned the Maharajah's itinerary to include elephant and rhinoceros hunting. The trip started in Kenya and then moved onto the Serengeti plains where there was an abundance of rhinoceroses. I remember because it was one of the first safaris where I was allowed to travel with the expedition, instead of staying with the set-up and support crews.

"The Maharajah was in his late seventies but insisted on doing the 'kill' himself. He had already hunted zebras, impala, and wildebeest and was excited to face the real test when confronting the rhinos.

"The first night, we camped near Ol Doinyo Lengai—the Mountain of the Gods. This volcano still erupts every five to ten years. The setting was a beautiful campsite near the River Lena. The party rested overnight, planning to get up early the next morning and get information on the animals' movement from the local Maasai inhabitants.

"Dinner was served as usual under the moonlit sky. Tables were laid out with fashionable china and white tablecloths. A diesel generator powered the lights, which were throughout the campsite.

"Since the Maharajah was a vegetarian, he was served a special Indian menu. Everyone feasted on roasted impala and chicken curried Indian style. The Maharajah retired for the night after a round of cocktails, in preparation for the big day.

"The hunting party set out early. They followed the Maasais who quickly pointed Uncle Hardial and Uncle Rajinder to an area where they had seen a family of three rhinos.

"The chief tracker, Ole Nosa, came over to Rajinder and whispered, 'Bwana Raji . . .Kifaro, Hiko Huko,' which means 'there are rhinos over there.'

"We turned the Willys Jeeps and land cruisers in the direction of the sightings. Hardial, with his sharp hunter's eyes, was the first one to see the rhinos, which he spotted by their long horns. He guided the vehicles towards the animals.

"The rhinoceroses are among the most unpredictable of the big game animals; sometimes they can be shy, galloping away from humans. At other times, they can be as savage as any lion, charging towards intruders and even striking vehicles with powerful thrusts of their horns. Uncle Hardial instructed the Maharajah to step down and position himself next to a strong acacia tree, which was about fifty yards from the animal.

"Rajinder pointed out to Hardial and the Maharajah the unusual size and shape of the rhino's horns. Normally, the front horn is considerably longer than the rear one. This particular rhino had two horns that appeared to be the same size.

"About that time, the animal noticed the party and started pounding its rear legs on the ground, ready to charge. Hardial directed the Maharajah into position. The rhino's tail went up in the air and he thundered towards the hunters.

"The Maharajah lifted the heavy .404 caliber hunting rifle and pointed it towards the on-rushing beast. When the animal was about forty yards away, he fired. The impact of the gun was greater than he expected. The jolt was too much for him and he fell backward onto some thorny bushes as the bullet headed safely towards the sky.

"The rhinoceros was still charging, and Uncle Rajinder realized that the Maharajah was in terrible danger. He lifted his rifle, took careful aim, and then prepared to fire his heavy gun when he was sure of the target. The bullet from his first shot entered the animal's left temple, slowing the rhino's charge. With his second shot, he killed the beast, which stumbled and fell within ten feet of the terrified visitor from India.

"The shaken Maharajah was happy that he had his African trophy and even happier that he would live to tell the eventful story of the rhino hunt. He couldn't thank Rajinder enough for saving his life and practically promised him a kingdom of his own, if he ever visited Ranipur in India.

"The incident with the rhino didn't faze the Maharajah at all. He was anxious to move on to the next target on his list— an elephant. The party moved on to Dodoma in Central Tanzania where elephants had been causing havoc amongst the local maize farms. Tents were set up on a hill next to a beautiful natural spring where the water was cold and crystal clear.

"Local guides related tales of the enormous size of the tusks on the big bull elephant that led the herd. They said that they nearly touched the ground, and the bull had to drag them as he moved around.

"The hunters made an early start and were tracking by 6 a.m. The guides spotted elephant droppings only half an hour old and shortly after that, they heard the trampling of leaves, trees, and branches, the sound of birds flying high above the elephants, and frequent grunts from the huge animals.

"Hunting elephants was different than going after a lion or rhinoceros. Rajinder and Hardial constantly monitored the breeze, noting from what direction it was blowing. They did this to prevent the elephants from catching the scent of the hunters.

"Using powerful binoculars, Rajinder tracked the leader of the herd. His tusks were unbelievably long and almost touched the ground. Each tusk weighed 100 lbs., which would make this animal an impressive catch.

"After the rhinoceros incident in Lengai, Rajinder decided to accompany the Maharajah on this hunt. They started towards the elephant, stopping every now and then to check the wind's direction. As they approached the bull, it turned around and raised its massive trunk. In the same motion the huge animal trumpeted loudly, showing its anger at their interruption in the middle of his morning meal of baobab leaves. The elephant took a few giant strides towards the intruders.

"Whispering to the Maharajah to prepare himself, Rajinder instructed him to aim just below the left ear for the quickest kill. The elephant kept moving, which made aiming difficult. As it turned sideways, the Maharajah fired. He missed the target slightly and the elephant turned towards the hunters. Rajinder fired another shot, finishing the great beast.

"As the elephant fell, the whole area shook with the impact of its huge body. The rest of the herd stampeded away from the fallen leader as they heard the thunder of the gunshots and the sounds of their patriarch screaming and falling. Two of the younger bulls returned, circled the fallen leader and ran away. They would repeatedly turn back, come towards the dead elephant, stop halfway, raise their trunks and trumpet their sorrow, and then move away.

"Hardial fired a number of shots into the air to scare away the young bulls. After about twenty minutes, the herd slowly moved on, leaving their fallen leader behind. I have to admit, I was proud of my uncle's prowess as a hunter. For the rest of the trip, I daydreamed of the day when it would be me making the shot that saved a client's life.

"African members of the party spent the next half-day getting the tusks out, surrounded by flies that rose and settled like smoke from a campfire blowing in a breeze. The stench of the open carcass permeated the atmosphere.

"African servants and local guides packed as much of the meat as they could. The rest of the big bull elephant was left behind for the hyenas, jackals, and vultures who would feast on the remains for days.

"The Maharajah was ecstatic. He had a beautiful and unusual rhino horn trophy, and now he also had the long and heavy elephant tusks to take home. At the Dhillons' recommendation he decided to stop in Nairobi at the Zimmermann's and get his trophies stuffed and mounted before he took them back to India."

The Trial: Day Five

"They were constantly discussing the case, looking for ways to prove that SharanJeet was guilty. I finally had to leave, after we had an argument."

Mohinder Singh

Akash cleared a path for himself, his father, and his grandmother through crowds of reporters outside the courthouse. As the trial wore on, all the main players willing to talk to the news media had been interviewed, and now reporters were looking for a new angle.

Though neither he nor his father had been at Kijabe when his grandfather was killed, it seemed the reporters had decided that Mehar Singh's eldest son and his grandson could provide the fresh perspective they needed. The low hum of conversations inside the courthouse was like the calm after a bad storm compared to the cacophony of shouted questions outside. Akash and his father quickly took their seats as the day's testimony was about to begin.

The defense called the first witness on this, the fifth day of the trial.

"Your honor, defense calls Dr. J.F. Webster," Anderson said.

The physician came to the front of the courtroom and was sworn in.

Anderson asked, "Dr. Webster, have you treated the accused, SharanJeet Kaur Dhillon, while she has been in prison?"

"I have," the doctor replied.

"Is the defendant in good health?"

"No. When she arrived at the prison, she was very weak. She had bruises on one arm and an ugly scratch across her chest."

"And have you observed the symptoms which she has described to this court - the fainting spells, disorientation, and dizziness?"

"Yes. On the first occasion when I had come to attend to the health of Mrs. Dhillon, she appeared unstable on her feet and then she fell to the floor, unconscious. She has had four such fits while she had been under my supervision."

"And what would you say is the probable cause of these fainting spells, doctor?" Anderson asked.

"I could find no evidence of any physical disorder that could cause these symptoms. SharanJeet Dhillon appears to be in good physical health, as far as my examinations could determine."

"Then how would you explain her symptoms?"

"When there is no evidence of physical ailment or disorder, it is logical to look to other causes," Dr. Webster replied. "Probably a psychologist could more completely answer your questions."

"Thank you, Dr. Webster. No further questions, your honor."

On cross-examination, the prosecution asked the doctor if SharanJeet could have faked these "so-called fainting spells."

"Anything is possible," the doctor replied. "But it would be very difficult for Mrs. Dhillon to fool me."

"Difficult, but not impossible?" Howard asked.

"No. Not impossible."

"Thank you, doctor. No further questions."

Next, Mr. Anderson called Dr. J.C. Wilson. He explained to Justice Njonjo and the assessors that this psychiatrist was an expert on "hysterical personalities," and that his testimony would prove that SharanJeet was such a personality.

"Doctor, can you briefly explain, in layman's terms, what is meant by 'hysterical personality'?"

"Well, first and foremost," the psychiatrist began, "within the medical field, the term hysterical is not used in its colloquial sense but rather indicates a specific form of mental disorder."

"Can you describe the behaviors specific to this disorder?"

Dr. Wilson replied, "Patients with hysterical personalities

have an urgent need to appear important, although they exhibit an almost total lack of self-understanding. Their emotions are easily roused but are very shallow in nature. They tend to reflect or respond to the emotions of those around them."

"Doctor, would you say that a hysterical personality could have contributed to SharanJeet Dhillon's behavior towards her father-in-law?"

"Yes, definitely. Threatening to commit suicide if Mehar Singh did not refrain from behavior which she considered inappropriate is very much in the character of someone suffering from a hysterical personality."

The doctor replied, "Typically, a patient suffering from a hysterical disorder would have some sort of emotional outburst when belittled or derided. There is a strong tendency to play on the emotions of those around them and to try to arouse sympathy. People suffering from the disorder will threaten, or even carry out, acts of extreme violence to secure this attention."

"Are there any physical manifestations of the disorder?" Anderson asked.

"Oh, yes. Those suffering from hysterical disorder will make themselves physically ill to gain sympathy and attention. The illness is often psychosomatic, in that it is caused by the mental disorder, but the symptoms are real, and the patient is usually unaware of the true nature of the malady. In addition, fainting spells and seizures are not uncommon."

"Would you say that the behavior of SharanJeet Kaur Dhillon is consistent with hysterical personality?"

"I would say it's quite likely," the doctor replied. "Her history of sickness, the grandiose gesture of the 'attempted suicide,' even her behavior here in court—all these things indicate someone crying out for attention. It is not surprising that it was Mehar Singh's insensitive comments about her inability to have children which caused her to act out in a violent manner."

"Why do you say that, doctor?"

"Children are very important in the Sikh culture, and infertility is often thought of as a sign of impurity or personal weakness.

It is likely that this inability to become pregnant was the root cause of SharanJeet's developing a hysterical personality."

"To have this perceived weakness thrown in her face, especially by a family member, would be a serious emotional blow. That, coupled with the alleged suggestion of a liaison with her father-in-law, could easily have driven SharanJeet to violent action."

On cross-examination, the prosecution forced the doctor to back off from some of his stronger statements. The prosecution's case was clearly weakened by the psychiatrist's testimony, though all the physical evidence still weighed heavily in their favor.

In an unexpected move, Anderson recalled SharanJeet as a witness. After she took the stand, he said, "SharanJeet, the statements you made in court on Friday differ greatly from the signed statement you gave to the constables on the night of the murder. Can you please explain to the court why that is?"

SharanJeet testified, "Before the police arrived that night, I had one of my fainting fits. During the interrogation I was physically ill and mentally confused. I was afraid of what the family would do and think, since I had accidentally caused the death of the head of the family.

"I was afraid of my husband's brothers because they are very cruel, and if I had told the truth—that he met his death by an accident—they would have killed me."

"Did you at any time go to the servant's quarters and instruct Mwangara and the other African servants as to what they should tell the police?"

"No, I did not," SharanJeet replied. "I do not know why Mwangara has made up this story, but it is obviously a lie - it makes no sense. All the testimony, even that testimony which incriminates me, indicates that none of the servants witnessed Bapu Jee's murder. Why would I then go and tell the servants how to answer the constable's questions? If I was guilty, they could not incriminate me; and though I am innocent, this ridiculous claim that I told them what to say to the police only makes me look guilty."

"And what happened after the constables finished questioning you that night?"

"After the police closed the house," SharanJeet said, "we went into the village and stayed at the postmaster's home. The next morning, we came to Nairobi. When we got there, we went to the Sikh temple. At the temple, Kulwant confronted me. She was angry and irrational. She started slapping me and said that Bapu Jee's death was my fault, and that she would see to it that I was either hanged or imprisoned for life."

"Did anyone witness this attack?" Anderson asked.

"I don't know. I was still in shock from the murder of my father-in-law, and her attack was unexpected. I didn't really notice if anyone else was around. Most of the family was there, but of course they will support Kulwant's side of the story. They want me hanged as badly as she does."

"What happened after Kulwant allegedly attacked you?"

"I was taken to the hospital, and the following night they took me to prison."

"While you have been in prison, have you been well?"

"No, I have fainted several times. I can hardly keep any food on my stomach, and I am unable to sleep."

"Prior to the events of February 20th, had there been any trouble between you and any member of the Dhillon family?"

"No. Mohinder and I have always been very happy, other than the sadness of our not being able to have children. I was very fond of Bapu Jee, and I had only the greatest respect for him. I always thought that he was a great man and a great leader. I never had any disagreement with him until the day he made that horrible suggestion. I have always gotten along well with my family and was especially close to my sister-in-law, Kulwant. That's why I cannot understand the manner in which she has turned against me."

Michael Anderson called SharanJeet's husband, Mohinder Singh, to the stand. He testified that SharanJeet was frequently sick without warning and that on several occasions, she had suffered from "fits" which caused her to faint without warning.

He emphasized that SharanJeet was very unhappy at not having a child. He said she had even "borrowed" a child from her husband's elder brother in order to satisfy her maternal instincts.

"Would you describe your marriage to SharanJeet as happy?"

"Oh, yes. SharanJeet and I love each other very much. It is sad that we've had no children, but that's the only cloud that has cast its shadow on our lives."

"Had the defendant ever been alone with Mehar Singh before the incident on February 20th?" Anderson asked.

"No," Mohinder replied, "I don't believe she had. It's rare for my mother to be away from the house, and SharanJeet frequently travels with me on business. We don't like to be apart, but there were duties at home which she needed to help with since my mother was away." Then he added wistfully, "I wish she had gone with me."

"Your father never reported to you any questionable conduct on the part of your wife?"

"No, and if he had witnessed such conduct, he would have told me. Bapu Jee was always conscious of anything that would bring shame or dishonor on the family."

"You were in Dar-es-salaam when the crime took place?"

"Yes, I flew back as soon as I received the news of my father's death."

"And where have you stayed since you returned to Kenya?"

"At first, I stayed at the home of my brother-in-law, Bawa Singh, here in Nairobi."

"Why did you leave your brother-in-law's house?"

"They were constantly discussing the case, looking for ways to prove that SharanJeet was guilty. I finally had to leave, after we had an argument."

"Could you recount that disagreement, to the best of your memory, please?"

"Certainly," Mohinder said. "On the morning before the preliminary inquiry, Bawa and another of the brothers were discussing the case. They turned to me, and Bawa said, 'We've wasted two nights on Kulwant, trying to teach her the story of the man in the car. Now it's up to you. You must side with us, so that Bapu Jee's death will be avenged.'"

The Trial: Day Six

"Do you not realize that if you memorized the
testimony of another, you are not giving your own
testimony before the court?"

Michael Anderson

Sitting with his grandmother near the front of the courtroom,
Akash winced as the prosecution called Dalbir Ram, the village
postmaster, to the stand. Anand was known to be "guptish,"
someone who was very insecure and frequently would lie to
compensate for his lack of self-confidence. If Mr. Howard could
keep Anand's testimony limited to the things the postmaster
could actually have witnessed, he could help the case. But if he
was allowed to wander at all, the old man would probably lie
so much that his testimony would be discredited.

"Mr. Anand, would you please describe to the court the
events of February 20th, as best as you can recall?"

"I was summoned to the Dhillon house by Mehar Singh's
daughter, Kulwant. When I arrived, I found the old man lying
on the ground near a flight of steps leading to the main door."

"And what happened after you arrived at the Dhillon household?"
Howard asked.

Anand said, "The old man was lying on the ground at the
point of death. The accused told me that four Africans had
killed Mehar Singh and then run away," the witness declared.
"She did not say how he'd been killed. In order to save his life,

I wanted to carry him inside the house.

"Then I heard a shot. I was surprised and left the body at once. I went around the back of the house and saw the accused. She said she had fired the shot to scare the Africans. She had a pistol in her right hand. I did not see any strangers in the compound."

"So, at no point that evening did you see these Africans whom Mrs. Dhillon claims she was trying to scare away?"

"No. I never saw any Africans."

"And afterwards, did you hear the victim's daughter, Kulwant, threaten SharanJeet, or see her attack or harm the defendant in any way?"

"No," Anand said, "I did not hear Kulwant say, 'Tell me who killed my father and I will have my revenge,' and I did not see her hit or attack SharanJeet or throw water on her."

"Thank you, Mr. Anand. No further questions, your honor."

Mr. Anderson rose from the defense table to cross-examine the postmaster.

"You stated before the court that you saw no Africans standing outside the compound, is that correct?"

"Yes, that's true," answered Anand.

"But didn't a number of the young African boys from the village follow you and Kulwant back to the Dhillon home, to see what all the excitement was about?"

"Yes, but I only meant that there were no strangers. SharanJeet wasn't firing the gun to scare off those boys."

"So, although you told the court there were no Africans outside the compound, you now say the African boys from your village were gathered there?"

"Yes, they were there."

"All the boys of the village?"

"I don't know that. I had no time to waste counting them."

"If, as you say, you had no time to waste counting them, then how can you say with certainty that there were no strangers among them?"

"It was only the boys from the village."

"Only a moment ago, you stated that you saw no Africans

outside the compound. Yet now you claim to know, without having checked carefully, the precise composition of a crowd of Africans gathered outside the compound?"

"What are you trying to say? Are you calling me a liar?"

"I am not calling you anything, Mr. Anand. I am merely asking you, is it not possible that the four strangers SharanJeet Kaur Dhillon saw that day could have been hiding among the crowd of African boys outside the gates of the Dhillon home? Before you answer, please remember that you've already told the court that you did not examine the group of boys carefully."

"Well, I suppose four men could have hidden in the crowd," the postmaster said grumpily.

Mr. Anderson continued, "Other than my cross-examination, your testimony has been very similar to that given in the lower court. Would you agree with that statement?"

"Of course it is," Anand replied. "I paid close attention."

"In other words, you have learned it all by heart?"

"Yes."

Justice Njonjo interrupted. "You have what...memorized what by heart?"

"The testimony that SharanJeet gave in the lower court. I learned it by heart because I knew that I would be required to tell the court."

"Do you not realize," Anderson asked, "that if you memorized the testimony of another, you are not giving your own testimony before the court?"

"But it was the same!" the postmaster exclaimed. "What she said and what I heard that night, there is no difference. I'm not lying."

"Whether or not you are lying is not at issue," Anderson replied. "You were asked to tell us what you saw and heard that night, and instead you repeated back someone else's testimony, which you had memorized for that purpose. Since you admit you memorized all you have told us, your own statements can neither corroborate nor contradict that testimony."

"I have no further questions, your honor."

Chief Justice Njonjo stood, and stated that court was adjourned until 10 a.m. the next morning. Akash helped his grandmother to her feet, and they joined the crowds filing slowly out the door.

The Trial: Day Seven

"She told all the servants to tell the police they
were away at the time of the shooting."

Mwangara

Although he, too, believed his Aunt SharanJeet to be guilty,
Akash had to admit that Michael Anderson was doing an excellent job of defending her in court. He began the trial's seventh
day by stating before Judge Njonjo and the assessors his earnest
belief that some of the witnesses had been tampered with.

Mr. Anderson asked for the indulgence of the court. He was
concerned as to the nature of the questions he was asking a
Crown witness during cross-examination of the Kijabe murder
case at the Supreme Court.

"It is my submission that this case has been built up on a
family "fatina" and that, in their effort to exact revenge for the
murder of their father," Mr. Anderson declared, "this family has
caused false or misleading statements to be placed before the
court. It is of the greatest importance that we should get at the truth."

Chief Justice Njonjo agreed that there had already been
much about the case that he did not like.

Continuing his cross examination of the Kijabe village postmaster, Dalbir Ram Anand, Mr. Anderson asked, "Is it not true,
Mr. Anand, that in the statement you made before the magistrate
at the arraignment, you said that you did not at any time see
the accused with a firearm."

"I . . .I don't remember," Anand answered.

"Request permission to approach the witness, your honor." Anderson crossed to the witness stand and placed a piece of paper in front of the postmaster.

"Do you recognize this document?" he asked.

"Yes, I . . .it's the statement I gave before the magistrate."

Anderson pointed his finger to a spot on the paper.

"Can you please read this sentence before the court?"

Anand hesitated, then read haltingly, "No. At no time did I see SharanJeet with a weapon."

"But yesterday, you testified that she had a pistol in her right hand, is that correct?"

"When I first arrived at the house I did not see anything in her hand. After I heard a shot fired, I then noticed she was holding a pistol."

"Why did you not tell this story earlier?"

Anand replied, "The magistrate did not question me in detail on this point."

"Postmaster Anand, I suggest that there are two reasons why you changed your story. In your earlier statement, you clearly remembered what you had told the police, and you repeated to the magistrate exactly what you had told the police. Is that correct?"

"Yes."

"Since then, you've had ample opportunity to discuss the case and your testimony with the deceased's family. Perhaps they have 'refreshed' your memory?"

"No, that is not so."

"During the arraignment, did you not stay at the home of Bawa Singh, son-in-law of the victim, in Nairobi?"

"Yes, I did."

"And are you staying there during the present proceedings, as well?"

"Yes, I am."

"Isn't it true that Hardial, and Rajinder , the deceased's sons, and Kulwant, his daughter, are also staying there?"

"Of course - they're family."

"And naturally all of you discuss the case quite frequently?"

"No," Anand said. "It's not necessary to discuss it."

"So you've never heard—or participated in—a discussion of this case, outside of the courthouse?"

"Well, on one or two occasions I might have been present when some family members were discussing the case."

"Yesterday, didn't I see you leave the court with Bawa Singh and his brother-in-law, Hardial?"

"Yes."

"Did you discuss the evidence you had given?"

"I don't remember the specifics of the conversation—whatever I was asked, I told them."

"Did you spend time discussing what line the cross-examination might take?"

"No."

"You swear, under oath, that you *never* discussed the evidence you were going to give today with the Dhillon brothers?"

"Not particularly," Anand answered, "as I have no special interest in the case."

Anderson asked, "What do you mean by 'not particularly?' Are you saying that you actually did discuss it?"

"They did not influence my testimony at all," he answered.

"Were they pleased with the evidence you have given?"

"I don't know."

"From what you've heard of family conversations concerning this case, were the brothers worried about possible harm to their father's honor?"

The witness replied, "It's possible they were."

Anderson pressed the point.

"Were they, or were they not, concerned about their father's honor being besmirched by these proceedings?"

Anand agreed that, yes, the brothers were concerned about damage to Mehar Singh's reputation. With that admission, Anderson dismissed the witness.

Next, Mr. Howard, the Crown Counsel, called Mwangara, the 60-year-old African employed by the Dhillons.

"Mwangara, please describe as clearly as you can recall, the events that transpired last February 20th."

In a barely audible voice, the old man testified, "There was much confusion. We all heard the gunshots, 'though we did not yet know that Mehar Singh had been killed. I was in the servants' quarters, calming some of the other servants and trying to decide if one of us should go up to the main house and see what had happened. Suddenly Mohinder's wife SharanJeet came up to us. She told all the servants to tell the police they were away at the time of the shooting."

There was a faint murmur and muffled conversation until the judge's icy stare restored silence.

Continuing his testimony, Mwangara stated, "SharanJeet said, 'If any one of you is asked what happened, you say that you weren't present at the house.'"

"And what did you do then?" Howard asked.

"I asked her to please go away," but then she said to me, 'You, Mwangara, instruct the others to say that you'd gone shopping for vegetables at the time.'"

Mwangara said she left after he asked her to go for the second time.

The judge asked the assessors and the witness to leave the court while Mr. Howard asked for a ruling on a point of evidence. He wished to ask Mwangara if a certain statement he was alleged to have made to the police was true.

Chief Justice Njonjo ruled that he could not allow Mr. Howard to proceed with this, as it would either be a leading question or be tantamount to cross-examination, and neither was allowed to the prosecution. The prosecution then called another witness, Ranjit Singh, who said that the accused was his friend's daughter.

"Were you present when the police inspector questioned SharanJeet Kaur Dhillon?" Howard asked.

"I was."

"In what capacity?"

Ranjit answered, "While the inspector was taking her statement,

I was there to translate the inspector's questions into Punjabi, so SharanJeet could understand them."

"And did the accused understand the questions and give her statement freely, under no duress?"

"She understood the questions," Ranjit said, "but at the time, the accused was weeping and it was difficult to get a statement from her. She often had to be asked two or three times before answering a question."

"And after the statement was taken, did Inspector Steenkamp read it back to SharanJeet?"

"Yes he did, but. . ."

"Thank you. No further questions, your honor."

On cross-examination, Michael Anderson began, "You state that there was some difficulty in obtaining SharanJeet's statement, because the defendant was weeping, is that correct?"

"Yes, that's true."

"I find it curious," the defense attorney said, "that other police officers have gone out of their way to state that Mrs. Dhillon showed no outward signs of emotion, yet you say she was weeping. How do you explain this?"

"I cannot," Ranjit replied. "Anyone present in the room could clearly see and hear her sobbing. I only report the truth as I observed it from that night."

Michael Anderson continued, "It is a great shame that others are incapable of doing the same."

Mr. Howard immediately objected to the statement, and Anderson withdrew it. He addressed the witness again.

"One last question. After the statement was taken, in English, by Inspector Steenkamp, was it read back to the defendant in Punjabi before she was asked to sign it?"

"No," Ranjit said. "Steenkamp read the statement to her in English, then she signed it and they left."

"In your opinion as a translator, does SharanJeet understand written English?"

"No. If she understood English well, then I would not have been called in to translate."

"Then there is a reasonable possibility that SharanJeet was not even aware of the contents of the statement that she was signing, is that correct?"

"Yes, that's correct."

"Thank you. No further questions."

Mr. Anderson called the defendant to the stand again.

"SharanJeet, did you come up with the idea of lying to the constables on your own?"

"No," she said. "It was suggested to me."

"Who suggested it?" Anderson asked.

"I can't say. I am in enough trouble already."

"By following this advice, you have strengthened what would have been a much weaker case against you. Whoever told you to lie to the constables is no friend. I ask you again, please tell the court who gave you this advice."

SharanJeet looked visibly shaken, even terrified. "I cannot," she said. "Even if it would save me, I. . .you just don't understand. It would be worse than jail."

Anderson looked as though he wanted to continue this line of questioning, but it was clear that SharanJeet would give no answer.

"Thank you, SharanJeet," he said. "No further questions, your honor."

Mr. Howard began his cross-examination by attacking SharanJeet's last statement.

"Isn't it true, Mrs. Dhillon, that your outrageous claim that someone counseled you to lie to the constables is itself a lie, designed to explain away the discrepancies between your testimony here in court and the sworn statement you gave to the police on February 20th?"

"No," SharanJeet said. "That's not true. I did as I was told - they said the evidence would support the story I told the constables, and that Bapu Jee's sons would have no reason to come after me."

"Then who, Mrs. Dhillon? Surely you don't expect this court to believe that you were acting on the advice of some mysterious figure whom you refuse to reveal? Name the person or persons who gave you this advice, or admit that they do not exist - your lies make a mockery of this proceeding."

"I've told you the truth. . .I can't say more," SharanJeet replied, nearly weeping.

"The truth," Mr. Howard interrupted, "is that you lured Mehar Singh to his death, and then, not content with merely taking his life, you've now done your best to destroy his reputation, as well."

"No. That's not so. . ."

"You planned the murder because you were afraid you would be sent back in disgrace to your parents. You sent for your father-in-law at a time when you knew that no one else would be at the house, and a few seconds after he entered the house, you shot him."

"No," SharanJeet shouted. "That's not the way it happened. I've told you the truth and related the story exactly as it happened."

"Will you agree, then, that Mehar Singh sustained three gunshot wounds at your hands?"

"I have no idea how he came to be wounded - I have explained to the court that I have no clear memory of that sequence of events."

"You have no memory? Do you seriously expect this court to believe that you struggled to the death with your own father-in-law, and you 'don't remember' how he came to be wounded?"

SharanJeet's attorney objected that Mr. Howard was badgering the witness, but Justice Njonjo ruled against him.

"I cannot help what you or the court believes. I have told you the truth."

"Isn't it true, Mrs. Dhillon, that you planned the story about the African robbers well in advance? Isn't it also true that you carried out the crime in such a manner that the evidence would be consistent with that story, and that all your statements on the day of the tragedy supported that story?"

"I . . .don't know," SharanJeet answered. "I was very upset at the time, and I was afraid of what Mehar's sons would do if they thought I had caused his death. I said the first thing that came into my head."

"Mrs. Dhillon, why don't you admit that Mehar Singh never made any improper suggestions to you, and that no struggle took place. You killed your father-in-law in cold blood, didn't you?"

"That absolutely is . .not. .true," SharanJeet responded in a shrill voice that sounded near its breaking point.

Mr. Anderson objected again, and this time Justice Njonjo agreed that this line of questioning was getting them nowhere. The objection was sustained, and the prosecution stated that they had no further questions for SharanJeet.

Before adjourning the hearing until Monday morning, Chief Justice Njonjo repeated the request he had made earlier in the proceedings that the assessors should not discuss the case with others.

The Trial: Day Eight

*"The witnesses who have testified so far have been
threatened by the deceased's sons. The witnesses
are fearful of these ruthless young Sikh men who
are concerned about a blot on their father's honor."*
Counsel Anderson

Bawa Singh was called to the stand on the eighth day of the
trial. He stated that he was employed by the Public Works
Department in Nairobi, and that he had arrived at the Kijabe
mansion where the murder allegedly took place.

Cross-examining, Mr. Anderson asked Bawa Singh if the
chief topic of conversation at his house, where most of the
family staying during the trial, was not the death of the old man.

Bawa Singh agreed.

The case for the prosecution ended at noon. Among the last
witnesses for the Crown was a government analyst who gave
his opinion that the bullets and cartridge cases found at the
scene were fired from the pistol exhibited in the court.

As Counsel Anderson started the case for the defense, he
asked Bawa Singh if the principal point in these discussions
was the old man's honor. Justice Njonjo interrupted the questioning
and asked what was meant by "honor." He pointed out that
there were several kinds of honor, with one type related to morality.

Responding to Justice Njonjo, Mr. Anderson responded that
this was a critical cultural issue. "It is my case," he said, "that
the witnesses who have testified so far have been threatened by
the deceased's sons. The witnesses are fearful of these ruthless

young Sikh men who are concerned about a blot on their father's honor...testimony of these witnesses has been tampered with and what has been presented to the court is not all truth."

Jumping up quickly in protest, the opposing attorney Mr. Howard pointed out that independent witnesses would have to prove such an allegation.

Continuing, Mr. Anderson declared that his case was that "this old man met his death by accident. The circumstances in which the accused had the revolver have been explained by her. They arise to a great extent by a remark made by the deceased, which has come to be interpreted by his family as a blot on his honor and on their family name."

Justice Njonjo said he did not want to be kept "in the dark about the defense." He indicated that if there was any question of the old man's honor, he would allow the prosecution to call rebutting evidence.

Mr. Anderson went on to say that he would call medical evidence to show that the accused was "a hysterical personality" who might behave "in a dramatic manner." The questioning of Bawa Singh continued. Under further questioning, and before he was dismissed, Bawa Singh stated he had never seen or heard of the accused having a fit.

Mr. Anderson then cross-examined Assistant Inspector Price, who had provided testimony that he had taken the accused's statement. Price said the questioning started at about 9:50 p.m. and ended after midnight.

Mr. Anderson persisted, "While Mrs. Dhillon's statement was being taken, when you yourself could not understand anything, was the statement being signed by Mrs. Dhillon explained to her by any one who was present there?"

Mr. Price said, "I have no recollection of that. She spoke English well enough for me to understand."

After relentless questioning, Assistant Inspector Price admitted that Bawa Singh had helped to explain some of the accused's statements.

Mr. Anderson then dramatically suggested that the statement

had not been taken in a fair situation. "This extraordinary interrogation, with the corpse still present and the relatives standing around, is hardly an opportune time to get a true coherent statement, wouldn't you agree?"

Mr. Price replied, "The accused answered everything. She gave her statement coherently. . in a voice which appeared normal to me."

Under further rugged questioning by Mr. Anderson, Mr. Price agreed that it was not "the ideal place" to take a statement.

Chief Justice Njonjo decided that he wanted to visit the crime scene in Kijabe along with the assessors. The trial was adjourned for a day as the group made the 40-mile trip to Kijabe. SharanJeet and her escort accompanied Njonjo, as did the Crown Counsel, Mr. A.G. Howard, and the defending barrister, Mr. Anderson. The hearing was scheduled to resume the following morning, with evidence observed at the scene of the crime to be entered into testimony.

Justice Njonjo spent the morning in Kijabe being shown the Dhillon mansion, the adjoining Gurudwara, the post office, and the bullet holes in the building. The group had lunch at the Kijabe Inn before returning to Nairobi.

The Trial: Day Nine

"I have nothing to say...I've already said
everything that I wanted to. I am ready for
your judgment, your honor."

SharanJeet Kaur

In his summation before he passed judgment, Justice Njonjo recalled that SharanJeet's main defense was that her father-in-law had made a most improper suggestion to her. However, he declared that, like the assessors, he did not believe that story.

The justice said that if the prosecution's case rested alone on the evidence of Kulwant, then he would hesitate somewhat before convicting the accused of the murder. He indicated that Kulwant's story regarding the man in the car and the subsequent quarrel between the deceased and the accused was less than credible.

Chief Justice Njonjo continued to say that the case did not by any means rest on Kulwant's testimony alone. There was the fact that three bullets had been fired and, furthermore, there had been testimony that, after the deceased had been shot, SharanJeet had approached Africans employed by the deceased and asked them to say they were not present during the incident. Though SharanJeet had tried to discredit Mwangara's statement, no one had presented the court with a valid motive for the servant to lie. By her own testimony, it was quite clear that SharanJeet had made up a false story with regard to the shooting. Her credibility was further damaged by her later suggestion that the deceased had been killed by four Africans.

Justice Njonjo declared that he could see nothing unfair to the accused in the manner in which her statement to the police had been taken, except that it might have been ideal if fewer people had been present.

SharanJeet's statement, which she later told the court was largely untrue, appeared to be an account well thought out beforehand in order to bolster her story.

SharanJeet's statement, he declared, smacked of scheming. The justice confessed that he was unable to believe that the deceased had ever made the improper suggestion alleged by the accused. Other than SharanJeet's own testimony, no evidence had been given to support the notion that Mehar Singh had ever shown any tendency towards such inappropriate behavior. Mrs. Dhillon's allegation was, in fact, contrary to everything known of his character.

In the witness box, the justice said, the accused had been cool and calm, but on cross-examination it appeared that many of her statements were lies. He pointed out that frequently she had given answers consisting of nothing more substantial than, "I don't know," or "I don't remember," and in most cases, her answers strained the boundaries of credibility. It appalled the justice, he said, to think that anyone present could not remember the incidents.

Justice Njonjo stated emphatically that he did not believe the accused's evidence, and he believed the pistol was ready for firing when she took it from under the pillow. He was convinced that she had loaded it. There was no evidence that she was acting in defense of her honor as a woman, that she had suffered provocation at the hands of the deceased, or that she had lost self-control.

Giving his grounds for saying that the case did not justify a verdict of manslaughter, the judge stated that the three shots had been fired from the pistol. If one shot alone had been fired, there might have been justification in finding that the pistol was fired by accident. But three shots? No, the judge said, three could be nothing except a deliberate assassination.

"Like the assessors, I can come to no other conclusion than that the accused deliberately fired at the deceased with the intention of killing him, and that she did kill him. I do not accept the defense story that it was an accident, nor am I able to find grounds for coming to the conclusion that it was a case of gross or wicked negligence which would amount to manslaughter. I therefore convict the accused of murder as charged."

A packed courtroom rumbled with varying emotions as it heard Mr. Justice Njonjo utter these words when concluding his judgment in the Kijabe case in the Supreme Court on Saturday morning.

Asked if she had anything to say and if she had any thoughts as to why the sentence according to law should not be passed, the accused, who had been allowed to remain seated in the dock replied in a tone of grim resignation, "I have nothing to say . . . I've already said everything that I wanted to. I am ready for your judgment, your honor."

In passing sentence, Mr. Justice Njonjo said, "I assure you this is one of the most painful duties which falls to a judge, and since you are a woman, it is more painful. You have been most ably defended by your advocate, Mr. Anderson. It is quite obvious he has devoted much time and talent to your defense and he has prepared thoroughly. He has considered every possible point which could be urged in your favor.

"The prosecution's case," Chief Justice Njonjo added, "was conducted with fairness and according to the laws of the Kenyan judicial system, as is to be expected of the Attorney General's Department." Then he pronounced sentence before the hushed crowd.

As the Chief Justice prepared to pronounce his judgment, there was a minor outburst in one of the public galleries. Before continuing, the judge warned that if there was further noise or disturbance, the galleries would be cleared.

"I, Chief Justice Njonjo, presiding over this court, find the defendant, SharanJeet Kaur Dhillon guilty of the charge of committing murder on the person of Mehar Singh Dhillon and sentence her to be hanged by the neck until dead."

SharanJeet emitted a loud scream and fainted as soon as Justice Njonjo made the announcement. In the corridors and precincts of the court, large numbers of Asians waited silently to hear the verdict. As soon as the verdict was announced, the courthouse was in an uproar and the Kenya Police Askaris who were on standby had to evacuate the courthouse.

Michael Anderson rescued SharanJeet from her slumped position on the floor and lifted her gently into a chair as he asked that someone bring her water. There was a short delay as she was revived and then the proceedings continued.

SharanJeet was informed of her right to appeal within thirty days, and then, escorted by a European policewoman, she walked quickly from the dock. Led away in handcuffs through the back entrance to the court and into a waiting prison bus, SharanJeet was ordered to be held in prison in the Nairobi facility until being transferred to confinement in an unannounced location.

SharanJeet's attorney immediately presented an appeal but the Court of Appeals ruled that there was no foundation for a new trial and no new evidence of substance. The appeal was denied.

The trial, the circumstances surrounding the trial, and the negative publicity given to SharanJeet outraged the entire Asian community. The Indian High Commissioner, Apa Pant, initiated a petition on SharanJeet's behalf. He wanted to obtain as many signatures as possible to request clemency and, thereby, halt the first execution of an Asian woman in Kenya. The petition gained momentum. More than 70,000 signatures were collected in a few days. Asians, Europeans, and some Africans from all over Kenya, from Nairobi to Kisumu, and from Mombasa to Nyeri, signed the document. The petition was presented by Apa Pant and a number of Asian community leaders to Governor Titterton and a plea for clemency was made to Justice Njonjo.

After a week of deliberation and with the approval of Governor General John Titterton, SharanJeet's sentence was reduced to life imprisonment.

She was kept in prison in Nairobi for two weeks and later transferred to the one in Gilgil, about forty miles from the city.

Chapter XIX

*"Muhammad (the Prophet) In the name of Allah,
Most Gracious, Most Merciful. Those who reject
Allah and hinder (men) from the Path of Allah,
Their deeds will Allah bring to naught. But those
who believe and work deeds of Righteousness,
And believe in the (Revelation) sent down to
Muhammad - For it is the Truth from their Lord, -
He will remove from them their ills and improve
their condition."*

THE HOLY QUR-AN

The Asian community was distraught over the verdict. The
Asians felt dishonored by the spectacle of the trial, and they
had suffered politically as they had lost a powerful spokesper-
son who had brought the Asian point-of-view to the bargaining
table. The verdict which sentenced the first Asian woman to be
hanged was extremely unpopular, and there was widespread
sentiment that, for some reason, SharanJeet had been framed
and that the real killers were still on the loose. In general, the
allegations didn't pass "the smell test," and speculation persisted
underground and in private circles that his death had been
politically motivated. The death raised fears among potential
Asian candidates as to their safety if they were to become powerful
in the Kenyan political arena in an environment that wasn't
suited for non-black Africans.

The Dhillon household also was in disarray after the loss of their inspiration. The family had spent so much time at the trial that their businesses had suffered. Gathering at the house in Muthaiga, family members were disheartened and on the verge of giving up on life completely. It was as if the light had gone out of their lives. With their leader slain, there was little desire to carry on.

After a few days filled with many intense meetings, the family began to put the pieces of their lives back together. Rallying around the youngest brother, Hardial, the brothers decided to banish Mohinder Singh, the murderer's husband, from the family.

Santokh was chosen to break this news to their mother. Satbir Kaur surprised them with her reaction; without hesitation, she gave her immediate blessing to this plan of her sons.

In fact, Satbir Kaur was angry and told Santokh, "Tell him I don't want to see him or his wife ever again. He should never talk to me or come near me. As far as I'm concerned, both of them died the day my husband was killed."

Businesses all over Maasai land and in Nairobi owned by the Dhillons had to be taken care of, and many business activities were out of control as they had been neglected during the trial. Each son was assigned responsibilities with set goals and direction. One by one they took off in different directions to put their affairs in order.

Depressed and weary, Akash wanted to leave London and return to Kenya, but the family persuaded him to complete his law education before he returned home.

Hardial traveled extensively within Maasai land. The sawmill at Mau Narok, stores in Loliondo and Narok, and the game lodge at Ngorongoro Crater in Tanzania, were quite distant from each other and all required his attention.

Gradually Hardial, Rajinder, and Santokh regained control of the family's vast holdings and finances. The slow and painful recovery process had started.

Akash returned to London, but he felt restless and impatient. Grown quiet and withdrawn, he had no desire to talk with anyone except Anar. Though it was a trying time for the young lovers, it drew them even closer.

Shortly after his return from Kenya, Akash began to have a strange and recurring nightmare. He would wake in the middle of the night, sweating and close to screaming, and feeling an enormous weight on his chest which he couldn't push off. It was as though a person or object was lying on top of him, pressing him down. The dream was always the same. An old Sikh man wearing a white turban with a long white beard, waving a long round stick, would walk up to Akash. The old man would gently nudge Akash, wake him up, then touch a wrinkled hand to his face and whisper, "Akash, Akash, wake up, you are wasting time. Don't forget your mission, I am waiting. This has to be done and only you can do it. Remember we want revenge, revenge." As soon as he had delivered this message, the old man disappeared from view.

When the dream was over, Akash would stay up most of the night, unable to sleep. The only person who knew about the dream was Anar.

Akash was convinced that SharanJeet did not plan and execute the murder of his grandfather on her own. Through the way she sat in the Courthouse in Nairobi and arrogantly spun her web of lies, she had seemed supremely confident that someone was going to take care of her. She was fearless. In the back of his mind persisted the thought that he must return to Kenya and track his grandfather's assassins and the powers behind the plot.

He decided that the day he passed his bar exam, he would return home and investigate the circumstances surrounding his grandfather's death. He belonged back in Kenya, he knew it. Nevertheless, he would have to wait a year to implement his plan, while he worked in England to gain legal experience.

Eight months remained before Anar graduated and then she would have the choice of spending time in Britain or returning to Kenya as a reporter for the English *Sunday Times* newspaper. The series she had written on Mehar Singh had cemented her reputation as an up-and-coming young journalist, and her future looked bright.

While finishing his assignment with the law firm, Akash started planning his return to Kenya. Akash was going to try to land a position in the prosecutor's office in Kenya. That would give him the connections and political experience he needed to follow in Mehar Singh's footsteps. He longed to fulfill the political ambitions that he had spoken of with his grandfather. While trying to obtain an appointment with the government, he planned to start his own law practice. With just the family ventures, the Dhillons had enough business contracts, business disputes, and other issues to keep him busy.

Chapter XX

*"They move like moth, looking at burning all
around, Without delay they line up ready to fight,
duty bound, They play jokes with death, and like
lions they roar, Wherever they stare and rebuke,
enemy is no more."*

Rabindranath Tagore
In praise of Sikh bravery

Akash decided to throw a going-away party as he started packing for the trip back home. The building he lived in had a huge party hall that could accommodate as many as three hundred people.

The list of guests included most of the Kenyan friends whom Akash and Anar had met in England, fellow students from Oxford and Cambridge, as well as sports acquaintances from Akash's hockey and cricket circles.

Anar undertook the responsibility of arranging the party. She secured a live band that played music from the fifties and sixties. Food was to be catered from the Jewel of India in Kensington, and the cooking was to be done on the Tandoor clay oven at the party. Everyone was asked to dress up in a sports outfit related to tennis, soccer, cricket, hockey, rugby or another sport they enjoyed.

The party started at 6 p.m. on a warm summer Saturday evening. Guests showed up early knowing that they were in for a lot of fun, good food, and dancing at any party thrown by Akash.

Musicians began playing around nine and started off with

some Chuck Berry, Ray Charles, and Little Richard numbers, all favorites of Akash's.

"Come on, let's dance," a voice called out to Akash. He turned to see Valerie, his friend Khurshid's girlfriend. Akash had lost touch with her for a long time. After a warm embrace, they were off dancing. His friends loved him, his music, and parties.

Couples danced to the slow numbers, holding each other closely and kissing; others laughed and joked with their friends. No one wanted the party to end, so the celebration finally wound down at 6 a.m. They decided to go for breakfast and stay with Akash, who was flying back to Nairobi that afternoon. The whole crowd from the party was at Heathrow to give him a warm sendoff.

Before returning to Kenya, Akash made a stop in the Seychelles. He had always wanted to see the islands where his grandfather had stopped on his sea voyage from India to Africa many years ago. He wasn't disappointed; the islands were every bit as beautiful as his grandfather had described to him.

Akash walked over much of the islands, observing the beautiful fair-skinned and blue-eyed women. Stopping in the bars, he wondered if he was near a place his grandfather had visited. Walking through a field outside of town, he sensed that this was the same field where Mehar Singh had introduced the sport of kabbadi to the Seychelles islanders. His grandfather would be glad to know that the essentially Indian sport he'd taught the islanders was now an international sport with a World Cup tournament with countries like the U.S, India, Pakistan, Britain, Canada, Fiji, and Singapore all competing for top honors and prize money.

After an invigorating stay in the islands, he completed his journey back to Kenya. Akash's arrival was cause for round after round of celebrations since his friends and family had been waiting for this day for years. He visited them all; it seemed as though he was driving from party to party throughout Kenya. Everyone wanted to make sure the young attorney was properly welcomed on his return to Kenya, and some of the people he visited he hadn't seen since he left to go to school at Oxford.

Once recovered from all the parties and celebrating, Akash began looking for office space in Nairobi. Since he wanted to follow his grandfather's lead and enter the political arena, he had applied for positions within the government. As a public defender or an assistant to the prosecutor's office, working within the system would allow him to make political contacts.

His desire was to work for the prosecutor's office and eventually rise to the level where he was allowed to try major cases. This was where he could do the most good, where he could use the law to do what it was intended to do: protect the people of Kenya from lawlessness and corruption.

Akash was certain he would eventually get the job he wanted. With his prestigious degree from Oxford, his litigation experience in England, and his family connections, he should have attractive job prospects. The wheels of government turned slowly, so he acquired office space in Nairobi and set up a private practice while waiting for the hoped-for appointment.

His law offices were in the city center on the top floor of the Kenyatta Conference Center. The prestige location had a magnificent view of the capital and was conveniently located within easy sight of the law courts in Nairobi.

Akash wanted to establish himself, build a reputation for his young practice, and start pursuing his ambitions as quickly as possible. With the full financial support of his family as well as the benefit of their political connections and reputation, he was taking his first steps towards success.

A born politician with instincts rooted in his genes, Akash arranged for the *East African Standard* and *Daily Nation* reporters to interview him. He was barely settled in his office when the newspaper printed a short biography containing his credentials beside an interview in which he discussed his prominent political family and background.

In the interview, Akash revealed his desire to follow in the footsteps of his grandfather. He told reporters that he wanted to go into politics and hoped someday to be the charismatic leader Mehar Singh had been. He announced that he wanted to make sure that Kenya was not forever deprived of the positive influence his grandfather had been on behalf of Asians in Africa. He wanted to walk in his grandfather's tall black boots which ended just above his knees.

In the favorable interview, he spoke eloquently of his grandfather and his early life, his first years in politics, and the times they enjoyed together in Mehar Singh's early campaigns. The interviews provided glimpses of his grandfather's achievements, celebrated the old man's influence on Akash, and described how the family had migrated to Africa and settled in Kenya.

The article generated much interest. Everyone—the business community, politicians, Asians, Europeans, and Africans—was anxious to see how young Akash fared. His grandfather's fame and the Dhillon family name could ease his way and open doors for him, but the article also put pressure on the young attorney. Suddenly he was living his life in a fishbowl, and everyone was curious to see how he would measure up against his grandfather who had forged a path for himself into African politics at a time when Africans of Asian descent had no place in politics.

For a few months, Akash was busy with Dhillon family contracts and litigation. Family businesses had grown considerably over the past years, and there was plenty of work to keep him busy. At the same time, this was an excellent way to begin his legal career, as he came to know the Kenyan judicial environment and made contacts with peers. As yet, however, he was rarely called upon to appear in trials.

In his business travels throughout the three East African countries of Kenya, Uganda and Tanzania, he made numerous business contacts and allies. His travels even took him to the island of Zanzibar, where he saw old Arab dhows similar to the small craft on which his grandfather had sailed from India to Africa.

Four months after returning to Kenya, Akash got the news he'd been waiting for. He was assigned to the prosecutor's office in the capitol of Nairobi.

Eager to get involved in his first major case and show his mettle, Akash was thrilled. He had gotten his feet wet with contract work for the family, but now he had something to cut his teeth on. As he became involved in his new job, it seemed as though his opportunity would not come. Though he got to work on many important cases, he was only assisting and they weren't his cases.

He prepared legal briefs and handled case research, which assisted in bringing criminals to justice, and tried many lesser cases on his own. Nevertheless, Akash was anxious to prove his knowledge of the law and his skill at oratory and legal rhetoric as primary prosecutor on a major case.

One day his opportunity came. The big case he wanted finally arrived, and he knew immediately that it would be controversial and explosive. It would surely make—or break—his career. It began with a desperate phone call from the daughter of Colin McKenzie, Member of Parliament for Machakos. The McKenzies and Dhillons had been friends for years as Mehar Singh had developed a close relationship with Colin. For two generations, the McKenzie family had been farmers in Kenya on a 3,000-acre wheat farm in Elmenteita close to the Dhillons' sawmill in Mau Narok.

After he put the phone down, Akash rushed to the hospital. He pushed the Range Rover to its considerable limit, speeding along the twisting, bumpy road from Muthaiga to Nairobi as fast as possible. When he arrived at the hospital, he stormed in and demanded to be taken to Elizabeth McKenzie's room.

When he saw her, his breath caught in his throat. Elizabeth's body was completely bandaged, she had a broken nose, and the skin around her left eye was an ugly shade of purple and nearly swollen shut. Her lips were grotesquely enlarged and red, her cheeks were puffed up, and there was swelling on her neck. Akash and Elizabeth had been friends since childhood and, as children, they had played together on the farm in Elmenteita and at the sawmill in Mau Narok. Akash could scarcely believe what he was seeing.

Elizabeth started crying as soon as she opened her eyes and saw Akash sitting by her side. She had difficulty speaking with her damaged and oversized lips. But her eyes communicated the resilience and fire that he knew to be inside his strong but broken friend.

"Akash," she said, weakly reaching for his hand, "I'm so glad you could come." She paused. "It was horrible."

He said, "Shhhhh. Don't try to talk yet, Elizabeth. I'll be here with you tonight. We can talk when you're stronger."

"Thank. . .," she started to say, then she abruptly eased into a drugged sleep, as the Demerol they had given for the pain took effect.

Sitting by her bedside throughout the night, holding her hand, Akash thought back on the times they had shared as children. He was enraged at the pointlessness, stupidity, and violence of what had been done to her.

Elizabeth felt better the next morning, and after a shower, she was able to talk. She'd gone to a party at the State House in Nairobi accompanied by her boyfriend Chris. After the festivities, they'd joined a group of friends and continued on to the Kenyan Finance Minister's residence in Westlands.

The Westlands party had the same atmosphere as all the "high society" gatherings in Nairobi, with an abundance of food, drinks, marijuana, and women. It was a party like hundreds of others they'd been to, and they had no reason to fear that this one would turn out badly.

At the party was Hilton Koinange, the young Finance Minister, a brilliant scholar and graduate of the Massachusetts Institute of Technology in the United States. A member of a rich Kikuyu family that had been in politics for generations, he had been credited with strengthening the Kenyan economy and enforcing the Exchange Control regulations controlling the outflow of funds from Kenya to England and other countries.

A little tipsy, Elizabeth had gotten separated from Chris and was wandering through the mansion, trying to find him. She ended up in the west wing of the huge house with a couple of young Africans. The next thing she remembered, the two young Africans were dragging her into a bedroom. She struggled, kicking and fighting, but the men were too strong for her. They pushed her onto the bed, just as Koinange walked into the room.

The two Africans held her while Koinange unbuttoned his trousers. Elizabeth couldn't believe what was happening.

She fought fiercely with her attackers, digging her nails deep into their bodies. She ran away from the bed toward the door, but they grabbed her and Koinange punched her in the stomach. This made her buckle over, and the two Africans tossed her on the bed.

She lay there, unable to catch her breath, and incapable of resisting as Koinange raped her. She began to scream, and one of the Africans covered her mouth and then gagged her with his handkerchief. The house was spread out, and the bedroom door was closed. With the distant noise from the party, there was no way anyone on the outside could suspect what was going on.

The young Africans were enjoying themselves, as they watched Koinange while Elizabeth lay sickened and in shock. She tried to think of some way to escape, something she could do to stop the attack, but there was nothing. She had never felt so helpless—or so violated—in her life. After Koinange finished, the other two took turns.

One of the men sat in front of Elizabeth and held her face, turning her head and forcing her to look at what was going on, while the other violated her. The stench of stale sweat permeating from the man on top made her want to vomit. She tried to close her eyes but they forced her to keep them open. It seemed to go on forever, an endless nightmare of pain and humiliation, until finally she blacked out.

She remembered regaining consciousness on the bedroom floor, her clothes bloody, her body aching, her face swollen, and the lower part of her body completely numb. She saw the phone next to the bed and slowly crawled on her hands and knees towards it. She painfully made her way across the short distance, reached the phone, and dialed her father's number.

No answer. She was desperate and wanted to get out of the house before Koinange or his friends came back to attack her again.

Fortunately she was on the ground floor and the windows were not locked, so she managed to reach the window. Her arms seemed superhumanly strong as they enabled her to pull her body over the ledge and fall onto the lawn. The main street was 400 yards away, and she started the long crawl. She couldn't remember the number of times she passed out from exhaustion. Her bleeding weakened and alarmed her, but she finally reached the main street.

A prominent Indian businessman, Jagat Singh, was on his way home from a night out at the Sikh Union Hockey Club in Pangani when he saw someone crawling in the middle of the road and slammed on brakes. He was able to stop in time, just before his car ran over Elizabeth. Disembarking, Jagat Singh cautiously walked toward the body on the tarmac road and touched it. He heard a groan and saw the woman's lips contort in pain. Singh was a big man. Over six feet tall and close to 300 lbs., he sported a long dark beard that was untied and scruffy. He picked Elizabeth up and cradled her in his arms as he placed her in the back seat of his Mercedes 450 SL.

Once she was settled, he got behind the wheel and sped to the Tom Mboya Hospital. He carried her into the emergency wing, where she was immediately admitted and seen.

In shock and weak from loss of blood, Elizabeth identified herself and said she had been raped by a member of the president's cabinet and wanted the police to take a written statement. The police came and questioned her. After they left, she called Akash.

The young attorney cringed as he listened to his friend relating her traumatic ordeal. He reassured her over and over again that he was there for her, and that he would take care of everything. He realized the seriousness of the incident and the political implications. He knew it would be a difficult situation, however, as Koinange was a Government Minister and would use all the influence of a powerful Kikuyu politician to see that justice was thwarted.

When Akash was ready to leave, Elizabeth looked into his eyes and pleaded with him, "Please, please, Akash. Go after the bastards that did this to me, and put them away for good." Then Akash noticed her eyes brighten as she caught sight of figure behind him.

"Chris," she exulted to a young man carrying flowers and rushing to her bedside, "I'm so glad you're here."

Chapter XXI

"His martyrdom was a great event in the Iron Age,
He accomplished this feat for the protection of Saints.
He laid down his head, but did not utter a groan,
He suffered martyrdom for the sake of Dharma,
He laid down his head but not his principles."

Guru Gobind Singh Jee on
his father Guru Teg Bahadur's martyrdom

Leaving the hospital, Akash felt on fire. Like a bloodhound, he smelled the scent of the opportunity ahead to show his mettle in the law courts, and he was internalizing the pain that his childhood buddy was going through. He would have done anything to take that pain away, but it was too late. The only thing he could do for his friend was make sure her attackers were brought to justice.

First, Akash had to get a copy of the police report, to determine the magnitude of the charges against Koinange. Then he would meet with Colin McKenzie and get his agreement on the strategy in the litigation.

Elizabeth had promised Akash that she intended to testify at the trial in spite of the pain it would cause to relive the attack. She could endure the pain, she said, as long as the attackers were punished.

The police report was as Elizabeth had related it to Akash. She had described her attackers in appearance and by name.

Akash drove to Machakos, about fifty miles east of Nairobi,

to meet with Colin McKenzie. Their meeting was solemn, short, and to the point. Colin had thought about the incident, the ramifications to his image, his family's future in Kenya, and the confrontation with the powerful and ruthless Kikuyu politicians. His first priority was to see the men punished who had attacked his daughter.

The family friend who had grown into an attorney explained the details of the case to Mr. McKenzie, and he emphasized that, in spite of the relative strength of the case, it was imperative for Elizabeth to testify on the stand. This would be emotionally draining and publicly humiliating for everyone, especially for her, as she faced her attackers in court.

Colin McKenzie was firm. "Let's make sure we prepare well and go in with all our guns and put these young punks away for good. Do whatever it takes to make sure they get what they deserve."

"Yes, Mr. McKenzie," replied Akash, "You know this is more than just a court case to me. Elizabeth has been my friend for years. I intend to thoroughly research and prepare the case. The men who attacked your daughter will not get away with this."

Like Koinange, the Kenyan Attorney General was a Kikuyu by the name of Richard Ware. He had been informed by the police commissioner of the details of Elizabeth's statement.

The implications were extremely far-reaching for the government and president. The first step Ware had taken was to inform the president of the alleged involvement of his Finance Minister, Koinange, in the alleged rape of Elizabeth McKenzie, daughter of the Member of Parliament, Colin McKenzie.

Ware called for Koinange and his two friends to come and see him immediately. Koinange was expecting this. He planned for his two friends, Winston Waturo and Mwangi Ethegi, to take the blame for the attack and to deny knowledge that he was even in that part of the house at the time Elizabeth McKenzie claimed she was raped. In return for their cooperation, he would take care of them financially and make sure they were out of prison within a few months.

The three of them arrived at the Attorney General's house, and the maid showed them into the living room. A tall Kikuyu in his mid-forties, Richard Ware was a suave, polished, and successful lawyer in Kenya who had been schooled in England.

The Attorney General came straight to the point and asked Koinange, "Did you and your friends rape this European girl?"

Koinange spoke next. "Let me explain the whole incident. The McKenzie woman is obviously trying to frame me. I was nowhere near her at that time.

"Winston and Mwangi had followed Elizabeth, who was so drunk that she had no idea where she was going. They followed her into the bedroom. She then made advances towards them. They were reluctant at first, but she was persistent in her demands, and finally they decided to do what she insisted upon. After all, Elizabeth is an attractive woman. Now, in the cold light of morning, she is coming up with this ridiculous rape story to try to protect her reputation."

Ware listened carefully and then, as he scanned the police and medical reports, he asked Koinange, "How do you explain her injuries and the blood all over her body?"

Koinange replied, "She must have had an accident after she left my house. She was very drunk, you know."

Ware turned to Winston and Mwangi, "What do you two have to say to all of this?"

Mwangi quickly replied, "Koinange is telling the truth; that is exactly the way it happened. Winston and I are the ones who should be blamed, if anyone is held accountable. But the European woman started this whole thing. She is the one who asked us to go to the bedroom. It was all her idea."

Ware sensed that they were not telling the truth and that there was something wrong. However, as Attorney General he had no choice except to protect his Finance Minister and the other two scoundrels as much as possible. A scandal of this type involving a high-ranking member of the president's cabinet could cause them all a great deal of political damage. He spoke firmly, anger creeping into his voice.

"Listen to me carefully. I'm not sure I believe your version of the story, but we have no choice politically. We'll stick to this version of events. Just make sure that none of the three of you let slip anything that doesn't support this story.

"None of you should talk to the press or anyone else, under any circumstances, and you two (he pointed at the Africans) are to avoid meeting with Koinange. If you must see each other, make sure it's in a private place and make sure you're not followed or spotted. It would be better if you're perceived by the media as casual acquaintances, rather than close friends. Koinange, distance yourself from these two as much as possible.

"If there are problems, contact me here or at my office. Never mind the time—call me day or night. We all have to be very careful."

After the three left, Ware poured himself a strong gin and tonic with Wairagi, the local Kenyan Gin. Sitting on the verandah facing the Nairobi skyline, he started imagining how the defense should proceed for the three Africans. It would take a resourceful defense attorney, and maybe more than one, even if they had the Attorney General in the shadows coaching them. Those three idiots could ruin everything, he thought. If anyone witnessed this attack, then Koinange would go down. And if he was found guilty of a crime this heinous, the president would be wounded politically. After all, Kenyatta had entrusted Koinange with an important position in the cabinet.

Ware knew that Colin McKenzie was a fighter and would stop at nothing to avenge the assault on his daughter. He had to find the perfect attorney to defend the case. He was up against the young Asian Akash Dhillon, who wanted to make a name for himself. According to reports he'd received, the young attorney and the victim in the case had grown up together. On top of that, Koinange was a Kikuyu, and the Kikuyus had always been the political enemies of the boy's grandfather. It was going to be a tough fight.

Chapter XXII

*"Since there is no self, there cannot be any life after
life of a self.*
Therefore abandon all thoughts of self.
*But since there are deeds and since deeds
continue, be careful with your deeds.*
*All beings have Karma as their portion: They
are heirs of their Karma:*
They are sprung from their Karma:
Their Karma is their kinsmen:
Their Karma is their refuge:
Karma allots beings to meanness or to greatness."

Sayings of Buddha

Back in London on assignment for the paper and covering a
series of meetings between Kenyatta and the British Prime Minister,
Anar was counting the days before she would travel to see
Akash. She called him in Nairobi at least once a day and she
wrote long, rambling letters in which she poured out her heart,
letting her mind roam freely over the thoughts and emotions
conjured by her love for him.

My dearest Akash,
*I miss you and I love you more than ever; more than
words can express.*
Now that I am a journalist let me write reporting on my

feelings for you. Perhaps I can even wax a little philosophical.

There are moments in life when one wishes that time would stand still, that everything would stay the way it is, forever. Such happy times could be periods of emotional or physical joy, mental stimulation, or times when we feel a oneness with the world, or with someone close to our heart. The thoughts and feelings one experiences are so unique, joyful, soothing, and pleasant. We feel as though we are on top of the world and want to stay there.

Such a moment could be a time of great achievement in academics, sports, business, or career, but more often those moments of transcendence come with the birth of a child, the closeness of family, or the first kiss of a new love.

Memories of wonderful times can be triggered by listening to a piece of music, the lyrics of a song, or words heard during a conversation. Though these moments are private, we get the urge to tell everyone and share that overwhelming inner happiness.

But when love is the source of these feelings, those moments are carved much deeper in the mind. Feelings of transcendence, the desire to share this feeling with everyone around you, that connectedness to the one you love—these feelings are stronger, and the degree of emotional satisfaction or physical happiness is at a higher level. In a situation where two individuals are in love, there are bound to be moments of joy and fulfillment. There are times when we wish we had a crystal ball and could gaze into the future, so we could see the friendships that might develop or know how long they might last.

From afar, I recognize and can distinguish a change in you, although I'm sure you don't perceive that. This could stem from the fact that I am getting to know you as only a soul mate knows its true other self.

I confide in you, which I have never done with another person. This trust is based on knowing that you and I respect our unique bond and relish our intimacies.

I wish you could open up to the level that I do, and this might happen with time. As I often remind you, "let it out." Whatever is on your mind, say it. Otherwise the thoughts or words that are within you will stay within you. If you can express them and not hurt anyone, they should be let out.

The level of communication we have is incredible. Is it because I love you so much or is it because you are a good listener? You smile when I'm mad and say things to you that I shouldn't. You understand me completely—and maybe love me a little bit—or perhaps you love me too much, and thus ignore all my faults. Is love blind?

My love for you is so strong and deep that I find it difficult to believe that I, or anyone else, could love another human being so much. As I always say, wherever I am, whatever I'm doing, or whoever I'm with. . .if you ever need me. . . I am there for you, my love.

I love loving you. You are my own special miracle. The time and days we share are my blessings. The memories we make are my treasures. Every time I see you, you take my breath away and make my heart skip a few beats. The laughter, the silly jokes, and the gentle moments we share, are exquisite and make me smile when I am blue. The togetherness we have is my "dream come true" and the understanding we feel for each other is something I have never had with anyone.

If anyone ever asked me what part of my life you are . . . I would have to look at them, smile, and unhesitatingly say — the best part. The happiness you give is something I will never be able to get enough of. I love having you in my private world and having you to love. I will never stop loving you in this lifetime and if there are other lives to follow, then I will love in each of those lives, too.

One of the best presents I can give you is the poem by Algernon C. Swinburne which reminds me of you:

Ask nothing more of me, sweet.
All I can give you I give

Heart of my heart, were it more,
More would be laid at your feet:
Love that should help you to live,
Song that should spur you to soar
I do love you,
Anar

Strengthened by her letters and fortified by her love, Akash was wasting no time preparing his case for trial. He knew that the defense would deny the rape and allege that Elizabeth invited the sex.

Akash had a great deal of physical evidence, from photographs of Elizabeth's injuries, to the doctor's reports on her condition when she was admitted. But even though doctors agreed that Elizabeth's internal injuries were consistent with rape, the physical evidence was purely circumstantial. Even if they managed to prove that she was raped, Koinange and his friends could claim she was raped after she left the party. Even medical testing of semen taken from Elizabeth wouldn't prove his case, as the two African professionals were going to admit they had sex with Elizabeth; they intended to claim that she initiated the contact.

His best chance was to get an eyewitness, but that would be next to impossible, as obtaining a willing witness from within Koinange's household would be problematical. First it would be difficult to get anyone present to testify against the powerful politician, even if they witnessed the attack. To make matters worse, there was the added problem that, with the noise and confusion of the party, it would be hard for anyone to know an attack was taking place. He spent the whole weekend thinking of ways to strengthen his case. Mentally he ran through a list of all the Africans he knew who might help and calculated the contacts they might have.

He finally thought of Joseph Ole Likimani, his grandfather's friend and former right-hand man. Likimani was reliable, knew everyone who was anybody in government circles, and had a large and influential following.

Akash called him. Likimani was pleasantly surprised to hear from his friend's grandson.

"Hello, my dear young Akash, I haven't seen you for months. How's the law practice going?"

"It's been progressing smoothly but uneventfully until last week, Joseph," he said. "Now it's coming along eventfully but not, I think, smoothly."

This enigmatic reply piqued Likimani's interest. "Tell me more," he said.

Akash briefly brought Joseph up-to-date on Elizabeth's case and the problems he expected to have in trying the case.

He told Likimani, "Joseph, I want a witness from within the Koinange household who might have seen or heard Elizabeth's struggle. Without that, I might be in trouble, although I wouldn't want Elizabeth or her father to know that. I know that the Kenyan Attorney General is manipulating things behind the scenes and could be too influential for me to wrestle a conviction based only on physical evidence."

Likimani thought for a moment, then said "My young friend, this is a hard one. You really know how to challenge me. But I want to get to the bottom of this, the same as you. Colin McKenzie was a good friend to your grandfather and has been good to me as well. Anything I can do to help young Elizabeth, I will. I'll make no promises, but I'll do what I can." He paused, looking thoughtful. "There is a Maasai named Saibulu who works in that house. I'll contact him. Let's hope for the best. I'll call you."

Akash went to see Elizabeth to see how she was recovering and to find any additional details she might have remembered.

"Elizabeth, let's go through the scene again. I know it's painful but we're grasping at straws to find something that's going to nail them."

Slowly they went through the day's and evening's events, over and over again, until the repetition seemed tortured. Elizabeth patiently reconstructed the events and relived the attack in nauseating detail. The more times she repeated the story, the more frustrated Akash became. She would make an outstanding witness. Every time she went over the events, even the tiniest details of her story were exactly the same. But as long as the Kenyan Attorney General was in the shadows on the side of the defense, the quality of her testimony, the physical evidence, the truth— none of it mattered. He needed nails for Koinange's coffin, and all he had were thumbtacks.

No matter how many times she repeated the story, Elizabeth couldn't recall anyone who had seen the two men forcing her into the bedroom. No one had interrupted them while she was being raped. Despite Akash's relentless questioning, her memory was unable to dislodge any recollection of anyone who had seen her, from the time they shoved her into the room until Jagat Singh rescued her and carried her to the hospital.

Akash kept waiting for Likimani to call. Desperately he hoped that Likimani could give him what he needed—a miracle witness.

Meanwhile, Koinange was getting worried. He wasn't sure if anyone saw them, and he wasn't even positive he could rely on his friends, Winston and Mwangi. He knew that they could be bought if the price was right. Concerned about his position in the president's cabinet, he decided he had to take the initiative. Any negative publicity could adversely effect his position.

Koinange made the strategic decision to try to scare the Asian attorney or the European girl, Elizabeth. The Asian might be easy to intimidate, he thought, since he was new to politics and would be careful about stepping on the toes of the wrong people.

Koinange called his mentor Charles Lare.

"Charles, can we meet? I need to discuss something that can't wait," pleaded Koinange.

They decided to meet in Limuru, a beautiful small town on the outskirts of Nairobi. The drive from the capital runs through soil that is red and vegetation that is green all year round. Fertile acres of coffee and tea plantations provided delightful visual companionship on the ride.

After the customary greetings, the two Kikuyu politicians

ordered a couple of Tusker export beers. Koinange confessed, "I'm in trouble and I need help, or I'm finished as a politician. I might even be put away for a long time in Marsabit or some other God-forsaken remote outpost with Somalis as my compatriots."

He told Lare the truth and confessed to the rape.

"How could you be so stupid? Of all the people—Colin McKenzie's daughter! You must be out of your mind. Were you high on Marungi or some other drug?"

The KANU vice president paused for a minute or two, scratched his head and spoke almost in a whisper, "We have to go after the Asian attorney. I have the man to take care of him. I know the man. . .Malefu Njoroge will do the job."

Njoroge had been Lare's aide during the campaign to undermine Mehar Singh's growing political career.

"Leave it to me. Njoroge is a good man, and he has experience in dealing with this family. We'll get together and plan something."

Chapter XXIII

*"Therefore let the scripture be your authority in
deciding what should be done and what should not
be done. By knowing what is prescribed by the scriptural
injunctions, you should perform your work in this world."*
The Bhagavad Gita

It was after midnight when Akash received the phone call he'd been waiting for all day.

Likimani had been drinking and his voice boomed loudly through the phone, "Akash, get ready, son. . .we have a witness. Saibulu is our man. He'll meet us tomorrow for lunch at my house. Be there."

Excited and restless, Akash tossed and turned and couldn't get back to sleep the rest of the night. It was early as he drove up the magnificent circular driveway to Joseph's house in Parklands. Likimani had built a mansion modeled after one which an Italian Count, Vittorio De Sica, had constructed in Milan.

Likimani had traveled all over Europe and bought some of the world's finest antiques, paintings, and statues to make his mansion a true showcase. He had one of the most exclusive art collections in East Africa.

Saibulu was there, waiting as Likimani welcomed Akash. They got down to business, as Akash wanted to know what Saibulu had seen.

"Please, tell us what happened on that night," he said.

"It was after midnight," Saibulu began, "and I had gone

over to that part of the building to get a bottle of Amaretto for one of the guests. As I went past the bedroom, I heard a scuffle and a woman screaming. It sounded as though she was struggling, and I could hear her crying. I recognized Koinange's voice as he told someone to cover her mouth. It was quiet after that. Though I knew I might get in trouble, I was afraid for whoever was in the room. I decided to sneak around the outside of the house and peek through the window. I saw them. .Koinange . .and. . .they were doing it."

When he had said this, Saibulu started to weep.

"I. . .I should have called the authorities," he said. "I should have done something to help that poor girl. Instead, I kept quiet, and just went back to the party with the bottle of Amaretto, as though nothing had happened."

"Are you sure that it was Hilton Koinange that you saw?" asked Akash.

"Yes, I am positive."

"Are you willing to make a statement to the police?" asked Akash.

Likimani interrupted and said, "Yes, he will. I've already discussed that with him. Don't forget, he's a Maasai and Koinange is a Kikuyu."

Akash was pleased with the way things were going. He finally had something solid to work with. He called Elizabeth and briefed her about the progress of the case and he stressed the importance of her testifying, especially now that Saibulu was ready to corroborate her testimony.

"That was all we needed," he said. "Now, even with the possibility of the Attorney General attempting to influence the outcome of the trial so he can save face for the government, we should still be able to get a verdict in our favor."

Elated, Akash went home to have a small celebration. As he drove towards home, his mind drifted into another world, dreaming. . .

He drifted back in time to a day in late September in Kenya. The temperature was balmy and a cold tropical breeze was blowing full force. As the wind whistled down the deep canyons

and ravines, all that he could hear the winds say was. . . "Anar.
. .Anar. . .Anar." Over and over again, the sound of her name
rolled off into the distant escarpment and across the vast Rift Valley.

This was all he thought of as he drove down the Langata
Road in his black Mercedes SL. The top was down and the fast
German car screamed around the corners, tires screeching, gripping
the road as though it was riding on rails. The car swayed to the
left, to the right, and as he straightened the wheels coming out
of the sharp bends, the sleek black shone brightly in the reflection
of the full moon which silvered the African night.

Speeding around the winding roads, his thoughts were of
Anar, as always. He was convinced that his mental process was
ruled by one perpetual thought which started with her image
in his mind as he awoke in the morning, remained with him all
day, and went to bed with him when he dozed off at night and
dreamed private dreams of her through the evening.

What would life be without her? It was impossible to imagine.
When he awoke in the morning, the first thing he did was
whisper her name. All day long, he thought of where she was
and what she might be doing. And the rest of the time he was
planning when he might see her or talk to her on the phone.

He shouted at the top of his voice,

"Anar, I love you....".

He picked up a couple of bottles of wine, and decided to
relax and cook a special treat, sautéing his favorite jumbo
Mombasa prawns in lots of butter, spices, and garlic.

In the kitchen, peeling the prawns and sipping on imported
red wine from Marseilles, he didn't notice the first knock at the
door. He had turned on a jazz record—Dizzy Gillespie playing
"The Champ" on the trumpet—and he'd been transported to
a different world by the hot jazz, sipping the wine, and the
sweet aroma of the sizzling prawns.

The second knock was forceful, and it disturbed his musical
tranquility. He wasn't expecting anyone, so he opened the door
and, before he could react, three Africans were inside the house.

They pushed their way into the kitchen and pushed Akash

back against the kitchen wall with his hands behind his back. The leader of the three was a tall, well-built Kikuyu, and he was the first to hit Akash. He punched him below the stomach and then followed with a lifted knee to his crotch. The big African kept punching the young attorney as the other two restrained Akash. In spite of his injuries, Akash struggled furiously, certain that he was fighting for his life.

After the leader had finished, one of the other Africans, a young, slightly built Kikuyu took over.

By this time, Akash's lips were bleeding, his left eye was nearly swollen, and he was having difficulty standing up. He could hardly breathe for the pain in his chest, and he was afraid they might have broken one of his ribs and punctured a lung. He heard himself gasping for air, and each time his lungs expanded, he experienced a shooting pain in the left side of his chest. His ribs throbbed and ached.

After the second attacker was finished, Akash was on the floor and only half-conscious. He kept his eyes closed and pretended to be unconscious. He could barely decipher their words through ears that had been pummeled and damaged.

The younger attacker called out to the leader, "Malefu, come on. Let's get out of here, before someone comes or we are noticed."

The big African called back, "Wait, I have to find out what he has in here. There might be some evidence that he has collected against Koinange and the others. He's passed out, anyway."

Akash heard this, yet lay still, hoping to escape more brutal torture—or worse.

"Mehar Singh must be turning in his grave. First, we take care of him, and now his grandson. They can't mess with the Wa Kikuyu. This should be a lesson to everyone, once again; once again," the leader boasted.

Akash couldn't believe what he heard. He wanted to get up and confront them. But he couldn't reveal that he was conscious, or they would surely finish the job they'd started.

One of the Africans came over and lifted Akash's head from the floor, then released it. Akash forced himself to remain boneless and didn't cry out when his head struck the floor.

"I think we're done here," the leader said. "Leave him. He will live, but he'll remember us for a long time to come. Leave the note next to him. Let's go."

Akash lay perfectly still until he heard a vehicle start up and drive away. Then he rolled onto his back and picked up the note. With his eyes swollen and half shut, he had difficulty reading the simple, hand-written note:

"LEAVE KOINANGE ALONE. IT IS NOT YOUR
BUSINESS. WAHINDI."

Akash could hardly rise to his feet after they left and when he tried to do so, everything hurt. He crawled to the edge of the sofa in the living room, got up on the soft cushions, and passed out.

The first thing Njoroge did after leaving Akash was call Charles Lare, "He won't bother us anymore. He should be scared stiff after the beating he got today. I didn't find any evidence though."

"Well done, your reward will be coming. Let your accomplices know that."

Chapter XXIV

"Say to the believing men that they should lower
their gaze and guard their modesty:
That will make for greater purity for them: and
Allah is well acquainted with all that they do."
THE HOLY QUR-AN

Akash woke to the sharp sound of the phone ringing. His whole
body was in pain. It hurt even to lift his arm to reach for the
receiver. When he finally picked it up, it was Anar.

"Where were you, my jaan? I've been calling for the last half
hour. I got so worried—are you all right?"

Akash could hardly open his mouth. He mumbled,
"Where. . . are. . .you?"

Anar could barely make out his words. She thought they
had a bad connection.

She said, "I'm in Nairobi. I flew in last night. I'm coming
over right now."

Akash fell back into a semiconscious state. It still hurt to
breathe, and he didn't have the strength or the will to move.

Anar had the key to the apartment and let herself in. When
she saw Akash, she screamed, "Oh my God...what happened,
who. . .never mind, let me call the ambulance."

Akash was rushed to Nairobi General Hospital. Once he
was admitted, Anar called his parents.

Doctor Chopra, a Dhillon family doctor for two generations,
attended Akash. The preliminary diagnosis was that one of his

lungs was badly damaged, two of his ribs were broken, and he had a hairline fracture on his right jaw. The good news was that there was no surgery required. He would be able to go home after a week or so.

Recuperation was slow, but Akash was lovingly spoiled by Anar, his family, and friends. They played cards and board games, watched movies, and read books to him. Though he could do nothing about the case while in the hospital, Akash never let Elizabeth and the ordeal she had been through wander from his mind. As he strengthened physically, he became mentally even more determined to see her attackers brought to justice.

He called Elizabeth from the hospital to tell her the saga about meeting Saibulu and being severely beaten by supporters of Koinange.

He assured her, "There's nothing to worry about. We have Saibulu as a witness, and he's going to testify and put Koinange and his buddies away for a long time. So stay put, bear with me, and once I'm ready, I'll call you."

In the meantime, Lare informed Koinange that his man Njoroge had taken care of Akash.

"He won't bother us anymore," Lare said. "I'm sure he'll take a long time to recover, and that should keep him out of our way."

The Kenyan Attorney General Richard Ware learned about the beating after Akash had filed a police report detailing the assault. Akash had even been able to identify Malefu Njoroge as one of the assailants. Ware wasn't pleased with this turn of events. Beating up Mehar Singh's grandson was going to create quite a stir, and once the newspapers found out, it was going to be trouble for everyone.

He was right. The *Daily Nation* headlined the attack,

"MEHAR SINGH'S GRANDSON ASSAULTED BY KIKUYU EXTREMISTS."

Written by a local Goan journalist, Joey DeSouza, the article described the attack in detail and hinted at a political motive. The journalist recalled the assassination of Akash's grandfather and editorialized the view that this was a politically inspired attempt to kill the young attorney, rather than a random act of violence.

Ware took the initiative and called on the president to bring him up-to-date on the developments in the McKenzie rape case and the subsequent beating.

After listening to Ware, Kenyatta ordered, "I want this stopped immediately. The rape case should be tried. Leave the young Dhillon alone. Do you understand?"

"Yes sir, I'll handle it." Ware answered. He turned and left the room.

The McKenzie rape case was scheduled to be heard at the law courts in Nairobi. Ware had been working secretly in the background with the lawyers responsible for defending Koinange and his two accomplices. Their strategy was as predicted. They would plead "not guilty" and force Akash to prove otherwise.

Akash had kept to himself the fact that there had been a witness to Elizabeth's attack, and this was going to surprise everyone. In the meantime, the witness Saibulu had taken a leave of absence and had gone to Narok in the Maasai District to be with his ailing father.

Trial judge Manohar Madan, the first Asian Judge in Kenya, had a reputation for being extremely strict in murder and rape cases. The pretrial proceedings were merely a formality, as the Africans pleaded as they had planned.

In his opening statement, Akash mentioned that he would prove that there was a rape which took place and that he intended to have not only Miss McKenzie testify but also an eyewitness. This shocked Koinange and the defense attorneys and took them completely by surprise.

Koinange quickly reassured his attorney, "No one saw us. . .it can't be true. He's just bluffing."

After the preliminary proceedings, the case was adjourned until the next morning.

Koinange invited Winston and Mwangi to come to his house, so they could try to think of who this mystery witness might be. They reanalyzed the evening's events, trying to think of who had access to that part of the building.

"It could have been a guest," Mwangi pointed out.

"No, there's no need for anyone to visit that part of the house. It has to be a family member or a servant."

"Okay, let's check each of the servants. Bring them in, and we'll question them," Koinange replied.

They assembled the servants and asked if anyone had visited that part of the building on the evening of the party. None had.

"Is anyone missing?" asked Koinange.

"Yes, Saibulu is not here," one of the maids whispered.

"Speak up woman, what are you saying?" shouted Koinange.

"I said, Saibulu was here, but he's gone to be with his father, who is ill."

Koinange's face grew flush, as the heat of understanding—and a feeling of betrayal—permeated his whole being. He withdrew to have a private word with his friends. Quietly and under his breath he said, "Oh yes. . . and he is a bloody Maasai after all. .I should have fired him a long time back ...they are all friendly with the Dhillons. It has to be him. Winston, you and Mwangi leave right now; go find him. Here are the keys to my Range Rover. He must be in Narok; I think he lives on the outskirts of Narok near Wyaso Nyiro. Take the Loliondo road. I want him out of the picture. Take my revolver, and use it if you have to. Do you understand me?"

"Yes, sir," replied Mwangi.

Winston and Mwangi drove as fast as they could to get to Narok. They had an idea where Saibulu's parent's lived—in the manyatta off the main road. It was almost 11 a.m. by the time they found the Maasai village with its mud huts. They couldn't risk going in during the day, so they decided to get off the main trunk road and sleep for a few hours until it was dark.

Saibulu had planned to stay with his parents until Akash called him to court in Nairobi to testify. A dutiful son, he supported his parents as well as some other families in the Maasai Boma. He'd grown up in these hills, herding cattle and playing with other village boys. Saibulu had become a legend in the local manyattas during his teens when he had been attacked by a herd of buffaloes walking home from the local dukas. In the manyatta, he'd heard the elders describe the buffalo as the most dangerous animal in Africa and declare that the only way to escape a buffalo was to lie flat on the ground. The African buffalo's horns were shaped in such a way that it is almost impossible for them to harm a flat object. Saibulu remembered what the old Laibonis had talked about and lay flat for close to three hours till the buffaloes became distracted and trotted off. He had never attended school and had gone to Nairobi with one of the village elders. There he'd met Koinange's chef, who offered him a job as the house boy. Now, years later, he was an old man.

At his parents' home, Saibulu knew that if the Kikuyus found out about his being a witness, they would come for him, but he didn't know they already had discovered him. When the Kikuyus burst into the hut, Saibulu was unprepared and alone, as his family had gone to the adjacent village to a wedding. He stared at Winston and Mwangi as they pointed the revolver at the Maasai.

Placing his hands under Saibulu's armpits from behind, one of them pulled the servant up from the dirt floor in the dimly lit surroundings. There was a struggle, but the intruders overpowered Saibulu. They pushed him to the floor and held him down.

"Now, tell us, why are you hiding?" asked Mwangi.

Saibulu responded, "I'm not hiding, I came to see my family and will be going back soon, in a day or so."

"Aren't you testifying for the McKenzie woman in Nairobi?"

"What. . .what are you talking about. I know nothing about any testifying," protested Saibulu.

He knew he was in trouble, but he thought if he could break away from them, they would never be able to find him in the dark. He knew the land around Narok and thought he could escape and hide from his intruders if only he could get an opening. Saibulu placated the aggressors as they continued to question him, and he vehemently declared that he had no idea what they were talking about.

Finally he decided to make a run for it. Picking up a handful of dirt and throwing it in Mwangi's eyes, he began to run. Mwangi was expecting this, and the moment he saw Saibulu get up, he fired and kept firing as the servant attempted to disappear into the dark night.

The first bullet was all that was needed to slow him down; it caught Saibulu in the right thigh. He stumbled as he fell. Winston and Mwangi grabbed and dragged him to the nearest acacia tree. They hung a rope on the strongest branch and tied a noose around the Maasai's neck. Then they forced him to stand on a stool as they tightened the noose.

"*Now*, are you going to tell us about testifying for McKenzie?" Winston asked Saibulu.

"Go to hell.. both of you."

"No, you will," retorted Mwangi, as he kicked the stool away. Saibulu gasped for air as he was left swinging from the tree.

The Kikuyus made sure he was dead before they left. Now the only eyewitness to Koinange's attack was dangling on a rope from an acacia tree.

Chapter XXV

"Eternal God! Thou art our shield,
The dagger, the knife, the sword we wield.
To us protector there is given,
Timeless, Deathless, Lord of Heaven,
To us all steels's unvanquished flight,
But chiefly Thou, Protector brave,
All-steel, wilt Thine own servant save."

Guru Gobind Singh Jee

Joseph Likimani dispatched his personal driver to Narok to pick up Saibulu and bring him to the trial. The testimony of Koinange's house boy was going to be crucial to Akash's case; without it, it would be difficult to prove that Koinange, Winston, and Mwangi had raped Elizabeth McKenzie.

When Likimani got the news of Saibulu's death from his driver, he called Akash immediately. Akash was devastated. With the Kenyan Attorney General on the side of the defense in the background and determined to save face for the Kikuyu political machine, Akash doubted he could win the case without the servant's testimony.

Though the physical evidence supported the case that Elizabeth had been assaulted, there was no way to prove that the assault occurred at the party, or that Koinange and his two lawyer friends were the guilty parties. Semen samples and other medical evidence that could have supported the possibility of their guilt had conveniently disappeared after being handled by Kikuyu lab technicians, and without evidence or eyewitness testimony, it would be their word against Elizabeth's.

"Dammit, Joseph, it was that bastard Koinange," Akash said. "I know he had Saibulu killed. He had to do it to save his skin.

"I'm not sure where we go from here. They're guilty as hell, yet I know they're going to deny any guilt. It will be their word against Elizabeth's. She'll be raped again in court."

Likimani tried to reassure him. "Let's slow down a little and think things through," he said. "Maybe there's something we can do."

Akash knew he had to tell Colin McKenzie about Saibulu's death before he saw it in the press. He decided to drive to Machakos and break the news to Elizabeth and her father in person. Akash called ahead to inform Elizabeth that he was coming to discuss the case and asked if her father was going to be home.

"Yes," she said. "He's out now, but he should be back within the hour."

"I'll be there as soon as I can."

The drive from Nairobi to Machakos was on the main highway to Mombasa and passed through Embakasi, next to the Jomo Kenyatta International Airport, through the Athi River and into Machakos. It took about an hour to get there and, throughout the drive, he tried to decide how to break the dreadful news which was the last thing that the McKenzie household wanted to hear.

Colin welcomed Akash at the door and offered him a drink. Akash not only wanted a drink, he needed one to bolster his courage for what he had to tell Colin and Elizabeth.

"I'll have a large vodka and tonic, please," he said.

After the three of them were seated in the lobby, Colin said, "Well, how're we doing with the trial?"

"Mr. McKenzie, I'm afraid that. . .well, I have some terrible news." He paused and braced himself for their reaction to the bombshell he was about to deliver. "The eyewitness, Saibulu, has been murdered. We suspect, but can't prove, that Koinange and his assassin friends are responsible.

"Without the servant's testimony - well, I don't want to say we have no case, but it's going to be much more difficult. The lab specimens that might have incriminated Koinange have mysteriously disappeared. That leaves the testimony of the admitting doctor, which will prove that you were assaulted, but how, when, and by whom? The testimony of Koinange and his friends, and your testimony, will be the critical factors.

"In any normal rape case, this would be enough. But with Koinange pulling out all the stops and rallying his political supporters around him, including the Attorney General, and with Judge Madan trying the case, I'm afraid we have a struggle on our hands. I'm going to request a continuance, based on the murder of our eyewitness and hope we can recover the 'missing' physical evidence or find something else to incriminate them before the case comes to trial."

Elizabeth was the first to react. "I don't believe this. How could you let Koinange's men get to your only eyewitness? I thought Saibulu was under some sort of witness protection. This is stupid, this is crazy...I don't see how you could let this happen. Now what do we do?"

Akash sat silently, his head bowed in defeat and embarrassment. He had no answer. This woman—his friend—had been violated, and her attackers deserved to be punished with the full weight of the law. Instead, it appeared that the law was going to betray her and allow these criminals to go free, and perhaps he had been negligent.

Colin McKenzie was furious. He paced back and forth in the foyer like a caged tiger, muttering to himself.

"These animals raped my daughter, and there's nothing we can do? I've given my life for this country, loyally served it, and in return, I'm betrayed. My daughter, my blood, is betrayed."

Akash responded. "Colin, Joseph Likimani and my staff are working to find another angle we can use to prove their guilt. But unless we're able to turn up new evidence, I'm afraid we have to face defeat. There's just no way we can win without evidence. If we go to trial and Koinange is acquitted, we can't retry the case because of double jeopardy. The only strategy is to postpone and hope something turns up."

"I've had enough," Elizabeth said defiantly, her voice breaking. "Daddy, I can't live here anymore. I'm not sure I even feel safe here. I want to move to London. Can I?"

A look of pain crossed Colin's face but he said staunchly, "Sure, honey, we can talk about it." He put his arms around his daughter's shoulders encouragingly as he spoke.

"Please," Akash said. "Don't make any hasty decisions. I understand your wanting to be free of this nightmare. But Joseph Likimani is helping us, and he's extremely resourceful. It looked hopeless in the beginning, don't you remember? Yet we found an eyewitness. So we may turn up something that will bring these men down."

"Do what you can," Elizabeth snapped, "but I'm not going to count on you or some miracle breakthrough. I'm going to make preparations to move to London. If you find something before I leave, then I'll testify, but if you can't find a way to bring these men to take responsibility for what they've done. . .you can't expect me to stay here and see them walking free. They've not only disgraced me, but they've caused me to lose my relationship with Chris. It's been very strained with him since this happened, and I don't have reason to remain here."

Akash excused himself and left. He felt remorseful, as though he'd been lacking in vigilance, but there was nothing he could do to change the past. This case was certainly a lesson in how much he had to learn as a lawyer. He decided to call on the only person who made him see the light and believe that there was still good in the world.

Akash parked his Mercedes in the driveway next to Anar's Range Rover. She'd rented an executive home in Langata in an exclusive, gated community. It was private, spacious, and well protected.

She opened the door and ran into his arms. As she hugged him tightly, he responded by kissing her lightly on her soft, moist, and inviting lips.

They hugged and held onto each other as though they were starving men finding food for the first time in days. Anar broke away and said, "Let's go inside where it's warm and cozy."

The interior of the house was decorated exquisitely by Anar. With excellent taste acquired through her refined family background and extensive international travels, she had developed a unique sense of style. Furniture had been carefully selected and shipped from Spain and Portugal, and the color theme was predominately black, her favorite color.

She poured him a stiff vodka and tonic. "What's happening with the trial? You seem upset. Tell me about it," she said, snuggling beside him on the couch.

Dejectedly, Akash went through the setbacks they'd experienced, including the murder of Saibulu and the disappearance of medical evidence. He described Elizabeth's feelings of disappointment and embarrassment as well as her father's anger and desire for revenge, and then he confessed his own feelings of inadequacy and helplessness. This was the sort of situation that had motivated Akash to study law, and yet he now felt powerless to bring Koinange and his men to justice. He now realized, he told Anar, that book learning was often no match for "street smarts."

Anar had never seen her soul mate look so dejected. "You know, this isn't right," she said. "We know those three are guilty of rape. Njoroge even confessed to your grandfather's murder. There has to be someway we can get to them."

Anar was always the more logical of the two. She thought for a while, then continued, "I have a strategy I'd like to propose, but first let's open a bottle of wine and relax. We'll strategize later. This has to be done right. It'll take time to come up with a fool-proof plan, and we need to get a grip on our emotions so that we can objectively develop a plan."

Akash agreed that he was too distraught to think clearly, and they decided to go to the Inter-Continental in Nairobi City Center for a night out to have dinner and wind down. They called and made a reservation at the Rusty Flamingo, a restaurant on the tenth floor with a spectacular view of Nairobi's skyline.

The manager, Alban Fernandes, was a client of Akash, and he'd played cricket and hockey for Kenya. He welcomed the young couple and guided them to a table with a grand view of the city lights.

Anar and Akash were deep in conversation and halfway through their meal, when someone came up to their table and interrupted them. To Akash's amazement and anger, it was Koinange.

"Good evening, Attorney Dhillon. Fancy meeting you here. How've you been? All set for the trial?" The sneer in his voice and smirk on his face were unmistakable and obnoxious.

Akash had to restrain himself from getting up and punching the arrogant Kikuyu. He couldn't believe it—this man not only believed himself so far above the law that he could get away with raping Elizabeth and murdering the witness, but he even had the nerve to gloat about it in public!

"Yes, I'll be there. We're ready and will see you in court. Good night...Koinange," he replied in an icy tone, as he dismissed the arrogant attorney like a servant.

It was obvious to Koinange, too, that he had been treated like a servant boy whose entrance had not pleased his master. He managed a weak smile and said, "Very well, then. You two have a good evening, and enjoy your meal." He had a smug, self-satisfied look on his face as he went back to his table.

As soon as Koinange was far enough away that he couldn't see, Anar touched Akash's arm to calm him. She could see the anger in his face and knew he was boiling.

She refreshed his memory about what they'd been discussing before they left home as she asked, "Don't you want to hear about my suggestion?"

"Yes, of course," he said, as though emerging from a trance. "Between dinner, and. . . him, I'd almost forgotten. Tell me about this plan of yours," encouraged Akash, silently admiring the way in which she had steered his animal passions into a positive area.

"Okay, first there's our man, Koinange. And he's linked to Njoroge. We know this from what you overheard when his men were assaulting you."

Akash nodded. She continued. "Now, since we can't seem to get anything solid on Koinange, you may have to pursue this from another angle. Njoroge doesn't have Koinange's finesse or Koinange's connections. He's more brutal, but he's also sloppier. You can follow his trail and see where it leads. Once you have the goods on Njoroge, it might be a simple matter to get him to turn on his boss."

Akash smiled at his intelligent and beautiful strategist who constantly amazed him with her cunning and resourcefulness.

He replied. "I have a feeling that Elizabeth's rape, and even my grandfather's murder, are only the tip of the iceberg with Koinange. He's so addicted to power that he doesn't know when to stop—he does things just to prove he can get away with them and that could prove his downfall."

She replied. "Leave this to me. After all, I *am* an investigative journalist, and I want to get my next major story as badly as you want to win your first big case."

Akash leaned towards Anar and said, "It's a wonderful plan, meri jaan. With luck, we may even be able to get Njoroge on the ropes in time to have him testify against Koinange in the McKenzie assault case. Let's sleep on it, and we'll work out the details in the morning."

They spent the rest of the evening reminiscing about the times they had shared in England and reliving fond memories of trips they'd taken. Anar was behind the wheel as they left the Inter-Continental, deftly handling her powerful Range Rover. They were quiet on the drive home, thinking of the challenge that lay ahead as Akash prepared to do battle with Njoroge and Koinange.

Akash was half asleep when Anar pulled into the driveway of her villa, and she had to nudge him awake. He followed her into the foyer. Exhausted from the day's stress, he collapsed into the soothing comfort of soft clean sheets on a firm mattress, folded Anar into his arms, and immediately fell into a deep, dreamless sleep.

Chapter XXVI

*"Whenever you take a step forward you are bound
to disturb something. You disturb the air as you go
forward, you disturb the dust on the ground
You trample upon things. When a whole society
moves forward this trampling is on a much bigger
scale and everything you disturb, each vested
interest, which you want to remove, stands as
an obstacle."*

Indira Gandhi, 1967

Anar felt a growing excitement that she had rarely experienced. She knew she was preparing to confront some of the leading political figures and criminals in Kenya in this search for the truth that she had become a part of and committed herself to.

But that's what had drawn her to journalism: the power it had, at its best, to bring down people who felt they were above the law. She loved the way journalism had the unique ability and sacred trust to expose the truth, no matter the consequences, without bowing to political influence, coercion, and corruption. Yet Anar knew that the press was far from perfect. She was aware that, at its best, it functioned as a watchdog branch of government, checking the power of those who would abuse the public trust by bringing their untoward activities into the cold light of day.

Anar decided she had to get to Njoroge, either directly or through one of his subordinates. He was the key to Koinange, she sensed, just as she sensed that he was the weakest link in the chain mail armor that seemed to protect the finance minister. She felt certain Njoroge was also the key to the truth about Mehar Singh's murder.

Anar made arrangements to visit the Dhillon house in Kijabe where Mehar Singh's murder took place. She wanted to look over the scene of the crime to get a feel for what might have happened and to talk with servants.

After driving into Kijabe, just off the road from Nairobi to Nakuru, Anar turned right onto the steep dirt road leading up to the small town on the base of the Rift Valley Escarpment. She drove past the post office and through the center of town, passing small shops and the Skoni, or farmer's market. At the other end of town, she saw the bus station, a school, and at the end of Kijabe road, the police station.

She went in, presented her press credentials, and asked one of the Askaris if she could obtain copies of all the police reports on Mehar Singh's death. When he asked why she needed them, she explained that she'd been doing a series of articles for the *Sunday Times* on the slain Sikh leader, and she wanted background information.

She was surprised when the officer gave her what she requested, but then, Mehar Singh's murder was considered solved. Since the policeman had no reason to suspect that there could be possible political ramifications caused by the investigation she was launching, he had no reason to deny her request. Besides, it was doubtful that police reports on old cases would contain information not available elsewhere.

After acquiring the documents, Anar turned back toward town. She took the steeper side road leading to the Dhillon family mansion, which was halfway between the town of Kijabe and the rail station. On the left side of the road, she passed the Sikh temple where Kulwant had been teaching when Mwangara came to fetch her and call her to the murder scene.

As she traveled in Kijabe, she realized what a beautiful place it was and she understood why Mehar Singh had decided to settle there. Kijabe was at the edge of the Great Rift Valley

Escarpment and overlooked a breathtaking scene across the valley with animals roaming and dust blowing across the horizon. On a clear day, you could look across the valley and see for miles and miles. About 6,000 feet above sea level, the climate was cool and the winds often blew at a strong place. Anar had learned in her childhood studies that Kijabe meant "windy" in the Maasai dialect. There was a hot water spring with sulphur in it at the foot of the slopes, and people came from far away to enjoy the healing, medicinal qualities of the spring. For the entrepreneur and businessman Mehar Singh, Kijabe was central in terms of access from Nairobi, Nakuru, and Narok. It was centrally located in the heartland of Maasai land where Mehar had begun his traveling duka business, which had helped him make his fortune.

After Anar pulled in through the tall, gated entrance and parked her Range Rover, she approached the main house and arranged to meet with the African servants, introducing herself as Akash's assistant. Perhaps because they'd always had a special affection for the young Akash, they were very willing to talk. She questioned them about that fateful day of the murder and she examined them individually against the statements they'd given the police and the testimony they'd provided in court.

She met with Mwangara, the 60ish house servant who'd called the police after discovering the murder. The stories they gave her matched what she'd read in newspaper accounts of the murder. They said nothing to contradict statements they'd made at the arraignment and trial, and they added little to what she already knew. Mwangara politely provided a tour of the main building and showed her holes in the wall where bullets had ended up on that fateful day in February.

Driving back to Nairobi, she speculated on the huge amount of research she needed to conduct at the Nairobi Public Library in addition to her intensive scrutiny of the newspaper reports on Mehar Singh's assassination. She spent most of the week reading through reports in the *East African Standard* and the *Daily Nation* searching for clues. The guilty party in all the articles was the daughter-in-law SharanJeet. It was a unanimous verdict and unchallenged opinion throughout all accounts she read of the murder. It seemed strange that there was no mention of anyone else who could have been responsible. Somehow it didn't pass the "smell test" for a journalistic bloodhound like Anar.

She compared original police reports with court transcripts. It took her many hours to go over the paperwork, and it seemed as though her work would be futile. But after hours of tedious work, Anar's tired, bloodshot eyes spotted something that didn't make sense.

"That can't be right," she said aloud. But when she rechecked the documents, she saw it again.

The names of the ballistics expert assigned to the case and the forensics examiner who performed the autopsy on Mehar Singh were different from the names of the men who delivered that testimony in court.

Anar picked up the phone and called the newspaper, asking to speak to her friend Paul Sandhu. When he came on the line, she said, "I need you to run a couple of names for me, and see if you can get me addresses."

"Hang on a second—let me get to my papers." She heard papers shuffling and books falling to the floor, as Paul cleared his habitually cluttered work space. Then he came back on the line. "Okay," he said. "Give me the names."

Anar read the ballistics technician's name first. It only took Paul a second to come back with, "Subject deceased. Died in a car accident, on - hey, aren't you writing the series on Mehar Singh?"

"Yes," Anar answered. "Why do you ask?"

"Well, judging from the dates, it looks like this guy had his accident less than a week before he was scheduled to testify in the murder trial."

Anar said, "Probably just a coincidence." She didn't want anyone to get too interested in her research. From the sound of things, it might not be good for her health.

"Yeah, I guess. What's the other name?"

Anar read off the coroner's full name, half expecting to learn that he, too, had met with an untimely death. But instead, Paul read back an address in Narok. She wrote it down, then had him repeat it back to her, to make sure she had copied it correctly.

"Thanks, Paul," she said. "If I get anything decent out of this, I owe you lunch."

After he hung up, she turned the land rover around and headed for Narok. With luck, she might finally have found a lead.

It was nearing dark when she pulled into the driveway of Temur Ahmed's modest home. Before she could knock or ring the bell, the door opened a few scant inches, the safety chain still in place.

"What do you want?" a gruff male voice asked.

"I want to speak with Temur Ahmed," she said. "Is he here? He used to be a forensic examiner over Kijabe district."

"He used to be a lot of things," the man said. "Now, he's just a tired old man who's afraid of his own shadow."

"I'm sorry to bother you," Anar said, "but do you mind if I come in?"

Anar found herself looking into the eyes of Temur Ahmed, a short man in his seventies, his head covered by an oversized cloth hat. He was wearing the traditional long white collarless shirt which fell to below his knees with a loose pyjama, and he walked half bent over because of his bad back. His good humor radiated from the broad smile he flashed which revealed tobacco-stained teeth. Anar noticed the thick gold chain around his neck with the word "Allah" written in Urdu, and then her eyes focused on the two rings he wore on each hand with their shining emeralds and ruby stones.

"Sure, why not," the old man said, with a shrug. "What harm can it do now?"

Anar began, "Mr. Ahmed, do you mind if I ask you a few questions about an old case?"

"What do you want to know about Mehar Singh's autopsy?" he asked.

"How did you know. . ."

"Who else would you want to know about? It's always the same - 'Why were you on vacation during the trial? Why did you retire so soon after that case? What are you hiding?' Same questions, same answers. Never does any good."

"Mr. Ahmed, I'm not here to bother you, but my fiancée is Mehar Singh's grandson. He works for the prosecutor's office now. We have some reason to believe that there were others involved in Mehar Singh's death, and we're trying to discover any information that might help."

"Why dredge all that up now? He was a great man, but he's just ashes now - the courts are satisfied, the daughter-in-law is safely behind bars. What purpose will any of this serve?"

"If we're right, Sir, justice will be done. The people whom we think were involved have committed other recent crimes, too— just lately, one of them raped Elizabeth McKenzie, the Member of Parliament's daughter."

"Rape? Why would someone with that much power and money want to commit rape?"

"We think rape is a control crime, sir. And for some men, there can never be enough power, control, or money," she answered. "But it appears there is enough power and money to keep this rapist out of jail. The only eyewitness was murdered at arms' length from him, so we can't link the suspect to the murder."

"That sounds like them, all right," Temur said. "I'm an old man now, and I don't have that much time left. If you really want to get them, I can help you. I want to leave this earth with a clear conscience when I go, and if I can help rid Kenya of murderers and rapists, then I should do so."

"You have information?"

"I have only proof that SharanJeet couldn't have worked alone. I can't stand up in court and tell you who her conspirators were, but SharanJeet Dhillon could not possibly have fired the shot that killed Mehar Singh."

Anar sat in silence for a moment, unsure of what she'd heard. She'd hoped for this news, and she'd suspected the truth, but she hadn't expected to hear him confess the truth so glibly.

"You can prove that someone else fired the fatal shot?"

"Easily," he answered. "The bullet wound to the temple is the one that killed him, and the angle of entry is all wrong for any location where SharanJeet could have been to fire the other three shots."

He grabbed a pencil and made a quick sketch on the back of an envelope.

"If Mehar Singh was here," he said, "and SharanJeet here, then the shooter that fired the bullet which killed him had to have been somewhere around here, almost perpendicular to SharanJeet's line of fire. Unless she can fire bullets around corners, she couldn't have killed her father-in-law. Of course, this is just a rough estimate. The real proof is in my report."

Anar said, "I'm assuming this isn't the same report that was presented during SharanJeet's trial?"

"No, of course not. I was ordered to go on 'vacation,' and the Chief Medical Examiner testified based on the coroner's report that his political cronies had produced."

"And the ballistics technician?"

"He's the main reason I'm helping you now. A totally honest man—rare, these days—refused to play ball with them, so they arranged an 'accident' before he could testify in court. His boss also presented an altered version of the ballistics report, although in his case it was probably more a matter of fear than political pressure that influenced his decision."

"Why haven't you said any of this before now?" Anar asked.

Temur Ahmed hung his head, obviously ashamed. "It was my wife," he said. "I used my copies of the original forensics report as insurance - as long as I had them, they couldn't do anything to us. But they said that if I ever went to the police, they'd take her first. And they made it clear what they'd do to her before she died."

"I'm sorry," Anar said. "I didn't come here to cause you any trouble . . ."

"That's all right," he said. "She's beyond all that, now. The cancer took her from me over a year ago. I've really just been waiting to join her, and I'll go easier, knowing that this is off my conscience. 'The truth will set you free,' it is said." The old man looked wistful as he appeared to reflect on memories of his wife and departed professional friend.

"Where have you kept the evidence?" Anar asked. Then she shifted gears. "I'd like you to come with me tonight and stay in a safe place, until my fiance can arrange some sort of protective custody."

"I'll grab a few things, then. It won't take a minute. I travel lightly these days. As to the copies of my report, there's one copy here and another copy in a place no one would think to look." A wide smile enlivened his face. "Behind the portrait of Kenyatta in the courthouse in Nairobi. Mzee is the last person most people would suspect of concealing evidence."

Chapter XXVII

*"The perfect way knows no difficulties, except that
it refuses to make preferences;
Only when freed from hate and love it reveals itself
fully and without disguise;
A tenth of an inch's difference and heaven and
earth are set apart.
If you wish to see it before your own eyes have no
fixed thoughts either for or against it."*

Sayings of Buddha

Like a bloodhound who'd caught the scent, the young journalist knew she'd found a major break in the story, and she wasn't sure what to do next. She knew she needed more information to nail the Kikuyus, though. She decided to visit others who had firsthand knowledge of the murder and find more information. She returned to Narok and the Maasai District townships to question Mehar Singh's African and Asian friends.

Everyone she spoke to had heard of the murder or read about it, but there was no new evidence; everyone believed the newspaper reports and the court's conclusion that the daughter-in-law SharanJeet was guilty. No one suggested any possible connection to anyone else.

She decided to go underground to try and obtain African contacts that might be able to incriminate Njoroge.

Her cousin Ali had left home when he was a teenager and moved to Limuru after getting involved with a teenaged

Kikuyu girl. Ali had married the girl and had been disowned by his own family. Anar was the only person in the family who maintained contact with him, and he had visited her many times when she was living in Nairobi before she left for England. She decided to contact him and see if Ali could help.

Ali had changed his name to Gichuru, and he now spoke the Kikuyu dialect fluently. He knew the latest gossip and news within the Kikuyu community. Anar called him in Limuru and explained the situation to him.

"I need to know how Njoroge was connected to the Mehar Singh murder case," she said. "We already know he was involved. We have that information directly from his own mouth."

Ali was reluctant to betray his Kikuyu friends, but after the loyal Anar pleaded with him, he offered, "Let me talk to some elders and see what comes up. Is this the same Malefu Njoroge who has a long scar on his left cheek?"

"Yes, how do you know that? That's him," Anar replied quickly.

Ali started by saying, "I know him. That bastard hurt my wife's sister. She was gang-raped and then thrown over the escarpment near the Italian church. Fortunately for her she came to rest against a tree. She was so badly beaten and injured from the fall that it took two days to crawl back to the main road, where she was picked up and taken to the hospital in Kijabe. She'll be more than willing to help us, though she has a speech impediment from that unfortunate incident."

"My God, that sounds so much like what his friends did to Elizabeth McKenzie. That's exactly the sort of information I need. Why don't you start there? Ask her questions, and let me know what you get. Ali, this is very important. If we can get the information I need, the rapist Koinange and his henchmen will go down. Please try your best, not just for my sake, but for your wife's sister and all the girls in his future whom this man will harm. He thinks he is above the law - or that he is the law."

"I'll do everything that I can," Ali promised, not looking terribly happy about it.

Chapter XXVIII

"To those who are good to me I am good,
And to those who are not good to me I am good,
And thus all get to be good."

Saying from Taoism

When Anar got home, a black woman in uniform was waiting outside in a Police Land Rover. As Anar approached the woman, Anar admired the tall and gorgeous lady who walked with a purposeful elegance and proud air which illuminated the sharp features which were classic Maasai in nature. The police woman addressed her by name, "You are Anar Khan, right ?"

"Yes, what's wrong?"

"Nothing's wrong, I have some personal business I'd like to discuss with you."

Anar invited her in and offered her a soft drink. The woman obliged and, after sitting down, she straightened herself and crossed her long beautiful legs. Anar studied her sculptured face and felt awed by this regal beauty.

"My name is Harriette, I am Saibulu's sister...you know what happened to him." The woman stopped speaking momentarily, trying to regain her composure. "My brother was a gem of a human being. He helped his family and everyone around him. We were very close. This is just so unfair...his being killed for just being at the wrong place at the wrong time during a disgusting rape by those powerful and arrogant Kikuyus."

"Yes, that was terrible. I'm sorry."

"I want to avenge his murder, if it's the last thing I do. It feel it is my duty to make sure justice is done. I know that the attorney Akash Dhillon is your friend. Maybe he can help."

"I'll discuss meeting you with Akash and will contact you soon," Anar promised. "Akash will know what to do."

After Harriette left, Anar lay down on the couch and started thinking about Temur Ahmed, Ali, and now Harriette. She knew that at some point soon a confrontation or meeting with Akash's aunt was going to be inevitable. It was crucial now, since there was strong evidence that another person had helped to kill—or had killed—Mehar Singh.

Ali went straight to his sister-in-law's village after seeing Anar, and he found her in a mud hut with a thatched roof in Thika, about thirty miles from Nairobi, living with her grandmother. Nyandiki, a pretty girl with a shaven head, was barefoot and wearing a loose frock. In a display of her instinctively warm nature, she hugged Ali before they both sat down facing each other on the short wooden stools made by the local villagers. Ali explained how he was trying to help his cousin Anar and desperately needed more information on Malefu Njoroge. Nyandiki was more than willing to describe the way they gangraped and assaulted her, and she cursed Njoroge throughout the conversation. The brutal assault was still etched in her mind in a vivid fashion.

Ali asked if she knew of any connection between Malefu Njoroge and the murder of the Asian politician, Mehar Singh. She said she knew of nothing to connect Njoroge to the assassination but suggested that he talk to her grandfather. The old man, Manyiro, was in his seventies but his intellect, memory, and senses were still extraordinary. He wore a pair of black cotton shorts with a thick green blanket wrapped over his upper body, which exuded the stale odor of sweat. According to the old Kikuyu traditions, his ear lobes had been cut and they hung loosely, containing small pieces of wood inserted through the ear lobes. With a mouth full of shining white teeth, he was chewing on a small branch of acacia and rubbing the chewed end against his front teeth like a tooth brush. The branches were commonly used by the tribes for cleaning their teeth. As he spit and chewed on the branch, he would wave and point his brown cane to make a point. His head was clean shaven and he wore sandals made out of old tires tied together with strings.

Ali began by asking if he remembered when Mehar Singh was killed in Kijabe.

Manyiro's eyes lit up and he said, "Of course I do, he was quite a man, "Mwanake" they called him, the strong one. His daughter-in-law shot him. But Njoroge was behind it all, along with his half brother Charles Lare, who was the brains of the operation . . ."

Ali interrupted him. "Did you say Lare?"

"Yes, he and Njoroge are half brothers. Charles Lare has taken care of that goon for years. Malefu has no sense at all, but Lare keeps him around to do all the dirty work."

"Go on," Ali said.

"The Asian woman who shot Mehar Singh had a gambling problem and was deep in debt; Njoroge knew that. They paid her a lot of money to kill the Sikh leader. They had to eliminate him, otherwise Charles Lare was going to lose his position as the number two man in KANU."

Ali was in shock. He never expected the old man's information to be this good. He asked Manyiro, "How do you know all this, and how can we prove Njoroge's connection with the murder?"

"I heard it from Njoroge's own mouth, and so have others whom I could name. He drinks heavily, and the more liquor that gets into him, the more stories that come out of him. Proving it might be difficult, but Njoroge likes to brag about his adventures and experiences. In the right situation, or if he lets his guard down, then he'll talk. And maybe that's the only way to prove his connection to the murder."

Ali wanted to avenge his sister-in-law's rape and see Njoroge brought to justice. This was his opportunity, and he was ready.

Ali had difficulty controlling his excitement. He called Anar and related his conversations with his sister-in-law and

Manyiro while informing her about SharanJeet's gambling and Lare's relationship with Njoroge.

"I'm going to get these guys. Give me a few days to plan, then I'll call you," Ali promised Anar.

Chapter XXIX

"For this purpose I was born,
Understand all you pious people,
To uphold righteousness, to protect
the worthy and the virtuous,
To destroy all evildoers, root and branch."

Guru Gobind Singh Jee
From the Bachittar Natak

The next morning, Anar decided it was time to face Akash's aunt. She drove to Gilgil to visit SharanJeet Kaur Dhillon.

When the guard on duty informed SharanJeet that she had a visitor named Anar, she expressed surprise that anyone would want to see her, but she reluctantly agreed to come out and meet her.

Anar introduced herself as a journalist who was a close friend of Akash, and SharanJeet's eyes lit up when she heard that name. SharanJeet had a special fondness for her nephew as they used to play gin rummy and other games in Kijabe. She asked Anar about Akash, "Is he still that handsome gentleman I adored?" Her interest seemed quite genuine.

Anar felt herself blushing involuntarily. "Yes, I guess so," she replied, realizing anew that her beloved had always been attractive to women.

Prison had not been good to SharanJeet—she'd lost too much weight, and her eyes were sunken and deeply set as though she hadn't been sleeping well. Her face was lean and she walked slowly with a noticeable hunch.

Anar started with simple pleasantries, to relax her subject. "How are you doing?" she asked softly, genuinely wondering how this frail woman was coping with the harshness of prison life.

SharanJeet shook her head despondently as she looked away.

As they sat at a table with Askaris watching from a distance. Anar began to question SharanJeet.

Akash's aunt was reticent, refusing to answer questions that related to the crime, stating that all of the information Anar wanted was in court papers.

"You don't understand," SharanJeet announced. "Whatever I tell you won't matter. I'm here for good. It won't bring Bapu Jee back, it will only cause me more pain and trouble. Now go, please."

Frustrated, Anar snapped, "Why are you protecting them? Can't you see that whoever is behind this has already betrayed you? You're going to be left here to rot, until you die in prison, while they're allowed to go free. And for what? You don't gamble anymore..you can't.. and now.. there's someone who has evidence that there was another killer."

SharanJeet was startled. She stood up and moved away from the table, turning her back on Anar. "How did you know about my gambling ...and what's this about someone having evidence?"

Anar pleaded with SharanJeet to sit down, and she began to tell the frightened woman about the meeting with Temur Ahmed in Narok and the original ballistics report being hidden. She also told her about Ali's trip to Thika and Lare's relationship with Njoroge.

SharanJeet spoke softly, nearly stammering, "I don't believe this is happening.. I read the articles that you're writing on Bapu. . . Mehar Singh, for the *Sunday Times*. I heard the guards talking one day about how you've been working with Akash to find evidence against Koinange and Njoroge and researching the original murder case. I had no idea you had found all this out."

Anar replied, "Akash and I believe there's more to the murder of Mehar Singh than most people know. We think that Koinange, and perhaps Charles Lare, were involved in Mehar Singh's assassination. Is there any information you can give me, anything at all?"

SharanJeet hesitated for a moment, then said, "All right.. You should tape this conversation. Once these men find out I've spoken with you—well, even in prison, witnesses willing to go against Koinange have been known to disappear. The tapes will give you and Akash the evidence you need, even if something should happen to me. And because I asked you to tape the conversation, and it was done with my full knowledge, the tapes should be admissible as evidence in court. I hope you have several blank tapes with you. This is going to take some time, and reveal a few things for everyone." Suddenly SharanJeet paused and a pained expression crossed her face before she continued. "I guess I've learned a lot about the law and courtrooms, haven't I?" Then she added wistfully, "More than I ever wanted to know."

Anar was prepared as she excitedly set the tape recorder down and positioned it properly to get the best possible sound. She said her name aloud, and had SharanJeet do the same, then played this back, to make sure the recorder was picking up everything they said and recording it clearly. When she was satisfied that the equipment was functioning properly, she said to SharanJeet, "I'm ready, can we start?"

SharanJeet took a deep breath, sighed heavily and said, "This whole mess started because of my problems with gambling. Mohinder, my husband, tried to get me to stop betting and playing at cards, but I couldn't seem to kick the habit. At first, it wasn't a big deal. His family had plenty of money, and I seemed to win nearly as often as I lost, so I wasn't falling behind.

"But gradually, my gambling problem got worse and worse. Soon I was so deep in debt that I needed financial help desperately. I was afraid to go to Mohinder, for fear of what he'd do when he discovered how much money I'd lost at the tables. I couldn't possibly go to Mehar Singh.

"The Kikuyus followed me, and as my troubles got worse, they gradually reeled me in. They knew of my weakness for gambling and my growing debts. They exploited that weakness, making sure that no matter how far behind I got, the house always extended more credit.

"Soon I was so far in debt that I had no hope of ever paying back my markers. That's when Njoroge approached me about killing Mehar Singh. They offered money—enough money to pay off all my bad debts and still be set for life. At first, I ignored them and refused to accept their offer. To my shame, when they finally threatened to reveal my gambling debts to my husband, Mohinder, I agreed to do what they asked.

"I made a terrible mistake. I shot Akash's grandfather . . .I still don't know how I had the courage to do it. But I did commit that terrible crime and then spouted that ridiculous story they made up about his making sexual advances towards me. My father-in-law never did that." She paused, then continued. "That fateful day changed my life and everyone else's. I think of it every day and wish we could put time back. I was so nervous and scared when I picked up the gun. I remember that I was trembling and praying at the same time. I'd gone in and out of the house so many times, debating as to whether I should or shouldn't...then I kept thinking of my gambling debts and my husband. I don't know what gave me the courage in the end to aim the gun and fire those shots that changed everything." She paused and Anar could see the remorse on her face. "Oh, it might have been so different." Then SharanJeet broke down sobbing as tears streamed down her face. "I should have killed myself that day and not harmed Bapujee."

Anar was amazed at the statement SharanJeet was giving. She was confirming their suspicions about Malefu Njoroge and his connection with Mehar Singh's death.

"Please, SharanJeet," she said, putting her hand on the older woman's arm, "continue."

SharanJeet asked for a drink of water, then proceeded with the next part of her story.

"You were correct to suspect that Charles Lare was involved. If you follow the stench of Koinange and his pet viper, Njoroge, they will always lead you back to Lare. He was at the meeting where they laid out the plan to kill Mehar Singh. He was the one who promised to pay me the money if I killed Akash's grandfather and discredited his name. He was supposed to deposit $200,000 in my numbered Swiss account right after the killing." Then her countenance took on a sad look.

"I've checked into my account in Zurich. The money isn't there; it was never deposited. Not only did they frame me and then try to get away with it, but they didn't even give me the payment they promised, so I could clear my gambling debts and save my husband's name. I will not let them escape."

This was more than Anar had dared to hope for. SharanJeet was not only incriminating Lare and all his men, but she had specific dates and times when she met with the conspirators. This was a blockbuster story sure to land Anar's byline on the front page of every paper in Kenya. More importantly, if they timed it right, they should be able to bring down Lare and his gang.

SharanJeet finished her statement, saying, "I agreed to perform the killing because I felt I had no choice. I was desperate, and I would've done anything they asked to get out of the situation. I can now see that I was stupid. They had to eliminate Mehar Singh. Lare knew there was no way he could beat Akash's grandfather in the presidential election. I hope this gets them. I'm in prison anyway, deprived of any real life and reputation and removed from my husband's love. I'm already dead in many ways."

Anar stared at the tape recorder, almost in shock. She'd expected a bombshell, but this was more of a nuclear warhead. SharanJeet's information went far beyond the wildest suspicions she and Akash had. This was nearly enough to topple not just Lare, Koinange, and his men, but the whole government. She would have to handle this story delicately, or she could cause irreparable damage to Kenyatta and all the government.

She snapped out of her silence when she realized that

SharanJeet had stopped talking.

Anar counseled SharanJeet, "I don't know what to say. I could thank you but I know you're only doing this to get even with your accomplices. I'll hand this tape over to Akash and the authorities, and let them handle the situation. They'll know what to do."

SharanJeet responded, "I realize you have no reason to trust me, but you can believe me when I tell you this. You must be very careful and cautious about this information. You're dealing with people who are ruthless and cruel, people who have killed before to save their skins and will not hesitate to do so again. Be very careful, and please, take the tape to Akash first.

"The two of you can discuss how to handle this situation, once he's heard the tape. Before you go to the authorities, make sure you've safeguarded the information on these tapes. And take care of yourself. Lare has friends and influence at every level of government. Be very careful."

As Anar left the prison, her mind was swimming in a sea of thoughts and ideas. They had the evidence they needed to take Koinange down, if only they could find the right way to use it before Lare and his men found out what they had. The drive back to Langata was an invigorating and stimulating one for Anar as she started planning the next step. She couldn't wait to tell Akash what she had.

Chapter XXX

"Chirian se main baz turaaun sawa lakh se
Ek laraun, tabhe Gobind Singh naam kahaun.
Unless I raise one to stand against many,
cause sparrow to spurn the hawk, a single Singh
faces to fight hundred thousand,
then alone I will call myself Gobind Singh."

Guru Gobind Singh

It was just after six a.m. when the phone rang. Anar knew it had to be Ali as he was always up early and had difficulty restraining his excitement.

Ali was almost shouting,

"I have a great plan...this will get Njoroge for sure. Malefu has a nasty temper and, not only that, he's well known for his weakness for booze and women. When you combine that with his monstrous ego and loose mouth, we know we can play on his vices."

He updated her on the details to trap the Kikuyus. She listened approvingly and then asked him to repeat several key details before telling him, "I have just the right person to work with you. Her name is Harriette. Ali, you've never seen anyone so breathtaking and so gorgeous. She'll knock anyone out with her looks and her figure. I'll have her get in touch with you."

Ali contacted Balwant Singh, a Sikh friend who owned the Western Electric Supplies Store and enlisted his aid. Ali described the scenario, laid out his plan to trap Njoroge, and explained the risks involved.

266

Balwant Singh was affectionately nicknamed "B.S." by his friends and for good reason. He always had an answer for anything. Once he heard Ali's plan he quickly agreed to record the evening's conversations. He'd always been a fan of "Mission Impossible" and had seen enough episodes to know how Peter Graves and Greg Morris did this almost every week. The opportunity to join in on a spy mission was all the incentive he needed,

Ali explained, "We'll plan a party, and tell James that it's a celebration for Njoroge that he'll never forget. We'll set him up, and once we have him, he won't hesitate to give us Lare."

They decided to have the party in Kabete, a suburb on the outskirts of Nairobi, not far from Limuru.

"We'll invite some of his friends and women that he likes. We have to get him drunk and mad. From what Nyandiki's grandfather said, once he is in this condition, you can't stop him from talking - and his favorite subject is himself and his exploits."

It seemed optimistic to hope that Njoroge's undoing would be his tongue loosened with booze, but Njoroge was an arrogant moron by reputation, so anything was possible.

Balwant Singh drove and checked out a sleazy African bar in Kabete which served African food and beer and loudly played the local African music. Ali was chosen to invite Njoroge and Koinange to the Sombrero Club. The reason they provided for the invitation was to celebrate the fact that Koinange was going to win the case against the McKenzies. Ali played the two of them against each other, telling Njoroge that it was Koinange's idea and letting Koinange think that Njoroge arranged the celebration for him.

Ali also arranged for a couple of ringers to ask the right questions that would push Njoroge's buttons and make Njoroge angry after he was drunk.

Harriette met Ali outside Kabete to go over the details of her role for the night. Ali was stunned as he caught sight of the Maasai woman. Now he knew what Anar meant when she was describing this goddess-like creature who was dressed in a provocative, low-cut dress that enhanced her irresistible figure. He had no doubt that Njoroge would confess to anything under the influence of this vixen.

About twenty people were at the party, and Koinange had recklessly brought his friends Winston and Mwangi to celebrate with him, even though he'd been advised to keep his distance from them. Njoroge came alone. The party was loud with talking, laughing, and the rhythmic beat of the African pop music.

Ali had assigned two hired women to take care of the men in every way that they wanted. Koinange was happy to drink and talk.

The party was in full swing when Harriette approached Njoroge, who by that time had finished half the bottle of scotch. Sitting close to him, she took a sip out of his glass and looked at him invitingly. As Njoroge looked her over intently a couple of times from head to toe, she put her forefinger into her lips and started sucking it. Njoroge was excited, and he asked her name as he moved closer to her.

She replied, "I'm Harriette, but they call me dynamite.. it can be ignited if the man is right."

The challenge was too much for Njoroge, and he snapped back, "Why don't we go upstairs and check the strength of the explosives."

Harriette helped him off his feet as he grabbed the bottle of scotch and stumbled towards the stairs. They went into the first room that was unoccupied. Balwant Singh had ensured that this room would be vacant and wired for the recording.

Njoroge collapsed on the bed as he dragged her towards him. Harriette pulled away as she teased him, "Hey, wait a minute, let me at least prepare myself."

Harriette had her back towards him as she noticed the wire leading to the tape recorder.

Njoroge watched her undress as he ran his hands over her back. She poured him another drink and took a sip before handing him the scotch. Then she came around and lay down next to the huge frame of the Kikuyu. She turned her head sideways at his clumsy effort to kiss her lips. She wanted to get his confidence and started by moving her hand to his lower body and undoing the zipper.

She whispered, "I have never been near anyone so powerful and strong. I want to feel those muscles and be around you for a long time." Then she pushed back from him and looked into his eyes. "You should be in politics instead of doing other people's dirty work." She could practically see his ego ballooning in front of her eyes as she continued her flattery. "You think of us black Africans first and foremost. We need someone like you up there. We native Kenyans have to stick together." Then she brushed against him, her breasts touching him. He was clearly aroused. He smiled, showing his stained teeth.

"I like you...Harri.......now come here," as he fondled her breasts.

Njoroge turned the beautiful Maasai woman onto her back and was on top of her in a flash as he started taking his pants off. Harriette hugged him and whispered in his ear, "Hey, big man, the next time you want any killing done, I'll do it for the next president of our country. Now tell me, what's this rumor I keep hearing about you getting a woman to do your killing for you?"

He was surprised, half looked at her and asked, "What do you mean? Who was killed?"

"The Asian leader, Mehar Singh."

"Stop that...let's explode."

"That's what everyone is saying, Njoroge has no balls and women do his dirty work."

"Me with no balls, listen, woman . .if you have a problem, go ask Lare, he has all the answers."

"What do you mean?" asked Harriette. She knew that Njoroge was furious and getting angrier by the minute.

"You heard me, now leave me alone and get out of here."

"So, it was you and Lare who killed the Asian," shouted Harriette.

Njoroge slapped Harriette and was getting ready to hit her again as she pushed him and jumped out of bed.

"You are just a coward and scum. The rumors must be true."

Njoroge shouted, "Listen to me, you. . . I had to finish the job. The Indian woman couldn't hit an elephant at close range. She kept missing the old man. I had to finish the job and put him away. I had to. My single shot put him away. I had to do it! There was no way we could allow a Kala Singha Wahindi to be leader of KANU or Kenya.

"Lare is the guilty one, why are they blaming me? I only acted on orders given to me by the great Charles Lare, who thinks he's God's gift to Kenya and to all of us. Now leave me alone - I want another drink, Kwaheri."

Harriette wrapped her dress around her and ran out of the room as she wiped the blood off her cut upper lip. She hurried to get away before Njoroge could grab and hit her again.

After Mwangi saw Harriette rushing towards her Toyota, he ran upstairs to check on Njoroge and found his friend nearly passed out and half hanging off the bed. Mwangi dressed his Kikuyu friend and helped him get down the stairs and out through the side door to the waiting Datsun pickup.

Balwant Singh and Ali watched them leave, then came into the room to check on the tape. After listening to half of the tape, Ali was jubilant as he said, "We have enough on Lare. Let's get out of here before they come back and figure out what we've done."

Chapter XXXI

"Tu thakur tum pah ardas
you are the lord; we pray to you
Jeo pind sabh teri ras
you have favoured us with our being and body
tum mat pita hum balak teray
you are my mother and father
we are your children
tumari kirpa mah sookh ghaneray
in your grace lie many comforts."

Ardaas - Sikh prayer

Akash was out of the office when Anar called, so she left a message for him to meet her in the evening for a celebration. She decided to take Temur Ahmed to the house and rest for a while before she met Akash.

In the meantime, Ali called Anar but she wasn't available. He decided to go by the villa that night and present his news in person, so he drove from Thika to Nairobi. It was about 5 p.m. when he rang the bell at Anar's villa. She was surprised to see him, but once she saw his face, she knew something exciting had happened.

"What is it, Ali? What did you find out?"

"We have him," Ali answered. "Not just Koinange - we have Vice President Lare as well. Harriette was fantastic. Njoroge confessed on tape. Just listen and you will see what I mean."

Anar went to the living room and sat next to the tape player.

271

She knew that whatever she was about to hear was going to be spectacular, she could tell by Ali's excitement.

Once she'd heard the tape, she said to Ali, "I'm dreaming. I must be. This is incredible. What's going on? First, I get a tape from SharanJeet and now this. I can't believe it. Akash should be home soon. He'll know what to do."

With this latest news, Anar decided that Akash should listen to the tapes even before they celebrated.

She called his office again, and this time he was in.

"Meri jaan, we have something, come on over right away. There's someone here you should meet, and I want to listen to these tapes."

"What tapes? What are you talking about?" he asked.

"You'll see soon enough. Come home, jaan—this can't wait."

When Akash arrived home, Anar mixed drinks and explained the whole story about the medical examiner who had autopsied Mehar Singh. Akash laughed when he heard where the other copy of the coroner's report was hidden.

"Temur Ahmed is sleeping and snoring away," Anar said. "Ali has offered to stand guard when you or I are not available. That way we won't have to rely on anyone who might be working for them."

After the revelation concerning the coroner's report, Akash wondered how anything else they had discovered could possibly compare. But by the time he'd listened to the tapes, he was smiling and shaking his head in disbelief. After they heard the tapes a few times, Akash walked over to the bar and poured himself another vodka and tonic, then eased himself onto the sofa next to Anar.

"Considering he was drunk at the time and didn't know he was being recorded, Njoroge's confession probably isn't admissible in court," he said. "Of course, he probably won't know that. We could use it to pressure him into making a mistake by 'arranging' for him to hear the tape, if we can manage to 'delay' his lawyers' arrival until after he's heard the tape.

"At any rate, we won't even need it," he said. "This is amazing.

Between SharanJeet's testimony and the medical examiner's evidence, we have everything that we wanted, and much more. But. . .what are we going to do with it?" Akash asked.

"I thought you'd know, you're the brains," teased Anar.

Akash knew that whatever happened next would be critical for his family and for him and, unless he was careful, for Kenya. Kenyatta was still president, and no one wanted to endanger the great man's reputation. But smaller scandals than this one had toppled administrations stronger than Kenyatta's, and the fact that the corruption went as high as the KANU vice president made the situation grave and threatening.

Akash knew he needed someone to advise him, someone with experience in dealing with the Africans and Kikuyus and someone who could also understand the political ramifications of the situation.

"Of course," Akash realized. "Ole Likimani."

"What about him?" Anar asked.

"He understands complex political situations better then anyone, and he always knows what to do. He thinks like my grandfather. Let's call him."

He called Likimani and asked, "Joseph, can you meet with me? Some new evidence has surfaced, and I have to make some difficult decisions about how to proceed from here. I desperately need some advice. Would it be possible for you to come?"

"Of course, Akash," Joseph answered, "just tell me where and when."

"We need to move as quickly as possible. Can you come to my house tonight? Say, in an hour or so?"

"I'll be there," Likimani said. "Naturally, I assume you'll have plenty of spicy Indian food and Waragi on hand," he said, joking. "After all, you know I don't work for free. And don't forget my favorite pappadums and green chilis, just the way I like them."

Akash laughed, remembering the older man's fondness for Indian curries, which was surpassed only by his love of the Kenyan Waragi gin.

When Likimani arrived, he offered his grandfather's friend a drink. After pouring Waragi and tonic, Akash explained Ali's story and recounted how they'd captured Njoroge's confession under the pretense of throwing a celebration party. He described Anar's trip to Kijabe, her visit to the prison, and her meeting with SharanJeet.

Akash said, "I hope you're prepared for this. The scope of this new evidence is much broader than anything I was expecting and I don't know what to do with it. This is going to blow your socks off. I just hope that once you've heard the tapes, you'll be able to advise me. My grandfather trusted you so much, and I know he would be happy to see me turn to you. I don't want to mess anything up here, so I'm seeking your wisdom. And your experience."

He told Joseph about the medical examiner who'd performed the autopsy on Mehar Singh, and then Likimani sat in stunned silence as he listened to the tapes of SharanJeet and of Njoroge. He replayed them several times, leaning closer, with his ear close to the recorder.

After a long pause, Likimani asked, "I'm shocked. Well, my young Dhillon, what's your plan now?"

Akash replied, "I'm not sure. We know that it was Njoroge who killed my grandfather. He should be punished. And SharanJeet has probably paid her dues. I don't feel sorry for her, as she did try and kill Bapu Jee and then wounded him. But Lare has to be held accountable."

He thought for a moment, then added, "I want to give this to the newspapers and break it wide open. Let's expose the culprits!"

Likimani smiled at the bold confidence and enthusiasm of the young attorney. How like his grandfather he was. Mehar Singh would be proud. They were cut out of the same cloth, and Likimani could see it clearly now. Both were brave doers and fearless leaders.

The older and wiser one replied, "Wait just a minute, and let's think this through. You asked for my advice, young man, and I will give it to you, as I once advised your grandfather." Likimani paused and looked up at the ceiling as though measuring his words carefully. Then he spoke. "You have a good idea but let's give it to the papers at the same time that we set up a meeting with the president and expose his high-level corruption to the old man himself. I'll set up the meeting with Mzee and you can come with me."

This instantly made sense to Akash, and the attorney nodded his agreement. And even though Akash had met Mzee twice, he would feel more comfortable with the Maasai being there.

Joseph added, "We'll prepare our words carefully. Kenyatta is a Kikuyu himself, and incriminating a high KANU official is going to upset him. He's a fair man, but this will make him look bad, and it's going to make the Kikuyu look bad. Still, no matter how angry he is, he won't be able to ignore this evidence. It's too momentous."

Akash anticipated that once the president heard this bombshell, he would try to reprimand Lare privately and prevent the story from becoming known. Akash felt he had to make sure that Kenya and the world knew about this before Kenyatta took action.

After Likimani left, Akash and Anar decided to celebrate and went to the best Chinese restaurant in Nairobi, the Mandarin Queen, overlooking the law courts and the Kenyatta Conference Center.

Now it seemed they had found the evidence they needed, and it was as though a great weight had been lifted. They ordered a second bottle of wine, as they spoke of lighter subjects and more frivolous times.

Anar asked, "If our lives were to end right now, what would you want to remember about us?"

Akash thought for a while and said, "There are so many good memories, but the best one would be the memory of you in Barcelona. That time when we were in the swimming pool and we were resting on a float. You had my baseball cap on sideways, and you were at the other end of the float.

"You looked in my eyes, and said, 'Never stop loving me,

my love. I love you so much, meri jaan.' That memory stands out in my mind."

"How about you?" asked Akash.

"I think of the silly things you always say to me. Then a smile covers my whole face and I feel all warm inside."

As they finished their meal and left the restaurant, Akash put his arm around his true love and led her to the Mercedes which would take them home.

Chapter XXXII

The dawn of a new day is the herald of another sunset.
Earth is not thy permanent home, for life is like a
Shadow on the wall. Even as thy friends have departed,
So thou too must go. Thou hast lived this life as though
It were everlasting, but the Messenger of Death forever
Hovers near.

Sikh Funeral Prayer

Not only was this story going to exonerate Akash's aunt and bring down Lare and Njoroge, it was going to be Anar's big break as a journalist. Akash asked her to write the story, and when the news broke throughout the country, it would be under her byline.

After they got home, Anar worked all night preparing her story. She wrestled with every word, carefully editing it to make sure that the crimes Njoroge and Lare had committed were powerfully conveyed. She wrote of Akash's beating by Njoroge, covered some of the Mehar Singh murder reports, and then disclosed the medical examiner's evidence and SharanJeet's embittered statement, both of which were supported by Njoroge's taped confession.

Akash stayed up with her for most of the long night. He was pleased with the finished stories. There was no doubt in his mind that this was the best writing Anar had ever done, and the reports would have exactly the effect they desired when they appeared in the national press.

Akash wanted the news to go to the *East African Standard* and *The Nation*, as well as to the Reuters syndicate before he saw Kenyatta.

His meeting with the president was arranged for the same morning that the newspapers were scheduled to break the story. This was to insure that there could be no second thoughts after the meeting, and the president would have no time to block the news stories.

The headlines read, **"KANU VICE PRESIDENT CHARLES LARE. . . MURDERER?" "IS LARE GUILTY?"** and **"SHARANJEET IS INNOCENT!"**

The meeting with the president was set up at 6 a.m., as Kenyatta liked to start his day early. The morning papers hadn't reached the president's desk as yet.

Akash was nervous as he anticipated his meeting with the president of the country. He had tossed and turned all night, feeling nervous and scared about the old man's reaction to the news of corruption among high trusted officials. He got up earlier than usual and took a long time dressing. He checked the tapes that he had copied several times, just to be sure. As he was walking out the main door, he looked up at the portrait of Mehar Singh and caught the eye of the patriarch. A feeling of relief came over him, as he felt suddenly warmed by the assurance that he had his grandfather's blessing. He drove to pick up Likimani and then they headed north towards the State House. They were both quiet as Akash turned his black Mercedes through the high gates after being checked and waved through by the smartly dressed Askaris on duty. The long driveway led to the president's residence, a majestic colonial palace with high ceilings and pillars inside that communicated the prestige of its occupant. Outside, the immaculately kept gardens full of colorful tropical flowers and acacia trees also insinuated the importance of the regal dwelling. As the two men disembarked, they noticed the early morning dew glistening on the green

Kikuyu grass and colorful flowers. Diligent gardeners were already at work manicuring the gardens so they could avoid the heat of the day. Akash parked in front of the main structure and the men approached the long series of steps approaching the entrance. There they were met and escorted to the study by the president's secretary.

They met the president in his study. Kenyatta was casually dressed with his khaki safari suit and a pair of leather sandals.

"Jambo Mzee?" Likimani greeted the president and started by formally introducing Akash.

Kenyatta was in a joyous mood and greeted them, "Jambo, habari ya sibui." He remembered him as Mehar Singh's grandson.

"Mehar Singh was a fine man, an African, a true Kenyan, and a brother. He knew his people and their problems. Truly a great man, and we all miss him very much," the president said.

After the president offered them Kenyan coffee and snacks, Likimani started the conversation by informing Kenyatta, "Mr. President, Akash has uncovered something very serious. It involves one of your senior ministers and we have undeniable proof. We've brought some new evidence for you to examine and two tapes for you to listen to. I'm afraid they will shock and disappoint you."

Kenyatta was taken aback. "Well, this is a nice way to start my day. What is it? Who is it? Come on, tell me."

"First, this is a copy of the original coroner's report on Mehar Singh's death. It proves beyond a doubt that there was a second shooter, and that SharanJeet could not have made the fatal shot. The rest of the story is on these tapes," Likimani said. "They will clarify the situation better than either of us could."

As they played the tapes, Kenyatta picked up his flywhisk from his desk. He kept swishing it around, as he stared out the window at the garden, his eyes unfocused. He kept shifting in his chair, swiveling it from side to side, and swinging the flywhisk at nothing. The more details he heard, the more upset he became, and he started swinging the flywhisk faster and faster as his anger mounted.

When the tapes had finally finished, Kenyatta rose and paced around the room a couple of times, talking quietly to himself under his breath as he attempted to pull his thoughts together. "Lare always wanted to be number two and he wouldn't be the vice president today if Mehar Singh was still alive. That's the damn truth. As for Njoroge, he's a mercenary punk who does exactly what Lare wants." He paused. "Does anyone else know about this?"

When Akash told him about the impending newspaper reports, Kenyatta lost his cool, "You idiots! You should have talked to me first. This is ridiculous. I should have known first. I haven't even seen the newspapers yet, and you're telling me that the whole world knows this story."

"Both of you handled this all wrong," Mzee said, clearly agitated. Then he looked at Likimani. "Joseph, I'm especially disappointed in you. You should have known better, and you should have acted sensibly. How long have you known me, and this is the respect I get? You should have come to me. You know this isn't the proper way to do things. Now, please, both of you, just leave me alone, I have some thinking to do," Kenyatta said, dismissing the two visitors.

As they were leaving, the president's under secretary walked in with the morning's newspapers. He glanced at the visitors and recognized them but chose not to acknowledge them.

Kenyatta read the newspapers, to see just how bad his government and his officials were going to look. Then he asked his undersecretary to summon Lare to his office.

There were no formalities from the president. As soon as Lare walked in the door, Kenyatta asked him, "Have you read the newspapers this morning?"

"No, not yet," Lare replied. "Why? Should I have?"

"Listen to these tapes and then tell me what you think I should do as the president of Kenya."

After Lare had finished listening to the tapes of SharanJeet's statement and Njoroge's confession, his shoulders drooped. He was shivering as he said, "That Njoroge, I should have had him killed a long time ago. He can't keep his mouth shut.

"I was only trying to protect us Kenyans. I didn't want an Asian leading our country. This had to be done. I did order the killing and Mehar Singh's daughter-in-law was more than willing to do it, but she couldn't finish the job, so Njoroge had to step in. Now, I guess it's all over for me. I have no choice but to resign immediately."

The president was furious, and he glared at Lare as he announced the decision that he'd reached.

"No," he said, "that's only the first step. You have to resign and then be tried as an accessory to Mehar Singh's murder. You'll have to face the consequences of your actions. That's the only way I can prove to the public that you were acting on your own, and that I was not involved in your crimes in any way. That's how I want it. Now, get out of here, you moron. You disgust me."

As Lare walked out of his study, Kenyatta called the Nairobi Chief Commissioner of Police. Charles Lare and Malefu Njoroge were arrested later that same day and held in the maximum security facility in Nairobi.

Chapter XXXIII

"Why, ungrateful man, repine,
When this cup is bright with wine?
All my life I've sought in vain,
Knowledge and content to gain;
All that Nature could unfold
Have I in her page unrolled;
All of glorious and grand
I have sought to understand.
'Twas in youth my early thought,
Riper years no wisdom brought,
Life is ebbing, sure though slow,
And I feel I nothing know."

Omar Khayyam

The next morning Charles Lare was charged as an accessory to the murder of Mehar Singh. Njoroge was charged with the murder of the Sikh leader.

They were transferred to the maximum security prison at Kamiti, near Kiambu, to be held there until their trial. The confessions of Njoroge on tape and SharanJeet's evidence provided the prosecution with enough ammunition to ensure a conviction.

In order to facilitate his wife's release, Anar told Mohinder Singh, SharanJeet's husband, about the evidence against Njoroge and about the taped confession in which he admitted to firing the bullet that killed Mehar Singh. He contacted Michael Anderson, the Scottish attorney who had defended SharanJeet in her original trial, to reopen the case and try to free her.

Anderson contacted the Chief Commissioner of Police in Nairobi, Peter Essaga, to get written statements from Lare and Njoroge. Anderson requested to be present at these sessions.

On the drive from Nairobi to Kamiti, Anderson traveled with Mohinder Singh.

"I never thought my dear SharanJeet would ever be freed or have the chance to be free," Mohinder lamented. "She is a good woman who made a terrible mistake and the possibility of her having a second chance in life…I have to thank God." The elation in Mohinder's voice was apparent.

Anderson was met at the prison gates by Essaga and Akash. The Police Commissioner escorted the party to Lare's cell. The minute Anderson saw Lare, he realized what a transformation had occurred in the debonair jetsetter. Wearing the khaki safari suits so common in Kenya, Lare looked tired and dejected. His clothes were wrinkled with stains from sitting on the dirty prison benches, quite a contrast to the neat and immaculate dress for which he was known. As Lare listened somberly, Anderson informed the former KANU vice president that the taped confession of Njoroge had implicated him as the person who actually ordered the murder of Mehar Singh.

Lare knew he was finished as a politician. He was on the way to a possible death sentence as an accessory to the murder. He decided to take his only opportunity to get even with his ruthless stepbrother.

Lare told Essaga in his statement, "Njoroge had orders only to observe the Indian woman in Kijabe on that day in February but not to do any killing. We wanted to stop the political career of the Sikh leader, but she was the one who would kill him, motivated by personal reasons. The plan was for her to kill and then dishonor him by making up a story about his character.

"Njoroge panicked and shot Mehar Singh when he saw that the SharanJeet woman had failed. But I had nothing to do with the actual murder. That was all Njoroge's doing."

As Lare finished his statement, Essaga escorted Anderson and Akash to the opposite wing where Njoroge was being detained. As they approached Njoroge, Anderson knew exactly what he had to say to ignite the spark with the temperamental Kikuyu.

He informed Njoroge, "Malefu, we talked with your brother, and Charles told us exactly what happened that day in Kijabe when Mehar Singh was murdered. Now, we know the facts; we know that you decided to kill the old man on your own initiative, after you saw that SharanJeet had failed. Of course, you are welcome to give us your version of events. . .if you like."

Njoroge knew he was in trouble—trouble so deep that there was no way out. He'd always relied on Charles to bail him out of his difficulties, but now his brother was in just as much trouble as he was. There was no one left to save him, and it looked as though Charles was willing to throw him to the lions to save himself.

His life had ended with his outburst at Koinange's celebration party in Limuru.

He told Essaga, "Lare can say whatever he wants, but he's the one who masterminded Mehar Singh's murder. Charles Lare was going to benefit by eliminating the popular Sikh. I was only a pawn in his bloody plan.

"As we'd planned, I was in Kijabe with Winston Waturo and Mwangi Ethegi to observe the day's events and watch SharanJeet kill her father-in-law. All three of us were in the compound of the Dhillon estate in Kijabe, and we saw her fire the shots.

"Her hands were trembling and she only managed to hit his wrist with the first bullet and then his arm with the second one. Her third shot hit the fence on the east side of the mansion. After the three shots, Mehar Singh was still standing on the steps of the house.

"It was obvious she wasn't going to finish the job. I had to do something. I fired from behind the shed that overlooks the front of the house. I had a .32 similar to the gun that SharanJeet was using, and my bullet did not miss. I caught him in the temple and he went down immediately. I didn't go there intending to kill him, but I had no choice."

Anderson was pleased with the statements. He made sure that Commissioner Essaga had both the prisoners sign the transcripts of their testimony.

Anderson looked at Mohinder Singh, tears running down his cheeks, as he met him outside the prison and gave him the thumbs up sign. As they strode to the prison gates, the smiling trio of Essaga, Akash, and Anderson appeared jubilant with what they had achieved related to the two Kikuyus.

"Get ready to see your wife. She will be freed soon. Malefu Njoroge and Charles Lare signed their confessions. SharanJeet should be exonerated."

"Thank you . . . thank you so much, Michael." Mohinder Singh had tears running down his cheeks.

After Anderson finished speaking with Malefu Njoroge, it was Akash's turn. This was the moment he'd waited for, the chance to confront his grandfather's murderer and to bring Koinange to justice.

"What do you want?" Njoroge spat, as Akash sat down across from him at the table. "You come here to gloat?"

"No, Njoroge," Akash answered in a calm, reasonable tone. "I came to offer you a chance to make things easier on yourself, if you'll help me get the ones who are really responsible. We know you were only acting on orders."

"But the Chief of Police said that Charles told them I acted on my own. . ."

"We can't use you against Lare. It's going to be your word against his, and you'll have to hope you can win on the force of the evidence. But we can deal, if you're willing to give us evidence against Hilton Koinange, specifically evidence about the rape of the McKenzie woman."

Njoroge was silent for a moment, and Akash was almost afraid he would refuse to testify against the Finance Minister. But then the other man slumped in his chair, and said, "What the hell. If it helps me, I'll tell you what you want to hear."

Akash obtained Njoroge's permission to tape their conversation and then began questioning him. Njoroge revealed everything. He told Akash how Koinange had gone to Lare and admitted to the assault, pleading for help to get him out of trouble. He confessed he'd ordered them to hold Elizabeth down and gag her while the assault was taking place, and he revealed the story they'd made up to cover themselves when Elizabeth went to the police. He detailed how Charles Lare, at Koinange's request, had arranged for Akash's eyewitness to be murdered before he could testify against the powerful finance minister.

By the time Njoroge was finished talking, Akash had everything he would need to get a rape conviction on Koinange. He was elated as he thought of the scene to come, when the arrogant politician would be arrested.

The Chief Prison Officer at the Kamiti Prison was a huge Jaluo tribesman named Lucas Odhiambo, nearly seven feet tall and weighing over 300 lbs., with huge eyes that bulged out of their sockets. Odhiambo dominated the prison workers and the prison inmates. Odhiambo was from the same village as his idol, the politician Oginga Odinga, who had run against Charles Lare and lost during the election that had put Mehar Singh in the KANU secretary's office.

The arrogant and proud Kikuyu Charles Lare had frequently taunted and insulted Oginga and the Jaluos in public. Now Lucas Odhiambo had an opportunity to get sweet revenge for all those years of being put down by them.

Odhiambo contacted Oginga Odinga, informed him that Lare had been brought to the prison, and asked the Jaluo leader for his advice on dealing with his new charge.

Odinga's response was firm. "Do what you have to," he said. "Do what we must. But make sure that none of us are incriminated. This man is a well-known figure who is clever, manipulative and has a lot of visibility."

Odhiambo met with three of his most trusted prison officers, Onach Mere, Nashon Kinoch, and Paul Odiango. They were all Jaluos. They had to be, so that he could be certain of their loyalty. He explained the situation and made them aware of his plan for the Kikuyu politician. He swore each of them to secrecy and was confident that these were men he could trust. They were highly motivated as they had seen the Jaluo subjected to ridicule at the hands of Lare and his minions.

The plan was executed at dusk. Lare had strategically and intentionally been detained in a distant wing of the prison building. When the evening meal was served to Lare, two Askaris came into the cell behind the prison guard who was supposed to serve the prisoner's meal. As Lare sat down to start his meal, the three guards jumped him and quickly stuffed his mouth with pieces of cloth.

They tied ropes around his hands and feet. Then a noose was slipped around the neck and tied to the ceiling beams as Lare stood on a chair. The noose was tightened. After the chair was kicked away, the choking, kicking, and groaning prisoner died within minutes. Once they were certain he was dead, his hands and feet were untied, so it would look as though he hanged himself. Lare was found hanging in his cell early the next morning.

Kenyatta did not appear to be pleased when he was informed of the death. He wanted to know how this was allowed to happen.

"What kind of prison system do we have here?" he asked. "This prisoner was waiting to be tried on a national crime. He was detained in a maximum security facility. How can he have committed suicide when he was supposed to be watched by prison guards around the clock?"

But in reality, the president knew exactly what had happened. He was well aware of the make-up of the prison in Kamiti and who was in charge. Kenyatta had in fact deliberately ordered the Attorney General, Richard Ware, to have Lare transferred to Kamiti.

The president was quietly relieved that finally, this thorn in his side, this rogue elephant in the jungle of Kenyan politics, had been removed.

It didn't take Michael Anderson long to go through the judicial process and get SharanJeet freed. She'd felt that she had paid her dues for the attempted murder of Mehar Singh. SharanJeet was not the one who had fired the fatal shot and she had suffered enough in prison.

Chapter XXXIV

"Humata, Hakhata, Hvershta"
I praise aloud the thought well thought,
the word well spoken,
and the deed well done.

Part of a Zoroastrian prayer

Akash returned to the Inter-Continental and entered the Rusty Flamingo escorted by three armed Askaris. He had called ahead and learned that Koinange was dining there tonight. Calmly, but barely able to control his excitement, Akash headed towards the finance minister's table. As he neared the booth where Koinange and his date were seated, he turned toward them.

"Attorney Akash," he said. "What an unexpected pleasure to see you again." Looking past Akash at the stern-looking Askaris, he added, "Though I must admit your taste in, shall we say escorts, has deteriorated. The young lady you were with last week was much more pleasant to look upon."

"I'm afraid my 'date' tonight is not here for looks," Akash said. "It seems a friend of yours has developed quite a singing voice, now that he's changed his tune." He turned to the stunning blonde sitting with Koinange. "I'm sorry to interrupt your evening, miss, but I'm afraid the finance minister will be going to bed without his dinner."

Hilton started to rise from the table in a fury, and one of the Askaris put his hand on his sidearm in warning. "What is this

289

all about?" Koinange demanded.

Akash pulled the official documents out of his pocket and read them aloud.

"Hilton Koinange, you are hereby remanded to the custody of the Nairobi City Police department. There, you are to be incarcerated until you are arraigned on the charges of first-degree rape, assault and battery, obstruction of justice, and conspiracy to commit murder in relation to the recent assault against Elizabeth McKenzie. Officers, please arrest this man."

As the Askaris lifted him from his seat, spun him around, and handcuffed him, Koinange sputtered and spat curses incoherently at the officers, at Akash, at anyone in range. The polish that had characterized the finance minister was gone, washed away in a wave of violent rage. He struggled with the Askaris as they escorted him out of the restaurant, making an even bigger spectacle than the one Akash had planned.

As they exited the Inter-Continental and walked toward the waiting police car, Anar and her photographer were waiting to catch the exclusive pictures of the powerful politician's arrest. Later, Akash would give her all the details, allowing her to publish the most complete report of the Kikuyu leader's downfall.

Akash and Anar were having lunch at the New Stanley as Akash opened *The East African Standard* he'd brought with him. A look of shock crossed his face, and then he held up the paper so that Anar could read the headline: "Former Kenyan finance minister Koinange Found Dead In Prison."

"Apparently," Akash told her, "Lare had already taken out a contract on Koinange before he was even arrested." Akash reached across the table and poured Anar another glass of wine. "He must have realized that Njoroge would implicate the Finance Minister in order to save himself. Koinange was a part of Charles Lare's inner circle and could have used that information to bargain with, after he was arrested."

"So Koinange was killed by another prisoner who was paid by Lare's supporters? But what about Njoroge's death?"

"As near as we can tell, that was Koinange's doing. It's really kind of ironic. He never intended to turn state's evidence against Lare; instead, he had arranged for Malefu Njoroge to be killed by a corrupt prison guard. In the end, justice was served. Except for Charles Lare, it was the criminals who dispensed the sentences."

"So what do we do now?" Anar wondered aloud. "With all of this behind us, what comes next?"

"Next?" Akash leaned across the table and kissed the last of the red Marseilles wine from her soft lips. "*We* come next. And for a while at least, I want as little as possible to do with big cases - or anything else that keeps me away from the woman I love."

Chapter XXXV

"All my wishes have been fulfilled, I lack nothing.
God's victory resounds through the world and all
my woes have passed."

(Suhi, M. 5 : Guru Granth Sahib jee)

They had been married over a year. With his work in bringing
Lare and his cronies to justice, Akash was being assigned to
prosecute many important cases, and each victory in court
increased his notoriety. On the strength of his success, he was
preparing to run for the Member of Parliament representing
the Maasai District. Finally, he had the opportunity to follow
in his grandfather's footsteps.

Anar started a new national newspaper named,
"MWAFRICA", meaning "The African." The new publication
focused its editorial slant more directly on the issues and concerns
of local East Africans. With news coverage geared towards the
average black Kenyan, it was gaining popularity daily. Most of
the journalists Anar employed were Africans.

Akash rested in an armchair on the private beach on the
small Greek island where they were on holiday and listened to
the ocean waves beat against the rocks. It was one of the warmest
days of the year, and the hot Mediterranean sun was beating
down on him and gradually penetrating the strong sun block
he had applied.

The beauty of their surroundings made it seem as if all the
swimmers, sunbathers, picnickers and joggers were in a heavenly

paradise without a care in the world. What a place to relax and bask in the triumph of his recent accomplishments. SharanJeet was out of prison and a free woman, and he was certainly glad about that, but as he luxuriated in the sun, Akash thought over the events which had occurred after her release from jail, as Mohinder had recounted them to him. After SharanJeet had been freed, Mohinder had contacted his oldest brother, Santokh, in an attempt to mend fences. Mohinder related all the new developments, including the confessions of the Kikuyus and the information about their gambling, and Santokh had agreed to talk to his mother. The matriarch had agreed to let SharanJeet and Mohinder visit her at the mansion. Nervously but eagerly hoping for a rapprochement, they had complied with her request and as they had approached Manjee, they had both knelt down in front of her in respect as they apologized profusely for all the family turmoil. SharanJeet mournfully admitted that she had committed a horrible blunder because of her gambling addiction, but she begged for forgiveness and said that she never meant to kill Bapu Jee. Crying soulfully, Mohinder's mother had listened.

"You did fire those shots to kill Bapu Jee," she finally said to SharanJeet, "and you did intend to murder him. I am alone without him, and my life has been ruined. I know you have suffered time in jail, but I...can't forgive you. Both of you, please...go away." Then she had asked her son Santokh to help her to her bedroom.

As the cool breeze flowed in from the ocean towards the mainland and brushed his body, Akash realized that his grandfather's death and the subsequent events had given him a lesson in human relationships which he would never forget. He wondered whether Mehar Singh would be happy with his wife's bitterness. As he reflected on her anger and the rift in family relations which remained, he realized that most widows are still left with an honorable image even after their loved one passes. In Manjee's case, however, not only Mehar Singh's body but also his reputation had been murdered. Perhaps that's what she couldn't forgive. The young woman who had been transplanted from India as a teenager was now left alone as an old woman in this rugged land called Africa without her husband in her old age and without a firm, strong, wholesome image of him to hold onto. The thought occurred to him that perhaps the jury was still out on the forgiveness issue. Perhaps he would approach Satbir Kaur when he returned from vacation to see if he could soften the old lady's heart. Perhaps that was what his grandfather would want. Then Akash found himself wondering what the old man would think of the way he had handled himself as a young attorney. He realized that he might spend his life living in the shadow of that great patriarch, wondering what he would think of this and that. But what a great, long shadow that family legend had cast, and what a great man Mehar had been.

He wished the breeze had lasted longer to temper the heat of the sun. He reached for the margarita at his side; if the vagrant breeze wouldn't cool him, then the icy drink could cool and warm him at once. Relaxed, he started to doze off. Every now and then he was woken by delighted screams coming from the girls who were playing volleyball on the beach. As he slipped into a light sleep, his mind drifted into the grasp of dream . . .he heard a distant female voice, singing.

"You are for me and I for you, my love . . .we were made for each other . . .it is written in the wind . . .it is written on the waves . . . the winds echo our names as they blow through the canyons, the valleys and the mountains . . . you are for me and I for you."

He looked for the singer but there was no one around. The voice kept getting closer and closer. He was tossing and turning, trying to find the singer with that fascinating and beautiful voice, but he couldn't see anyone. He tried to shout; he wanted to ask everyone around him if they knew where she was.

The dream ended abruptly as he felt someone caress his face gently and kiss him lightly on the lips.

He opened his eyes and there was Anar, looking down at him. They both smiled and he folded her into his arms; in that embrace, time seemed to stand still - did they hold each other only for minutes, or was it an eternity?

At last, his dreams had become reality.

APPENDIX: CHARACTERS

A.G. HOWARD: .... PROSECUTING CROWN COUNSEL

AKASH: .... MEHAR SINGH'S GRANDSON

ALI: .... ANAR'S COUSIN

AMOLAK SINGH: .... SIKH PRIEST (GYANI)

ANAR: .... GRAND DAUGHTER OF SHAHBAZ KHAN

BALWANT SINGH: .... ALI'S SIKH FRIEND

BAWA SINGH: .... MEHAR SINGH'S SON-IN-LAW

BHARDWAJ: .... POLICE INSPECTOR IN CHARGE OF THE CID

CHAND SINGH: .... SIKH TRADER IN MAASAI LAND

CHARLES LARE .... VICE PRESIDENT OF KANU

CHUNILAL AGGARWAL: .... INDIAN ENTREPRENEUR

COLIN MCKENZIE: .... MEMBER OF PARLIAMENT FOR MACHAKOS

DALBIR RAM ANAND: .... THE POST MASTER AT KIJABE

DEE: .... ANAR'S FRIEND IN LONDON

DHARAM SINGH: .... SIKH PRIEST (GYANI)

DR. H.M. ARNELL: .... GOVERNMENT MEDICAL OFFICER

DR. J.C. WILSON: .... MEDICAL EXPERT

DR. J.F. WEBSTER: .... MEDICAL EXPERT

ELIZABETH MCKENZIE: .... AKASH'S FRIEND AND COLIN'S DAUGHTER

H.G.POTTER: .... KENYAN ASSISTANT INPSECTOR

HARBANS SINGH: .... MEHAR SINGH'S BROTHER

HARDIAL SINGH: .... MEHAR SINGH'S THIRD SON

HARRIETTE: .... SAIBULU'S SISTER

NYANDIKI: .... ALI'S SISTER-IN-LAW

HARRY FOSBROOKE: .... DISTRICT COMMISSIONER FOR NAROK

HARRY NEWTON: .... ENGLISH ENTREPRENEUR

HILTON KOINANGE: .... FINANCE MINISTER OF KENYA

JAGAT SINGH: .... INDIAN BUSINESS MAN IN NAIROBI

JAMILA: .... ANAR'S AUNT IN LONDON

JASBIR KAUR: .... AKASH'S MOTHER AND SANTOKH
SINGH'S WIFE

JOGINDER SINGH: .... FAMOUS KENYAN RALLY DRIVER

JOMO KENYATTA: .... KENYAN LEADER

JOSEPH OLE LIKIMANI ...... MAASAI POLITICIAN

JUDGE MADAN: .... FIRST ASIAN CHIEF JUSTICE IN KENYA

JULIUS NYERERE: .... TANZANIAN PRESIDENT

KALA SINGH: .... SIKH PIONEER AND MEHAR SINGH'S
FRIEND

KARANJA: .... GARDENER AT KIJABE

KHUSHAL SINGH: .... SIKH PIONEER IN KENYA

KIPRAGUT: .... AFRICAN HERDSMAN AT LOLIONDO

KOCH KEINO: .... KENYAN POLICE INSPECTOR, ASSIS-
TANT

KRISHAN LAL: .... INDIAN DOCTOR

KULWANT KAUR: .... MEHAR SINGH'S YOUNGEST DAUGHTER

LAIBONI DANGOIYA: .... MAASAI TRIBAL LEADER

LOTOBONYE SANGURA:.... KENYAN POLICE CONSTABLE

LUCAS ODHIAMBO: .... CHIEF PRISON OFFICER AT THE KAMITI
PRISON

MAHARAJA OF RANIPUR:. INDIAN PRINCE

MAKORA MASHARIA: .... JOMO KENYATTA'S AIDE

MALEFU NJOROGE: .... CHARLES LARE'S AIDE

MANYIRO: .... NYANDIKI'S GRANDFATHER

MANZUR KHAN: .... ANAR'S FATHER

MEHAR SINGH DHILLON: PATRIARCH OF THE DHILLON FAMILY

MICHAEL ANDERSON: .... SHARANJEET'S LAWYER FROM SCOT-
LAND

MICHAEL KARIUKI:............. CHIEF SECRETARY OF KANU

MILTON OBOTE: .... UGANDAN LEADER

MOHINDER SINGH: .... SHARANJEET'S HUSBAND AND MEHAR
SINGH'S SECOND SON

MUSTAFA MOHAMMED: ... KENYAN POLICE CONSTABLE

MWANGARA: .... THE SENIOR HOUSE SERVANT AT KIJABE

MWANGI ETHEGI: .... KOINANGE'S FRIEND

NASHON KINOCH: .... PRISON GUARD

NIKA SINGH: .... SIKH PIONEER

OGINGA ODINGA: .... KENYAN POLITICIAN AND LEADER OF KADU

ONACH MERE: .... PRISON GUARD

ONDIKI: .... CHAND SINGH'S WIFE

PAUL ODIANGO: .... PRISON GUARD

PETER ESSAGA: .... NAIROBI CHIEF OF POLICE

PETER NJONJO: .... SUPREME COURT JUDGE

PYARA SINGH: .... SIKH PIONEER

RAJINDER SINGH: .... MEHAR SINGH'S YOUNGEST SON

RANJIT SINGH: .... PUNJABI INTERPRETER

RICHARD WARE: .... THE KENYAN ATTORNEY GENERAL

SAIBULU: .... MAASAI SERVANT WORKING FOR HILTON KOINANGE

SANTOKH SINGH: .... MEHAR SINGH'S OLDEST SON AND AKASH'S FATHER

SATBIR KAUR: .... MEHAR SINGH'S WIFE

SHAHBAZ KHAN: .... INDIAN PIONEER AND ANAR'S GRAND FATHER

SHAMBOO DUTT: .... INDIAN ENTREPRENEUR

SHARANJEET KAUR: .... MEHAR SINGH'S DAUGHTER-IN-LAW

SULEIMAN: .... CHEF

SUNDER LALL: .... SHARANJEET'S BROTHER-IN-LAW

T.S. SHERIDAN: .... SUPERINTENDENT, PROSECUTOR

TEMUR AHMED: .... FORENSIC EXAMINER IN KIJABE

TOM KAPLANGET: .... CHIEF EDITOR OF THE *DAILY NATION*

TOM PRICE: .... KENYAN POLICE INSPECTOR

UDHAM SINGH: .... SIKH PIONEER

WARIA MOHAMMED: .... SOMALI LEADER

WINSTON WATURO: .... KOINANGE'S FRIEND

GLOSSARY

ABA-JAAN .... URDU WORD FOR FATHER

ACACIA TREES .... TALL AFRICAN TREES GROWING IN
THE PLAINS WITH DISTINCTIVE
THORNS

ASA-JI-DI-WAR .... MORNING SIKH PRAYER WHEN SUNG
BEFORE DAWN - AMRIT VELA - IT
PRODUCES A FEELING OF INNER
REPOSE AND PEACE.

ASANJA .... MAASAI WORD FOR LOVERS

ASHES .... ENGLAND AND AUSTRALIA PLAY EACH
OTHER IN A SERIES OF CRICKET
MATCHES WITH THE HISTORICAL
"ASHES" AT STAKE.

ASKARIS .... SWAHILI WORD FOR POLICE MAN

BAISAKHI .... A SIKH HOLY DAY, WHEN THE KHALSA
PANTH WAS INCEPTED

BAOBAB TREES .... AFRICAN TREES WITH THICK TRUNKS
THAT GROW LIKE THEY ARE UPSIDE
DOWN

BAPU JEE .... PUNJABI WORD FOR FATHER OR
GRANDFATHER

BOMA .... MAASAI CATTLE CORRAL

BUI-BUIS .... ARAB WOMEN ON THE COAST WEAR
BLACK VEILED AND SWATHED HEAD TO
TOE CAPES

CHAANGA .... LOCAL ALCOHOLIC DRINK BREWED IN
THE MAASAI MANYATTAS

CHAGGA .... BUSINESS SMART TRIBE LIVING AT THE
BASE OF KILIMANJARO

CHUNNI .... INDIAN WOMEN WEAR A SCARF
WRAPPED LOOSELY AROUND THE

NECK, TRAILING OVER THE SHOUL-
DERS AND DOWN THE BACK

DHOW .... SMALL SHIP WITH LATEEN SALES USED
MAINLY ALONG THE COAST OF ARABIA,
EAST AFRICA AND INDIA

DUKA .... SWAHILI WORD FOR A SMALL GROCERY
SHOP

GURBANI .... THE GURU'S WORD, A SINGING
MESSAGE

GURU .... IN SIKHISM MEANS ENLIGHTENER

GURU GRANTH SAHIB .... THE SIKH RELIGION'S HOLY BOOK
CONTAINS THE DIVINE HYMNS AND
MUSICAL MEASURES OF GURU NANAK
AND FIVE OTHER GURUS PLUS THIRTY
OTHER HINDU, SIKH AND MUSLIM
SAINTS FROM ALL WALKS OF LIFE

GURUDWARA .... A SIKH TEMPLE

GYANI .... A SIKH PRIEST OR HOLY MAN

HARAMBEE .... SWAHILI PHRASE, "LET'S PULL TO-
GETHER"

JALUO .... SUB SECT OF THE LUO TRIBES THAT
SETTLED ALONG LAKE VICTORIA,
MAINLY FISHERMEN AND
FARMERS, ACTIVE IN POLITICS

KABBADI .... SPORT PLAYED IN VILLAGES IN THE
PUNJAB, NORTHERN INDIA

KADU .... KENYA AFRICAN DEMOCRATIC UNION,
KENYAN POLITICAL PARTY

KALA SINGHA ....: NAME GIVEN TO EARLY SIKH PIO-
NEERS BY THE AFRICANS

KANU .... KENYA AFRICAN NATIONAL UNION,
KENYAN POLITICAL PARTY

KIBUIS...................................... OLIVE WOOD IS STRIPPED CLEAN ON
THE INSIDE AND IS USED FOR FRESH
MILK

KIKUYU .... BANTU SPEAKING PEOPLE WHO MAKE

UP THE LARGEST TRIBAL GROUP
KENYA. TRADITIONALLY AN AGRIC
TURAL PEOPLE, THE KIKUYU LONG
RESIDED IN SEPARATE FAMILY HOME-
STEADS.

KIRTAN .... THE GURU'S MESSAGE WITH ADDED
MUSIC, A COLLECTION OF HYMNS,
KIRTAN IS THE MEANS BY WHICH THIS
IS TO REACH THE SOUL

KOMBI .... A VOLKSWAGEN VAN

LAIBONI .... A MAASAI WITCH DOCTOR

LAMBARDAR .... PUNJABI WORD FOR VILLAGE HEAD OR
CHIEF

LANGAR .... TEMPLE OF BREAD, LANGAR IS SERVED
TO ONE AND ALL AT A GURUDWARA

LAYONIS .... UNTIL HE IS CIRCUMCISED, A YOUNG
MAASAI IS CALLED A LAYONI

LELESHWA .... A SILVERY WHITE AFRICAN BUSH,
COLOR CAUSED BY A FINE WHITE
FLUFF GROWING ON THE UNDERSIDE
OF THE LEAF AND THE YOUNG STEM

LOLIONDO .... A SMALL OUTPOST ON THE KENYA AND
TANZANIA BORDER, A MAASAI WORD,
NAMED AFTER TREES GROWING IN
THE REGION

MAASAI .... A COURAGEOUS NOMADIC TRIBE IN
EAST AFRICA DISTINGUISHED BY
THEIR BRIGHT RED ROBES AND CATTLE

MAKAMBA .... TRIBE IN KENYA SETTLED AROUND
MACHAKOS ON THE
OUTSKIRTS OF NAIROBI

MANDAFU .... SWAHILI WORD FOR COCONUTS

MANJI .... PUNJABI WORD FOR ELDERLY MOTHER
OR GRANDMOTHER

MANYATTAS .... A GROUP OF MAASAI HUTS

MATATU .... SWAHILI WORD FOR A PICK UP TRUCK

KIKUYU REBELLION AND UPRISING AGAINST BRITISH RULE IN KENYA THAT BEGAN IN 1952 AFTER A LONG BUILDUP OF RESENTMENT CAUSED PRIMARILY BY APPROPRIATION OF LAND.

.... AN EXPRESSION MEANING "MY LOVE"

.... MAASAI WARRIORS

...ΚÉ .... KIKUYU WORD GIVEN TO SOME ONE WITH A LOT OF PHYSICAL STRENGTH

MWANANDA .... MAASAI WORD FOR CATTLE AUCTION

MZEE .... SWAHILI WORD FOR A RESPECTED OLD MAN

NDITO .... MAASAI DAUGHTER

NGIBOT .... MAASAI CIRCUMCISION CEREMONY

PANGA .... SWAHILI WORD FOR A LONG KNIFE

PUNJABI .... INDIAN DIALECT SPOKEN IN PUNJAB IN NORTHERN INDIA

POSHO .... SWAHILI WORD FOR GROUND MAIZE OR CORN

RUNGU .... A ROUND WOODEN CLUB IN THE MASAAI LANGUAGE.

SALWAR KAMEEZ .... COLORFUL BAGGY TROUSERS WORN WITH A LONG TUNIC WORN BY SIKH WOMEN

SANGAT .... A SIKH CONGREGATION

SAVANNA .... REGION OF GRASSLAND WITH SCATTERED TREES AROUND THE EQUATOR

SHABAD .... THE GURU'S MESSAGE WITH ADDED MUSIC

SHIFTA .... SOMALI REBELS

SIANGIKI .... YOUNG MAASAI GIRLS

SIKH .... IN SIKHISM, A DISCIPLE

SIMMI .... SWAHILI WORD FOR A SHARP LONG KNIFE

SKONI .... SWAHILI WORD FOR A FARMER'S MARKET

SOMALIS .... RESIDENTS OF SOMALIA, COUNTRY
BORDERING KENYA ON THE NORTH
SWAHILI .... DIALECT SPOKEN IN EASTERN AFRICA
THE KOP .... LIVERPOOL FOOTBALL CLUB (SOCCER)
SUPPORTERS IN ENGLAND
UHURU .... SWAHILI WORD FOR FREEDOM
URDU .... INDIAN SUB-CONTINENT LANGUAGE
SPOKEN IN NORTHERN INDIA AND
PAKISTAN
VOCO .... FUEL THAT WAS A MIXTURE OF
KEROSENE AND DIESEL

Pally at age 6

Pally Dhillon was born in Kijabe on January 1, 1944. His grandfather, Kehar Singh Dhillon, migrated from Punjab in the early part of the twentieth century when the British Colonialists were recruiting Indians to work on the Railway Construction Project.

The early part of *Kijabe* is factual and relates the life of the author's grandfather. Dhillon's parents were both born in Kenya. Pally Dhillon went to school in Nairobi, Kenya, and then moved to London, England to attend college. Dhillon joined the computer industry in England in the early 1960s and has established a reputation as a highly respected professional on all aspects of computing. He has traveled extensively in Kenya, Canada, Iran, Europe and the U.S. on assignments.

Dhillon's interests are reading, sports, technological innovations and trends. Involved in field hockey all his life, he has been active in USA field hockey on the west coast as president of the hockey association and as a player, coach, and organizer. He has traveled all over the world to play hockey and to watch Olympics, World Cups, and other sporting events. He organized the medal ceremonies and announcements for hockey at the 1984 Olympics in Los Angeles. He plays golf on a regular basis.

Pally today

This is Dhillon's first book; he is now at work on a second book about Sikh pioneers in Britain. He has two daughters, Salena Zanotti, a medical doctor, and Asha Dhillon, an attorney.

Picture taken in 1914, Sikh pioneers in Kenya

Picture taken in 1920, Sikh Traders in Masaai Land

About Sikhism

Mehar Singh Dhillon was a Sikh, and he subscribed to basic principles of Sikhism. With approximately 2 million practicing Sikhs in the world, the religion is a monotheistic faith. It recognizes God as the only One, as He who is not subject to time or space, and as He who is the Creator, Sustainer, and Destroyer of the Universe.

In Sikhism, ethics and religion go together. The inculcation of moral qualities and the practice of virtue in everyday life is a vital step towards spiritual development. Qualities such as honesty, compassion, generosity, patience, and humility can be built up only by effort and perseverance. The lives of the Gurus illustrate that they lived their lives according to their code of ethics.

Sikhism is a modern, logical, and practical religion. It believes that normal family life (Grasth) is no barrier to salvation. It believes that it is possible to live detached in the midst of worldly temptations and ills. A devotee must live in the world and yet keep his head above the usual tensions and turmoils. He must be a soldier, scholar, and saint for God. Sikhism also places much emphasis on discipline.

Sikhism is well suited to the needs of modern life. It believes in the individual and his right to develop his personality to the maximum extent possible. According to Guru Nanak, every man has power or merit; he is a part of the divine. He is not a useless weakling, a mere product of the chain reaction of Karma. The Sikh is essentially a man of action with an overwhelming sense of self-reliance. He should invoke the Guru's blessing at every step in his life and ask for his Divine Favor or Grace.

Sikhism is both modern and rational. It does not foster blind faith. Guru Nanak exposed the futility of meaningless ritual and formalism. He questioned the superstitious practices of his time and he brought about a revolution in the thinking of his people.

In Sikhism, women have equal status with men. They have social equality and religious freedom.

Sikhism insists on a practical kind of faith. Just as one cannot swim without getting into the water, Sikhism believes that one cannot know spirituality unless one believes in God. Sikhism enjoins faith in the Fatherhood of God and brotherhood of man. Sikhism enjoins us to love God. We cannot love God if we love ourselves. Ego is at the root of all evil and our sufferings. If we concentrate on God and on singing his praises, we subordinate and even drive ego out of our minds. Only then can we acquire those great qualities and virtues which we associate with God.

About Kenya

Kenya is one of the most interesting and exciting countries on the East African Coast. It straddles the equator and shares a border with Somalia, Ethiopia, Uganda and Tanzania. Its coast is lapped by the Indian Ocean and it shares the vast waters of Lake Victoria with its western neighbors. The Rift Valley and central highlands area form the backbone of the country, and this is where Kenya's scenery is most spectacular. The humid coastal belt includes the Tana River estuary and a string of good beaches. Western Kenya takes in the fertile fringes of Lake Victoria and some prime game parks. The vast, arid northeastern region is where Kenya is at its wildest and most untouched.

Tourism is the mainstay of the economy and is helped by the picturesque game parks teeming with lions, buffalos, elephants, leopards and rhinos combined with zebras, antelopes, wildebeest and others. Kenya's climate varies enormously from place to place. The Rift Valley offers the most agreeable weather, while the arid bushlands and semi-desert regions can range from daytime highs of 40 degrees Celsius to lows of about 20 degrees Celsius at night. Western Kenya and the eastern coastal fringe are generally hot and humid year round. Nairobi, Kenya's capital, is cosmopolitan, lively, interesting, pleasantly landscaped and a fun place. Nairobi sprang up with the building of the Mombasa-to-Uganda railway. Originally little more than a swampy watering hole for Maasai tribes, it had become a substantial town by 1900.

The largest port on the coast of East Africa, Mombasa is hot, steamy and historical. This town of about half a million people dates back to the 12th century. A Muslim haven for centuries, it was attacked by the Portuguese in 1505 and burnt to the ground. It was quickly rebuilt only to be reduced to rubble again by an embattled Mombasa ruler during the long fight against the Portuguese. Mombasa's Old Town is a testament to this tumultuous era. Filled with ornate wooden shopfronts and balconies, it is a constant source of delight for the observant wanderer. The old quarter's most prominent attraction is Fort Jesus, which dominates the harbor entrance. Begun in 1593 by the Portuguese, it changed hands nine times between 1631 and 1875. Now a museum, the fort is a fascinating mixture of Italian, Portuguese and Arabic design.

Kijabe, the small village that bears the name for this book, is just off the road from Nairobi to Nakuru. Arriving in Kijabe, one would understand why Mehar Singh decided to settle there. Kijabe is at the edge of the Great Rift Valley Escarpment and overlooks a breathtaking scene across the valley with animals roaming and dust blowing across the horizon. On a clear day, you can look across the valley and see for miles and miles. About 6,000 feet above sea level, the climate is cool and the winds often blow at a strong pace. Kijabe means "windy" in the Maasai dialect. There is a hot water spring with sulphur in it at the foot of the slopes, and people come from far away to enjoy the healing, medicinal qualities of the spring. For the entrepreneur and businessman Mehar Singh, Kijabe was central in terms of access from Nairobi, Nakuru, and Narok. It was centrally located in the heartland of Maasai land where Mehar began his traveling duka business which helped make his fortune.

PREP Publishing Order Form

You can order any of our titles through your favorite bookseller! Or send a check or money order or your credit card number for the total amount*, plus $3.20 postage, to PREP, Box 66, Fayetteville, NC 28302. If you have a question about our titles, e-mail us at preppub@aol.com and visit our website at http://www.prep-pub.com

Name: _____

Phone #: _____

Address: _____

E-mail address: _____

Payment Type: ☐ Check/Money Order ☐ Visa ☐ MasterCard

Credit Card Number: _____ Expiration Date: _____

☐ $10.95—KIJABE, AN AFRICAN HISTORICAL SAGA. Pally Dhillon, Author

☐ $25.00—RESUMES AND COVER LETTERS THAT HAVE WORKED. Anne McKinney, Editor

☐ $25.00—RESUMES AND COVER LETTERS THAT HAVE WORKED FOR MILITARY PROFESSIONALS.

☐ $25.00—RESUMES AND COVER LETTERS FOR MANAGERS. Anne McKinney, Editor

☐ $25.00—GOVERNMENT JOB APPLICATIONS AND FEDERAL RESUMES: Federal Resumes, KSAs, Forms 171 and 612, and Postal Applications.

☐ $25.00—COVER LETTERS THAT BLOW DOORS OPEN. Anne McKinney, Editor

☐ $25.00—LETTERS FOR SPECIAL SITUATIONS. Anne McKinney, Editor

☐ $16.95—REAL-RESUMES FOR SALES. Anne McKinney, Editor

☐ $16.95—REAL-RESUMES FOR STUDENTS. Anne McKinney, Editor

☐ $16.95—REAL-RESUMES FOR TEACHERS. Anne McKinney, Editor

☐ $16.95—REAL-RESUMES FOR CAREER CHANGERS. Anne McKinney, Editor

☐ $16.95—REAL ESSAYS FOR COLLEGE & GRAD SCHOOL. Anne McKinney, Editor

☐ $16.00—BACK IN TIME. Patty Sleem

☐ $17.00—(trade paperback) SECOND TIME AROUND. Patty Sleem

☐ $25.00—(hardcover) SECOND TIME AROUND. Patty Sleem

☐ $18.00—A GENTLE BREEZE FROM GOSSAMER WINGS. Gordon Beld

☐ $18.00—BIBLE STORIES FROM THE OLD TESTAMENT. Katherine Whaley

☐ $20.00—(hardcover) WHAT THE BIBLE SAYS ABOUT... *Words that can lead to success and happiness.* Patty Sleem

_____ **TOTAL ORDERED (add $3.20 for postage)**

* PREP offers volume discounts on large orders. Call (910) 483-6611 for more information.